ALSO BY T. E. CRUISE

Wings of Gold: The Aces
Wings of Gold II: The Flyboys

Published by
POPULAR LIBRARY

WINGS *of* GOLD

BOOK III

THE HOT PILOTS

T. E. CRUISE

POPULAR LIBRARY

An Imprint of Warner Books, Inc.

A Warner Communications Company

POPULAR LIBRARY EDITION

Popular Library® and the fanciful P design are registered trademarks
of Warner Books, Inc.

Cover design by Mike Stromberg
Cover illustration by Mark Skolsky

Popular Library books are published by
Warner Books, Inc.
666 Fifth Avenue
New York, N.Y. 10103

 A Warner Communications Company

Printed in the United States of America

First Printing: March, 1989

10 9 8 7 6 5 4 3 2 1

BOOK I:
1954–1960

DULLES ISSUES WARNING ON INDOCHINA—
Secretary of State Warns That the Rest of Southeast Asia
May Fall Like Dominoes Under Soviet Domination—
New York Gazette

FRENCH/COMMUNIST SHOWDOWN IN VIETNAM—
French Forces Prepared for Red Assault at Dien Bien Phu—
U.S. Increases Financial Support to French Military
Operation—
Detroit Telegraph

GC-909 MAKES MAIDEN FLIGHT—
GAT Liner Introduces Jet Transport in America—
Aviation Trade Magazine

EASTERN BLOC SIGNS WARSAW PACK—
Iron Curtain Unites Against NATO—
Washington Star Reporter

SOVIET LEADER DENOUNCES STALIN—
Khrushchev Calls for Decentralization of Power—
Los Angeles Gazette

AIRPORTS RUSH TO MODERNIZE—
Public's Love Affair with the Air Catches Facilities
Unaware—
LaGuardia Airport to Spend $30 Mil. to Accommodate
Jets—
New York Business Journal

RUSSIANS LAUNCH SATELLITE—
Congress Calls for Inquiry as Reds Make Great Leap in Space
Race—
Milwaukee Sun

NASA INTRODUCES PROJECT MERCURY TEAM—
 Nation Salutes First Seven Astronauts to Explore Space—
 Miami Daily Telegraph

KENNEDY WINS MARYLAND PRIMARY—
 Massachusetts Senator Neutralizes Religious Controversy—
 November Race Shapes Up: Kennedy vs. Nixon—
 Boston Times

RUSSIANS SHOOT DOWN U.S. SPY PLANE—
 SOVIETS DISPLAY WRECKAGE—
 Captured Pilot to Be Charged with Espionage—
 San Francisco Post

CHAPTER 1

(One)

Gold Aviation and Transport
Burbank, California
21 July 1954

Herman Gold stood with his hands on his hips in the doorway of the acre-sized assembly hangar. The hangar was windowless but cool due to air-conditioning. It was lit to operating room intensity by hundreds of overhead light fixtures. The partially completed, Gold Commercial 909 jetliner prototype gleaming beneath those lights was 153 feet long and 42 feet high, and had a wing span of 145 feet. The jetliner was surrounded by plywood scaffolding from which the technician teams in their turquoise and scarlet company overalls swarmed like gaudy ants busy at some gargantuan, metallic beetle.

The streamlined GC-909 jetliner was Gold Aviation and

Transport's latest and most expensive endeavor, a graceful and lithe silver bird meant to seduce the airlines from their outmoded and aging fleets of piston-engined airplanes. Today, however, Gold was wondering if the 909 jetliner was going to turn out to be his company's most expensive flop.

Gold was fifty-five years old, with light blue eyes, freckles, and a wreath of curly, crimson hair around his ears that had long ago thinned on top to strawberry-colored fuzz. He was tall and thin, except for his damned potbelly. He'd been waging war against his paunch for the last twenty years. So far in his eventful life it had been one of the few battles he'd ever lost.

Gold had been born Hermann Goldstein, in Germany. An orphan, he had grown up in the streets of Berlin but had managed to pull himself out of the gutter by learning a mechanic's trade. During World War I he had served as an N.C.O. in the Kaiser's Imperial Air Service. He'd been a pilot, one of the aces who'd flown with Von Richthofen. His twenty confirmed kills had been four more than was necessary in those days to earn Germany's highest military decoration, the Blue Max, but he'd never received his medal, or any of the honors due him, because he was a Jew.

Soon after the war he'd made the decision to come to America, where he shortened his name to Herman Gold. He briefly worked as a truck mechanic on New York's Lower East Side, until a newspaper advertisement led him to a job as a pilot in a barnstorming troupe that was about to tour the country. He eventually ended up in Southern California.

This was during Prohibition, when an experienced pilot who could fly at night could make himself a great deal of money bringing in hooch from Mexico. In less than a week Gold had earned five thousand dollars, and although he had never been proud that he'd broken the law of his adopted country, it had been that money which had allowed him to start Gold Express, an air transport operation between Los Angeles and San Francisco.

Gold Express had made its first flight in 1921, and from the start had been a successful enterprise. In 1923 Gold had been able to rent a warehouse on the Santa Monica waterfront. There he established Gold Aviation, an aircraft design firm. In 1925 GAT suffered a string of setbacks, but things improved by 1927. It had been in '27, the same year that Lindbergh made his historic flight across the Atlantic, when Gold Aviation sold its first airplane design, the G-1 Yellowjacket, to the United States Postal Service. The Post Office ended up buying hundreds of the airplanes. It had been that cash infusion that had allowed Gold Aviation and Transport to build on 109 acres in the Burbank desert.

In the twenty-five years since, GAT prospered. During the '40s, flush with cash thanks to its wartime military contracts, the company bought out its surrounding neighbors, including the bordering movie studio, to become a sprawling complex; a vast, manufacturing metropolis that employed thousands on round-the-clock shifts to turn out fighters, bombers, and transport crafts for the military and international commercial aviation markets.

And after all of those years, and airplanes built, and hundreds of millions of dollars spent and earned, you'd think it'd get a little easier, Gold brooded as he watched the men in their overalls fussing over his company's latest and greatest silver bird. But it wasn't getting any easier, Gold knew. Aviation research and development costs had escalated enormously. Today, despite GAT's extensive resources, the company's future was pinned to the success of this awesome, shiny 909 jetliner, just as that future had been wagered back in 1927, when an exceedingly young and nervous Herman Gold presented his single engine, open cockpit G-1 Yellowjacket to those skeptical buyers from the Postal Service . . .

Gold walked through the hangar, and then turned the corner around a line of parts bins to look for his chief engineer Don Harrison. He found Don conferring with several team foremen in the work space that Don had walled off with banks of filing cabinets. Don Harrison was thirty-three. He was tall and broad-shouldered but a little soft around the edge, like a football player who'd been riding the bench too

long. He had wide-spaced hazel eyes and thinning blond hair
that he wore slicked back from his high, domed forehead.
As Gold watched, Don went to one of the filing cabinets,
pulled out a scrolled blueprint, and then unrolled the drawing on a drafting table. He pushed his tan, round-framed
eyeglasses up from the tip of his nose, and began to move
his index finger rapidly across the drawing in order to make
some point to the foremen, who nodded.

"Problem?" Gold asked, coming up behind Don as the
foremen went back to work.

Don turned around, a weary smile on his face. "Nah, just
putting out fires. You know what I mean?"

"You solve one problem and up pop two more." Gold
nodded, thinking that Don looked beat. There were deep
shadows beneath his red-rimmed eyes. The kid hadn't
shaved in a couple of days; his complexion beneath his
sparse blond whiskers was pale and his face was drawn.

"I think you could use some sleep," Gold said, frowning
as he regarded Don's baggy slacks and wrinkled shirt and
tie. "How long have you been here?"

"Forty-eight hours," Don said, and before Gold could
protest, added, "I've been napping in my office." He turned
back to his drafting table. "Don't worry. I intend to take a
nice long rest once this baby gets airborne."

Gold flinched. The kid had sounded exactly like Teddy
Quinn. For over thirty years Teddy had been Gold's chief
engineer and his closest friend, until Teddy died of heart
failure, back in '51.

"You know, Don, that crap about taking it easy in a little
while was just what Teddy used to say," Gold warned.

"But I *mean* it." Don grinned. He winked at Gold. "It just
might even be a honeymoon . . ."

"You mean you and that Forrester woman you've been
seeing might tie the knot?" Gold put his arm around Don's
shoulder, hugging him affectionately. "That's great news,
my boy . . . I'm very happy for you—"

"Hold on, Herman." Don laughed. "I haven't asked her
yet . . ."

"But you're planning to, right?"

"Yep . . ."

"Good! She'll accept. I'm sure of it. You've been going with her, how long?"

"About six months," Don replied. "I know that's not very long . . ."

"Nonsense!" Gold chuckled. "It's plenty! I knew my Erica maybe six *minutes* when I felt in my bones that she was meant for me."

"Well, your opinion of Linda means a lot to me, Herman," Don said quietly.

Gold smiled appreciatively. He'd been emotionally distraught over losing Teddy, and for a long time Gold had put off hiring a new chief engineer. He'd simply been unable to bear the thought of trying to fill his old friend's shoes, even though he knew that it was costing his company productivity as GAT's heart and soul, its R & D department, drifted leaderless. When Gold had finally been able to bring himself to begin his search he'd known that Teddy's replacement would have to be exceedingly talented to ever have a hope of measuring up to his predecessor. It hadn't taken long for Gold to discover that if he wanted the best and the brightest to head up his research and development department, there was only one choice: Donald Harrison.

Gold had kept his promise to Harrison to involve the young man in all aspects of the business, and had been impressed by his versatility. Unlike many talented but technical sorts who couldn't get beyond their narrow specialties, Don had an innate business savvy; the ability to comprehend the big picture. It hadn't taken long for Gold to discover that having the young man by his side as a protégé was an asset, not a liability. Since then, a strong friendship had developed as Gold had come to rely on Don as a sounding board as well as a creative source, much as he had relied on Teddy.

"I must say that Linda seemed like a wonderful girl from the times that Erica and I have gotten together with you two," Gold said. "Bright, beautiful—a wonderful girl . . .

You know, I never told you, but I met her once some years ago . . ."

"Really, how?" Don asked.

"Oh, she's a big newspaper reporter now," Gold said, chuckling, "but when I met her she was just starting out at some wire service, so I granted her an interview . . ." He paused. "I think she wanted to interview me about how the Air Force was using our MT-37 cargo transports during the Berlin Airlift . . ."

"I thought you didn't like granting personal interviews?"

"I didn't then, and don't now," Gold replied. "But this one I granted as a favor to my son."

"Steven knew her?" Don began, and then snapped his fingers. "Of course. We all met in Washington, back in 'forty-seven, during those hearings on the B-45 bomber." He shook his head. "Funny, though, I don't recall Linda ever having mentioned that she and Steve had become friends . . ."

"Say, now that you and Linda and Steve are all together again in Los Angeles, maybe you and Linda could fix Steve up with a date?"

"Somehow I don't think Steve needs much help in that department." Don chuckled. "Anyway, his leave is just about up, isn't it?"

"Yeah, but it wouldn't hurt to get him introduced to a nice girl," Gold murmured. "A girl who'd lure him home more often . . ."

He didn't want to say anything about it just yet to Don, but the other night, over dinner, Steve had brought up the possibility of leaving the Air Force and coming to work at GAT. Gold, though overjoyed over the prospect of at long last getting his only son to come into the business, was doing his best to play it cool concerning the idea. He was worried that if he pushed too hard Steve would back off. It wouldn't be the first time that had happened between father and son . . .

"Well, I think that I'd like to have some private time with Linda before we start double-dating." Don laughed. "Our romance has been pretty much progressing via the telephone these last few weeks, thanks to the rush work on the 909."

"I see . . ." Gold frowned apologetically.

Don glanced at Gold. "I know that expression on your face only too well . . ."

"I'm afraid the 909 is going to continue to keep you apart from your girlfriend for some time to come."

"What's happened?" Don sighed, removing his glasses to rub the bridge of his nose.

"I came here to tell you about it directly from my meeting with the delegation from the airlines," Gold said. "We've got a big problem with them concerning the 909."

"The airlines reps seemed to like our airplane just fine this morning, when you gave them a tour of the prototype—"

"They'd still like it fine if the 909 were the only game in town," Gold muttered. "But it isn't. The delegation told me that they'd been over at Amalgamated-Landis, where our friend Tim Campbell recently hosted a tour of a plywood mockup of his AL-12's interior cabin."

"Big deal!" Don replied. "Like you just said, it's fucking plywood! We've got a real, *metal* airplane, just about ready to fly—"

"Nevertheless, after his presentation Campbell was able to write some substantial orders for his jetliner," Gold said. "Those orders *he* wrote are the orders that *we* didn't get today."

"I don't understand it—" Don began to fume.

"Then listen a minute," Gold said. "And you'll understand only too well. Number one, Campbell is building the AL-12 longer and wider than our 909."

"That I know," Don said. "I worked for Campbell, remember? Who do you think did the initial design work on the Al-12?"

"Number two, the AL-12 is being touted as having transatlantic cruising capability."

Don's jaw dropped. "Herman, that plane was not capable of intercontinental flight when *I* worked on her—"

"Well, she is now."

"How did Campbell pull it off?" Don wondered, and then frowned. "I should have expected something like this. I should have warned you . . ."

"No." Gold shook his head. "Nobody knows Tim better than I . . ."

And wasn't that the truth? Gold thought bitterly. There was now such bad blood between the two of them that it was hard to believe that there had once been a time when Gold and Campbell had been business partners, and friends . . .

Gold met Campbell back in 1925, during the period when Gold Aviation was suffering its setbacks. Gold needed cash, and made the rounds to the banks looking for a loan, but he found bankers' doors that had once been open to him were now closed.

Only a junior bank officer named Tim Campbell was willing to talk. Campbell argued convincingly that Gold Aviation was topheavy with creative types; that what was needed was a money man to keep an eye on the fiscal bottom line. Gold, thinking at the time that he had little to lose, hired Campbell, and thanks to Tim the company not only survived but also thrived, eventually going public.

Campbell became increasingly important to GAT as the corporation's financial dealings—and the world—became more complex. It was Campbell who expertly piloted GAT through the shoals of the Great Depression, and it was thanks to him that GAT's air transport division expanded to become Skyworld Airlines. Gold was content to let Campbell run Skyworld, and keep financial watch over the entire company, while he and Teddy Quinn indulged themselves by hovering over their drafting tables dreaming up new airplane designs.

Eventually, however, the inevitable, simmering disagreements about GAT's corporate direction finally boiled over, and when they did, it was only natural that someone as bright and talented as Tim Campbell would think that he knew best. Campbell waged a vicious stock battle to seize control of Skyworld. In 1933 Campbell walked away with Skyworld in his pocket, but Gold was able to make him pay dearly for his acquisition. Since that bitter parting of the ways the two men had remained overtly cordial, but Gold had never forgotten how Campbell had vowed to get even for the way that Gold had managed to win the final hand of their high-stakes, stock market poker game.

In 1946 Campbell bought a huge block of stock in the aircraft building firm of Amalgamated-Landis, getting himself a seat on the board. He eventually took control of that company.

Now, Gold knew that it was Campbell's thirst for vengeance that was making Tim strain A-L's resources in a come-from-behind sprint to build and market a jetliner. If the AL-12 could steal away the GC-909's orders, GAT—and Herman Gold—would be ruined, and Campbell's revenge would at long last be realized.

"I guess we always knew that Tim Campbell was going to be able to leapfrog us when it came to technical features," Don said broodingly. "But that's only because Campbell bribed an airlines executive to hand over the 909's spec sheets and blueprints," he added angrily. "If Campbell hadn't had GAT's design to use as a jumping-off point he never could have caught up so fast—"

Gold shrugged. "As Tim likes to say, there's only one rule: 'Don't get caught.' The bottom line is that considering his jetliner's advanced features, it's no wonder the airlines are willing to wait to buy the AL-12 instead of our 909."

"So what's the answer?" Don asked, sounding dejected.

"The interim answer is to do some fast redesigning . . ."

Don burst out laughing. "You're kidding!"

"Do I look like I'm kidding?" Gold replied. "I've salvaged some of our initial orders—and stolen back a few from A-L—by promising to lengthen the 909's existing fuselage to accommodate extra passengers. Our plane will still have less capacity than the AL-12, but at least some of the airlines are willing to accept the compromise because we can deliver units sooner, which means they'll have a jetliner fleet faster."

"You said 'interim solution,'" Don reminded. "What's your long-term strategy?"

"We must get started immediately on a redesign," Gold said. "I want a bigger, wider 909; an intercontinental version. I told the airlines boys we would have a proposal—a detailed three-view drawing, performance specs, projected cost, and delivery schedule—by the end of the month. In return, they promised to hold off confirming their orders with A-L."

"You want a new airplane designed within two weeks," Don muttered. "My department will have to work around the clock—"

"I don't care what it costs," Gold declared.

"That's good," Don said dryly. "Because it's going to cost a lot."

Gold waved the matter aside. "This thing between Campbell and me is personal. Maybe someday I'll tell you about it . . ."

Don nodded, smiling wryly. "Well, I guess I have some work to do . . ."

"And we'd better get Rogers and Simpson on the horn and give them the good news," Gold said sarcastically.

"They're not going to be happy," Don agreed. "They busted their balls delivering the 909's engines on time. Now they're going to have to come up with something even more powerful . . ."

"Just tell them what we need and the date we need it on," Gold interrupted. "And if they give you any lip, tell them that if they can't handle the job we'll go to Pratt & Whitney, or GE—"

"Herman, calm down!" Don said. "You're pissed off at Tim Campbell. No need to take it out on the whole world."

"You're right," Gold sighed.

Don abruptly frowned. "Shit! I forgot that we've got those meetings in Washington next week. And Horton said they were urgent—"

"It's the CIA's style to call everything urgent," Gold grumbled.

"We can't stand them up—"

"You just like fooling around with all that top-secret stuff," Gold teased.

"Herman—What are we going to do about those meetings?"

Gold pondered it. "Okay, I'll go alone to Washington while you stay here and ride herd on the 909-I."

"The *what*?"

"The 909-International." Gold laughed over his shoulder as he began to walk back toward the hangar entrance. "I wish I could build them as easily as I name them."

(Two)

Don Harrison was dialing Linda's number at the newspaper when he was interrupted by the electrician foreman. Harrison wanted to give Linda the good news about how he was going to be in town next week, but the foreman said a wiring problem had him stumped, and his crew idled, so Harrison hung up the telephone and went to take a look. Then one thing led to another, and by the time he did get a spare moment to call Linda, he'd thought it over and decided against it . . .

Linda had lately been mildly complaining that he was too predictable, so why not surprise her? Why not keep the fact that he was staying in Los Angeles his little secret? That way he could get some solid work done during the next few days, which would give him the excuse to goof off one night and show up unannounced at her apartment with a bottle of champagne in hand.

It was unlike him—and exciting—to be so impetuous, but then it was also unlike him to have a swell girl like Linda. He began whistling merrily to himself as he went back to work. He was positive that she would enjoy the surprise, just as he'd enjoy the opportunity while Herman was away to spend some time with his girl.

CHAPTER 2

(One)

**Malibu, California
27 July 1954**

Steve Gold carried his sandals as he walked along the waterline, up to his ankles in the surf that broke in frothing bubbles on the sand. He pretty much had the beach to himself due to the day—it was a Tuesday—and the weather, which was overcast. Steve didn't mind the fact that the beach was deserted. He liked being alone; always had. And a quiet beach was his favorite place, next to being in the cockpit of a fighter jet.

Steve was twenty-nine years old. He was six feet tall and weighed 170 pounds. He had blond hair, cut moderately short so he could easily deal with it in order to look presentable, and squint lines etched vertically on either side of his nose and around his brown eyes, thanks to the long hours spent scanning the sky from various fighter cockpits. Steve was an Air Force lieutenant colonel and a fighter ace, with fourteen and a half confirmed Japanese kills during World War II, and six MIGs accounted for during the Korean conflict.

The fifth MIG he'd shot down had been especially sweet because it had given him twenty and a half official kills: *one half* kill more than his old man had tallied during World War I, when Herman Gold had flown with the Red Baron.

Actually, Steve had even more kills, but they weren't official. Back in '41 he'd flown a volunteer stint with the Flying Tigers in China, during which he'd knocked down five Japanese airplanes while taking part in one awesome and glorious dogfight over Rangoon. Unfortunately, the kills could not be added to his official tally because he'd only been seventeen years old. When the Flying Tigers had learned that he'd lied about his age in order to join up, they booted him home and wiped clean their records of any trace of him . . .

Steve now grinned as he thought about how Pop still enjoyed busting his balls about that, ribbing him that if the kills weren't official it was as though they'd never happened. Steve knew his father was just kidding; his old man was real proud of his son's war record.

Steve continued walking with his feet in the water. As he passed a retaining wall that divided the beach and had been blocking his view he saw that there was another person out here today, after all. It was a woman wearing a black bikini, a wide-brimmed straw hat, and sunglasses. She was semi-reclining in a white canvas sand chair, with her legs—*nice, long, legs*—stretched out on a red and white striped beach towel.

As he approached he saw her glance at him, and then look away in that kind of initially bored, disinterested way that he liked so much in women because it made things so much sweeter when he got their attention in bed. The closer Steve got, the better she was looking. He was figuring that it was worth a shot to try and strike up a conversation—

And then he realized that he was looking at Linda Forrester—

At that instant she gave *him* a double-take. He knew that she had recognized him by the way she quickly grabbed a book off her towel and ducked her head into it. It was obvious that she was just as flustered as he about this chance encounter, and like him, didn't know what to do . . .

He was still far enough away to credibly pretend that he hadn't recognized her. He could just turn around and walk back the way he'd come, but that seemed cowardly. He wasn't about to let her think that he was *afraid* to talk to her. On the other hand, he didn't want to cause any uncomfortable awkwardness . . . At least, no more than they'd both already experienced with each other . . .

So what the fuck was he going to do? He couldn't just keep on walking past her, and pretend not to see her . . .

He looked out at the ocean, and decided that the way out of this mess was to go for a swim. What the hell—He was feeling hot; a dip would be refreshing. It would also give Linda the chance to pack up and move away down the beach if she preferred not to talk to him. If she did so, he'd take the hint.

But if she stayed . . .

He shrugged off his terry-lined, shirt-jac, its pockets bulging with his car keys, wallet, and sunglasses. He put the garment down on the sand, took his cigarettes and lighter from the pocket of his boxer swim trunks, and laid them on top. He put his sandals on top of everything, and then ran out into the cold, clean water. When he was in up to his waist he pushed off, swimming with strong strokes until he was out beyond the point where the waves broke. He splashed around for a while, either floating on his back or treading water, watching the sun glint on the aquamarine sea as he thought about Linda Forrester.

They'd met in 1947, on a sultry summer Friday afternoon in Washington, during the Senate B-45 bomber hearings. Steve had been a captain assigned to the Air Force's Office of Public Information, and she had been a free-lance journalist, hired by Amalgamated-Landis to do a puff piece on their young engineer Don Harrison, who was in Washington to testify on behalf of the bomber he'd designed. Steve still remembered how happy he'd been when he'd found out that the relationship was strictly business between the bookish young engineer and the knockout brunette with shoulder-length curly hair and blue eyes to die for.

The next day had been a Saturday. Linda had asked Steve if he wouldn't mind showing her around Washington. The sight-seeing excursion had ended up in Steve's apartment, and finally, in his bed. The spark they'd lit that Saturday afternoon back in 1947 had burned fitfully for five years. It wasn't like they were boyfriend and girlfriend, or going steady, or anything like that. Hell, they'd only managed to get together for a weekend maybe half a dozen times a year. In between their get-togethers, he saw plenty of other women, and if he knew Linda, she saw plenty of other men, but somehow they'd always made the effort to get back to each other. Steve didn't think it was love—at least it didn't seem to him to be like the love they wrote about in books— but the sex had always been outstanding, as had their friendship . . .

Funny how the relationship had always remained less than the sum of its parts, Steve now thought as he began to swim back toward shore.

The end of the relationship had come two years ago, at Chusan Air Field in Korea, where he'd been serving with the 44th FIS, an F-90 BroadSword fighter-interceptor squadron. Linda, a senior correspondent for the *Los Angeles Gazette*, had been part of a contingent of reporters on a tour of the front. As soon as Steve had learned that Linda was on her way to Chusan he'd bribed an airman a couple of bucks to get the key to an out-of-the-way storeroom in Operations Center. He and Linda had enjoyed themselves on the cot he'd stashed in the storeroom. For that couple of days Steve had thought that life was as good as it could get: By day he'd had MIGs to joust with up in the sky, and by night there'd been Linda, waiting for him in the sack . . .

It had been outstanding, all right, but during their third night Linda had gotten all mushy, starting in about how she loved him, and maybe they should be thinking about marriage... In hindsight, he guessed that he'd probably been a bit too emphatic about how marriage wasn't likely. Not then, and not ever...

Well, good old Linda hadn't been much interested in joining him in the sack after hearing *that*. The contingent of journalists had moved on, Linda with them, and that had been the last Steve had seen or heard from her, except for her postcard from Japan a week or so afterward, letting him know in a couple of terse, scrawled sentences that the two of them were through, as if he hadn't already gotten *that* message loud and clear...

In the time since, he'd had no contact with her. It had been as if they'd never met. He'd been home in Los Angeles on leave for almost a month now, but it had never occurred to him to call her. Sure, he'd thought about Linda a couple of times... He guessed he even missed her... a little...

But she'd been *real clear* about how as far as she was concerned they were through. He knew how to take a hint.

As he swam back he resisted the temptation to see if she was still there. He wondered which way he'd bet if this were a wager: Would she stay, or leave? It wasn't until he was striding out of the ocean, the breaking waves pushing at the backs of his knees, that he allowed himself to look. She was still there; still reading, or maybe pretending to be reading...

It didn't matter. She was still there, and that was all he needed to know.

He slicked back his dripping hair, gathered up his things, and confidently walked toward her.

(Two)

The mid-morning sun was bright against the page of Linda Forrester's book. After a couple of stabs at trying to concentrate she decided that she wasn't in the mood for reading. She felt guilty as she tossed aside the copy of James Baldwin's *Go Tell It on the Mountain*. Friends at the paper had been after her to read the book since it came out last year, but it was tough going at the beach.

Anyway, it seemed like I spend my whole life generating print, or else absorbing it, she thought as she wiggled her toes in the warm, white sand. *Today is supposed to be a time out* . . .

She closed her eyes, leaning back against the chair canvas, listening to the shrieking laughter of the gulls swooping above the crashing surf. As she baked in the sun she thought about going into the water. Maybe later.

She sat up slightly, opening her eyes as she reached for her beach bag, and rummaged through it looking for her suntan lotion. It was then that she saw him walking toward her along the waterline. She didn't recognize him at first, but merely registered his presence, thinking that he was a good-looking guy wearing a short-sleeved cabana top and matching bathing trunks in a yellow-on-black paisley print. From the way he moved she could tell that he was fit and athletic.

It was as she was looking away that something clicked in the back of her mind: She did a quick double take, peering at him from over the top of her sunglasses. As he came toward her his image wavered like a mirage in the wriggling heat waves rising up off the hot sand.

But of course he wasn't a mirage, she thought, a little perturbed and a little pleased as she watched Steve Gold coming toward her. Nope, he was no mirage. A bit of a dream, he might be—although there'd also been nights since she'd seen him last when he'd been leading man in her nightmares—but today he was very real.

As she stared at him now she was able to guess from the almost imperceptible falter in his stride that he'd also recognized her. She quickly snatched up her novel; the book was on her lap upside down, but what the hell; he was still too far away to notice.

She took quick peeks at him while she pretended to read. He was just standing there about thirty yards down the beach, shuffling his bare feet in the sand as he looked out at the ocean. She guessed that he was trying to decide if he should come over... She wondered what he was going to do—and what she should do if he *did* come over...

She couldn't figure out what he thought he was up to as he abruptly took off his jacket, emptied his pockets, and went slogging into the water. Then she realized that this was his way of giving her a chance to beat a retreat.

What *nerve*! What *ego*! It'd be a cold day in Malibu when the likes of *him* could run *her* off—

She flung aside her book and angrily smoked a cigarette while she waited for "The Creature from the Black Lagoon" to get tired of splashing around out there with his fellow cold fish, and come say hello. Finally she saw him swimming back toward the shore. She removed her straw hat and quickly ran her fingers through her tousled curls to fluff them out, thinking that she'd been wearing her hair shorter since she'd seen him last. She then plopped her book back on her lap, this time right side up.

She watched as he shook the water out of his eyes, put on his top, and came swaggering over like the conceited lug that he was. He probably thought that she was going to be an easy touch just because he hadn't managed to scare her off the beach. Well, she had news for him...

"Hi there, blue eyes." Steve grinned, coming up to her. "I thought it was you."

Linda pretended to go back to her book. "What the hell are you doing here?" she murmured, trying hard to sound like she didn't in the least care.

"Enjoying the view," Steve said.

She snuck a peek at him staring down at her, and then quickly averted her eyes. The way he was staring made her acutely aware of just how little of her oiled, tanned body was hidden from view by her skimpy black bikini.

Then again, she thought wistfully, it was kind of silly—and late—to be feeling modest. It wasn't as if the two of them didn't already know every square inch of each other's bodies, *outside and in . . .*

"Mind if I sit down?"

"It's a free beach."

"I'll take that as a 'yes.'"

He settled down beside her on her towel. She was about to tell him to get the hell off, but then decided, *Why act childish? Why let him know that he's still under my skin?*

His unbuttoned beach jacket gaped open as he took out of his pocket a pack of Pall Malls, allowing her a glimpse of his broad chest and his flat stomach. She was remembering how she'd used to run her fingers over his hard belly, and how he'd reacted when she'd touched him there, and then she thought that maybe *he could tell* that she was looking at his body—

She quickly looked up into his eyes, which were so extraordinarily brown. He seemed to be looking right through her.

"Want one?" he asked, his own cigarette dangling from his lip.

At first she didn't quite understand, but then she realized that he was holding out the scarlet cigarette pack. She nodded, taking a cigarette, and then leaned toward him to accept the light held cupped in his hands against the sea breeze. *That* was a mistake, she thought as she saw him devour her cleavage with his eyes.

"What *are* you doing here?" she asked again. She knew that Steve had won the Medal of Honor, and had been promoted to lieutenant colonel for having shot down some famous North Korean honcho fighter pilot. The Air Force, wanting to get a leg up on the other service branches when it came time to do battle for appropriations, had put their newest war hero on a public relations tour. Every newspaper in the country, including her own, had run pieces on him, and she remembered the big cover story on Steve that *PhotoWeek Magazine* had done.

"Last I heard you were traveling around, selling the Air Force to the Cub Scouts," she said. "Or was it vice versa?"

Steve chuckled. "I was, but the Korean War ended. The Air Force decided that maybe the Cub Scouts would rather hear from test pilots, so the war hero has been retired from public speaking."

"Too bad . . ."

"Nah, I'm glad," he said. "It was getting to be a chore reciting that speech they wrote for me. Toward the end it felt like the story I was telling had happened to somebody else. I'm still assigned to the Air Force's Office of Public Information, in Washington."

"It sounds as if you've been grounded. Don't you miss flying?"

"I keep my hand in," Steve said. "I've got clearance at Andrews to evaluate TAC aircraft for Brigadier General Howard Simon, who's involved in R & D for the Air Force out of Patterson Field, in Dayton, Ohio . . ." He winked. "And who happens to be a friend of my dad."

"How convenient for you," Linda sniffed.

"It's not like being in a front-line TAC squadron, but it's better than nothing."

"What are you doing here?"

"I had some leave coming, so I decided to come home to sunny California."

"You've turned into a beachcomber?" she asked lightly.

"Not really. I'm here in Malibu to do my old man a favor. He owns a bunch of lots along the oceanfront—"

"A bunch?" Linda gasped. "Are you kidding?"

"Nope. You've got to hand it to my old man. He doesn't miss a trick. Way back when, right after Pearl Harbor, he bought up a lot of this oceanfront for a song. I guess everyone else was expecting the Japanese fleet on the horizon at any moment . . . Anyway, now he's building houses on the lots."

"I saw that construction." Linda nodded.

"I'm kind of keeping an eye on the project for him . . ." He trailed off.

Sure you are, she thought sarcastically. *What are you*

doing? Trying to count the building lots and come up with the same number twice?

She knew that Steve had dropped out of high school, and that in the Air Force had barely managed to pass his high school equivalency exam. By his own admission she knew that he was no genius, and that during peacetime the Air Force brass racked their brains trying to think of a place to park Steve Gold while they waited for another war to come around so that they could strap him into a fighter plane. Shooting down enemy airplanes was the one thing he could do, and to his credit, he did it better than almost anyone else . . .

"What are *you* doing here?" Steve asked her. "Slow day in the news business?"

"Actually, the opposite. The past week I've been working long hours pulling together a biographical Sunday supplement piece on the life of Jackie Cochran."

"Oh, right," Steve said. "The first woman pilot to break the sound barrier in a Sabre jet—"

Linda nodded. "Anyway, the piece got done, sliding in under the wire, just like usual. I decided I needed to get out of the office for a while."

"Well . . . Good for you . . ."

They were silent for a few moments, smoking their cigarettes. She wondered who was going to bring it up first. He did.

"Well, you seeing anybody these days?"

She glanced at him skeptically, but he seemed totally sincere. *Could Steve not know that she was involved with Don Harrison, the man who was chief engineer at his father's company?*

"Yes, I *am* seeing someone . . ."

"Oh . . ." He leaned forward to bury his cigarette butt, and then scooped up a handful of sand. He began to let it trickle through his fingers. "Is it serious?"

No, he didn't know about Don, she decided, remembering from her past experiences with him that either through innate honesty, or just plain dumbness, he'd never lied to her. Not even when it might have suited his purposes to do so, like on that last night they'd spent together in Korea. That night she'd let down her guard, revealed her feelings, and so had he when he'd coldly—but sincerely—set her straight about where he stood . . .

"Yes, it's serious," she murmured, watching as he moved his hand slightly to let some of the sand trickle down onto her toes.

"So it's serious . . ." Steve echoed. "Is it *love*?" He looked at her then, and she thought he was mocking her.

"Maybe it is love!" she said furiously, tossing away her cigarette. "And what the hell would *you* know about the subject, you sonofabitch?"

"Nothing," Steve said, holding up his hands in surrender. "I'm incapable of love. You told me that yourself, remember?"

"I sure do," Linda declared firmly. "And I was *right* . . ."

"So, uh, where is this guy?" Steve asked, pretending to be looking around. "He can't be too bright—"

"Oh, *he* can't be too bright?" she curtly interrupted.

"—letting a beautiful woman wearing next to nothing hang around this beach all by herself . . ."

"It just so happens that he's away in *Washington*. On *important* business," Linda said, miffed.

"That's funny. My old man's in Washington for a few days, as well. What kind of business is your boyfriend in . . . ?"

"Chemicals," she said off the top of her head. The truth was that she didn't know why Don and Herman Gold periodically went to Washington. She'd asked about it once, and Don had said something about it being classified, so she let it go. Sure, she was a reporter, but she was also a good American. She happened to agree with Senator McCarthy that the press had no business doing the Communists a favor by compromising Americans doing important work for their country.

Anyway, she would have lied to Steve, no matter what. She couldn't *possibly* bring herself to tell him that she was involved with Don Harrison. Steve knew her too well. At the mention of Don's name he would have burst out laughing, knowing *exactly* what she was up to . . .

The irony was that her relationship with Don wasn't as calculated as Steve would think; not *exactly*, at least. For example, she and Don had become reacquainted by purest chance. Last December her newspaper had sent her to Las Vegas to cover an aviation industry convention. Her editor had told her to emphasize the hot competition between GAT and Amalgamated-Landis to build the world's next great commercial transport: a jetliner. When she'd seen Don on the convention floor she'd immediately decided that he was the perfect interview. For one thing, he'd worked for both companies; for another, she already had his bio on file because of that free-lance piece she'd done on him back in '47.

She'd had no contact with Harrison since that free-lance piece, but when she reintroduced herself he'd been very polite. He agreed to an interview, and had even been gracious enough to offer to escort her around the convention. She quickly took him up on his offer, and thanks to Don she'd gotten access to industry VIPs she never could have approached on her own.

Once they were back in L.A., Linda had called him, thinking only to repay his kindness by offering to treat him to a nice dinner on her expense account. He'd accepted her invitation, and that evening perhaps both had indulged in too much wine because after driving her home he'd made a clumsy, groping pass at her—

Which she had gropingly, clumsily accepted . . .

She'd known even then that it was a terrible mismatch. Everything about him that evening had telegraphed to her that he was inexperienced with women; that he was going to misinterpret her acquiescence; take it much too seriously. But she'd been weak, and Don was attractive, in his way. And it had only been a couple of months since she'd broken off with Steve. She guessed that she'd been on the rebound . . . that she'd been horny . . .

And the rest, as they say, is history. The day after what

had been a night of adequate but forgettable sex she'd come home from the office preoccupied with work to find a dozen roses on her doorstep. A few minutes later a delivery man had arrived bearing an iced bottle of champagne. Then, as she'd known it was going to, the telephone had rung. It had been Don, asking if he could come over...

Reminiscing about it now, Linda remembered how she'd stood there with the phone against her ear, listening to his breathing as she pondered what to do with this sweet creature so trustfully resting in her palm. She'd thought about how lonely her busy life had lately seemed since she'd ended things with Steve Gold. She'd thought about how she wasn't getting any younger, and about how her news correspondent's life—the drinking and cigarettes, the lack of sleep and decent food—were catching up with her. She'd thought about how much of life was passing her by; for instance, didn't she want children?

And then she'd thought about what a solid bet as a husband wealthy, brilliant, young Don Harrison would be... She'd *known* that she could have him if she wanted him...

"Yes, darling," she breathed into the telephone. "Do come over, right away..."

And he'd kept coming these past six months, at first shyly, but then boisterously, limbs flopping and tongue lolling in bliss, like a newly adopted puppy. And her initial opinion of him had been right: He was so inexperienced in love that he thought that what they had was *real*...

Then again, who's to say who's the biggest fool among the three of us, Linda now brooded. *Steve and I once had the real thing, but that hadn't turned out to be any joy ride, either...*

"What do you say I come by your place tonight?" Steve suddenly asked.

She looked at him, not quite believing that he could be so crude.

"You fucking bastard—"

"Yes," he said calmly, looking into her eyes. "That's

right. I am. But that's what you want. I can tell. So what do you say?"

He's right, she thought. *He does know exactly what I want.*

She thought about the consequences.

There *are* none, she persuaded herself. Eventually Don would get up the nerve to ask her to marry him, and when he did she would say yes. Once they were engaged she would be true to him. She would stick to her part of the bargain—

Then stick to it now, nagged her conscience.

But Don hadn't yet proposed, she argued. The deal hadn't yet been made—

And to hell with the rationalizations, Linda finally thought. What it came down to was that Don was all the way across the country in Washington, so he would never know. That's all that mattered. It made no sense to pretend that she had virtue—whatever the hell *that* was—when what she really had was an itch that only Steve knew how to scratch . . .

"How's seven-thirty?" she asked lightly, trying to make a joke of it. His index finger began to trace a figure eight on her thigh just above her knee. She couldn't keep from flinching. "How's seven?" she amended. He lifted his hand to her breasts. With his index finger he began to lightly trace a circle around her left nipple, so very swollen beneath the black nylon of her bikini top.

"Steve . . ." she pleaded, thinking that at any moment somebody could appear on the beach to see him touching her so wantonly, but she knew that something like that didn't matter to *him*. The bastard just didn't *care*, just as she knew that there was no way she had the will to deny him.

Not even to push his hand away. . .

"How's now?" she asked hoarsely, and began gathering up her things.

CHAPTER 3

(One)

Central Intelligence Agency
Washington, D.C.
27 July 1954

Herman Gold was beginning to wonder if he'd died in a plane crash during yesterday's flight to Washington and gone to hell. That would explain why this meeting with Jack Horton and his crew of spooks and Air Force personnel was going to drone on forever.

It had been about four years since the CIA had first asked Gold to put his best engineers to work developing and perfecting aerial reconnaissance techniques and equipment. In those days the periodic progress meetings that took place at CIA headquarters had proceeded with just Gold, CIA man Jack Horton, and Air Force General Howie Simon in attendance. None of the three had liked beating around the bush, so decisions had always been made quickly. As time passed, however, the attendance at the meetings had grown, to now include over thirty people from the Air Force and from various departments of the "Company," as Horton liked to call his spy outfit.

It was too bad, Gold now thought as he struggled unsuccessfully to stifle a yawn. As was always the case, the bigger the committee the less work that got done because no decision could be made until everybody had put in their two cents, in order to justify their presence. Today's meeting was a prime example. It had begun at nine in the morning, and had continued without breaks for the last five hours. They'd worked right through lunch, munching on ham and cheese on white bread, and sipping bad coffee out of cardboard cups as the bureaucrats made their inane comments concerning the various projects going on inside GAT's top-secret workshop, code named "The Candy Store." The Candy Store was a guarded building with blacked-out windows in the center of the Burbank complex. It was where Gold's best and brightest engineers worked aviation engineering magic at the behest of their government.

"All right, then, I suppose we can move on to new business at last," Jack Horton sighed from his black leather swivel chair at the head of the long rectangular conference table.

Horton was in his forties. He favored dark gray or blue suits, white shirts with tab collars, and always, a red tie. He was tall and thin. He wore his dark hair in a crewcut through which the top of his head was beginning to show, and had a thick bottle brush mustache seeded with gray. The area in front of Horton was covered with bits of napkin. He'd developed a nervous habit of shredding paper when he wasn't using the sheets to polish the thick lenses of his black, horn-rimmed eyeglasses.

"Herman—?" Horton began.

"Hmmm?" Gold replied languidly, looking up from the opposite end of the table. He'd been doodling a sketch of the 909-I on his legal pad.

"A couple of days ago I attended a meeting at the White

House," Horton said self-importantly. "It was a meeting attended by the highest level of government—"

Gold had to smile. *These Foggy Bottom guys*, he thought. *Why not just say the President has issued some orders, and be done with it?*

"The meeting concerned the increased difficulty we're experiencing conducting effective reconnaissance flights over the Soviet Union. The Russians have increasingly been challenging us—even on our border flights—and meanwhile the highest levels have called for a way to conduct even deeper penetrations of Russian airspace."

"We've been talking about this for years," Gold said crossly. "You want to go deep over Russia, which means you have to go high. The Candy Store has come up with a series of airplane proposals which you fellows have seen. The problem has always been money."

"That's all changed, Herman," Horton replied. "There's been an increased insistence from the highest levels for adequate reconnaissance."

Gold thought, *Trust Ike, the new President, and an old military man, to understand the value of solid aerial reconnaissance in dealing with an enemy* . . . "So tell me what you decided," Gold said. "And I'll tell you if it's possible."

"My people in Dayton have compiled a preliminary spec sheet," Major General Howard Simon said as he passed a manila folder down toward Gold.

Howie Simon was a taciturn, white-haired, blue-eyed old eagle in his early sixties who worked out of the Air Force's R & D center at Wright-Paterson AFB, in Ohio. He and Gold had worked together on many projects down through the years, and in the process had become good friends.

Gold opened the folder and quickly scanned its contents. "Hmmm . . . You want at least a seventy-thousand-foot ceiling and an extended cruising range . . ." Gold closed the folder. "The rest I can read later. I can tell you right now that this airplane is going to have to be extremely light to get that kind of performance . . ." He tore a sheet of paper off his yellow legal pad and quickly folded it into a glider shape, which he held up to Simon. "Have you fellows considered building her out of paper?"

The Air Force personnel laughed. The CIA spooks didn't. Gold consoled himself by remembering that a sense of humor was not high on the list of the Company's qualifications for employment.

"The other thing you should keep in mind is the time factor," Horton said. "We're going to need our new bird—"

"Not bird," Herman interrupted dourly. "No bird was ever built this light. What we're talking about is an insect. A *light-weight* insect. Say, a mayfly—"

"Very well, then." Horton smiled patiently, as if he were dealing with a recalcitrant child. "This Mayfly must be ready within a year."

"I'll have to clear the decks to pull it off," Gold said worriedly. "Put everything else on hold and put the Candy Store team on it full time." He trailed off, wondering how the hell he was going to juggle his staff. The 909-I had to get built, as well . . .

"National security is at stake, Herman," Horton intoned.

It's always at stake, it seems, Gold thought. "I've got some questions."

"Of course." Horton nodded expectantly.

"My first concerns the funding," he began. "As I've been telling you for years now, designing airplanes is a very expensive endeavor." Gold looked from Horton to General Simon. "So who's picking up the check this time, boys?"

"Well," Horton began smoothly, "considering that we're talking about building an entirely new airplane from scratch, I would think that the project falls within the budgetary boundaries of the Air Force."

"Nice try, Jack," General Simon scoffed. "You know quite well that the Air Force has been told in no uncertain terms that this is a Company operation."

"Why is that?" Gold asked.

"The Air Force can't take the risk of sending uniformed personnel over Soviet airspace," Simon explained. "The Russians could interpret that as an act of war. The way it's been worked out is this: The Air Force will lend its technical expertise, and officially discharge those pilots who wish to volunteer for the flight program. Accordingly, since this is officially a Company operation the Company can pay for it."

"Okay, Howie, you've made your point," Horton sighed. "Herman, the Company will pay, all right. We'll get the money to you through the usual channels."

"Good," Gold said. "I'm prepared to start on this first thing, but I have two preconditions. Number one, if I promise to build you an airplane that meets your specs in the time allotted, you've got to be willing to cut me some slack to do it. Agreed, Jack?"

Horton shrugged. "Sure. Why not?"

Gold laughed. He glanced at General Simon. "Howie, that means I don't have to check in for approval with your Dayton people—" Gold's arm swept the room. "Or anybody else involved concerning what the Mayfly looks like, and what's she made out of; if my engineers working on her have changed their socks, and what they had for breakfast that day. Agreed?"

Simon looked uncomfortable. "That's not how we're accustomed to working, Herman . . ."

"*You* don't have the money, and *no one* has the time for us to get tied up in the usual red tape," Gold said firmly. "I'll keep you apprised of our progress as I submit my vouchers, but as long as the work is going smoothly, I'll expect Dayton, and everyone else to butt out. Agreed?"

"Agreed . . ." Simon reluctantly sighed.

"You said you had two preconditions?" Horton asked.

Gold thought again about how his engineering department was going to have its hands full trying to design and build a prototype intercontinental jetliner better than Tim Campbell's AL-12, *and* design and build a Mayfly prototype. And then he thought about how good old Jack Horton seemed to have connections in virtually all government agencies.

"I'll have to discuss the second one with you in private, Jack," Gold said.

Horton studied him a moment, and then nodded. "Let's get on with new business . . ."

The meeting lasted another two hours. When it was finally over, Horton sidled over to Gold while he and the others were packing up their briefcases.

"Herman, come take a walk with me. I don't think you've seen my new office . . ."

(Two)

"Okay, what's on your mind?" Horton murmured as he led Gold through the narrow, crowded corridors that interlinked CIA's imposing stone buildings in Foggy Bottom, near the State Department.

"How's your influence with the CAB?" Gold asked softly.

"The Civil Aeronautics Board?" Horton frowned. "I know some people over there. Why?"

"The CAB inspects commercial aircraft before issuing them a certificate of airworthiness," Gold said. "Without such a certificate, an airplane is grounded."

"Yeah, so?"

"I'd like you to use your influence to get the CAB to take a closer look at A-L's preliminary specifications for its new transatlantic jetliner."

"You sonofabitch." Horton laughed, shaking his head. "You want me to help you give Amalgamated a black eye—"

"I want you to *suggest* to the CAB that they ought to take a closer look at the AL-12," Gold repeated carefully. "That's all I want. Knowing that the CAB was for some reason interested in taking a closer look at Amalgamated's new airplane would make the airlines think twice about ordering it. That'd rob A-L of its momentum, and that would be a tremendous load off my mind. It would also be a load off the minds of my engineers, who could then divert their attention from my own jetliner endeavor to lend themselves to your very crucial Mayfly project."

Horton nodded. Gold smiled, knowing that the deal was done. The CIA man stopped at a pair of mahogany double doors with gleaming gold knobs.

"Come on in and we'll have a drink on it," Horton invited.

"Certainly, Jack," Gold said, following Horton in.

Horton's new office *was* plush, Gold thought. Jack had abandoned his previous office's antique front parlor look for art deco. Everywhere Gold looked he saw rich black leather upholstery and gleaming silver inlaid with ebony on a wall-to-wall sea of crimson carpeting.

"This office *is* much bigger than the one you used to have," Gold remarked.

"Doesn't everyone's office get bigger over the years?" Horton asked.

"I wouldn't know," Gold said, settling into an armchair as Horton crossed the room to the liquor cabinet. "Mine were always big."

CHAPTER 4

(One)

West Hollywood, California
27 July 1954

The heavy traffic surprised Don Harrison. It was almost seven-thirty in the evening, supposedly well past rush hour, but there were still logjams of cars on the road; an endless procession of lemon headlights and flaring, cherry tail lamps, glowing like neon in the gathering dusk.

Harrison gunned the Hudson Commodore's powerful V-8 to take advantage of a clear stretch on Sunset. The traffic delays were especially irritating because he'd purposely left his office at GAT late in order to miss the brunt. He'd spent that quiet time after everyone else had gone home making some progress emptying his in-box. The paperwork always piled up when Herman was away.

Harrison turned left onto Havenhurst, gliding past a pair

of teenage boys loitering on the corner. The boys nudged each other, pointing at the white convertible.

Harrison enjoyed their admiring glances. The Hudson was flashy, all right; so flashy that he almost hadn't bought it. His father had certainly disapproved, calling the purchase an extravagant waste of money. His father was a Ford man, and on his advice Harrison had always bought Fords: perfectly adequate little hump-backed hardtops . . .

It had been Herman who'd convinced Harrison to get a car with style. It had to be a big car, Herman had decreed. With a big engine, the better to take command of the road. And it had to be brightly colored and a convertible, so that people could see it coming and see who was driving it.

Now, when the admiring glances came Harrison's way he felt proud, the way he felt when he had Linda on his arm.

Linda loved the Commodore. She loved to drive it, and Harrison loved to let her. He would watch her in the same admiring way as other men when she was behind the wheel, her dark curls ruffling in the wind. He would admire her, and wonder at his great good fortune to be in love with her.

His parents had been right, Harrison thought as he parked beneath the tall palm trees in front of the Capullo de Rosa Apartments, the bungalow court where Linda lived. You work hard and you get the rewards. In school you get good marks. In life you get the job, the car, the girl . . .

Harrison glanced at the dashboard clock. It had taken a long time to get here, all right. It was almost eight o'clock. *Better late than never*, he thought, and then he chuckled. *Of course, you couldn't be late if you weren't expected—*

He was truly feeling pleased with himself for thinking up this surprise. It had been a struggle not to call Linda to let her know that he was in town these past few days. He knew that Linda was home tonight. Before leaving the office he'd called to check, hanging up as soon as she'd answered, of course. He couldn't wait to tell her that it had been him on the line . . . So he was predictable, huh? Well, he'd show her . . .

He grabbed the bottle of champagne he'd picked up on the

way over and got out of the car. The champagne was warm, but a half hour in the fridge would fix that. He smiled, thinking that he and Linda would have no trouble wiling away a half hour...

He entered the apartment court through the low archway, passing by the tenants' garages as he made his way along the terracotta walk that ran from the street to the far rear courtyard. Linda's apartment was way in the back, on the second floor, overlooking the swimming pool. Like always, as he made the journey to her door he couldn't help reminiscing about their first night together. How intoxicating it had been to hurry with her in his arms, past the backlit, splashing fountains and fragrant tropical gardens. At some point at her door, while she'd been fumbling through her bag for her keys, she'd turned toward him, and their mouths had locked for a long and passionate kiss. At that moment Harrison had felt larger than life; that he was forty feet tall, up on the silver screen, in some wild and romantic movie. He had felt that this could not be happening to him, because such things had never happened to him.

He'd been to bed with only two girls in his life before Linda, and neither time had the experience been much to remember, but many times he *had* fallen in love with girls who belonged to other men, or girls he saw walking down the street whom he did not know and would never see again. When it came to girls, it was a lot like the situation concerning the practical Ford versus the snazzy convertible. The girls who took an interest in him, and whom he felt comfortable approaching, had always been so ordinary, while the glamour girls for whom he'd lusted had always seemed so far out of reach—

Until Linda. Beautiful, glamorous Linda.

Yes, Harrison thought. *It was exactly like his father had said: You work hard, you get your reward.*

He walked quickly, trying to ignore the snatches of conversations and the tinny spurts of radio music and talk from the televisions leaking from the apartments that he passed. This place was certainly pretty, but the tenants lacked privacy. When the breeze was still, and people had their windows open, you could hear everything. Linda had said she didn't mind, but then she traveled so much her apartment was more like another hotel room than home.

Things would change when they were married, Don thought as he reached Linda's building, and made his way up the outdoor staircase to her second-floor apartment. *An apartment was no place to raise children.*

He knocked on the door, and waited. There was no answer, and it seemed pretty quiet inside. He hoped that she hadn't gone out during the time it had taken him to drive there, or if she had, that it was just for a moment . . .

He decided that it made no sense to stand outside wondering about it, and used the key she had given him to enter into the dark vestibule. "Linda?" he called out uncertainly, groping in the shadows for the light switch. He found it and flicked it on.

He wandered into the small living room, and saw her straw beach bag on the tan sofa, and a yellow and black garment of some kind lying crumpled on the peach carpet.

"Linda—?" He went into the galley kitchen, and was putting the champagne in the fridge when he heard hushed murmurings. He went back into the living room. The whispering was coming from behind the closed bedroom door. As he stared at it the bedroom door opened and Linda came out.

"Jesus Christ, Don!" she gasped. Her hair was mussed. She seemed flushed. She was wrapped in a sheet that left her shoulders bare. "What the hell are you doing here—?"

"That's a hell of a way to greet me." He laughed, walking toward her, spreading his arms wide to give her a hug.

His smile faded as he got closer. "Oh, Christ," he whispered, recoiling as he smelled her within the warm, close confines of the living room. *A bitch in heat,* flashed through his mind, and then he glimpsed movement in the bedroom through the partially opened door.

"Who's in there, Linda?" he demanded fiercely. "Who—?"

The words died in his throat as the door swung open and

Steven Gold, wearing just a pair of bathing trunks, stepped into the living room.

"Linda?" Don stared at her. Despite his rage he desperately hoped that she might tell him something to make this all right; to make everything not be ruined . . .

"I'm sorry, Don," Linda murmured, looking away.

He nodded. "There's some champagne in the refrigerator," he said, struggling to keep his voice steady as the waves of humiliation and loss washed over him. "You two enjoy yourselves . . ." He could hear the trembling in his voice. He looked down at his hands. They were shaking. It seemed that not only Linda, but also his own body was betraying him . . .

"Look, Don," Steven Gold said, taking a step toward him. "I want to—"

"Oh?" Harrison cut him off fiercely. "You want to apologize for *being* here, or maybe for my *catching* you here?"

"Don—" Steve began again.

"I don't want to talk to you," Harrison said flatly. It seemed to take forever for him to make it to the front door, to open it, to step out, and to shut the door behind him. As soon as that door was closed he broke into a run down the stairs. He had his fists clenched, and was shaking his head, willing himself not to cry. It would be even worse if he let himself cry.

He ran to his car, started it up, and pulled away, ignoring the outraged horns and squealing brakes of the drivers he cut off. He came around the corner onto Sunset on two tires, and then floored the Commodore, getting it up to fifty, wildly swerving to miss the cross traffic as he ran red lights, as if he could outrun his shame.

And as he drove through the soft California night he saw clearly that it was Steven Gold who had stolen his girl. He knew that he could not physically compete for Linda with a man like Steve. He supposed that he should have known that all along. His father could have certainly told him . . .

But there would be other arenas in which to confront Steven Gold, Harrison knew. He would think about it. He was an engineer, possessing a creative and logical mind. He would distract himself from his pain by thinking about this the way he might think up a solution to an aeronautical design problem.

And he would come up with a blueprint for getting even.

(Two)

Linda Forrester watched Steve stare at her front door.

"Why didn't you tell me it was Don you were going with?" he demanded.

"What good would that have done?" she asked dejectedly. She was feeling cold, and pulled the bed sheet a little closer around her bare shoulders as she slumped on the sofa.

"Well, for starters, I could have told you that he didn't go to Washington with my old man," Steve said.

"Touché." She laughed thinly as he went to the sideboard where she kept her liquor.

"You want a drink?"

"A big one," Linda murmured.

He poured two generous scotches, straight up. He brought them over, sitting down beside her.

"I'm sorry, blue eyes," he murmured. He set the glasses on the coffee table and gently took her hand in his. "I guess I screwed things up for you . . . I'm really sorry—"

"Don't be," she said. "I invited you here, remember?" She smiled grimly. "Anyway, you've done a good deed tonight . . ."

"How so?" Steve asked, puzzled.

"You saved Don, right? He'll never know what a favor you did him by putting him off a woman like me . . ."

"Don't say that—"

"Why not?" she began curtly. "It's true, isn't it? I had that poor chump by the short hairs, but now he can thank his lucky stars he found out about me before it was too late. Maybe now he can find himself a *nice* girl. A *good* girl. Not a *tramp* like me—"

"You're no tramp," Steve said, picking up his drink. "I don't want to hear you saying that, because it isn't true."

She had to smile then. "I guess that's the nicest thing you ever said to me . . . Thanks . . . *pal*," she added softly, taking the other scotch and clinking her glass against his. "We're two peas in a pod, you and I."

"How so?"

She took a long pull of her drink. "We're not the marrying kind."

CHAPTER 5

(One)

GAT
Engineering Department
28 July 1954

Susan Greene was at her desk outside Don Harrison's office when her telephone rang. It was the main switchboard. Mr. Gold was calling long distance from Washington to speak to Mr. Harrison.

"Good morning!" she said when her father came on the line.

"Good morning to *you*, maybe," he replied. "But it's lunchtime *here*, and hot as blazes . . ."

"Poor you," Susan said. "When are you coming home?"

"I've got another couple of days here, I'm afraid."

"It's a long trip this time around . . ."

"Yeah. Something's come up. A new project. The meetings are endless . . ." She could hear his exasperation. "Honestly, the way they like to have meetings, it's a wonder the government gets anything done . . ."

"Well, the world can't be run like GAT," she teased.

"And why not?" he asked jovially.

Susan laughed. She looked around to make sure that no one could overhear her, and then said, "Come home soon, Daddy. I miss you."

Sometimes the secrecy made her feel silly, but there was a point to it. She used her married name at work to keep people from knowing that Herman Gold was her father. She wanted people to relate to her for herself; not because she was the boss's daughter.

"I miss you, too, sweetie. Put Don on the line for me, would you?"

Susan hesitated. "Um, he's away from his desk . . ."

"Oh . . ." Gold said, sounding disgruntled. "He knows I call every morning about this time. Is everything all right?"

"Everything's fine."

"All right, then. I doubt that I'll be able to call later. I'll be tied up in these damned meetings. I'll call tomorrow. Good-bye."

Susan hung up the telephone, feeling guilty that she had lied. Everything wasn't all right. Don hadn't come to work this morning.

For anyone else to miss a day of work was one thing, but since Don had started at GAT a couple of years ago he hadn't missed a day. He'd even come in that time he was so sick with that terrible cold and the company nurse finally had to come around to insist that he leave so he wouldn't risk infecting the rest of the department. What's more, she was his secretary, so even if Don had decided to take a day off, he certainly would have called to let her know . . . Not that he would ever remotely consider not coming in when her father was away, as well . . .

Calling Don at home had only compounded the mystery. There was no answer at his apartment, but when she called the apartment building's front desk the concierge said that Mr. Harrison was at home . . .

She'd been wondering what to do when her father had called, and had decided not to tell him of her concerns. There was nothing he could do about it all the way across the country, and anyway, he'd sounded like he had enough on his mind without her further burdening him with her female intuition . . .

She reached for the telephone, thinking to call back the concierge and ask him to use his pass key to see if Don was all right. The telephone at the other end was ringing when Susan thought, *How embarrassing if the man rushed up there, perhaps with the police, and Don was only sleeping—*

Linda Forrester popped into her mind. *And what if Don wasn't sleeping alone?*

"Lyndon Tower Apartments," the concierge answered.

Susan quickly hung up. Don had a girlfriend, let *her* check on him . . .

She went back to her work, but she couldn't concentrate. After another half hour of fretting and watching the clock she decided to try Don's apartment again.

She was listening to his telephone ring, and thinking that if she didn't hear from him by noon, she'd just have to grit her teeth and call Linda Forrester at the *Gazette* to see if she knew Don's whereabouts—

The telephone rang and rang. He wasn't home. She was about to disconnect when he picked up.

"Hello? Hello?" he mumbled anxiously as though he were half-asleep. "Linda?"

"No . . ." she replied, feeling peeved and angry and hurt, the way she'd felt months ago when after only a few weeks of dating, Don had abruptly jilted her in order to pick up with Linda Forrester. "It's Susan . . ."

He didn't reply. What an indignity to have to add, ". . . at the office—?"

"Oh . . . Susan . . ."

"No need to sound so disappointed," she said, forcing lightness into her tone. "I was worried about you . . ."

"Yeah . . ." he grunted.

"Don, what's wrong?" she demanded, concerned all over again because the way he was acting was just not like him. "Are you sick?"

"Yeah . . . Sick . . ."

"I'm calling a doctor—"

"No! I don't need a doctor," he said quickly. "I need . . ."

"What? What is it? What do you need?"

"Company. Would you come over—?"

She hesitated, thinking, *Where was Linda Forrester?*

"Please, Susan . . . I need someone to talk to."

"All right. I'll come. At lunchtime. See you then."

(Two)

It was a little after one in the afternoon when Susan found a parking space on Wilshire Boulevard, a block down from Lyndon Tower. She didn't immediately get out of her lemon yellow, bug-eyed little Triumph TR2; she just sat there by curbside, lightly gunning the motor, wondering if she had the nerve to go through with this.

On the drive over she'd put the pieces together, remembering how Don had answered the telephone bleating *"Linda? Linda?"* like some goddamned, lost little lamb. Okay, so he'd had a romantic setback; it happened to everyone, God knew. Likely it was just a lover's spat, but wasn't it just like Don to take it so seriously?

The question was did she really want to be his shoulder to cry on? Could she bear to be relegated to that status, considering her own, simmering resentment over the way he'd dumped her for that sexpot?

But then again, she supposed that she had to go to him. She'd said that she'd come, so now he was expecting her, she told herself as she got out of the Triumph. And anyway, she'd already arranged for one of the other girls in the department to cover her telephone until she got back . . .

Lyndon Tower was a Spanish-influenced, art deco building, rising up eight stories behind the palm trees lining the boulevard. The apartment house was painted a pale lavender, and frosted like a wedding cake with statues and modernistic friezes. It was a ritzy address, with all the amenities, including a uniformed doorman who tipped his cap to Susan as he held the door.

The lobby was done in an Oriental motif by way of *Terry and the Pirates* and the Technicolor division of the prop department at MGM: Everything was brilliantly lacquered orange and red, with lots of green porcelain dragons and burnt sienna lions cluttering up the place. There were groupings of armchairs and low tables with fanned-out arrangements of newspapers in the lobby, and as Susan strode past on her way to the concierge a couple of men looked up from their reading to watch her go by.

Susan smiled. When Don had jilted her it had made her feel drab and frowsy, but in her saner moments she was objective enough to know that she was a pretty, brown-eyed blonde. It was true that she was a big girl, with a full figure, but she'd always been big, just as she'd always been athletic. Now, at thirty-one, her body was still as sleek and youthful as when she'd been a teenager, thanks to a rigorous routine of tennis, swimming, and golf. Strangers she met were always shocked to find out that she had a ten-year-old son.

She knew she looked especially good today, thanks to her new suit. Its gray silk ankle-length skirt and belted jacket fit her curves so well that she'd made the quickest little detour home in order to change into it before seeing Don. (She was not above rubbing salt in Don's wounded heart by showing him just what he'd missed out on by taking up with that skinny little Linda Forrester who was giving him so much grief.)

At the front desk she said that Mr. Harrison was expecting her, and then waited as the concierge telephoned upstairs.

"Sixth floor, apartment D, miss," the concierge told her. "The elevators are just around the corner..."

She had butterflies in her stomach as she rang for the elevator, and then during the ride up. *What the hell was she going to say when Don started in whining about his beloved Linda—?*

"Sixth floor," the operator said, sliding open the elevator door, and then Susan was walking like a condemned prisoner on the last mile down the carpeted, sconce-lit corridor to apartment D.

When she got there she found that the door was ajar. It squeaked somewhat on its hinges as she pushed it open.

"Susan?" she heard Don call out.

"Yes—"

"Come in . . ."

She entered through a short hallway, going past the coat closet, into the large living room. The walls were painted pale gold with white trim, and dotted with tasteful landscapes in ornate, gilded frames. There was light blue wall-to-wall carpeting, and furniture upholstered in a cabbage rose chintz, arranged around an oval coffee table with a mosaic top and curved, brass legs. The room was tasteful and immaculate, but obviously unlived in, like a display behind the plate glass window of a furniture store.

Susan smiled, thinking that she knew Don well enough to guess that cabbage rose chintz was beyond him. He must have sicced an interior decorator on the place, and now poor Don probably felt like a guest in his own home; and yet the notion of having everything "just so" because it was the proper thing to do fit Don to a tee.

"Don?" she called. "Where are you?"

"In the bedroom . . ."

Oh, great, Susan thought. *No way*, she decided.

"Well, I'm *here*," she said sweetly. "Aren't you going to come out and see me . . .?"

She stifled her shock as he came staggering into the living room clutching a fifth of vodka, looking and smelling like he'd just crawled out of a sewer.

"My God, what's happened to you?" Susan demanded.

He didn't answer, but just stood swaying in his rumpled

clothes, his hair dangling in greasy ringlets down his fore-head. She watched him stumble over to a wall, lean his back against it, and then slide down to the carpet. He stayed there, with his head sagging, his knees drawn up, and the bottle on his lap, like some back alley derelict.

"Just how drunk are you?" Susan demanded.

He shrugged, looking up at her with bleary eyes. "Not very. I've been trying, but every time I get close I get nauseous and have to stop . . ."

She couldn't help laughing. "But you did drink all that vodka?"

His grin was horrendous. "Second bottle . . ." he said proudly. "First was gin . . ."

"Well, I wouldn't brag about it." Susan scolded, her smile fading. "From the looks of you it's clear you can't hold your liquor . . ."

He looked away, shaking his head. "Can't hold my booze," he muttered thickly. "And can't hold my woman . . ."

Oh, shit, here we go, Susan thought. *He's going to start blubbering about Linda Forrester.*

"Okay," Susan began briskly, thinking to head him off, wrap this up, and get the hell out of his apartment and back to work. "I guess it's clear you had a little tiff with Linda. These things happen. No doubt she's just as upset as you are . . ."

Fat chance of that, she thought. It would be like expecting an alley cat—and she *did* mean *alley* cat—to be remorseful while it was licking the canary's feathers off its claws . . .

"Don, I'm sure that if you just telephoned Linda you two could make up, and everything would be all right and . . ."

"We're through—" Don cut her off. "I caught her with—"

"Yes?" she asked. He'd paused abruptly, and now he was looking at her so strangely. "What are you trying to tell me?" She knelt beside him on the carpet.

"I—I caught her with another man!"

"I'm sorry." *And I'm not in the least bit surprised—*

"I went to see her last night, and I caught her with him . . . I—don't know who he was . . ."

"Oh, Don," she sighed, taking his hand. "I'm really so sorry for you."

"Yes," he murmured, eyeing her. "I think you really are . . . and after I treated you so shabbily . . ." He looked wistful. "But then you *know* what it feels like to lose someone . . ."

"You mean my husband, I suppose?" Susan asked quietly. When Don nodded she said, "Well, yes. I suppose I do . . ."

"How did you get over it?"

"Get over it?" she echoed. "It's been ten years since I lost Blaize, but I still . . ." She trailed off, shaking her head. "It helps to know that he died doing what he wanted to do, for a good cause. He'd struggled for so long to be an RAF fighter pilot, and God knows the war he fought was just and right . . . It also helps to know that he died a hero, and that my husband lives on in my son . . . I think it was knowing that I had to carry on for the sake of Robbie that kept me from crumbling to pieces . . . But you asked me how did I *get over* my loss, and so I have to tell you that if the loss is genuine, you never *do* gt over it—"

She could feel herself getting all unsettled inside, so she clamped the lid on her memories, shook herself, and then said brusquely, "But drinking yourself sick isn't going to help anything." She reached over and took away the vodka. "I think you should take a shower, eat something, and then just go to sleep. I know it sounds trite, but you really will feel much better in the morning—" She began to stand up.

"Wait—" Don implored. "Where are you going?"

"I've got to get back to the office . . ."

"No! Stay!" He seemed to be trying to make a joke out of his desperate plea. "You're my secretary, right?" he grinned. "Well, today we're working outside of the office."

"Oh, Don," she said, uncertain. "I'm not sure it would be appropriate."

"Suzy, I just need somebody to be with," he said. "You

know how that can be, don't you?"

"Yeah . . ." she said after a moment. "I know. . ."

So what if she didn't go back to work today, she thought? The other girls could cover the telephones for the rest of the afternoon, and she didn't have to be home at any specific time for her son, who today was out sailing with his uncle.

Her brother Steve had always shown an interest in Robbie, but never more so than during this month's leave from the Air Force. For her part, Susan had encouraged her son's relationship with his uncle. Now that Robbie was becoming a young man, she was grateful that the boy had a strong father figure to whom he could relate. Her father spent as much time as he could with his grandson, but his schedule was hectic, and anyway he was getting on in years. Even when he'd been younger Herman Gold hadn't been the type to go running on the beach, or play catch, or do any of the other things that amused a ten-year-old, although Robbie did look forward to flying with his grandfather in his private plane.

". . . You just wait here," Don was saying. "Maybe make us some coffee, while I shower and shave. Then we can go out. We can go for a drive along the coast. Wouldn't that be nice? Out by the water, where everything's cool and clean and fresh . . ."

He took hold of her hand and squeezed it gently. Susan thought, *How good to be held again, even that little bit*. Don was looking at her with such need in his eyes, and wasn't that what *she* needed: to be held and cherished?

"Okay," she said. "You get cleaned up. I'll make us some coffee."

CHAPTER 6

(One)

GAT
7 April 1955

Herman Gold's huge corner office was located on the top floor of the main building. It had a commanding view of GAT's sweeping airfields, and the majestic, tawny California hills beyond the factory complex's boundaries. The office had wall-to-wall, moss green carpeting, and was furnished with sofa and armchair groupings upholstered in supple, burgundy leather. Custom-built display cases laden with mementos highlighting Gold's decades in the aviation business lined the oak-paneled walls, beneath his collection of commissioned oil paintings of GAT airplanes in flight. Gold's desk chair was a wine-hued, leather throne. His oak, marble-topped desk was the length and width of a dining room table. Gold had been surrounded by these—and other—trappings of wealth and power for so long that he scarcely noticed them. If pressed, he would have admitted that he took them for granted; that he'd had so much for so long that he'd become jaded.

Today, however, was different. Today he was as excited and happy—and goddamned *grateful*—as a kid on Christmas morning over what good fortune had seen fit to present him.

When his secretary told him over the intercom that she'd located Don Harrison and had him on the line, Gold snatched up the telephone.

"Don, it's me. I've just got off the phone with my son—"

"Oh, how *is* Steve these days?" Don asked a trifle coolly, Gold thought.

"You should know as well as I do that he's doing just fine in Washington." Gold laughed. "You've been spending so much time with Suzy and Robbie; whenever *I'm* with my grandson he never shuts up about his Uncle Steve at the Pentagon . . ."

"Yes, that's true," Don admitted. "But when Robbie gets off on that kick of his about Steve I suppose I just shut it off."

What an odd thing to say, Gold thought. "Well, anyway, you'll never guess why I called! It's just the greatest news—"

"Just spit it out, Herman," Don replied, sounding amused. "What is it? Something about the 909?"

"No! No!" Gold impatiently cut him off. "It's better than business—"

"Now I *am* stumped." Don chuckled. "What's up?"

Gold took a deep breath. For so many years he'd been *dreaming* of the day when he could say these few words: "Steve's decided to leave the Air Force and come to work with us—"

"I see," Don replied, sounding like he'd just been told he was the target of a lawsuit. "In that case, Herman, you'll have my resignation on your desk by the end of the day."

"What?" Gold gasped, bewildered. "What did you just say?"

"I think you heard me."

"Then I can't *believe* what I just heard. Come upstairs and talk to me."

There was a pause, and then Don said, "All right, I'm on my way."

Gold hung up the phone, his mind in turmoil. What the hell could Don be thinking of? Did the kid think that Steve was meant to replace him? If so, that was a ridiculous notion. Gold loved his son, but when it came to ability, *ten* Stevies couldn't do what one Don Harrison accomplished around there.

Thanks to Don, the preliminary specs on the new 909-I had been delivered to the airlines on schedule. The airlines had been enthusiastic concerning the new, intercontinental version of the 909 jetliner, and introducing a second version of the 909 had presented an unforeseen benefit: GAT was now writing orders on *both* models. The airlines, presented with a choice, had decided to buy the smaller, more economical, original version of the 909 to use domestically, and the 909-I for international flights.

What was even sweeter to Gold than a ledger filled with black ink was the fact that GAT's ability to offer a choice scooped Amalgamated-Landis. Of course, it had also helped when the news broke that the Civil Aeronautics Board was taking another look at the AL-12. The bad publicity caused Amalgamated's stock to drop, and some of the airlines to rethink their purchasing plans. By the time the smoke had cleared, GAT had been able to grab away a solid portion of A-L's orders.

Gold knew that he had Don Harrison to thank for this good fortune. Sure, he had been able to use his influence to get Jack Horton to sic the CAB on poor old Tim Campbell, but nothing of lasting worth would have come of that ploy if Don hadn't completed the play by coming up on time with a magnificent set of plans for the 909-I, and also creating a brilliant marketing strategy to position the two airplanes.

Since then, Don had put his mark everywhere in the company, moving the engineering department out of the era of Teddy Quinn, and into a new age.

Last July, when Don had so abruptly and mysteriously ended his relationship with that Forrester woman, Gold had been concerned that the obviously emotionally distraught young man would allow his concentration to wander, and his work to suffer. That had not proved to be the case. Perhaps it had been Suzy who was responsible for Don's speedy emotional recuperation. She and Don had certainly become inseparable the last couple of months, and Suzy was very happy about that, Gold knew. As for Don, since he'd gotten back with Suzy he seemed more relaxed and at ease with himself. He'd never been brighter or more innovative. His inspired work on the Mayfly project was a case in point.

The Mayfly reconnaissance jet that had started out life as a whimsically folded paper airplane, had since evolved into a titanium-built aeronautical hybrid. The Mayfly prototype looked like a sailplane due to her pencil-thin fuselage, and albatrosslike, extended wings. She was gossamer light, designed to glide at seventy thousand feet with only periodic help from her idling—to conserve fuel—turbojet. It was this inspired concept of harnessing the wind that had allowed the GAT Candy Store to devise an airplane capable of carrying a man and a camera virtually anywhere over the Soviet Union for up to eleven hours at a stretch. The credit for the glider concept, and for the R & D team leadership that had turned the idea into sleek, bold, matte black reality, belonged to Don Harrison.

The intercom buzzed.

"Yes?" Gold demanded.

"Mister Harrison is waiting."

"Send him in—"

(Two)

"It's no joke, Herman," Don Harrison said. "If Steve comes to work here, I go."

"But why?" Herman asked, looked pained. "For chrissakes, Don. Why would you feel that way?"

Harrison leaned back in his armchair and regarded Herman, who looked so forlorn and distraught behind his big desk. *What would you say if I told you that the reason I hate your son is because I caught him fucking my girl?*

Make that ex-girl, Harrison reminded himself. "I've worked hard for GAT these past years," he began. "I feel that in some large part I'm responsible for this company's continuing string of engineering successes—"

"Absolutely," Herman replied, smiling. "Don, I think you're jumping to conclusions. All I want to do is bring my son into the company in some specific capacity. For instance, I could put him in public relations, or maybe sales. An ex-Air Force officer would be a perfect representative of this company in both the commercial and military sales markets." He paused. "Stevie wouldn't—or maybe I should say *couldn't*—replace *you*."

"You know that and I know that," Harrison replied. "But what would the rest of the world think?" *For instance, Linda Forrester*, he added to himself.

"Come on," Herman replied, sounding frustrated. "You've had nothing but triumphs here. You're even dating my daughter, for chrissake—"

Harrison held up his hand in warning. "I think it would be best if we left personal considerations totally out of what is primarily a business discussion."

"Business?" Herman echoed in seeming disbelief. How can you be so cold about this?" he demanded. "Can't you see that you're tearing me apart? This is my *son* we're talking about. Do you know how long I've waited for this moment?" Herman looked away; he let his voice drop and grow hoarse. "I thought we were friends, Don, not just employer and employee . . ."

Harrison wasn't sure, but he thought Herman's eyes looked wet.

"Oh, Herman, of course we're friends," he muttered, feeling terrible over how this was turning out. His resolve began to soften as he realized that what he was really doing was not getting back at the son as much as he was punishing the father. But then Herman glanced at him out of the corner of his eye, as if waiting for capitulation, and Harrison reminded himself that Herman Gold was a cagey old bastard, skilled at negotiation, and not above producing a crocodile tear should the occasion warrant it.

And then Harrison thought about how resentful and embarrassed he'd feel if he had to deal with Steve Gold on a day-to-day basis. He thought about what it would feel like to be with Suzy while socializing with Steve, and Linda Forrester... He once again imagined how Steve and Linda must have laughed once he'd left the apartment on that awful night in July; how they would laugh at him in the *future* if he backed down now...

"Try and be objective," Harrison said. "If Steve comes into the business you'll naturally have to make him second-in-command—"

"That's not true," Herman quickly interjected.

"Fine! Let's say for the sake of argument that you bring your son into the business and somehow convince him to take orders from me, not that I for a minute believe that would happen," Harrison added skeptically. "The fact remains that the world would still assume that it was *your son* who was running things *with you*." He shrugged. "I'm not willing to let Steve take the credit for my work, simple as that." He shrugged.

Herman's previously wet eyes had frosted over. "I just figured it out... You think you're *taking over* this company someday..." He smiled disdainfully. "Isn't that right, Don? Don't you think that you're the heir apparent? Isn't *that* why you want to shut out my son?"

"That's as good a version of the truth as any." Harrison shrugged, and was surprised to realize that in a way, it *was* the truth, as had been all of his previous arguments against bringing Steve in. Sure, he thought he deserved to take over if—or when—Herman was ready to step aside. Having Steven Gold around would only muddle what now seemed to be a clear-cut line of succession.

The more Harrison thought about it, the more it seemed to him that in a roundabout way Steve had done him a favor by drawing first blood. If Steve had not humiliated him Harrison never would have been cold-blooded enough to realize that by keeping out Herman's only son, he was advancing the likelihood that GAT would someday fall under his control.

"You gave me an ultimatum a while back," Herman said softly. "You threatened me with your resignation. Has it occurred to you that you've hurt me and angered me to such an extent that I just might accept your offer?"

Blood is thicker than water, Harrison thought. He studied Herman's deadpan expression, trying to tell if the man was bluffing. *After all I've done here, would he really let me go?*

"I would be sorry if you accepted my resignation," he said sincerely. "I would hate to leave, but I am prepared to do so." He paused, and looked Herman in the eye. "I would not have offered it otherwise."

Herman sighed. He seemed to sag just a bit in his chair.

He's backing down, Harrison thought but was scrupulously careful to smother any sign of glee in his own expression and demeanor: another trick in the art of negotiation that he had learned from Herman.

"You're asking me to choose between you and my own son—" Herman protested, and Harrison heard the heartfelt pain in that plea.

It was time to give Herman a way out; a rationalization he could use to soothe his hurt. It was time to tell the deepest truth of all—

"I like to think that, in a way, *I'm* your son, as well . . ."

Herman smiled, and Harrison knew he'd won.

"Don't worry, I'll figure something out concerning Steve," Herman sighed. "I'll tell him something—God only knows what . . ." He laughed ruefully. "I can't believe I'm doing this . . ."

"I'll get back to work," Harrison said, standing up.

"One thing, Don," Herman said. "Steve can never know about this conversation—"

Suits me, Harrison thought as he nodded. "And I think it would be best if none of this ever got back to Suzy."

CHAPTER 7

(One)

Near Andrews Air Force Base
Maryland
7 August 1955

Lieutenant Colonel Steven Gold's F-404 Starscythe was at fifty thousand feet when his gloved fingers nudged the throttle. He felt that lovely kick in the pants as the thruster ignited, and heard his own giddy intake of breath routed from his throat mike through the earphones of his helmet as the Starscythe leapt forward. Cloud wisps swirled past the plexiglass teardrop canopy as the screaming jet knifed through the gray blue sky.

The F-404 was the Air Force's newest fighter. She was being called the "manned missile" because of her speed, climb rate/angle, and ceiling specs. Amalgamated-Landis had built her in response to the complaints from the fighter pilots in the Korean War that their birds had lacked the performance of Soviet aircraft.

As far as Steve was concerned, the Starscythe filled the bill. She could do Mach 2, and she was the first combat bird to be able to break the sound barrier in a *climb*, gobbling up the sky at over ten thousand feet per minute. She was also a strikingly different-looking airplane, thanks to her stubby, unswept, pylon-tipped wings and T-shaped tail.

That was not to say that the F-404 was perfect, Steve thought as he banked his silver stilletto of a bird through the heavens. Amalgamated-Landis still had a number of flaws to address. The F-404's high performance capabilities made her a thirsty bird; her stubby, rocket-fin wings could not carry much ordinance; she had poor turn radius capabilities, and a nasty pitch-up problem that Steve intended to see about right now...

He checked to make sure that his safety harness was cinched tight, and then pulled back on the stick and went to afterburner. The Starscythe rose like the Buck Rogers rocket ship she so much resembled. Steve felt himself being flattened against his seat back as if a giant were pressing his palm against Steve's chest, squashing the air out of his lungs. As he climbed higher the sky turned a darker shade of blue. His altimeter read sixty thousand feet. He was approaching zoom ceiling. His eyes kept scanning his instruments. At the very last moment before his bird ran out of lift and her oxygen-starved engine flamed out, he dropped the jet's needle nose to go over the top.

Steve heard himself groaning from the G-pressure as the F-404 arced into her dive. Far below through the cloud breaks was the glittering band of blue that was the Chesapeake Bay, and to the west, the green and white city-state of Washington, D.C., but Steve had no time for sight-seeing.

Get ready, he told himself. *If it's going to happen, it'll happen now—*

Pilots had been complaining that during attack dives the Starscythe's chopped wings interacted with its tail fins to cause the nose to abruptly rise up, stalling the jet, and putting her into a flat spin. Brigadier General Howard Simon, whose pet project the Starscythe was, had called from Dayton to ask Steve to check the problem out, saying that the F-404 that was waiting for Steve at Andrews A.F.B. was one of the first off the Amalgamated-Landis assembly lines.

It gave Steve a real thrill to be one of the first to fly a new airplane like this, but not nearly the thrill he felt as his diving Starscythe's nose abruptly pitched up and his wings lost their bite. His helmet clanked hard against the canopy as the stumbling jet slid across the sky and went into its spin.

Well, this is where I wanted to be, Steve thought to himself. His instrument panel had gone from tranquil green to warning, buzzing amber/red. The Starscythe was falling like an autumn leaf and also twirling like a top as it fell, like a dog chasing its own tail. Steve watched the sky whip around sideways as his harness cut into his shoulders: At least the webbing kept him from being hurled against the steel and plexi walls of his cockpit like the little steel ball that catapulted around the walls of a spinning roulette wheel—

Thinking of which, Steve hoped that his number would *not* come up as he struggled to get the jet's nose down. He'd taken her up as high as she could go in order to leave himself enough room to recover from his purposely induced spin— At least that's what he was hoping.

He was down around thirty thousand feet when he finally got the Starscythe back under control. He leveled her off, and then came around to bring her back home to Andrews, taking deep breaths to slow the jackrabbit thud of his heart. As he called in for permission to land he was already mentally composing his report to General Moore. Beneath the green rubber oxygen mask his grin was as wide as the sky.

The ground crew was waiting for Steve as he taxied the Starscythe along the tarmac toward the hangars. He climbed down out of the airplane and walked toward the ready room with his helmet tucked under his arm.

"Steve! Wait up!"

He turned, and was surprised to see Jack Horton coming toward him. The wind caught the front of Horton's gray suit jacket, lifting it away, and Steve glimpsed the snub-nosed revolver in its high-ride, black leather holster on Horton's right hip.

"You must really be coming up in the world if your CIA credentials have the clout to get you into an Air Force restricted access area carrying a piece." Steve laughed, shaking hands with Horton. "It's good to see you again, Jack."

"Yeah." Horton grinned. "It's been a while."

Steve nodded. He and Horton had worked together on Capitol Hill to put a public relations gloss on the joint operation between the CIA and the Air Force to supply military aid to the French forces in Indochina.

Horton pointed to the Starscythe behind Steve. "Most guys would be spending a beautiful Saturday like this relaxing . . ."

"Who says I wasn't?" Steve smiled. "But what brings *you* out here on *your* day off?"

"Who says it's my day off?" Horton replied. "I came out here to talk to you about a business matter."

Steve wanted to get his ideas concerning the Starscythe down on paper for General Moore while they were still fresh in his head. "Tell you what, see if your credentials will get you into the cafeteria over at the main complex."

"I think I can handle that."

"Okay, you go have yourself a cup of coffee. I'll hit the lockers and then I'll join you."

"That airplane you were flying is new, isn't it?' Horton asked.

"Yeah," Steve replied. "She's got a few nasty habits, but nothing that can't be tamed."

They were at a table in the cafeteria, having coffee and doughnuts. It was after lunch, so the room was nearly deserted. Steve had showered, trading his sweat-soaked overalls for tropical-weight tan wool slacks, a light blue cotton shirt, and a green and tan, silk-weave single-breasted sport jacket. In his pocket was his rough draft report on the Star-scythe. On Monday he'd give it to his secretary to be typed up for General Moore.

"Over all, I'd say that Amalgamated-Landis had built the Air Force a good fighter," Steve continued.

Horton smiled. "Your father is going to be pissed."

"That's true." Steve laughed. "Even if GAT has temporarily pretty much gotten out of the fighter business in order to concentrate on commercial jetliners. The one thing my father can't handle is taking a backseat to anyone in anything." He paused. "But you didn't come here to talk about jet fighters. Outside you'd implied that you were here to see me on some sort of business?"

Horton tore a strip off his napkin and began to methodically shred it. "Let me start off by saying that I was very impressed with the way you handled yourself calming our little ruckus . . ."

Steve nodded. It had been tricky back in February smoothing out the Indochina flap. The French had been bracing to make their stand at Dien Bien Phu, while Eisenhower had been making speeches about what a tragedy it would be for the United States to get involved. Meanwhile, the President was busy authorizing hundreds of millions in military aid, and a dozen C-119 cargo transports to fly parachute drops to the French forces surrounded at Dien Bien Phu. The Air Force C-119s and their crews had belonged to the Air Force but had been transferred to Civil Air Transport, a CIA-backed operation. There had been concern on the Hill about the wisdom of letting the CIA get involved in the French fight. Ike had been able to silence the critics by warning that if the United States didn't lend an indirect helping hand in Vietnam now, the nation might find itself having to do the whole job later on, but then the shit really hit the fan when it leaked that Ike had authorized the sending of two hundred Air Force technicians to help the French maintain the CAT fleet of C-119 transports. For a while it looked as if the CIA's secret airline was going to get its wings plucked, but the concerted public relations campaign by the CIA and the USAF had saved the day.

"A bunch of us over at the Company have had our eyes on you since you helped smooth out things," Horton continued. "We don't forget, kid; not our enemies, and *especially* not our friends. My superiors have talked with your superiors, and I've gotten the okay."

"Okay for *what*?" Steve asked sharply. "Jack, nobody's talked to *me*—"

"I'm talking to you now. I'm offering you a tour of duty with the Company. You know as well as I do that some time working with us could really advance your career."

"I *do* know that," Steve murmured, intrigued. The CIA and the Air Force had done a lot of work together concerning aerial reconnaissance since the advent of the Cold War. Those Air Force officers who had "sheep-dipped"—taken a temporary tour of duty with the Agency—had moved quickly up the promotional ladder. "But you haven't told me what it is I'd be doing . . ."

"We've got a new spy plane," Horton said. "A plane that will allow us to go anywhere we want over the Soviet Union and take pictures to our heart's content."

"I've heard a little about that." Steve nodded. "This new bird you guys are building is supposed to be state of the art."

"It is," Horton said proudly. "It's code-named Mayfly—"

Steve laughed.

"What's so funny?" Horton demanded, sounding affronted.

"Well, hell, Jack, you've got to admit Mayfly is kind of a pessimistic moniker. I mean, everybody *knows* a mayfly only lives for a day . . ."

Horton stared at him, his eyes blinking rapidly from behind those black horn-rims. "Anyway, the May—*our spy plane*—is in the prototype stage. We've got to start thinking about recruiting and training pilots."

"Aren't you going to get them from the Air Force?" Steve asked.

"Yes and no. You see, officially this is strictly a Company

operation, but unofficially, the Air Force is working hand in glove with us, and is willing to *lend* us some pilots. The Air Force is willing to release them for the time they'll be serving with the Company, and then reinstate them with no penalties concerning promotion or retirement when we're done with them."

"It sounds to me like you're looking for volunteers," Steve said. "Is that what you want me to do? Volunteer to fly one of these babies?" He thought, *If taking snapshots of Red Square is what the future holds, getting out of the Air Force and going to work for Pop is looking better all the time.*

Horton shook his head, smiling. "You underestimate yourself, kid. You're far too valuable to be wasted in a cockpit."

Hearing that made Steve feel wonderful. That was the first time anybody important who wasn't *related* to him had suggested that he was good for something other than flying airplanes.

"Like you said, the pilots we need are going to have to volunteer," Horton continued. "We're willing to pay well to get them to work for us, but the job we're going to be asking them to do is going to be pretty dangerous. Nobody in his right mind would do it just for the money. These pilots are going to need to be *recruited, motivated,* and *trained*—" He paused. "That's where you come in. You're just the guy we need to get us those pilots and instill in them the *need* to *succeed.* You've got the wartime record and the reputation to make the guys we're after look up to you."

"It kind of sounds like public relations stuff all over again," Steve said doubtfully.

"It's not public relations, it's *leadership,*" Horton argued. "This is an important job, and it's going to take brains to pull it off. A lot of the top brass, in and *out* of uniform will be watching. You pull this off and you'll be able to write your own ticket: an assignment to the Joint Chiefs of Staff, the State Department . . ."

Steve had stopped listening when Horton had said the job required brains. Here was a job that required smarts, not just a chest full of medals, a handsome mug, and an expense account, and he was being tapped for it. If he could pull it off, and he knew that he could, a lot of people were going to be very surprised, as well as impressed . . .

"Well." Horton smiled. "I guess you'll want some time to think about it?"

"I don't need to think about it," Steve said. "I accept."

"That's wonderful!" Horton laughed. "But just like that? Are you sure?"

"I don't see how I can refuse." Steve smiled. "You told me yourself that it's an important job that will boost my career. Confidentially, I've been looking for a way out of my present assignment. I think I've about worn out my welcome up on the Hill, which means I've about worn out my welcome at the Office of Public Information."

"Hey." Horton shrugged. "You know what they say about blaming the messenger for bad news."

Steve nodded. Last summer he and the other Air Force personnel lobbying on Capitol Hill had found themselves caught in a cross fire between Congress and the President over who was to blame for the French defeat in Indochina. The shitstorm began when the French, realizing that they were losing at Dien Bien Phu, formally requested United States air power intervention. Ike, who had been warning that the rest of Southeast Asia would fall like dominoes to the Commies if the French were defeated, ordered the Joint Chiefs of Staff to draw a plan of action. The JCS came up with Operation Vulture: Sixty Air Force B-29 bombers escorted by 150 Navy fighters to hit the Commies dug in around the French, but Vulture was never able to get off the ground. Dien Bien Phu fell to the Commies toward the end of May 1954, and the French, humiliated and defeated, went to the Far East Peace Conference in Geneva with their tails between their legs. There they agreed to divide Vietnam into North and South, just the way the Commies wanted it.

"You've got to expect a certain amount of finger pointing over this fiasco," Horton was saying. "You know there was still a lot of bad blood on the Hill concerning China."

"There's a lot of bullshit up there, you mean," Steve grumbled, thinking about how the democratic leaders of Congress, anxious to get revenge on the Republicans for the way the GOP had branded Truman "the man who lost China" back in '49, were now claiming that Vietnam had been lost because Ike had vacillated. The President, through his Secretary of State, John Foster Dulles, was now laying down a double line of defense: that Indochina wasn't all that crucial to the security of Southeast Asia, after all; and that in any case, the responsibility of losing it rested with powerful Democrats like Senator Lyndon Johnson because they did not back Operation Vulture.

"What gets under my skin is that the one thing the entire Hill agrees on is that the Air Force is at fault," Steve complained. "The noninterventionists are blaming us for lowering America's prestige by getting involved in the first place, and the 'should'a-used-the-bomb' crowd is blaming us for not *finishing* the fight."

"Well, you've got to understand how badly everyone felt about this," Horton replied. "I mean, it was—and still is— just inconceivable that some ragtag band of barefoot Commie peasants could whip the French Army..."

"Barefoot Commie peasants?" Steve smiled ruefully. "I've heard *that* before. You weren't involved in Korea, were you Jack?"

"No, I sat that one out."

"You know that I didn't," Steve replied. "So let me tell you that until you've seen them in action you just can't imagine how effective those so-called peasants can be, especially when they're supplied with the best weapons the Iron Curtain countries have to offer."

"But if we'd only committed air power to the battle—" Horton began.

"No way," Steve cut him off. "I know that's been the Company's position all along, Jack, but air power couldn't have finished the job in Indochina any more than it could in Korea. You can't fault the Air Force brass for realizing as much, and what's more, realizing that when air power *did* fail, the Air Force would have been placed in an awful disadvantage compared to the other branches of the service when it came time to lobby for appropriations."

"So what are you saying?" Horton demanded. "That the United States was right to stand by and watch the French get whipped?"

"I'm saying that if you expected the Air Force to *start* the fight, you had to be prepared to bring in the Army to *finish* it. That's the way it worked in Korea: Air power could do only so much, and then it was up to the Marines and the Army to do the dirty job of digging out the enemy. Do you think the American people were ready for that? For another mobilization?"

"No way," Horton admitted. "This country hasn't the stomach for another war in Asia so soon after Korea."

"That's right," Steve said, and frowned. "But a simple thing like the truth won't stop the politicians from making the Air Force a scapegoat for their own, and the nation's lack of will. That's why I don't need any time to consider your offer. I'm all through being a whipping boy up on the Hill. I just don't have what it takes any more to play the diplomat, or to stand politely with hat in hand, hoping to convince a few powerful senators and congressmen to toss the Air Force a few coins." He paused. "As a matter of fact, I'll let you in on a little secret, Jack. I'd already decided to leave the service—"

"No kidding?"

Steve nodded. "Of course, now I'm staying in, so that I can do this job for you."

"Nobody in the Air Force I talked to seemed to know that you were planning on leaving," Horton said.

"That's because I'd been keeping my decision to myself," Steve explained. "I wanted to let this Indochina flap blow over before I went public with the news. I didn't want anyone to misunderstand my resignation. I didn't want the Air Force's enemies on the Hill to use my resignation as propaganda; to claim that my leaving the service was some sort of vote of misconfidence on my part against the Air Force."

"I see," Horton murmured. "What were you going to do once you were back in civilian life?"

"Work for my father."

Horton smiled. "That's kind of ironic, because, in a way, you still will be working for Herman. You see, our state-of-the-art spy plane is being built by your father's company."

"No kidding?" Steve said, feeling proud.

"But here's the thing," Horton cautioned. "We believe in compartmentalization; in other words, 'the need to know.' You can't tell anyone, *including your father*, about your tour with us."

"I understand." Steve nodded. "I suppose I'll have some kind of cover?"

"Your present Air Force assignment will work fine as your cover," Horton said. "I've already gotten an all-clear with your superiors for you to maintain your office at the Pentagon, but your present OPI duties will be reassigned. You can expect to do a lot of traveling."

Steve laughed. "I can't believe you already cleared this with the Air Force. I guess you were pretty confident that I was going to accept your offer...?"

Horton grew solemn. "I was confident that when your country needed you, you'd *be* there."

(Two)

GAT
Burbank, California
15 August 1955

Herman Gold was in his office going over some figures with Don Harrison when his secretary interrupted to tell him that his son was on the line. Gold put his finger to his lips to caution Harrison to remain quiet as he picked up the telephone.

"Steve!" Gold said, leaning back in his desk chair. "How are you, son?"

"Fine, Pop."

"You know, Stevie, I've been doing a lot of thinking about our idea concerning you getting involved with sales. I think the sales department is going to be the best place for you to start—"

"Pop, slow down a minute," Steve said.

"Yes, what is it?" Gold asked nervously, his son's tone of voice warning him that something was up.

"Pop, I've been trying to figure out the best way to tell you this for the past week, but I guess there *is* no best way, so I might as well just spit it out: I've reconsidered my decision to leave the Air Force. I'm staying in."

"But Stevie, I thought we'd worked it all out," Gold protested. "I thought that you'd come to the conclusion that the Air Force was a dead end for you—?"

"I thought it *was*, Pop, but something new has happened..."

"What do you mean, 'new'?" Gold demanded. "I don't understand what you're trying to tell me—"

"I know you don't, Pop," Steve said, sounding wistful. "But unfortunately I'm not allowed to tell you anymore about it. I wish I could..." he added earnestly. "Someday I will be able to tell you, and when I do, I'm confident that you'll think I did the right thing..."

"This new assignment—or whatever it is—must be pretty important for you to change your mind like this," Gold murmured.

"Pop, like I said, someday you'll understand, and when you do, you'll be proud..."

"I've *always* been proud of you," Gold fondly chided him. You should know that by now."

"Yeah, sure I do, Pop," Steve said softly. "But just wait till I can tell you about *this*," he added excitedly. "I *swear* it, Pop, you're going to be proud of me in a whole *new* way. After this, nobody will be able to say I'm not fit for the executive suite..."

"Well, I waited this long for my son to join me," Gold said philosophically. "I guess I can wait a little longer."

"Thanks for understanding, Pop," Steve said, sounding relieved. "Listen, I've got to go. I've got a lot to do. Give my love to Mom and Suzy. I'll call home in a couple of days."

"All right, son."

"Bye, Pop."

"Good-bye," Gold said, and hung up the telephone.

"Well?" Don asked. "Did it work?"

"Like a charm." Gold nodded. He pressed down on his intercom button, and told his secretary, "Get me Jack Horton."

"Good idea," Don said. "We ought to personally thank him for getting us out of this mess concerning Steve."

"We owe Jack one big favor, all right," Gold agreed. "And General Simon, as well," he added. "It was Howie who pulled the strings with the Air Force to get Jack the permission to recruit Steve . . ." He smiled. "And you know what, Don? I'm starting to think this is all going to work out for the best, after all . . ."

"Good," Don said evenly. "I wouldn't want there to be any resentment between us concerning my insistence that you find a way to keep Steve out of the company."

Gold shook his head. "I admit that I was pissed at you for a while, but not now. You can't imagine how excited and happy Steve was sounding. This tour of duty with the CIA is going to be just the thing to give him the confidence he needs."

"I want Steve to be happy." Don nodded. "Happy, and *far away* . . ."

CHAPTER 8

(One)

Gold Household
Bel-Air
Los Angeles, California
17 March 1956

Susan Greene looked out her bedroom window, and saw her mother sitting by the pool. Now's as good a time as any, she thought. She grabbed a terry cloth robe, put it on over her bathing suit, and hurried from the room. She needed to go through with this before she lost her nerve.

She ran barefoot down the hallway to the curved, marble staircase, and then she did something she hadn't done in over twenty years: She parked her rump on the banister and slid down it, catching a glimpse of herself in the foyer mirror as she landed flat-footed, flexing her knees and windmilling her arms for balance.

She burst out in exhilarated laughter, feeling such a tremendous rush of love for this house. Her father had bought it in 1927. It was a rambling, vine-covered, English colonial, sheltered behind stone walls in Bel-Air. There were gardens, one with a splashing fountain, rolling expanses of lawn, a swimming pool, and a four-car garage. A caretaker lived above the garage, and Ramona, the housekeeper who'd been with the family since Susan was a toddler, had a bedroom off the kitchen. A couple of girls came in during the week to help Ramona with the cleaning.

Susan had moved out of this house when she was nineteen; that was in 1941, when she'd married Blaize Greene. The couple had moved into Blaize's little apartment in Santa Monica, near the pier. In those days Blaize, an RAF reserve officer, and an engineer as well as an accomplished racer and test pilot, had been on loan to GAT in order to work on a joint American/British fighter plane prototype. Soon after they were married, the RAF had called her husband back to England, to take fighter pilot training at a base just outside of London. Susan had gone with him, and set up house in a rented flat near Russell Square. For several months Blaize had been able to pull strings to be allowed to spend some nights and scattered weekends with her in London. She became pregnant about the time he graduated from training school. She had only just begun to show when he was assigned to a fighter squadron with the RAF's Desert Air Force, in Libya...

It was after he'd been killed in action, and after her son Robert Blaize Greene was born, that she'd come back home with her baby to California, to her parents, and to the warm and comforting embrace of this house...

She walked through the downstairs, passing through the big rooms with their fireplaces, parquet floors, high, gilded ceilings, and mahogany paneling. She went out through the solarium's french doors, to the flagstone patio landscaped with shrubbery and redwood flower boxes.

Her mother, wearing a black tank suit and reclining on a duck canvas chaise longue beneath the shade of a eucalyptus tree, heard her coming and looking up, smiling. Her mother had just turned fifty-four years old, but she seemed much younger. Her appearance had a lot to do with it, Susan thought. Her mother still had a super figure, and wore her blond hair in a short, touseled, Italian cut that emphasized her youthfulness, as did her outlook on life. Her mother seemed proud of the laugh lines around her almond-shaped brown eyes and at the corners of her wide mouth.

Back in the 1920s and '30s, Erica Gold had been a famous pilot; a renowed aviatrix who'd helped conquer the skies along with the likes of Amelia Earhart and Beryl Markham. Her picture had been featured on magazine covers; her exploits had been documented in the newsreels. Today, her flying trophies and mementos were now proudly displayed in her husband's office.

Her mother's only imperfection—if you could call it that, Susan thought—was her nose. Her mother had broken her nose in some tom girl stunt when she was little, and it had healed with a slight bump on it.

Susan's father said that it had been that bump that had made him fall in love with her mother, first thing.

"I didn't think you were still home," her mother said. "I would have thought that since Robbie's with his grandfather you would have taken the opportunity to take off with Don on a beautiful Saturday like this . . ."

Susan shrugged, staring out at the shimmering, turquoise, rectangular pool. "I guess I wanted to talk about something."

"About what?" her mother asked, putting aside her magazine.

"Don's asked me to marry him."

"Well! Isn't that good news . . . ?" Her mother smiled tentatively. "What did you tell him?"

"That I wanted to think about it . . ."

"And have you?"

"I think I'm going to accept."

Her mother nodded. "You . . . *think* you are . . ." When Susan shrugged, her mother added, "Do you love Don?"

"I think I do," Susan sighed.

"Suzy, dear..." Her mother coughed, then cleared her throat. "This is rather awkward for me to ask, but... have you had... *intimate relations* with Don?"

"Yes, Mother." She grinned. "We've made love..." Wickedly, she paused.

Her mother rolled her eyes, exasperated. "*And?*"

Laughing, Susan said, "And it was fine. Seriously, we've been intimate for some months. I mean, we've certainly been going together a long time," she added defensively. "I guess I knew that Don was leading up to proposing to me. I guess I encouraged it, but now that he has I'm suddenly not sure. I mean, I think about Don, and I like to be with him, but if you're asking me if I feel for him what I felt for Blaize..." She trailed off, shaking her head. "I've thought about it a lot. Maybe you can *really* fall in love only *once*, and if, for whatever reason, that first love doesn't last, the next loves will be imitations of that first time."

"I don't think it's a question of verisimilitude as much as one of intensity," her mother said. "First love is always the sweetest."

"Then *you* were very lucky," Susan replied. "Your first love has lasted."

"Thirty-five years." She nodded.

"It was love at first sight between you and Daddy, wasn't it?" Susan coaxed. "Just the way it was between Blaize and me?"

"Yes."

"If something had happened to Daddy early on," Susan began, "do you think you would have remarried?"

Her mother smiled. "I think that I *probably* would have, if the right man had come along."

"But you wouldn't have loved him the same way you loved Daddy, right?"

"I think that you just hit the nail on the head," her mother replied. "You're right that I wouldn't have loved my hypothetical second husband the way I love your father, but *I would have loved him*, or else I would never marry him.

Likewise, I strongly urge *you* not to marry a man you don't love."

"Then what are you saying?" Susan demanded.

"I'm saying that you need to look inside yourself concerning your feelings for Don. To do that, you need to separate yourself from the past—"

"You mean forget about Blaize? How could I ever—?"

"You don't forget about him," her mother gently instructed. "I'm only suggesting that you need to stop thinking about him for a while, in order to think about what you feel for Don."

Susan smiled wryly. "What if I told you I wanted to marry Don for Robbie's sake? So that he would have a normal family; a father . . .?"

"I wouldn't believe it," her mother said firmly. "You and your son are already surrounded by family, and besides, you're too strong a woman to think that way."

"You're sure of that?"

"Of course I am. You're my daughter."

Susan had to laugh. How characteristic that last comment had been! "What you mean is that I can't disappoint *not* because of who *I* am, but because of who *you* are." She was aware of the bitterness in her tone. "It's the same trouble that Daddy has relating with Steve: the chip-off-the-old-block syndrome."

"What's that supposed to mean?" Erica asked coolly.

"That you mistake your confidence in yourself as confidence in me. *You're* perfect, and *you* produced *me*, so *I* must be perfect, as if I were one of Daddy's airplanes rolling off the assembly lines."

"I don't think I'm perfect, Susan." Her mother frowned.

Why am I getting us into this? Susan wondered. "Mother, please let's not fight."

"Fine . . ."

"I'm sorry I said what I did." Susan realized that she really was sorry. "I don't know what's wrong with me lately. I've been feeling so moody . . ."

"It's all right, dear."

"Maybe I should see the doctor," Susan mused. "I've been feeling so under the weather."

"Because you worry too much," her mother said. "But you know, you *do* have to be careful how to deal with Don," her mother warned. "You must remember he's very important to your father, and the company—"

"Dammit, Mother!" Susan exploded. "I'm talking about love, not business!"

"You're not being fair—"

"What does fairness have to do with anything?"

"Suzy, you're being childish," her mother scolded. She paused. "So what are you going to do?"

"Marry Don . . . I guess . . ." Susan shrugged.

Her mother looked troubled. "But you *do* love Don?"

"In my way, I really do." Susan nodded, and allowed her mother's relieved expression to relieve her own doubts, as well.

(Two)

Alexandria, Virginia
12 October 1956

Steven Gold woke up to the smell of coffee, and glanced at the alarm clock on the nightstand beside his bed. It was 11 A.M., Sunday morning. He was lying on his back, nude, beneath the sheet, in the bedroom of his apartment on Prince Street. Linda Forrester, who was also nude, except for a pair of tortoiseshell eyeglasses perched on the tip of her nose, was sitting at his bedroom desk, sipping coffee while she studied one of the assignment files she'd brought with her on this trip to Washington.

She'd flown in Friday night, and they'd spent the weekend together. Tomorrow she had an appointment to interview the First Lady about the rigors of the campaign trail. Nobody doubted that Ike was a shoe-in against Stevenson in next month's election.

Steve remained quiet. He didn't want Linda, just now absently twirling her fingers in her shoulder-length, dark brown hair as she read, to realize that he was awake. He liked watching her when she wasn't aware of him, and not acting all flustered and self-conscious . . .

She'd evidently been spending a lot of time at the beach, back home in Los Angeles. Her skin was tanned to the color of coffee with cream, except for her startlingly white breasts and bottom where her bikini had kept away the sun. She was sitting perched on the edge of the straight-backed desk chair, her sleek, pear-shaped ass splayed against the black leather upholstery. As she leaned forward to turn a page, her white breasts bobbed, and a slight fold of belly appeared, bisecting her navel. When she shifted her position, the chair's leather seat made a soft, moist, kissing sound as it briefly adhered to her thighs. Now she was bringing up one tawny leg and tucking it beneath her like a stork, to reveal her dark thatch.

She saw that he was awake and smiled. "Have you been watching me all this time?" she demanded, laughing.

"So I'm a voyeur." Steve grinned. "A dirty old man."

"Well, you're dirty, all right." Linda smiled. "But evidently not so old." She gestured toward his erection, sticking up like a tent pole beneath the sheet.

"Well, are you going to do something about this?"

She took off her reading glasses and tossed them onto the file, then stood up and came over to the foot of the bed. She grabbed the top sheet and whisked it away. Then she pounced.

He hardly needed to fondle her before she was wet, and eagerly reaching for him. He tried to roll over on top of her, but she murmured, "No," pinning him back, and he remembered that lately she'd been liking it better when she was on top.

"How many times will this make?" she asked as she straddled him.

"Let's see: twice Friday night, and five times yesterday," Steve said, sighing happily as she impaled herself upon him with a wiggle of her hips. "This is only number eight, but the day's still young."

She began to rock back and forth, reaching back to tickle his balls. "You have anything left in these?" she teased.

"Seek and ye shall find."

Her pace gradually began to quicken. He reached up to pull her forward so that he could nibble at her pink nipples, and she gasped, riding him even faster, her thighs flexing and hips pumping. They were both sweating now. The bed was rocking with their exertions. He groaned and squirmed as she ground herself against him, their bodies making wet, slapping sounds. He heard her first, soft moans, almost like whispers, and smiled. They were old flying buddies; knew each other's sign language by heart: Her whimpers told him that she was poised at the brink, and he took pleasure in concentrating on her; on starting her on the downward slope until she was out of control.

Her moans increased, as did her urgent bucking, and then her hot, wet mouth that had been pressed against his ear, lifted away. She orgasmed with her spine arched and her head rocked back, so that he was able to see her flushed face. Her eyes were closed, the lids tinged with blue. Her lips, which had been pressed together in a thin line—almost a grimace—abruptly blossomed wide to free her shrill cry.

He held her—cradled her, really—through her diminishing throes and flutters. It was when she was lying limp and docile on his chest that he cupped her ass and thrust into her, growling—then moaning—as he came.

"It's always so good between us," Linda whispered, sounding amazed. "Hasn't it always been so good?"

"You know it has," Steve said. They were lying side by side on the bed, sharing a cigarette. He had the black, plastic ashtray from the nightstand balanced on his chest.

"Steve?" she murmured, lightly tracing around his nipple with her fingernail.

"Yeah?" he asked, exhaling smoke. As she tickled his

nipple his cock stirred but stayed where it was: He wasn't goddamned Superman, for chrissakes.

"What would you say if I told you I was pregnant?"

"Holy shit!" Steve sat bolt-upright, spilling the ashtray to the bed.

"Hey!" Linda twisted away from the spilled ashes.

"Are you? Are you pregnant?" he demanded, thinking guiltily of the times—like just now—when he'd made love to her bareback. *Just one more chance*, he prayed. *Get me out of this one, and I'll never do it again—*

"Of course I'm not pregnant," Linda said, righting the ashtray and trying to scoop the ashes off the sheet. "I'd asked you what *if*."

"Well that was quite a scare you gave me," Steve muttered, relieved.

"Excuse *me*," she replied, sounding pissed off.

"What are you mad about?" Steve asked. He took the ashtray from her and ground out the cigarette.

"Who said I'm mad?" Linda groused. "I'm not mad . . ."

Steve shrugged.

"Okay!" she blurted, moving away from him to sit cross-legged at the end of the bed. "Maybe I'm upset over how you reacted to my 'what if.' Like my being pregnant would be the worst thing in the world."

"Well, it's not like we're married," Steve pointed out.

"Well, maybe we should be," Linda said carefully. "We've been together a lot this past year. And a lot's changed . . . Like the fact that you're going to leave the Air Force, even if you have been dragging your butt about doing it—"

Steve frowned.

"What?" Linda demanded. "Why are you looking at me like that?"

Linda had been the only person outside of his family who he'd told about his decision to leave the military, and she'd been happy over the prospect of his coming back to L.A., but then Jack Horton had recruited him for the spy plane project. Since then, Steve had ben stalling Linda, making up all sorts of excuses to avoid telling her that he'd changed his mind. Putting her off hadn't been difficult because she was so busy in her own career, going off on assignment for months at a time, and when they spoke on the telephone it was easy for Steve to rationalize that he ought to wait to tell her in person. Now, here she was. He knew he had to face the music.

"Linda, there's been a change. I'm staying in the Air Force."

"What?" She looked shocked. "When did this happen?"

"A while ago," he admitted.

"I see," she said evenly.

"I know I should have told you sooner—"

"Yes, I think you *should* have . . ." She was acting calmly, but Steve knew that she was struggling to choke back her anger.

"I didn't want to upset you . . ."

"May I ask why you've made this decision?"

This was going to be the killer, Steve thought. He longed to tell her why he was staying in, but he couldn't. She knew him better than anybody; she of all people would understand why it was so important for him to successfully complete this assignment; what personal vindication it would bring him—

But he couldn't tell her: not her, not anyone. The spy plane project was ultra top secret.

"You seem to be at a loss for words," Linda said bitterly. "Tell me this much, at least: Has the Air Force reassigned you?"

Steve thought about his cover. "No . . . I'll still be with OPI."

"Uh-huh." Linda nodded. "So, what you're telling me is that your situation is exactly the same, but that for some mysterious reason you've changed your mind and decided to remain in the Air Force, here in Washington. Only you couldn't find the decency to tell me. All this while you've been lying to me, stringing me along with false hope . . ."

She smiled thinly. "Now that I think about it, I guess it isn't such a mystery, after all . . ."

"What do you mean?"

"It's obvious, Steve! You've decided to stay in because of me! It's your way of keeping me at arm's length! It's all as clear as day to me! You realized that once you were in Los Angeles we'd be seeing much more of each other, and that obviously frightened the hell out of you, so you decided to stay three thousand miles away from me to avoid having to make a commitment!"

"Linda, that's just not true!" Steve insisted.

"It isn't? What *other* reason—besides avoiding me—*could* you *have* for remaining here in Washington doing what you yourself have admitted is a dead-end assignment?"

Jesus Christ, Steve thought. *I'm totally framed. Only the truth will convince her, but I can't tell her about the spy plane* . . . "I know how it looks, but you're wrong. Believe me, you are—"

"Then prove it!"

"Okay! I will!" he said desperately. "Why don't *you* move *here*?"

"Huh?"

"You move to Washington. Then we could be together." He took a deep breath. "And then, eventually, I guess we could be . . . married . . ."

Her anger momentarily lessened, but then her flashing blue eyes regained their frost. "You sonofabitch," she hissed.

"Me?" he blurted, surprised and confused by her reaction.

"You think you're *so smart*! You *know* I can't move here! I've worked hard for years to become a senior news correspondent in L.A."

"You could work for a newspaper here," Steve said.

"Oh, sure!" she snapped. "Just that easy, huh, buster? It so happens that jobs for women journalists at my level are few and far between, and don't pretend that you didn't know that!"

"I never thought about it," he admitted truthfully.

"Right! You didn't think!" She jumped off the bed and began pulling clothes out of her suitcase lying on the carpet in the corner of the room.

"What are you doing?"

"Getting dressed and going to my hotel."

"Aw, come on . . ." He tried to think of a way to delay her, to give him time to sweet-talk her out of her anger. "Don't you even want to take a shower first?"

"Oh, I'll shower, all right! At the hotel!"

"Linda, don't be this way! I *meant* it about you living in Washington. I'm sorry I forgot about your job. I was just trying to—"

"I *know* what you're trying to do." She was pulling on loose-fitting dungarees and a dark brown cashmere turtleneck. She'd been wearing that outfit, and her mink coat—she'd called it her Katharine Hepburn look—when he'd picked her up at the airport on Friday night, and she'd looked outstanding, turning heads as she strode through the gate and into his arms . . .

"You don't have to say another thing—" She was at the mirror above the maple lowboy, simultaneously dashing through her makeup routine and running a brush through her hair. "You're going to get exactly what you wanted: rid of me!"

"This is just ridiculous," he said lamely.

"I'll say it is." She gathered up the rest of her belongings, chucking them into the suitcase. "Our relationship has been ridiculous right from the beginning, but let me tell you something now. *We are through.*" She said it calmly but firmly. Steve could tell that she was dead serious. "We're finished. You won't hear from me anymore." She pointed her finger like a gun at his chest. "And *I* don't want to hear from *you.*"

She snapped shut her suitcase. "Oh, and Steve, darling," she said sarcastically, "should we by chance run into each other in the future, do me a favor? Pretend you don't know me—" She dropped her steady facade to shout in a rage, "Because by then, *I* will surely have forgotten *you!*"

She grabbed her suitcase and stormed out of the room. Steve stayed in bed, feeling dumbstruck and helpless; like a man trapped in a nightmare. He could hear her rummaging around in the apartment, gathering up her stray things, and then the closet door opening and closing as she grabbed her coat. She left the apartment slamming the front door so hard the window glass shook.

And he was alone.

He got out of bed and padded nude and barefoot across the blue wall-to-wall carpeting into the living room. Like the bedroom, the living room had brick walls painted white and a minimum of furnishings: He hated clutter. The living room contained a floor-to-ceiling wall unit crafted of maple to house his television and hi-fi equipment. Arranged around the "sound wall" was a dark blue tweed sofa and a pair of matching armchairs flanked by glass-topped brass end tables. A rattan chest with sliding doors he'd picked up cheap in one of the antique shops on King Street was placed beneath the living room's window, which overlooked a brick-walled garden.

Steve used the rattan chest as his liquor cabinet, and that's where he now headed. It was just a little after twelve noon, but considering what he'd just been through he figured a drink was in order. He poured a generous shot of vodka into a tumbler, and then went into the small galley kitchen to get himself some ice and tomato juice: He had no kitchen equipment beyond a coffee maker but prided himself on keeping the refrigerator well stocked with mixers.

He mixed his Bloody Mary, and then stood in the kitchen, taking long pulls of his drink, thinking about how Linda was probably standing on the corner, hoping to flag down a cab. *Good luck*, he thought. It wasn't easy finding a taxi in Alexandria on a Sunday . . . If he wanted to, he could pull on some clothes, run downstairs, and likely catch her before she was gone—

If he *wanted* to . . .

He thought about it; how he felt. Goddamn, what he felt was relief.

He drained his glass, rinsed it out in the sink, then went back through the apartment to the bathroom off the bedroom, to shower and shave. In the bedroom he paused to grab his smokes off the nightstand, lit one, and took it with him into the tiled bathroom.

He switched on the light. "Shit!"

Floating in the sudsy water in the stoppered sink were her pale blue lace panties. He stared at the damned things a moment, then sagged against the bathroom doorjamb. *She's really gone*, he realized, closing his eyes, feeling tired and dizzy.

Has to be the drink, he told himself. Gotta be a damn fool to gulp down a drink like that on an empty stomach. *No wonder you feel so unsettled; so bad . . .*

The awful way he was feeling had absolutely nothing to do with the fact that she was gone, he told himself. *Dammit, absolutely nothing!*

He snapped his cigarette into the toilet bowl. Then, swearing savagely, he scooped the panties out of the sink and ran with them dripping a water trail across the carpet into the kitchen, where he tossed them into the trash.

CHAPTER 9

(One)

**Burbank, California
12 January 1957**

It was six-fifteen on a smog gray Wednesday morning when Herman Gold nosed his Cadillac into the Desert-Vue Diner's lot. He found a parking spot between a taxicab and a delivery truck, near the door to the aluminum and pink railroad car eatery. As he walked toward the diner's entrance he thought that whatever desert this joint might once have "vued" had long since vanished.

The diner's rectangular patch of asphalt was bordered by a hardware store and a dry cleaner. Across the street was a used car lot where a line of elderly De Sotos, Packards, and Ramblers sat quietly rusting under tattered, flapping pennants. Behind the diner, green trash dumpsters had replaced the dunes.

As Gold went into the diner he was hit by the smell of burned grease and cigar smoke. Behind the counter a middle-aged waitress was dishing out doughnuts and refilling coffee mugs while the short-order cook was frantic at his bank of toasters and sizzling grill. The counter stools were all occupied by sleepy-eyed, quiet men in work clothes, eating or smoking, while hunched over their coffee.

Opposite the counter was a row of red vinyl upholstered booths, their windows overlooking the parking lot. None of the booths were occupied, Gold noticed, except for the one at the far end, where Tim Campbell sat waiting for him.

"Good morning, Herman," Campbell said, standing up to shake hands. "Long time no see, amigo."

"Yeah, it has been a long time," Gold said. "You're looking well." Campbell was in his mid-fifties, short and stocky, with a full head (damn the sonofabitch) of gray-tinged auburn hair, slicked down and parted in the middle. This morning he was looking natty in a gray and black striped three-piece suit, yellow shirt, and too much jewelry: gold I.D. bracelet, gold watch, diamond pinky ring, and diamond stickpin glittering in his purple and ivory paisley tie.

"Well, sit down, Herman," Campbell said.

Gold hesitated, glancing down at the cracked vinyl to make sure there wasn't smeared egg yolk, or something else on it. He happened to be wearing a new blue cashmere blazer, and it was likely going to have to go to the cleaners just from absorbing the odors in this place.

"Congratulations on your daughter's marriage," Campbell said as they settled in. "Don Harrison's a great guy. I'm sure they'll be happy together."

"Thank you," Gold said, feeling uncomfortable because his ex-partner hadn't been invited. "It was just a small ceremony. You know, the family, and —" *And a few close friends*, he'd almost said, grateful that the waitress had chosen that moment to come take their orders.

Campbell ordered the breakfast special: scrambled eggs, ham, home-fries, English muffin. Gold just ordered toast and coffee.

"You oughta eat," Campbell chided. "Breakfast is the most important meal of the day—"

"We decided to meet here because it was convenient to both of our offices, not for the cuisine," Gold replied. GAT was close by, and although Amalgamated-Landis had manufacturing plants scattered around the Los Angeles area as far away as Long Beach and El Segundo, its executive offices were in Burbank. "I haven't been in a joint like this in thirty years."

"Ah, I ate in places like this all the time when I was kid," Campbell sighed, sounding astoundingly sentimental about it. "As a matter of fact, I met my wife in a place like this. She was working the counter at a coffee shop near the L.A. State Normal school campus. I used to stop in there for coffee when I was working my way through night school."

Gold nodded. He knew that like himself, Campbell was a self-made man. Tim had run away from his poverty-level Providence, Rhode Island home when he was twelve, riding the rails across America until he was caught by the authorities, and committed to a midwestern youth camp, where he'd received a basic education. When he was sixteen he left the camp, going to work as a clerk for Western Union, at first in Tulsa, and later in Los Angeles. Meanwhile, he took night school courses in accounting and bookkeeping, eventually landing a bank teller's position at the Pacific Coast Bank in downtown L.A., where he'd worked himself up to junior loan officer by the time Gold had met him. Then Campbell left the bank to come to work for GAT. The rest, as they say, is history.

"That your car?" Campbell asked, looking out the window at the fiery red and gleaming chrome El Dorado convertible.

"Good guess," Gold said dryly, eyeing the battered autos and work vehicles that surrounded his shiny new toy.

"Nice," Campbell sniffed. "That's what I'm driving, over *there*—" He proudly gestured toward the dove gray, Mercedes-Benz 300 SL gull-winged coupe, parked on a diagonal, taking up two spaces in the crowded lot.

"I test-drove one of those," Gold said. "At the Mercedes place over on Wilshire." He made a face. "It was okay. A little small for my tastes. But I ordered one for Erica."

The waitress came with the food. Gold glanced distastefully at his toast. It was dripping with butter. At least, he *hoped* it was butter.

"Should'a ordered butter on the side," Campbell observed as he dug into his ham and eggs.

"You said that you needed to talk to me about something?" Gold asked, glancing at his watch.

Campbell nodded. "First off, I wanted to offer you my congratulations, and assure you that I harbor no grudge over the way GAT beat the shit out of Amalgamated-Landis concerning the jetliner competition."

"Thank you," Gold said, and then added carefully, "Tim, I heard that you were canceling production of your AL-12 . . . ?"

"Well, you got all the orders from the airlines," Campbell said. "What was the point of building an airplane nobody wants?"

Gold, assuming that was a rhetorical question, just sipped at his coffee, which wasn't bad.

"Of course, what really killed us was that Civil Aeronautics Board investigation . . ." Campbel set down his fork to study Gold. "Of course, you had nothing to do with that?"

Gold shrugged. "How could I have?"

Campbell smiled, resumed eating. "Just what I thought, Herman, old buddy. How *could* you have?"

"Well," Gold said. "If there's nothing else, Tim, I ought to get going—"

"There *is* something else." Campbell set down his knife and fork, and took out of his coat pocket a silver and onyx cigarette case with matching lighter. "The reason I asked you here was to make you a proposition."

"What kind of proposition?"

Campbell took a cigarette from the case and lit it. "How'd you like to sell me some airplanes?"

Gold burst out laughing. "I've heard of selling ice boxes

to Eskimos, but never anything as farfetched as GAT selling airplanes to Amalgamated-Landis."

Campbell smiled indulgently. "Actually, what I meant was, how would GAT like to sell some airplanes to Skyworld?"

Gold wondered: *What the hell are you up to, Timmy?* Skyworld Airlines had been the "transport" part of Gold Aviation and Transport, before Campbell had parted with the airline back in '33, after that major stock battle between the two partners.

"By the way," Campbell said. "While we're on the subject of Skyworld, Hull says hello."

Gold nodded. Hull Stiles was Gold's old buddy from his barnstorming days. Hull had been with GAT from the beginning, but he was an air transport man, not an aircraft builder, and so had chosen to go with Tim Campbell after the split. Campbell became the president of Skyworld, and Hull Stiles became the airline's CEO. Thanks to the two of them, Skyworld prospered, easily weathering out the turbulence of 1934, when FDR's administration charged that the entire air transport industry was operating as an illegal cartel. That was the year that the Feds invited new bids on domestic air route assignments, but stipulated that no airline that had previously held a route could participate. The airlines got around that by simply changing their names. Skyworld Airlines, for instance, became Skyworld, Incorporated on its new papers. A potentially more serious restriction was that no route contract would be awarded to any airline that still employed the same top-level people in its executive suite. Campbell got around that by resigning his position as president and putting Hull Stiles in full charge. Meanwhile, Tim stayed on, taking no salary, as Skyworld's chairman emeritus. Technically, he was no longer employed by the airline; he was merely an investor, but Hull remained Campbell's puppet, and no decision concerning Skyworld was made without Campbell's approval.

"I had lunch with Hull a few weeks ago," Gold said. He got together with his old friend regularly, and knew that Hull didn't mind being Tim's second. Hull enjoyed the nuts-and-bolts side of running the airline. Tim occupied himself with what he called "the big picture."

"But let's get back to your intriguing request to buy some airplanes from me," Gold suggested, signaling the waitress for a coffee refill. "Why don't you start from the beginning?"

"Easy enough," Campbell replied. "In the beginning, naturally, I expected Skyworld to buy AL-12 jetliners from Amalgamated-Landis."

"*Naturally*, since you have controlling interests in both companies," Gold smiled.

"Skyworld was at the top of A-L's order list," Campbell added. "And stayed loyal right through the CAB scare."

Gold grinned to himself as he remembered how upset Hull Stiles had been about that. Hull had complained that all the other airlines were canceling their orders for the suddenly controversial AL-12, and was worried that if Skyworld ended up being the only airline equipped with the jetliner, the traveling public would stay away.

"But when all the other airlines deserted us in favor of buying your GC-909, I saw the handwriting on the wall," Campbell continued. "I knew we couldn't allow A-L to go broke tooling up a production line to build airplanes exclusively for Skyworld. But when Amalgamated canceled the AL-12, Skyworld was faced with a new predicament—"

Gold nodded. "Canceling the AL-12 left Skyworld without any jetliners on order."

"And so, as hard as it is for me to accept," Campbell said, smiling wryly, "I now find myself sitting across from you, and asking if you'll sell me some airplanes. So what do you say?"

"There's no problem in my selling you 909s, Tim," Gold began. "But I can't promise you when you'll get them. GAT's commercial transport division is working at full capacity, but I've still got a three-year order backlog. All I can do is put Skyworld at the bottom of the list."

"Come on, Herman," Campbell scowled, disgusted. "All

I want is a half dozen airplanes, and you're telling me I'm not gonna see 'em until 1960, for chrissakes."

"I don't see a way around that," Gold said firmly.

"Maybe Skyworld oughta buy from Boeing or Douglas..."

"That's not much of a threat," Gold replied, thinking that Boeing's 707 had made its maiden flight, but that it was going to be some time before the Seattle-based aircraft manufacturer could gear up to fill commercial orders. Douglas was even further behind concerning its DC-8 jetliner.

"The competition is definitely on my heels with some fine airplanes," Gold acknowledged, "but at this moment, GAT is the only game in town when it comes to commercial jets. If you want some, you're just going to have to wait your turn."

"Now hold on, Herman," Campbell said, looking worried. "Maybe we can negotiate a way out of this unhappy situation..."

Gold shrugged. "I'm listening."

"You just told me that GAT is operating at full capacity?"

"Yes, I did."

"And you're years away from filling all your orders, and meanwhile you know that Boeing and Douglas are breathing down your neck, doing all they can to gear up to start stealing away the bottom two-thirds of your waiting list..."

"It's the price of success, I suppose," Gold replied. "We thought about subcontracting out the airframe manufacturing process, but the economics aren't there."

"That's right," Campbell agreed. "Subcontracting is out of the question when you're talking about an airplane like the 909, but what about outright taking over new manufacturing capacity?"

Gold shook his head. "Once again, the cost would be enormous—"

"*Without* a major cash outlay?"

"Get to the point, Tim."

"The point is that I'm desperate for those airplanes," Campbell said. "Skyworld's lifeblood is its domestic routes, especially its New York to Florida runs. A lot of our Northeast corridor competition is due to receive their 909s. Skyworld is not going to make it if all it can fly are prop planes. What I want you to do is push Skyworld to the top of your list, and in the meantime find a way to temporarily snitch a couple of 909s from somebody else's order, and immediately lend them to us, so that Skyworld can be first on its block with jet aircraft."

Gold thought: *It was certainly feasible*. GAT was about to deliver a large order—five 909s and ten intercontinental 909s—to Trans European Airlines, but the largely international carrier was entering into its post-holiday winter doldrums, while Skyworld was beginning its New York to Florida winter rush. TEA wouldn't need its full order until spring, which would roughly coincide with Skyworld's slower period, and by then, if GAT put Skyworld at the top of its list, the airline could take possession of some 909s of its own.

"Okay, I *could* do that for you," Gold said. "Now tell me why I *should*?"

"Because Skyworld will pay you a substantial leasing fee, and I, personally, will trade you three hundred thousand shares of Amalgamated-Landis, and give you an option on another two hundred fifty thousand shares, in exchange for two hundred fifty thousand shares of GAT."

"That would make me the major stockholder in your company," Gold said.

"And if you exercised your option you could take outright control," Campbell added. "Then, by selling off A-L assets you could finance the retooling of our Long Beach commercial transport plant complex, providing GAT with the extra 909 manufacturing capacity it so desperately needs to fill its orders before Boeing and Douglas can get into the act."

"The deal you're offering me will cost you a fortune," Gold pointed out.

"Sometimes you've got to spend money to make money," Campbell philosophically replied. "Let me be frank. When the Civil Aeronautics Board came after A-L the price of the company's stock fell; it fell even further when we announced we were canceling our AL-12 program . . ."

"In other words, you're taking a bath, and want to cut your losses by getting out," Gold said.

"I want out, all right." Campbell nodded. "This way I can get out and also help Skyworld to prosper. Plus, I can recoup some of my losses by getting in on the ground floor with a quarter of a million shares of GAT that will skyrocket when it becomes public that your company has doubled its 909 manufacturing capacity—"

"Separate checks here, gents?" The waitress had returned, and was reaching across the table to clear the plates.

"What kind of pie today?" Campbell asked.

"Cherry, apple, blueberry—"

"Apple, and more coffee for me—in a fresh mug," Campbell stipulated. "You, Herman?"

"Nothing," Gold said absently, pondering Campbell's deal. "I didn't like the sound of that last bit about you getting in on the ground floor of GAT." He frowned. "I'm not sure I want you back as a sizable stockholder."

Campbell raised his right hand. "Word of honor, amigo. No trouble."

"And I'm not so sure that you will make a killing on GAT stock," Gold warned. "If we do this deal it's going to be totally on the up and up. Full disclosure to the public and the Feds, who, I expect, will be all over us on what amounts to a merger between two major aviation concerns . . ."

"*Naturalmente*," Campbell said lightly. "We can also figure on the Defense Department getting into it on the national security angle, since both companies have military contracts . . ."

"It'll be months before we get the okay," Gold said.

"I understand that," Campbell said. "But there's nothing I can do to speed up that process. What I'm offering you is the best I can do to persuade you to give Skyworld the jetliners it needs *now*. Without your help, Skyworld will go belly up."

Gold nodded. "Okay, Tim." He reached across the table to shake hands. "You got yourself a deal."

Campbell grinned. "You know, it sure is a real pleasure doing business with you again, amigo."

"Apple pie and coffee in a fresh mug," the waitress said as she placed the food in front of Campbell.

"Put everything on one check," Campbell told her. "My treat," he said regally, winking at Gold.

(Two)

Harrison Residence
Brentwood
Los Angeles, California

Mrs. Susan Harrison's new house was a rambling, single-story ranch in the better part of Brentwood. It was set off from the road by an adobe wall, and further hidden from view by the overgrown landscaping that shaded the front porch. The house had a terraced swimming pool, set like a glittering topaz in a fragrant garden. A red brick path twisted its way through the wooded grounds beyond the pool, to a gazebo overlooking a goldfish pond, and then to a serenely isolated brick patio beneath shady eucalyptus trees.

The sprawling, easygoing house had seemed the essence of Southern California to Susan, and she had tried to furnish it remaining true to that spirt, with lots of leather upholstery, Shaker-style cedar furniture, Mexican pottery, and bright cotton rugs. There were rooms that remained empty—a lot of the furniture was still on order—but Susan had no doubt that in time this house would be a showpiece...

Whether it would ever feel like *home* was yet to be seen...

Susan was having breakfast with her husband and her son in the solarium when she mentioned that her brother was going to be in Los Angeles in the spring.

"Oh, really?" Don said absently between sips of coffee. The newspaper was propped in front of him. He was scanning the business section.

"You know what else, Don?" Robbie said excitedly. "When Uncle Steve comes in April, the two of us are going camping!"

Don seemed to flinch. He was frowning as he set down his cup, then crossly called for the maid to come take away the remains of his breakfast. "What about school, sport?"

"Don, it'll be spring vacation—" Robbie said.

"He's got a week off at the end of April," Susan elaborated, munching on toast.

"I see . . ." Don angrily looked toward the kitchen. "Where the hell is the maid? Damned woman is as lazy as they come," he complained.

"Well, what did you expect?" Susan said defensively. "I hired the best person I could find, but you've got to realize that gems like Ramona are few and far between."

"You know what else?" Robbie was busy bragging to Don. "Uncle Steve said he was gonna teach me to hunt."

Don shook his head, wincing. "Look, sport, I don't know if it's such a good idea for you to be spending your vacation with your uncle . . ."

"Huh?" Robbie's green eyes went wide. "Sure it's a good idea, Don," he said patiently.

Susan had to smile. At times like this her fourteen-year-old son was the spitting image of his father. In addition to his father's green eyes, thick, straight, coal black hair, and chiseled features, Robert Blaize Greene had inherited his father's determined air; once her son had set his mind on something, nothing could dissuade him.

"Hunting is dangerous—" Don began as the maid finally trudged in to clear the table.

"What you mean is that hunting isn't something sissy." Robbie was sulking. "Like chess, or model building, and that stuff *you* like—"

"Watch your tone, young man," Don warned.

"Don't tell me what to do!" Robbie snapped. "You're not my father!"

"Dammit!" Don exploded.

"That's enough, both of you," Susan said quietly but firmly. "Robbie, you go get ready for school."

"But Don said I can't go with Uncle Steve—" her son protested.

"Of course you can go with your uncle," Susan replied. Don looked about to say something, but she silenced him with her eyes. "But vacation is in April. School is *now*. Get going."

Don waited until her son had trudged out of the room. "That's just great," he complained. "I thought we'd agreed that we weren't going to contradict each other in front of him . . ."

"I'm sorry, darling, but whatever got into you?" Susan asked. "How could you think you could forbid him to spend time with his uncle?"

Don shrugged, looking away.

"I don't know why you developed this animosity toward Steve," Susan continued. "Whenever you see my brother you can hardly bring yourself to say two words to him."

"You're imagining things," Don said.

Susan sighed. She got pretty much the same evasive response whenever she queried her brother. Her intuition told her that something had happened between Don and Steve, but the two men were clearly determined to keep it from her.

"I guess I'm just a little jealous about the way that Robbie looks up to Steve," Don sighed. "Sometimes I think he can hardly abide me."

"Now you know that's not true," Susan soothed. "He is fond of you, but . . ." She hesitated.

"But he *loves* his Uncle Steve," Don said dejectedly . "Is that what you were going to say?" He ruefully chuckled. "I just wish Robbie wouldn't call me by my first name . . . I wish he would call me . . . Dad . . . or Pop. . . . Something like that . . ."

"Maybe he will, eventually, darling," Susan murmured. "But you can't rush the boy..."

"How long am I supposed to wait for him to come around?" Don demanded. "How am I supposed to compete with his war hero Uncle Steve, the fighter ace, the sportsman, the hunter..."

"You must be patient," Susan said. "Robbie's at that age where feats of physical prowess are important to him. When he's older, more mature, he will come around... Meanwhile, try to see things from *his* point of view. We did spring the idea of our marriage on him—"

"Suzy, we'd been going together such a long time—"

"And then we took him from his grandparents' house where he grew up, and moved him here."

"We're not even five miles away," Don muttered. "Chrissakes, Suzy, you take the kid over there most every day." He paused, looking sour. "So what *you're* telling me is the same thing *he* told me: that I'm not his father, and I'm not to forget that fact, right?"

Susan shrugged. "You're my husband whom I love, and my son's stepfather, but yes, you're correct in saying that you're not Robbie's father."

"Which means that as far as you're concerned, I have no authority over him?" he demanded, sounding angry.

"Oh, Don—"

"I want Robbie to spend that vacation week with us," he declared.

"You're making this so impossible for me," Susan said, feeling herself near tears.

"Will you back me or not?"

Susan shook her head. "I'm sorry, darling, but the decision is Robbie's to make."

"I see." Don was staring at her, and for an instant she thought she saw something unfamiliar and frightening in his eyes, but then he smiled. "Look at the time!" He stood up. "I better get going to the office."

"Darling? You're not angry with me, are you?"

"Of course not," he said. "But I've got to run. I've got a

meeting this morning with your father," he rattled on. "Don't want to be late—"

"I love you—" Susan beseeched.

He paused in the doorway. "And I love you, very much," he said quietly. "But that was never the issue we were discussing, was it?"

Susan had no reply to that. He shrugged and left.

She wished that she were going to the office with him, but Don had insisted that she leave her job in order to supervise their new household. Now, as she sat staring out the windows at her azure pool and her pretty gardens, she couldn't help feeling that her marriage had cast her in the role of referee in the never-ending sparring match that had arisen between her husband and her son.

"Goddammit," she morosely complained to the empty room, thinking that she loved them both so much; how could two people so beloved be causing her so much pain?

"*Goddammit—*"

(Three)

**GAT
Burbank**

"Something bothering you, Don?" Herman asked.

"No!" Harrison said, startled.

"You sure?" Herman was scrutinizing him. "You looked a million miles away—"

Harrison forced a grin. He was in Herman's office for their meeting. They were seated in armchairs, a coffee table littered with folders between them. The meeting had been going on for an hour, but Harrison had been having trouble concentrating. His mind *had* been elsewhere; brooding over this morning's confrontation with his stepson and his wife.

He truly loved Susan, and he'd started out feeling genuinely strong affection for Robert. Robbie had seemed to like

him, at first, but as Harrison became more seriously involved with Susan the boy had begun to hold him at arm's
length.

Now Harrison wasn't born yesterday. He was educated;
had read some psychology back in his college undergraduate
days. He understood what Susan had been trying to tell him
about Robbie's insecurities, but what Susan and Robbie
seemed to be ignoring were *his* feelings of insecurity. Why
couldn't they ever see it from *his* point of view? Why
couldn't they see that they were always playing it two
against one: mother and son against the "wicked" stepfather?
Take this morning: What had he asked for? Only the opportunity to spend some time with his stepson—

—who preferred his Uncle Steve. It made Harrison so
fucking angry! It looked like Steven Gold was not going to
be content with stealing away Linda Forrester. Good old war
hero Steve was intent upon destroying Harrison's marriage
by turning his stepson—and through Robbie, his wife—
against him . . .

"Everything okay at home?" Herman suddenly asked.

"Yes, of course!" *Jesus Christ*, Harrison thought, trying to
regain his composure. *What'd he, read my mind?*

"Good." Herman was nodding. "Then shall we get back
to the matter at hand? We were discussing the European proposal."

Harrison nodded. "What I still don't understand is why
you feel we have to build a new jetliner for the European
market when we've already got a perfectly good plane to sell
them."

"You mean the 909a?" Herman asked.

"Yeah, I do. When we designed a smaller version of the
original 909 intended for use on short domestic hops, I
thought it was in the back of our minds that the 909a would
be perfect for the European market?"

"I agree with you." Herman smiled. "Unfortunately, the
Europeans want nothing to do with it. They want a home-
grown airplane."

"That's just so stupid," Don fumed, frustrated.

"Ah, well." Herman shrugged. "We ran into exactly the same thing over there back in 'thirty-six, when we were trying to market our Monarch GC series of commercial transports. The Monarch series was state of the art then, and the Europeans were dying to buy them, but jingoistic national pride wouldn't let them. We got around that problem by subcontracting to the British firm of Stoat-Black, the manufacturer of our airliners for the European market."

"That's how you met Sir Hugh Luddy?" Harrison asked.

"Right. That's what started GAT's long association with Stoat-Black," Herman replied, leaning back in his armchair and fondly rambling on. "You know, that's how Susan met her first husband Blaize Greene . . . Blaize was a test pilot for Stoat-Black in those days . . ."

Dammit! Harrison thought, *If I'm not battling Steve Gold, I'm up against this sonofabitch of a ghost Blaize Greene—*

Herman must have read something in Harrison's expression. "Of course, that was all a long time ago," he said quickly. "The point is, our association with Stoat-Black turned out to be extremely productive, and profitable. That's why I'm so enthusiastic about this Skytrain project. GAT, along with Stoat-Black, will be entering into a consortium with the French firm, Aérosens Aviation, to be called Skytrain *Industrie*. Our transatlantic partnership's initial project will be to build a short-hop jetliner to be called the Skytrain *Pont* I."

"The preliminary specs for which," Harrison said dryly, "appear to be based on our 909a."

"I know it sounds crazy," Herman confessed. "Like we're reinventing the wheel. In a sense, we are, but we'll make some money doing it, and long-term, we alone of the American aircraft industry will have established a beachhead in the European market."

"But only as a member of the Skytrain *Industrie* consortium," Harrison pointed out.

"We can't get in on our own." Herman shrugged. "A slice of the pie is better than none."

One of Herman's secretaries appeared in the office doorway. "Excuse me, sir," she addressed Herman. "I've got Hull Stiles returning your call—"

"Tell Mister Stiles I'll be right with him," Herman told his secretary, and then asked her, "Did you get that delivery schedule from Tyson?"

Harrison perked up. Leo Tyson was the chief of the Commercial Transport production division.

"Not yet, sir," the secretary said. "He's working on it."

"How about Gleason, in sales?" Herman asked, standing up.

"He's out of the office," the secretary said. "I left word with his secretary that Mister Gleason is to call as soon as he comes in."

"What's up, Herman?" Harrison asked. "It sounds like you're selling airplanes to Skyworld?" When Herman nodded, Harrison complained, "But I haven't heard anything about this . . ."

Herman hesitated. "It's all happened rather suddenly. Just this morning, as a matter of fact."

"I see . . ."

"Don, if you don't mind, I'd like to take this call in private."

"Sure, Herman . . ."

"Hull, old buddy—" Harrison heard Herman laugh as he left the office. "Hull, old buddy, it looks like we're back in business again—"

Not my day at all, Harrison thought as he waited for the elevator to carry him down to his office in the R & D department. It seemed that here at GAT, as in his own home, he was the odd man out, the second choice after Herman's true son, Steve and Suzy's first husband, Blaize. That was why Herman was making deals without him, Harrison brooded. Why Suzy and Robbie were freezing him out at home. It evidently didn't matter how hard Harrison worked for Herman, or how much he loved his new family. As far as the Golds were concerned, he was a second-class citizen. Here at work he could be usurped at any time by Steven, Herman's flesh and blood, while at home he seemed unable to exorcise Blaize Greene's ghost from his stepson's heart—

Harrison's fists clenched. And, perhaps, not even from his wife's bed . . .

I want . . . I need . . . something, Harrison thought angrily. *Something to solidify my position on all fronts—*

The answer when it came to him seemed so astoundingly simple: another child! A boy, he hoped; a son of his own, one to fill the role and assume the surname that Robert Blaize Greene had so decisively rejected. Another grandchild would bring Harrison closer to Herman, thereby weakening Steven's hold on his father. It would no longer be two against one at home. Two against one at GAT.

The few times the subject of children had come up, Susan had been hesitant. ". . . All in good time . . ." she'd said. ". . . We mustn't rush . . . Too many changes for Robbie to absorb . . . We must consider Robbie's feelings . . ."

Well, Harrison thought. *The time was now, and Robbie would just have to deal with it because change was in the wind.*

Harrison knew he could prevail upon Susan. She would not, could not, deny him on this.

A son, of my own, Harrison thought. *Yes.*

Suzy didn't know it yet, but they were going to have a baby.

CHAPTER 10

(One)

Whetstone Air Strip
Nevada
22 May 1957

Steven Gold leveled off at ten thousand feet in his F-90 BroadSword jet fighter. Below him Whetstone's corrugated steel hangars looked like tin cans half buried in the sand. The CIA compound's tents looked like scraps of cloth, and its airstrip looked like a two-by-four plank of lumber lying at an angle against the tan and brown desert terrain.

Steve looked out past his BroadSword's gleaming, swept-back starboard wing, and saw the tiny black cross on the airstrip's ready line begin to crawl forward. He clicked his throat mike. "Chase Two, this is Chase Leader. Mayfly is taking off. Come on home, Chase Two. It's time to go to work."

There was a crackle of static from the earphones built into Steve's helmet, and then, "Roger, Chase Leader. This is Chase Two. I'm coming around."

Steve swiveled his head beneath the BroadSword's teardrop canopy until he saw Chase Two—the F-90 being piloted by Captain Chet "Lowball" Boskins—glinting in the sunlight as it made its sweeping turn back toward Whetstone.

"Say there, Lieutenant Colonel, *sir*," Boskins began in his easygoing Texas drawl. "Since I'm a Mayfly pilot in training, and technically no longer in the Air Force, do I still have to take orders from you?"

"I happen to be the highest-ranking Air Force pilot at Whetstone," Steve joked.

"You're also the *only* Air Force pilot," Boskins radioed back.

Steve laughed. It was true. The other Air Force personnel were either aircraft maintenance or aero-medicine specialists. Everyone else was either CIA, and that now included the Mayfly pilots, or GAT personnel—instructors or technicians—here to qualify the men that Steve had recruited to fly the Mayfly spy plane.

"Would you pokey little BroadSwords mind getting out of my way?" the Mayfly's pilot, Lieutenant Mel Evans, cut in. "I happen to be in a real airplane, here, and I've got places to go."

Steve banked his BroadSword to starboard in order to give the matte black, high altitude reconnaissance jet plenty of sky as it soared past on its incredibly long, thin, glider plane's wings. "I've seen it a few times already," Steve confided to Boskins, "but I still can't get used to the way that blackbird can climb."

"Affirmative," Boskins replied. "I'll never forget my first Mayfly flight. I left the ground and she acted like she wanted to go straight up. You've got to experience it to believe it."

Not much chance of that, Steve thought. The CIA was

very careful about who it allowed to drive its brand new toys.

For the last eighteen months Steve had been traveling across the country and around the world, visiting SAC air bases to chase down leads concerning likely pilot recruits. Once the Air Force and CIA gave him the okay on a particular guy, Steve would meet with him, explain about the problem the U.S. was having monitoring the Russians, and then pitch the Mayfly program. If the pilot was interested—and most of them were; these men were patriots—the Air Force gave him temporary leave from his present assignment to undergo a battery of psychological and physical tests to certify his fitness for the job. Those pilots who passed were then released from the military, with the promise that they'd be reinstated with no time lost for promotion or retirement, and given financially lucrative, two-year contracts with the CIA.

Next stop for the accepted pilots was Whetstone, for a lengthy and difficult course in Mayfly driving. The spy plane's outstanding abilities also made her a fragile and temperamental bird, quick to punish those who did not treat her with a full measure of respect.

Steve moved his BroadSword into position on the Mayfly's starboard wing while Boskins put his BroadSword on the spy plane's port side. The slender black bird was climbing fast, heading toward California. The two F-90s kept escort as long as they could, but within minutes the Mayfly was effortlessly climbing past 47,000 feet, operational ceiling for the BroadSwords.

"Blackbird, we are running out of sky," Steve radioed to the Mayfly pilot.

"Affirmative, Chase team," Lieutenant Evans called. "You boys get downstairs before you get yourselves nosebleeds. I got some flying to do . . ."

Steve watched Evans's albatross-winged, black dagger of an airplane climb ever higher, dwindling away until the Mayfly's tail pipe was a distant glowing speck; a twinkling star in the desert sky.

"She's gone for about six hours," Boskins said.

"It must be something to fly so high you can almost reach out and touch the stars," Steve murmured. The Mayfly could carry its pilot to seventy thousand feet: higher than any man had gone before. As a matter of fact, the opportunity to break altitude records was one of the selling points Steve had used in persuading some of the Air Force's top pilots to sign on as Mayfly driver.

"Say, Steve," Boskins began as he maneuvered his Broad-Sword into position on Steve's wing. "You flew a Broad-Sword in Korea—?"

"Affirmative."

"She was supposed to be one hell of a dogfighter in MIG Alley," Boskins continued.

"Well, I'm a little prejudiced, considering that she's GAT-built, but in my opinion she had her moments..."

"I sure would like the chance to see what she can do," Boskins said hopefully. "I've always felt like I missed out on the real fun, getting stuck flying ground support in a Shooting Star in Korea..."

Steve knew that the soft-spoken Texas jet jockey had earned his nickname because of his penchant for bringing in his F-80 low, and *staying* low, to more effectively bomb and strafe the North Koreans off the face of the earth. During his combat tours Lowball Boskins had proven that he had the guts to concentrate on the dangerous task at hand, steadily driving his airplane where he was told to drive it, and keeping it there until he was satisfied that he'd done his job. He'd been one of the first pilots Steve had recruited for the Mayfly program.

"I'd think a slow mover like this BroadSword would be boring to a hotshot, F-404 Starscythe jockey like yourself," Steve mused. Boskins had been stationed in Germany in a TAC fighter squadron, helping to keep a wary eye on the Red Bear, when Steve had looked him up.

"The F-404 is fast, all right," Boskins replied. "But the BroadSword is legendary for what it can do in a furball mix-up. I've always had a hankering to see what *I* could do with her..."

Steve looked around. The clear blue sky was empty of traffic, and below them there was nothing but miles of parched desert. "Tell you what, Captain. I don't see any harm in us burning up some kerosene playing tag."

"Just what I wanted to hear," Boskins exclaimed joyously. At that instant he popped his speed brakes, dropping back onto Steve's tail. "Ah, Lieutenant Colonel, sir? Don't look now, but you got one bad ass pilot on your six o'clock—"

Not for long, Steve thought. He cobbed his throttle and his BroadSword pulled away. Steve watched in his rearview mirror as Boskins began closing fast on his stern, and then Steve broke right, across his attacker's nose. Taken by surprise, Boskins began to overshoot. As Boskins followed Steve's turn in order to try and regain his position, Steve barrel-rolled. Boskins overshot, and Steve dropped down onto Boskins's tail.

Steve clicked his throat mike. "Rat-tat-tat, ole buddy. You're taking hits." Of course his BroadSword had no guns, or even a gun sight, but Steve had flown enough combat missions in F-90s to know when he was within kill range.

"Fuck!" Steve heard Boskins swear. Boskins began jinking his F-90, trying to throw off Steve's imaginary aim, and then dropped down into a steep dive toward the desert floor.

Steve stayed glued to Boskins's six o'clock, but as he followed Boskins down he was mindful of his altimeter unwinding. Fun was fun, but he didn't want Boskins getting carried away and drilling a hole in some cactus down there . . .

He needn't have worried. At fifteen thousand feet Boskins abruptly pulled up, causing Steve to shoot past as he hurried to come out of his own dive. Now Boskins was behind him, and likely licking his chops as he closed on Steve's tail: It wasn't a bad maneuver, just a basic and easily stymied one.

Boskins was about to drop down on his tail when Steve flipped the switch on his throttle, extending his own speed brakes. His BroadSword shuddered as it reared up in the sky. Boskins flashed past. Steve clicked the switch again and hauled in his brakes. He cobbed the throttle and once again settled down nicely onto Boskins's six o'clock.

"Rat-tat-tat, ole buddy."

"You keep saying that," Boskins muttered.

For the next ten minutes Boskins must have tried everything he knew—which wasn't much—and none of it worked. That didn't make Steve feel good; it worried him. He knew that Boskins was one of the Air Force's best fighter jocks, but Lowball had been trained in combat tactics well after the Korean War. Steve knew the current theory fresh from the think tanks of the desk jockeys who made the rules: Guns on fighters were obsolete. Today's Mach-two interceptors would engage the enemy over enormous distances—perhaps even out of visual range—blowing him out of the sky with radar-controlled air-to-air missiles. Let the machines do the work, the desk jockeys were saying. Let the pilot come along for the ride, if you must, but put blinders on his eyes to keep him glued to his ghostly green radar screens, and certainly don't waste the money we could use to buy more computers by taking the time to teach him aerobatics . . .

"I quit," Boskins said dejectedly, slowing down and coming around to head back toward Whetstone.

"Roger," Steve replied, relinquishing his six o'clock to pull alongside Boskins, who was staying very quiet. Steve could imagine how bad the guy was feeling. "Hey, buddy. Don't take it so hard."

"I couldn't break away from you once . . ."

"Don't forget I've logged hundreds of combat hours in this bird," Steve said. He thought, *And while you were in college, I was learning how to maneuver, not punch buttons on some computer.*

"I'm going to be hearing rat-tat-tat in my fucking sleep," Boskins sighed.

"And I've heard the *real* thing," Steve reminded him softly. "And that makes a difference. Anyway, think how badly you would have waxed me if we'd been flying Starscythes."

"Yeah! That's right!" Boskins brightened. "Once I got a radar lock on you it would have been bye-bye, Lieutenant Colonel..."

Maybe, but then again, maybe not, Steve thought. At least he'd managed to salvage a little of Boskins's self-respect. The one vital piece of equipment the Air Force hadn't yet figured out how to take away from a fighter jock was his ego...

(Two)

Whetstone
24 May 1957

Steve stood in the motor pool's doorway, waiting for the kid to bring around the Jeep he had requested. It was high noon; the thermometer mounted on the doorjamb read one hundred degrees, but Steve was willing to wager that the parched air inside the motor pool's corrugated steel building was far hotter than that.

Steve was wearing a USAF, rescue crew/test pilot issue, Indian orange, cotton flight suit, low-heeled black cowboy boots, and an Air Force flight satin baseball cap in blue, on which he wore his silver oak leaf. While he waited for his jeep he glanced again at the creased scrap of paper Captain Chet Boskins had left for him in his mailbox at the compound's Administration/Communication hut:

> *Urgently request that you meet me at the cave/1200 hours*
> *Steve, please be there!!!*
>
> *—Lowball*

Here it was already a little after noon, and it was going to take another ten minutes to drive to the cave, Steve brooded as he pondered the note's urgent, almost panicked tone. He wondered what was wrong? It wasn't like Lowball to lose it...

A Jeep came around the corner, pulling up in front of the motor pool. A young, blond, freckle-faced airman with a badly sunburned pug nose put the jeep in neutral, set the parking brake, and hopped out, leaving the engine running.

"Sorry for the delay, sir." He gestured over his shoulder toward the Jeep. "It took some doing to find her."

"No problem," Steve lied, thinking that it wasn't this kid's fault the compound was short on vehicles, or that Steve didn't have a Jeep personally assigned to him. He wasn't permanently stationed at Whetstone. He'd been there only a few weeks, and would be back in Washington in a few more days.

As Steve settled into the driver's seat he noticed that there was no key in the ignition. "Airman?"

The kid saw him looking at the tangle of wires drooping down from beneath the metal dashboard, and smiled apologetically. "Actually, sir, I *couldn't* find an available vehicle, so I kind of borrowed this one from Mister Cooper."

"Kind of borrowed," Steve repeated slowly. "From Mister Cooper . . ." Cooper was the CIA station chief at Whetstone.

"Yes, sir."

Steve was glad that he was wearing wire-rimmed aviator sunglasses with dark green lenses: They helped him to keep a straight face. "What you're telling me is that you hot-wired this?"

The airman nodded. "Just leave it running when you get to where you're going, sir, unless you know how to start her up without the key?"

"If I did, I wouldn't admit it, son . . ."

The young airman had difficulty stifling his own grin. "I filled her up, so you won't have any worry about running out of gas." He paused. "Begging your pardon, sir, do you think you might be able to return Mister Cooper's Jeep by, say fourteen hundred hours? That way I could put her back before he notices it's missing."

"I understand," Steve said. "For the record, Air Force personnel do not steal vehicles. Off the record, I appreciate what you've done."

This kid had gone out on a limb for him. Whetstone was officially a CIA operation, which meant the spooks had authority over the Air Force noncom personnel.

"I'll be back in plenty of time," Steve added, releasing the brake and putting the Jeep in gear. "If by any chance I'm not, as far as you're concerned, I never asked you for a Jeep."

"Thank you, sir," the kid said, looking relieved.

"Thank *you*, son."

Steve drove away from the compound's scattered clusterings of tents, trailers, and hangars, passing the airstrip where a matte black Mayfly was parked on the ready line. The spy plane looked dismal and dispirited with its long, thin, drooping wings propped up by wheeled struts to keep them out of the dirt, but as Steve had seen, once the Mayfly was airborne and those struts were jettisoned, the black bird could really limber up.

Steve had made this trip to Whetstone because he'd wanted the men he'd recruited to know that he took a personal interest in them, but being near the West Coast had also allowed him to squeeze in a week at the end of April to take his nephew camping in the Santa Ana Mountains. Steve was grateful for that time with Robbie. The camping trip almost hadn't come off. Back in March, Steve's sister had called to warn him to expect some blowback from Don on the subject. During that conversation she'd asked again why Steve and Don were so frosty with each other, and again, Steve had ducked the question. What could he say? *The reason your husband hates me is because he caught me screwing his girl, the one he really wanted to marry.*

When Steve had first heard about Susan's intention to marry Don he'd briefly considered coming clean with her, thinking that she ought to know what she was getting into, bringing the guy into the family. At the last moment he'd decided to butt out, figuring that everybody had the right to privacy about his past. Thinking back on it, Steve was glad that he'd kept his mouth shut. When he'd visited the Harrisons in April the couple had seemed deliriously happy with each other, and with Suzy's pregnancy. Their baby was due the third week in January.

Steve was really glad that he hadn't let that snafu concerning Linda Forrester spoil things for Don and Suzy. *Especially* now that Linda was ancient history for *everyone* involved . . .

The Jeep rattled and creaked as Steve steered around the worst potholes and rocks in the narrow, jutted road. The terrain resembled Death Valley: sparse vegetation in a dusty, arid land the leached out colors of dried blood and polished bone. There was a hot wind picking up. As Steve drove he hunched down, turning up his collar, grateful for his flight suit's long sleeves and trouser legs. The windblown swirling grit rasped unprotected skin, drawing blood like atmospheric sandpaper.

He reached the switchback turnoff for the cave. The steep, twisty, gravel-strewn incline up the butte was more a goatpath than a road, but the Jeep had all wheel drive. As he dropped the transmission into low and began the climb, scrub lining both sides of the road scraped against the Jeep's wheels and fenders. He kept glimpsing scurrying movement just ahead of his front tires among the rust-colored rocks and low, thorny bramble. He tried his best to ignore the slitherings and creepings. This was snake country, but Steve didn't mind reptiles; he'd seen his share of them during his tours of duty in the tropics. Snakes were no big deal, but back at Whetstone they had been having some trouble with tarantulas invading the compound at night. He did not at all care for those big, hairy mothers, striped like tigers, with a leg span as wide as a man's outstretched fingers. Nobody at Whetstone wanted to go near the fuckers once it was discovered that they could jump six feet in any direction, including right into your face, so the recommended procedure was to use the bugs for target practice. This drove the CIA spooks crazy because the only firearms on the compound were their ridiculously expensive, custom-built, silenced, long-barreled .22 caliber pistols that the pilots swiped out of the Mayfly survival kits.

Steve slowed down as he approached the cave entrance set in a jumble of the rock about twenty feet above a wide spot in the roadway. As Steve pulled up he thought he was too late because he didn't see another Jeep, but then he saw Chet Boskins beckoning to him from the cave's shadowy entrance.

Boskins was a slightly built, wiry twenty-seven-year-old, with short-cut, light brown hair and blue eyes. He was wearing sunglasses and a tan cotton baseball cap, a white T-shirt, and baggy, silver khaki fatigue trousers, with double-snap, bellows-type pockets, tucked into black, lace-up hiking boots. Around his waist was a canvas web belt from which dangled a pair of canteens, a sheathed survival knife, and a flapped pouch.

Steve, mindful of the engine's hot-wired ignition, left the Jeep's motor running, and set the parking brake. He did know how to restart the Jeep if he had to, but why bother? It had a heavy-duty cooling system so it wouldn't overheat. Because he was parked on a slight incline and couldn't use the transmission to hold the Jeep in place, he wedged a couple of good-size rocks behind the rear tires, and then made the easy climb up to the mouth of the cave.

"Sorry I'm late," Steve told Boskins. "I couldn't get a Jeep. By the way, where's yours?"

"I came cross-country," Boskins replied.

"You walked?"

"It's only about a mile as the crow flies," Boskins said, and then he grinned. "I won't say no to a ride home, however."

Steve followed him into the shallow cave, where it was at least fifteen degrees cooler, thanks to the underground spring that trickled down out of one of the cave's fissured walls to collect in the small pool the eons of dripping water scooped out of the cave's stone floor. At least fifty cans of beer bobbed in the pool. Boskins scooped out a pair of brews and tossed one to Steve. Thanks to its time spent immersed in the water the can was frosty cold. Steve sighed happily as he pressed the can against his forehead.

Boskins opened his beer with the church key he'd pulled from his belt pouch, and then tossed it to Steve, who opened his brew and took a long swallow. As he drank, the sweat came popping out of his pores almost faster than he could take the liquid in, but the cold beer nonetheless hit the spot.

This cave had been discovered by some of the pilots while on a cross-country training hike. Now, Air Foce supply personnel kept the cave stocked with beer, and hauled away the litter of empties that periodically carpeted the cave floor as those in the know spent as many evenings here as they could. The cave was kept a secret from the spooks, who had banned alcohol from Whetstone. Steve felt honored to have been let in on the secret; he was, after all, technically straddling the fence between the Air Force and the CIA.

Steve and Boskins settled side by side on a couple of the canvas camp stools that had been left in the cave, and lit cigarettes. "Your note had me upset, Lowball," Steve began. "What's wrong? You're not still upset over the way I waxed your tail the other day?"

"Nah." Boskins smiled. "I've already managed to forget that ever happened."

"Then what's your problem?"

"It's not just *mah* prob'em," Boskins said quietly in his languid, cowboy drawl. "We're all mighty upset about what's been going on, Stevie boy..."

"Why don't you start from the beginning?"

Boskins looked suspicious. "What you're telling me here is you don't know nothing about what I'm saying?"

"That's right," Steve replied.

Boskins extracted something from his belt pouch and tossed it to Steve. It tumbled through the air, glinting in the dim light coming in from the mouth of the cave. Steve caught it and held it up to the light.

"A silver dollar?" he asked, puzzled, turning the coin around in his fingers.

"Open it," Boskins said.

"Open—?"

"Just kinda twist it apart," Boskins explained. "And do it

careful like," he cautioned. "It'll be my ass if you lose what's in there."

Steve noticed an edge and pried the coin slightly open using his thumbnail. He then twisted it the rest of the way apart. Stuck inside with a bit of cellophane tape was a small straight pin. He looked up inquiringly at Boskins.

"A suicide pin," Boskins said.

"A what—?" Steve burst out laughing, thinking this was some kind of joke, but his laughter faded as Boskins frowned, straightfaced.

"The spooks told us that they developed some kind of new poison," Boskins said. "All you got to do is jab yourself with that there pin and according to the spooks you'll be dead quicker than a two-dollar blow job from a big-city whore."

"Holy shit," Steve murmured, holding at arm's length the half of the coin that contained the pin.

"'Course, that one there's *supposed* to be a dud," Boskins elaborated. "According to the spooks it ain't been dipped or soaked, or whatever."

"What are you doing with this thing?" Steve demanded.

"That spook in charge of survival training—"

"Woodrow Brown?"

"Yeah, *him*." Boskins scowled. "Ole woody-pecker Brown issued them to us last week, telling us that when we train we got to go with a full kit." He shook his head. "Some survival training. Guess we're only supposed to survive long enough to stick ourselves . . ."

Steve carefully fit together the two halves of the hollow coin, and then tossed it back to Boskins. "Look, Lowball, I'm not sure I see your beef . . . I mean, you were in Korea. You know what kind of treatment downed pilots received from the Commies. There's no reason to think the Russians are going to treat you any better."

Boskins looked angry. "What you're saying is that you agree with the spooks that if we go down we oughta kill ourselves? Save the diplomats the trouble of trying to negotiate us home?"

"I'm not saying that at all. I'm saying that if it comes down to it, whether you allow yourself to be captured alive is totally up to you. Nobody can force you to stick yourself with that pin. It's your decision . . . All the spooks have done is give you the option . . ."

"That's what the spooks tole us," Boskins said skeptically. "They said only us pilots can decide if death is preferable to being tortured into telling the Reds all about the Mayfly project. Only *we* can decide if it would be more honorable to die than to embarrass our country—*and* their fuck'n *agency*—"

"Right," Steve said.

Boskins spat. "But then they told us something *else*. That whatever we decided about *ourselves*, it was our duty to make sure that no part of the aircraft falls into enemy hands."

"How are you supposed to do that?" Steve asked.

"The spooks are putting a bomb in each airplane, right behind the pilot's seat. Our orders are to activate the fucker right before we bail out. And get this. *Supposedly*, we got seventy seconds before she blows, but I'll tell you something, Stevie. Not one of us pilots believes that." His smile was sardonic as he held up to the light streaming into the cave the phony silver coin. "Every one of us would bet our *bottom dollar* that as soon as we activate that bomb it's gonna blow. No way would we have a chance to bail out."

"You think the spooks want you to take the death before dishonor route whether you want to or not—"

"That's right, Steve. Did you know we're supposed to fly with no I.D. or personal effects? On one hand the spooks are telling us it'll be up to us to decide for ourselves whether to be taken alive or not, and on the other hand they want to make damned sure we're not carrying anything that'll identify us as Americans. You know the airplane don't carry no markings at all . . ."

"You guys don't think your country is going to be there for you if you get caught . . ."

"Right again." Boskins nodded firmly. "That's just what

we think, and I was elected the one to come tell you that we also think it stinks. We don't trust the people we're working for, Steve, and in our kind of work, that mean's there's gonna be trouble at some point down the line."

Steve nodded. "Your job is going to be tough enough without having to be worried about getting stabbed in the back."

"The bottom line is that we're Air Force men, used to doing things the Air Force way," Boskins continued. "The way you explained this assignment I thought we was taking part in a military reconnaissance operation. I never figured on being turned into a spy, or being treated like one by the enemy if I should fall into his hands."

"You guys deserve to know that you won't be forsaken," Steve agreed.

Boskins, nodding, looked relieved. "I knew you'd see it our way..." He paused. "A bunch of us were figuring that since you brought us in, you could fix things up for us..." He hesitated. "That is, if you got the clout..."

"I'll certainly talk to them about this, Lowball."

"You'll talk to Brown?" Boskins sounded pleased.

"Fuck Brown, and fuck his boss, Cooper, as well." Steve scowled. "I'll be back in Washington next week, and when I am, I'll go right to the top."

(Three)

Central Intelligence Agency
Washington, D.C.
25 May 1957

"Lieutenant Colonel, you can't go in there—"

Steve Gold had always coveted Jack Horton's secretary. From his previous visits here he'd learned her name was Joyce. She was an auburn brunette with hazel eyes and an outstanding set of tits. Today she was wearing a tan, thin wool dress that clung to her curves. Steve enjoyed watching her breasts bounce as she jumped to her feet, moving fast around her desk as if she were going to tackle him to keep him from getting past her.

He should be so lucky... He wouldn't mind a little un-armed combat with this one... But he did want to keep his confrontation with Jack Horton's doorkeeper down to a dull roar. He couldn't afford to attract the attention of building security. He was wearing his Air Force uniform, and pinned to his lapel was the laminated pass that Horton had arranged to be issued him, so he'd had no difficulty getting this far into the building, but he knew that he had no right to be here uninvited...

"Please, sir," she began again. "You know how busy Mister Horton is. You should have called for an appointment—"

"If I'd called for an appointment you would have put me off for a week," Steve chided, and then he smiled. "Why, I bet it'd be harder to get penciled in to see old Jack then it would be to get *you* to see me on a date..."

"Is that what you'd bet?" She tilted her head to look him in the eye, a slight smile playing at the corners of her mouth.

Made in the shade. Steve thought. "Uh-huh..."

"What happens when you lose your wagers, Lieutenant Colonel?" she asked playfully.

"I pay off." Steve paused. "Say this Friday night...?"

"All right... I'll write down my number..." She turned to bend across her desk to reach pen and paper, the tan wool stretching to mold her backside.

Outstanding upstairs and *downstairs*, Steve thought, tempted to tarry another moment to enjoy the view. *Business before pleasure*, he reminded himself. While she was occupied he tried to slide past her, but she was fast—he'd have to remember that—and managed to plant herself in his path.

"I'm sorry, sir," she said firmly, all business again even as she deftly unbuttoned the flap of his jacket's breast pocket to tuck away the folded slip with her telephone number. "Mister Horton is in a meeting. He mustn't be disturbed."

Steve caught a whiff of her perfume as he watched her button the pocket flap and smooth it down with a proprietary little pat. "I like a girl with nimble fingers, but what I have to say to Jack can't wait."

He placed his hands on her waist and gently, easily, lifted her out of he way, enjoying her startled protestations as her feet left the carpet. As he set down the flustered girl he winked. "On Friday night I'll pick up where I left off."

He opened the double doors to Horton's office. Jack was behind his hulking, black laquered desk, going over some papers with his assistant, Turner Layten, who was seated nearby in a spindly, straight-backed armchair. Horton glanced up, obviously surprised by the intrusion.

"I'm so sorry, sir," Steve heard the secretary feverishly apologizing from behind him as he stepped into the office. "I tried to stop him, sir, but—"

"She couldn't," Steve said pleasantly, finishing her sentence.

"That's all right, Joyce," Horton said.

"See, Joyce?" Steve said, glancing back over his shoulder at her. "I told you your boss was a great guy."

"Thank you, Joyce," Horton said. "Now, if you'll excuse us . . ."

"Yes, sir."

Steve gritted his teeth, trying not to wince as Joyce gave him a hard pinch on his butt before backing out of the office, shutting the doors behind her.

"This better be important, Gold," Turner Layten blustered. Layten was in his thirties. He was pear-shaped, with rounded shoulders, baby-smooth jowls, small gray eyes, and waxed black hair parted on the side. Like his boss, he was wearing a gray suit, white shirt, and red tie, except that his shirt had French cuffs, from which gleamed heavy rectangles of gold. "You've got a lot of nerve barging in this way," Layten continued.

Steve ignored him. Layten was a "yes man"; a fawning jackal to Horton's lion. Steve, who during his military career had been unable to bring himself to kiss ass, and had paid the price for it, despised Layten's breed. "Your secretary said you were in a meeting, Jack," Steve said. "But I don't see anybody."

"Goddamn it!" Layten began.

"That's enough," Horton said crossly, nervously fingering his mustache. Layten shut up like a clam.

Steve allowed himself to smirk. *Sure it was juvenile*, he thought, *but what the hey, nobody's perfect*.

"I wasn't aware you were back in town," Horton said.

"I just got back from Nevada yesterday." Steve looked around Horton's vast burgundy-carpeted office filled with curios. "I see you've added some new pieces since I was here last." He wandered over to the end table next to the black leather sofa and picked up a small tulip-shaped purple glass vase overlaid with silver. "For instance, this is new, isn't it?"

"Yes," Horton said. He seemed to flinch as Steve balanced the vase on his palm.

"I swear, Jack, you've got enough art deco stuff to open up your own shop on King Street."

"Actually, that's art *nouveau*," he said, his jaw clenched. "And it's *very* delicate, and very expensive. Please be careful with it."

So I'm a bull in a china shop, eh? Steve thought as he put down the vase. *Then beware my horns . . .*

"Anyway, Steve, to what do we owe the *unexpected* pleasure of this visit?" Horton's smile remained, but his eyes behind his black horn-rimmed eyeglasses were flat, dark gun muzzles.

Steve reached into his trouser pocket as he approached Horton's desk. "I came by to discuss this with you. It's a little something I got from one of the pilots at Whetstone," he added as he tossed the silver dollar onto the desktop.

Horton had to block it with his hand to keep it from skidding clear across the waxed surface and into his lap. He then gingerly picked it up and placed it carefully on his desk blotter. He and Layten took a moment to distastefully study it.

"You know you shouldn't have this . . ." Horton said.

"It's totally against regulations—" Layten rushed to agree.

"Keep your shirts on, guys," Steve replied, drawing up a chair and sitting down. "That's a *genuine* silver dollar, not the little door prize your boys were handing out to my pilots—"

"*Your* pilots—?" Layten snickered gleefully.

"Where do all you guys with two last names get that obnoxious, snorting-honking sort of laugh?" Steve inquired. "I mean, are you guys *born* with it, or do they bring in geese and hogs at prep school to teach it to you?"

"Is there a point to this, Steve?" Horton asked tiredly.

Steve nodded. "First, I wanted to know if *you* knew about what was going on at Whetstone, and now that I *do* know that, I want to know how you could condone handing out cyanide-dipped pins—"

"Actually, it's a shellfish toxin," Layten said earnestly. "We're quite proud of it. It's instantly fatal; a really great advance in the field . . ."

"You're up on your poisons, aren't you, Layten?" Steve asked.

"Actually, I was in charge of research and development of this particular toxin."

"Now how did I know that?" Steve mused. "Were you also in charge of the suicide bomb?"

"What 'suicide bomb'?" Horton interrupted.

"Come *on*, Jack." Steve scowled. "You know exactly what I'm talking about. Don't make things worse. You've already made some terrible mistakes with this poison pin crap, and this crap about putting bombs in the airplanes and expecting the pilots to detonate them before bailing out."

"The self-destruct device in each plane is timed to allow the pilot ample time to eject—"

"So you say!"

"You don't believe me?" Horton protested.

Steve had to give the guy credit. He actually managed to look hurt. He wondered if they taught acting classes at the

Company training center. "It's not what I believe that matters," Steve said calmly. "Your pilots don't believe you. You're facing a mutiny in the ranks at Whetstone."

Horton was shaking his head. "That's not the information that Layten has been relaying to me."

"Then you're a horse's ass for buying it!" Steve shot back.

Layten began to say something, but Horton held up his hand. "Let him finish," he said affably.

"Thank you." Steve nodded. He glanced at Layten. "Look, seriously, Turner, no offense to you, but you weren't there. I was."

"I'm in constant communication with Whetstone," Layten replied defensively.

"Then you're being fed false information," Steve countered, struggling to keep the scorn he felt toward Horton's lapdog out of his voice.

"My network is absolutely reliable," Layten said firmly, glancing anxiously at Horton.

Steve gave up on Layten. "Jack, you listen to me now. What you've got at Whetstone is a little cold war going on between your personnel and the pilots I recruited. It's easy to see how it got started: Your personnel are self-reliant lone wolves trained to operate behind the lines. From day one they're probably taught that they're expendable."

"That's true." Horton nodded.

"Are you saying that Air Force pilots are taught something different?" Layten demanded, looking amused.

"In a way, they are . . ."

"But the men you recruited were all fighter pilots: lone wolves, as well!" Layten said triumphantly.

Steve shook his head. "I can see how it might look like that to you . . ." He smiled. "To tell you the truth, I thought the same way once, but since then I've learned that despite how it might seem, flying a fighter requires *teamwork* and trust. First, you've got to trust your flight crew to see to it that your airplane is in top condition. Then you've got to trust your wingman to work with you during combat. Fi-

nally, if things should go wrong, you've got to trust S &
R—"

"Pardon?" Layten asked.

"Search and Rescue," Horton told him softy.

"Right," Steve said. "You've got to trust Search and Rescue to bust their asses to find you and bring you home safe
and sound. You plant doubts in a pilot's mind about *any* of
that and his morale and concentration—in other words, his
performance—is going to suffer."

"Dammit, you're right as rain." Horton nodded vigorously.

"Huh?" Steve blurted, taken aback by Horton's sudden
turnaround. "You understand what I'm telling you?"

"I certainly do: You're saying that we've inadvertently
planted a time bomb of a different sort, and now it's ticking
away. Unless we deactivate it it's going to blow apart the
entire project."

"Exactly," Steve said, vastly relieved.

"I can't thank you enough for bringing this to my attention," Horton said. "And I can tell you right know that I
intend to make some immediate changes. You just leave
everything to me."

"That's great, Jack. Let me thank you right now on behalf
of the men . . ."

Horton grinned benevolently. "But where's my manners?"
He snapped his fingers. "Layten, would you ask Joyce to get
us some coffee? Now then, Steve, I want you to tell me
more about what's going on at Whetstone. You've done a
first-rate job for us. I want *all* your input. Your opinion
counts . . ."

(Four)

"Excuse me, sir," Turner Layten said respectfully once
Lieutenant Colonel Steven Gold had left the office. "But
wasn't placing the bomb in the MR-1 the Director's idea?"

"More or less," Horton replied. They'd moved to the sofa

and armchairs in his office for their coffee. Horton now took a paper napkin from the coffee table and began to tear strips off its edge.

"The gist of the Director's memorandum was that nine times out of ten, a carefully selected, properly motivated individual's conscience will lead him to do the right thing," he lectured his assistant. "But every once in a while you might have to prod the recalcitrant onto the duly appropriate path with a judicious push . . ."

"Yes, sir . . ." Layten seemed to hesitate. "But sir, you told the lieutenant colonel that you would have the devices removed from the MR-1s . . . ?"

Horton nodded. The Mayfly had been reclassified the Meteorological Research 1 to coincide with the National Advisory Committee on Aeronautics' recent public announcement that the spy planes' flights would be for the purpose of studying weather patterns. "I tell people a lot of things, don't I, Turner?"

"Yes, sir. I do see, now, sir . . ." Layten was beaming. "But what do we do about the lieutenant colonel, sir?"

"We've done it already," Horton replied. "Now we need only continue to string him along."

"Yes, sir."

"But we do it with kid gloves," Horton added quickly. "I want Steve Gold treated with the utmost respect. He's made himself a lot of friends in high places, Layten. Friends in the Pentagon, and up on the Hill. If he were to go rogue on us the Air Force would be on our backs in an instant. You know that SAC is just itching for the opportunity to grab control of the MR-1 program. A controversy about how we're handling the pilots they've loaned us would be just the opening they'd need to pounce."

"But sir, how do we keep the lieutenant colonel from finding out that nothing has changed?"

"Steve's job is done. The pilots are in place. We're about to go operational. When we do, the pilots will be scattered to remote, foreign air bases. When that happens their little rebellion will fizzle, and Steve Gold won't know anything further about the MR-1 program unless we tell him."

"I see . . . Do we send him back to the Air Force?"

Horton pondered it. "No, I don't think so, Turner . . . I did his father a favor by taking him on, and now I'd like to increase old Herman Gold's indebtedness to me, by keeping his prodigal son out of his hair for as long as possible."

"And as you said, sir," Layten volunteered, "the lieutenant colonel has important friends, and as long as he's with us any friend of his will likely be a friend of ours."

"That's very good, Turner."

"Thank you, sir."

"We'll kick him upstairs," Horton mused. "Give him an important-sounding title: USAF/CIA liaison in charge of something or other . . ." He trailed off. "You see to it . . ."

"Yes, sir . . ." Layten hesitated.

"Something's bothering you." Horton smiled fondly. "I can always tell . . . Out with it, man . . ."

"Well, sir . . . It's just that the lieutenant colonel is somewhat lacking in finesse . . ."

"He's a simple man." Horton nodded. "But don't you ever confuse that sort of simplicity with stupidity," he warned.

"No, sir."

"I agree that Steven Gold is a bit too true blue for any covert operational purpose," Horton continued. "But that Boy Scout image of his plays well around town. We can get some mileage out of that, don't you think?"

"Leave everything to me, sir," Layten said, standing up. "I'll make sure that he's given all the perks, and kept happy."

"Just as long as you also make sure that he's cut completely out of the loop," Horton warned as his assistant took his leave. "There's no place for Boy Scouts in our sort of work."

CHAPTER 11

(One)

The Top Hat Grill
Los Angeles
4 February 1958

Herman Gold was having lunch with his son-in-law Don Harrison to celebrate the birth of his second grandchild. Both mother and the strapping baby boy the proud parents had named Andrew were doing fine. Gold's daughter Suzy would be home from the hospital by Friday, which was when his son Steve would be flying in from Washington for the weekend. Gold's wife Erica had planned a celebratory family dinner for Saturday night. Gold was looking forward to having everyone all together at last under one roof. He had even begun to hope that Don was ready to come around toward Steve.

Don had certainly mellowed these past nine months. It

seemed that the process of becoming a father in his own right had helped him to develop poise and self-confidence in the office. Gold had been relieved to hear that the situation had also improved in the Harrison household. Suzy had confided to her mother that the stress on her marriage had eased considerably with the advent of her pregnancy.

The only dark spots on the horizon concerned Don's continued animosity toward Steve, and the way that Don seemed to want to blank out his stepson Robbie's existence. Today, for instance, Gold had tried to steer the conversation around to Robbie, but Don had been unreceptive. When Gold had flatly come out and cautioned the man not to neglect his stepson, Don had dismissed the subject with a shrug, saying that he had always tried his utmost with the boy, but that Robbie was now a teenager; old enough to be held responsible for his own social behavior. Don had intimated that Robbie had never really welcomed him into the family, and that as far as he was concerned, the relationship between stepfather and stepson was a two-way street...

They were seated in Gold's usual corner booth at the Top Hat; one of the tables with a better view of the popular Wilshire Boulevard dining room. The restaurant was a favorite deal-making place for the Hollywood crowd, so you could always count on spotting some movie stars, who tended to not really resemble their doctored-up, autographed photos that lined the restaurant's walls.

Gold and Don had finished their lunch, and were enjoying themselves chatting as they worked on polishing off their second bottle of champagne. Don was puffing on a foot-long cigar, rambling on about how Andrew was destined for great things. The dining room was crowded, and Gold was slightly tipsy, so he didn't notice Tim Campbell and Hull Stiles threading their way through the closely packed tables until they were standing right near him.

Stout little Tim Campbell was dressed like a used car salesman in a very splashy, tan windowpane plaid three-piece suit, a burgundy shirt, and a white tie. Hull Stiles stood a little behind Campbell, towering over him like a tree. Hull was in his early sixties, but he was still a raw-boned, rangy old cuss, with big, callused hands, and ropey shoulders straining the meticulous tailoring of his staid, double-breasted blue flannel. Hull had ivory hair, slicked straight back from his forehead, and a matching fringe of close-cropped beard ringing his strong jaw. He had wide-set brown eyes, and skin that the sun had long ago permanently burnished to the color and wrinkled texture of worn cow-hide, thanks to his hundreds of hours spent in open cockpit aircraft.

"Herman, fancy running into you, here." Campbell smiled. "Hey! Don! I hear you're a new papa! Congrats, kid—"

"Thanks," Don said coolly.

Gold smiled, thinking that Don looked like he could hardly bring himself to shake Campbell's hand. Obviously he was still fuming over last week's announcement by the Feds. The proposed merger between GAT and Amalgamated-Landis had been disapproved under antitrust statutes, and for reasons of national security.

"Hull," Gold began. "Have you and Don met?"

Hull glanced questioningly at Gold, who remembered that the old pilot was a bit hard of hearing, due to all that time spent in close proximity to roaring aircraft engines.

"Oh, sure, I know Don." Hull nodded once Gold had repeated the question a bit louder to carry over the busy restaurant's bustle and clatter. "We met back when this young whippersnapper here was working for Amalgamated." Hull reached across the table, first to shake hands with Don, and then to clasp Gold's shoulder. "And you, you old rascal"— Hull flashed an easygoing grin—"You certainly look every bit the granddaddy, but tell Erica I think she much's too pretty to be a grandma twice over—"

"That's true, she is." Gold laughed. "You fellows have lunch yet?"

"We just finished," Campbell replied. "But we wouldn't mind joining you for a congratulatory drink—"

You mean, to congratulate yourself on your stock market

killing, you gloating sonofabitch, Gold thought as he and Don slid over to make room in the curved booth. This past year, while the government had plodded along in its decision-making process, Campbell had enjoyed watching the value of his Amalgamated-Landis stock soar as the speculators had hungrily bought in.

Gold snapped his fingers for a waiter and then sent him to fetch two more champagne glasses. The waiter returned with the glasses, but when he took the champagne from its ice bucket to pour, they saw that the bottle was almost empty.

"Another bottle then," Campbell said grandly. "And put it on my bill," he told the waiter.

"You can certainly afford it." Gold smiled. Tim must have had someone on the inside in Washington to tip him off on which way the Feds were leaning because he'd been able to take the Street by surprise, unloading a goodly portion of his huge holdings of A-L stock. By the time the word spread that Campbell was bailing out, Tim had already taken his profits. Through mutual friends Gold had learned that Campbell had come out of it all smelling like a rose, in large part recouping his losses suffered during Amalgamated's failed attempt to market its own jetliner.

"Somebody's got to win, and somebody's got to lose," Campbell said airily.

"And somebody's got to cheat," Don Harrison said pointedly.

Campbell eyed him the way a snake sizes up a bird with a broken wing. "Herman, you ought to teach your protégé here how not to be a sore loser."

"You think so?" Gold asked. "I would have thought losing was a topic Don would have covered in exhaustive detail during his time spent working with you—"

Campbell nodded, smiling thinly. "That's okay, amigo. I can take a little joke. Why not? I *won.*" He leaned forward, his elbows on the table, his expression now extremely serious as he stared at Gold. "I finally did it. I finally put one over on you the way you once hornswaggled me. How does it feel to be outfoxed, Herman? To know that I got the best of you coming *and* going?"

"What can I say, Tim?" Gold shrugged. "The facts speak for themselves."

"That's right! That's damned right," Campbell declared fiercely. "The facts don't lie."

"Take it easy, Tim," Hull Stiles urged, putting a cautionary hand on Campbell's sleeve.

"Take it easy, nothing!" Campbell snapped, shaking off Hull's touch. "And who are you anyway to tell me what to do?" he snarled. "I talk and you listen, remember?"

"Sure, sure, Tim—" Hull said, so meekly that Gold felt embarrassed for him. "All I meant was that we're all friends here, right?"

"Sure we're friends." Campbell abruptly giggled. He looked around. "Where the fuck's our waiter with the champagne?" he loudly demanded.

He's drunk, Gold realized, surprised, and a bit shocked. In all the years he'd known Tim, Gold didn't think that he'd ever seen him drunk . . .

"Why shouldn't we all be friends?" Campbell was rambling. "I got no beef. I'm happy. For a paltry leasing fee— for nothing, *for fucking pocket change*—my airline got the jump on all of its competitors." He stared gloatingly toward Gold. "Thanks to you, amigo, Skyworld enjoyed the use of those GC-909 jetliners you diverted to us, and *then*, thanks to the way I hornswaggled you into bumping us to the top of GAT's delivery list, we took possession of our own jet fleet."

"That's right, you did," Gold soothed, wanting Tim to calm down. The guy was unpredictable enough when he was sober.

"Don't you patronize me, you sonofabitch," Campbell snarled, his mood once again doing a 180. "I came out on top. I *did!*"

"You sure did whip his ass, Timmy," Hull urgently agreed.

Campbell pounded the table. "I got *everything* I wanted

out of Herman Gold, and for once in his life Herman Gold got *nothing*!"

"Well, that's not exactly true," Gold said sheepishly. He gestured toward the waiter who had appeared with a fresh bottle of champagne. "I'm getting a drink out of the deal . . ."

"Yeah, that's right!" Campbell laughed, calming down as though somebody had thrown a switch. "You're getting a drink . . ." Sighing contentedly, he nodded to the waiter who was showing him the label on the champagne bottle. The waiter popped the cork and poured a little into Campbell's glass. He tasted it, pronounced it satisfactory, and the waiter proceeded to fill their glasses.

"A toast then," Campbell said, raising his glass. "To the winners, and to the losers." He paused melodramatically. "I trust we all now *know* who we are . . ."

"To old times," Gold murmured, sipping at his champagne as he locked eyes with Hull.

Campbell tossed back his champagne in one gulp. "Come on, Hull. Let's get going . . ."

"Yeah, sure, Tim." Hull hurried to tag along behind Campbell as he stood up and strode away.

(Two)

"What an asshole," Harrison murmured, watching Tim Campbell and Hull Stiles go.

"Well, like I said before," Herman said, chuckling, "the facts do speak for themselves."

"I'm surprised you didn't *slug* the little bastard." Harrison shook his head. "*I* would have . . ."

"Well, now," Herman responded goodnaturedly. "You've got to take circumstances into account. For instance, he was drunk . . ."

"Yeah, I realize." Harrison nodded. "I mean, it was obvious he was tipsy, but still—"

"And there's a time and place for retaliation," Herman added, sounding somewhat mysterious, Harrison thought.

"What I still don't understand is how you allowed yourself to be duped," he said. "And I can't believe how well you're taking it."

"Thank you." Herman smiled. "I'm going to have a little more of Tim Campbell's champagne... Would you care for some?"

Harrison shook his head. "However, if you'll pardon me for saying it, Herman, I *do* feel you were naive to go into this deal," he scolded.

"Oh, really," Herman replied, sounding amused. He cocked one eyebrow. "How so, Don?"

"Well..." Harrison was a bit taken aback by Herman's continued genial manner concerning all this. "Well, for instance, I don't understand why you didn't use your connections in Washington to check out the deal before committing yourself..."

"I did," Herman said.

"You—you did?" Harrison was flabbergasted.

"Sure. I put a call in right away to somebody I know who has access to the right people to get the information."

"So you *knew* that the Feds would kill the merger?"

Herman laughed. "I knew the proposal didn't have a snowball's chance in hell within *hours* of making my deal with Tim. That's why I bought Amalgamated-Landis through a third party *early on*, before the announcement of the proposed merger drove the price up—"

"You bought Amalgamated...?" Harrison echoed weakly, feeling very confused. "Through a third party...?"

"So as to avoid any charges of insider trading," Herman said, dismissing the matter with a wave of his hand, as if it were a pesky fly. "And like Campbell, I sold my A-L holdings during the height of the hoopla on the Street concerning the proposed merger to make a tidy profit. Not as much as Tim made, but enough..." He paused, smiling. "By the way, since the origins of this deal, and your *son*'s origins seemed to coincide, I thought it appropriate that I put those profits into a trust for little Andrew..."

"Well, thank you, of course, but—"

"No, thank *you*." Herman laughed. "Money I can still make, no problem...New *babies*, however..." He trailed off whimsically.

"I'm getting a splitting headache," Harrison complained. "And it's not from the champagne. Please just answer me this: If you knew right from the start that this whole thing was a ploy by Tim Campbell, why did you go along with it? Why would you be so willing to help an enemy?"

"Who said he helped an enemy?"

Harrison looked up. Hull was back.

Herman was laughing. "You can hear pretty good when you want to, you old bastard—"

"You sound like my wife," Hull agreed jovially.

"Where's your master?" Don asked sarcastically, looking around for Campbell.

"Hey," Herman reprimanded him as Hull slid into the booth next to Harrison. "Don't go shooting off your mouth when you don't know what you're talking about."

Harrison pressed his lips together, feeling surprised and a bit insulted to be put down that way. "I'm just shocked at the way Hull lets Campbell treat him..." He heard the sulkiness in his voice. It mad him feel doubly embarrassed.

"Ah, Timmy doesn't mean anything when he talks to me like that," Hull confided, giving Harrison a friendly nudge with his shoulder. "He's like that little white poodle my wife's got. All yap, with little itty-bitty teeth, can't give you but a nip, and *that's* hardly ever..."

"So where *is* your yapping little poodle?" Herman chuckled.

"Oh, he's left," Hull said.

"I hope he's not driving?" Herman asked, concerned.

"Nope," Hull winked. "I took his car keys out of his pocket when he wasn't looking. The guy's so soused he never even knew. I fed him a song and dance 'bout how he must of dropped them somewhere in the restaurant, then I told him I'd come back in here to look for them, and put him in a cab."

"I don't think I ever saw him that juiced," Herman said.

"He doesn't usually drink much at all, that's why."

"He ought to watch himself . . ."

"Well, today was his big celebration, you see . . ." Hull's smile was like the sun coming out from behind the clouds. "Over besting you . . ."

Both men burst out laughing.

"What *is* going on here?" Harrision implored, confused and frustrated.

"Let me straighten you out, son," Hull began, taking a sack of Bull Durham and a packet of cigarette papers out of his pocket.

Harrison, watching Hull adroitly roll himself a smoke, thought: *Put this guy in work clothes and he'd fit right in on the GAT loading dock.*

"First off, Herman saw through Tim's scheme from day one," Hull continued, sticking his cigarette between his lips, and then producing a wooden kitchen match, which he flicked alight with his thumbnail.

"That much I already know," Harrison complained. "What I *don't* understand is why he played along."

"To help *me*," Hull replied, lighting his cigarette and ex-haling smoke. "You see, Tim may *control* Skyworld, but she's *my* airline. I *run* her. I made her what she is today."

"That's true," Herman interjected. "Hull and his brother ran the operation from its beginning, back when it still was a part of GAT."

"Your brother?" Harrison asked Hull, intrigued. "I didn't know you have a brother."

"Had," Hull muttered.

"Lester Stiles is dead," Herman said evenly. "He died in the cockpit when one of our transports went down, back in 'twenty-five . . . Anyway, the point I was making was that nobody knows the nuts and bolts side of the airlines business like this guy here . . ."

Hull smiled at the compliment. "Don, you can imagine

that I wasn't too happy about the fact that Skyworld was gonna get stuck flying AL-12s when the competition was flocking to the GC-909, but I knew there wasn't any way around it."

"It makes sense that Campbell would want his airline to buy from his aircraft company." Harrison nodded.

"But what really got me upset was finding out that the AL-12 was canceled," Hull continued. "That left Skyworld with nothing at all to fly. When Timmy told me about his scheme to con Herman into supplying us with planes I knew right away that Herman was too smart to fall for it. That's why I called him, and asked him to play along with the guy for my sake, on account of old times."

Harrison was skeptical. "Come on, you can't tell me that Herman went to all this trouble just to do you a favor? Why, the legal expenses alone are going to cost GAT a fortune, and what about all the industry feathers we ruffled by delaying other airlines orders so that we could bump Skyworld to the top of the 909 delivery list—"

Hull was nodding. "Now, I sure do know that Herman went way out of his way to do me this favor," he said quickly. "And I do appreciate it—"

"Bullshit!" Herman scowled. "I haven't nearly paid you back what I owe you—"

"What *you* owe to Hull?" Harrison repeated, staring at Herman. "Now I'm getting confused all over again."

"For starters, I owe him my life," Herman said firmly.

"Now don't you go running off about that," Hull grumbled.

"This man wants to know, I'm going to tell him," Herman declared. "You see, Don, back during Prohibition I did a brief stint flying booze from Mexico into California."

Harrison burst out laughing. "Oh, I'm sorry, Herman, but the thought of you as a bootlegger..." He broke up again as the two older men exchanged bemused glances.

"Kids," Hull sighed, rolling his eyes.

"They think they're the only ones ever been young," Herman commiserated. "Anyway, Don, I got myself into a scrape out in the desert with some crooked federal lawmen. There was some shooting. If Hull and his brother Les hadn't come to my rescue I wouldn't be here today, and that's a fact."

Hull was trying his best to busy himself with smoking his cigarette. Harrison thought the guy actually looked angry over Herman having brought all this up.

"And if that weren't enough," Herman continued, "if it hadn't been for Hull playing along, I never would have come out on top back in 'thirty-three, during my stock battle with Tim over control of Skyworld."

"But Campbell ended up with Skyworld," Harrison pointed out.

"Sure, but if Hull hadn't tipped me off in the beginning about what my partner Tim Campbell was doing behind my back, I might have lost my entire company. And it was Hull who at great professional risk played along with my final strategy. Thanks to him, all three of us came out of what could have been a financially mortal combat a little bloodied, but survivors."

"I've got to get going," Hull said, standing up. He shook hands with Herman. "Thanks again, for everything . . ."

Herman said, "Anytime, anyplace, I'll be there for you, the way *you've* always been there for me . . ."

"One last thing, Herman," Harrison asked as he watched Hull walk away. "Why did you have to go to such an elaborate ruse in order to help out Skyworld? When Tim Campbell initially approached you, why didn't you just tell him that you thought his deal was bogus, but that you were still willing to give him the airplanes on account of your friendship with Hull?"

"Business is business." Gold smiled, signaling the waiter for the check. "But *revenge* is sweet. By pretending to dance to Tim's tune, and then to eat a little crow for the guy, I hope that I've convinced my ex-partner that he's finally gotten the better of me."

"So what?"

"So *this* way I don't have to keep looking over my shoulder, waiting for Tim to plant a knife in my back."

"I'm beginning to understand," Harrison murmured. "The way you and Hull have worked it, Campbell thinks he's *already* stabbed you in the back."

"Um . . ." Herman grunted, preoccupied as he studied the tab that the waiter had presented him.

"What's the matter?" Harrison asked.

"Campbell," Gold muttered affectionately. "Don't you *know* that on his way out he collared the waiter, and told him to add that extra bottle of champagne to *my* bill, after all?"

CHAPTER 12

(One)

**Gold Household
Bel-Air
8 February 1958**

Susan Harrison was enjoying the family dinner being held in her parents' dining room. The room was lined with Japanese silk-screened panels and was softly illuminated by glittering Waterford chandeliers. A fire crackled in the hearth, and candles cast their rich glow on the linen-covered Georgian table that had been so elegantly set with sterling flatware, crystal, and fine china. Now the dessert plates had been cleared away, and the maid was coming around with coffee.

"And this is something very special for tonight," Susan's father announced from the head of the table, proudly holding up a long-necked brown bottle. "It's a German wine, one that is very rare in this country. It's a *trockenbeerenauslese*: a wine made from grapes allowed to dry in the sun while still on the vine."

He stood to pull the wine's cork, and then, smiling at Suzy, came around the table to pour her some in a small, ornately engraved, crystal dessert wineglass. "You should have the first sip," her father continued, his hand on her shoulder. "May my new grandson Andrew's life be as sweet as this wine."

Suzy tilted the glass against the candlelight. The wine was golden and moved slowly in the glass, like syrup. She took a sip. It was intensely sweet, almost like honey, with an after-taste like raisins. She found it a bit cloying, but she knew from the way her father was eagerly watching for her reaction that the stuff must be some big deal . . .

"It's delicious, Daddy . . ."

Her father nodded, handing the bottle to the maid, who went around the table with it. "The taste of that wine reminds me of my homeland," he sighed.

"Oh, Herman," Susan heard her mother scold. Erica got irked when Herman got maudlin about Germany. "You never tasted such wine in Germany in your life, and you know it!"

"That's true," Herman admitted, laughing. "This stuff cost a fortune even in those days. In Germany I never made enough money in a year to buy a bottle . . ."

For some reason Susan found that uproarious, but then the wine had been flowing freely all through the night, so that now she was more than a little tipsy. She felt deliciously sleepy, lulled by the twinkling candlelight, and by the sounds of the multiple conversations going on at the table.

Her parents were sitting at opposite ends of the table, looking radiant. Her husband was on her right. Robbie was across the table, sitting next to Steve. Her son, looking quite the young gentleman in his white shirt, striped tie, and blue blazer, was hanging on Steve's every word as he told of his work in Washington on behalf of the Air Force.

". . . of course the Bell Lab, X-series of rocket planes will be taking the Air Force into outer space," Steve was telling Robbie.

"I'm not so sure about that," Don interrupted.

"Pardon?" Steve asked politely from across the table.

Don looked past him, to Robbie, as he spoke. "Well, there's no point in telling the boy nonsense . . ."

"What do you think was 'nonsense' in what I was saying?" Steve asked tightly.

"Well, it's clear the Air Force no longer holds the monopoly it used to," Don replied.

"What's that supposed to mean?" Steve asked.

"Yeah, Don," Robbie piped up. "*Everybody* knows the Air Force owns the sky." He smiled at Steve, who winked back.

"Maybe they own the sky," Don said, "but Steve was talking about space . . ."

"Yeah, so?" Robbie demanded.

"Well, a few days ago this country launched its first successful space satellite, and according to our contacts in Washington, the bill to fund that agency—"

"What agency?" Susan interrupted.

"Don means the National Aeronautics and Space Administration," her father explained to her.

"Right." Don nodded. "The Air Force will be getting some stiff competition from NASA concerning who gets the funding to explore space."

"Aw, come on," Robbie exclaimed. Susan saw her son look anxiously at Steve. "That's just a lot of bull, right?" Robbie demanded.

Steve, his mouth compressed into a thin line, didn't reply.

"Steve, I take it you don't have much confidence in NASA?" Susan heard her father ask.

"Come on, Pop," Steve said disdainfully. "I don't expect Don to understand, but you're a pilot, like I am."

Oh, shit—Susan thought as Don stiffened in his chair. She glanced at her husband and could sense his anger. She wondered if Steve's slight was intentional, but then it wouldn't matter one way or the other, she brooded sadly. She knew that Don would retaliate.

"Well, from a business point of view, our people in Washington tell us that NASA is going to be getting the lion's share of the appropriations," Don said.

"Over the Air Force?" Steve asked skeptically.

"That's what we've heard," Herman interjected from the head of the table.

"You remember Burt Crenshaw, don't you, dear?" Erica asked Steve. "Well Burt's son-in-law is an aide to one of the senators on the appropriations committee . . ."

"GAT's Aerospace Division will be bidding on contracts to build components for the NASA rocket program," Don said.

Susan saw Steve's look of dismay. "Pop?" He glanced at the head of the table. "Pop, I thought you told me you were going to put the company's R & D resources into the Air Force's orbiting lab program?"

"Your father and I changed our minds about that," Don said.

"Well, if you ask me—" Steve began.

"No one did," Don said curtly.

"Come on now, Don," Herman said. "No need for that tone of voice . . ."

"Well if you *did* ask me," Steve continued, growing angry, "I'd tell you that you were making a big mistake. There's no way the Air Force is going to wave the white flag to NASA. We're going to push ahead. In a few years we hope to have our lab in orbit, and to be working on space weapons like lasers and particle beams—"

"Ray guns?" Don smiled. "Is that the kind of Buck Rogers stuff the Air Force has up its wild blue sleeve?"

"If that's what it takes," Steve said belligerently.

"You're living in a dreamworld." Don chuckled.

Susan saw her husband smile at Robbie, but her son was not smiling back. Robbie was not appreciating the way his uncle was being put on the defensive.

"You say that I'm in a dreamworld, but at least I'm out

and around," Steve told Don. "I'm not cooped up in a lab all day—"

"Oh, good," Don said sarcastically. "But before we get to hear your war stories, *again*, since you're the man of action around here you should be interested to know that we've heard that one of NASA's priorities is to select pilots to become space explorers. They're calling them astronauts."

"What's that got to do with me?" Steve asked.

"Well." Don smiled. "You're a pilot, right? Doesn't exploring outer space sound appealing to you?"

"Yeah, Uncle Steve, it sound's great!" Robbie exclaimed.

"There." Don chuckled, gesturing toward Robbie. "You've got your biggest fan here keen on the idea. I was thinking that maybe you ought to try out to be one of these astronauts . . ."

"Oh, really?" Steve fumed. "Did you and my father discuss *that* without me, as well?"

"It's just a thought, Steve," Susan heard her father try to placate her brother. "Of course, if you're not interested . . ."

He trailed off, sounding tentative. Susan wondered what was going on with her father. Usually he was so forceful, but tonight he seemed to retreat the more her brother and her husband bickered.

"It's obvious that these astronaut guys are going to be in the limelight," Don was telling Steve. "So I thought you'd be interested, that's all . . ."

"What's *that* supposed to mean?" Steve demanded. "That I don't like hard work? That all I want to do is hog the glory?"

"You said it, I didn't." Don smiled.

"You gonna be an astronaut, Uncle Steve?" Robbie asked.

"Yeah, *Uncle Steve*," Don mimicked gleefully. "You going to be an astronaut?"

"Stop it, Don," Susan heard herself murmuring. "*Both* of you, please stop . . ."

"Listen, Robbie, the way NASA runs things, these guys aren't going to be true pilots at all," Steve was busy explaining to her son. "They're going to be like . . . glorified white *rats* ... locked into tin cans..." Steve glanced angrily at Don. "Is that all you think I'm good for?"

"What I think you'd be *good for* is another topic," Don said coldly. "My point at the moment is only that it would be good public relations for GAT Aerospace if you tried out for the NASA program. If you're really interested in helping the company you'll do it. If not..." He shrugged. "It's time to put up or shut up, Steve. You're either willing to pitch in, or you're not..."

"You little *bookworm*—" Steve snapped.

"Steve!" Herman commanded. "Come on now, Steve, calm down... This is supposed to be a joyous occasion—"

Steve was glaring at Don. "Where does this *bookworm* come off telling *me* what to do?"

"Right." Don nodded fiercely. "You call me names because that's easier than admitting that you're too selfish—that you've *always* been too selfish—to do the right thing by your family, and the company!"

"Like *you* do the right thing, you mean?" Steve demanded.

"That's right, I do!"

"Stop it! Both of you!" Susan cried out, shocking them into silence. "Listen to yourselves, arguing like two little boys! And you, Don! You should be especially ashamed of yourself. This dinner is supposed to be a celebration of the birth of your son! What's wrong with you? Why can't you and Steve get along?"

She noticed Steve smirking and turned on him. "What's so funny?"

Her brother leaned back in his chair. "Yeah, Don. Why not tell her why we don't get along? Why don't you tell *everyone* what's really on your mind, old buddy?"

"What's he talking about, Don?" Susan asked, totally confused.

"I don't know what he means, honey," Don said nervously. He glared at Steve. "Just shut up, will you?"

"No! I won't shut up," Steve replied, looking amused. "You're pretty good at needling people, old buddy. You can dish it out, all right, but you can't take it. You know as well as I do the reason you hate me—"

"Shut up, I said—!" Don's chair tipped over as he jumped to his feet. He was trembling with anger.

"What's the matter, bookworm?" Steve taunted, the smile vanishing from his face. "I know you want to keep me out of GAT because you're afraid of the competition. Well, I don't blame you. You sure turned out to be inadequate competition concerning—"

Don snatched up his wineglass and hurled its contents across the table, into Steve's face.

"*Oh, my God*—" Susan gasped.

Her mother was ashen. Her father's stunned expression had melted into one of deep grief. Robbie looked like he was about to cry, and Don looked exhausted. He was still trembling, but his head was down and his hands hung limp by his sides.

Steve sat with the wine that had splattered the front of his shirt and suit jacket dripping down his face. "Well, I guess I've just had one for the road," he said mildly.

"You'd better go," Susan heard her father hoarsely whisper. "Please, it would be the best thing . . ."

Steve nodded, wiped his face with his napkin, and stood up. "Thanks for a lovely evening."

(Two)

Steven Gold went upstairs to the guest room he was occupying, changed clothes, and packed quickly. He telephoned for a taxi, and then went back downstairs with his valise, giving the dining room a wide berth. He was waiting for his cab at the front door when his father appeared in the foyer.

"I'm sorry, Pop," Steve said, setting down his valise. "I'm sorry the evening got spoiled—" He was choosing his words carefully, not about to accept responsibility for what he considered to be Don's fault.

"Where are you going?"

"I called a cab," Steve said. "I'll check into a hotel for tonight, and catch the first flight I can back to Washington tomorrow."

His father was looking old and gray. Steve felt his anger draining away, to be replaced with compassion. *Fuck it,* he thought. *I can't do much for him, but at least I can let him off the hook* . . . "Come on, cheer up, Pop." Steve forced himself to smile apologetically. "It was my fault tonight."

"No . . ." He put his hand on Steve's shoulder. "Don shouldn't have goaded you like that . . ."

"Pop . . ." Steve shook his head. "It was my fault, I tell you. The guy's so thin-skinned. I should have known better than to push him. I played with fire and I got burned, is all . . ."

"Steve?" his father began. "What you were talking about before . . ."

"What was that, Pop?"

"You were suggesting that Don had some reason other than the office to dislike you . . . ?"

"Ah, that was just the wine talking," Steve said quickly. "I was just shooting my mouth off . . ."

"Then there is nothing else?" his father prodded. "Nothing more I should know?"

Steve shook his head, grateful that he had another gift to give. "Nothing else you should know, Pop. I swear it to you . . ."

His father was nodding, looking satisfied. "The thing with Don, he's as emotional as he is brilliant . . ."

"Yeah, sure, Pop . . ." *He's brilliant and I'm dumb* . . .

"I haven't had the chance to tell you, but Don's devised a preliminary concept for a radio-controlled rocket engine," his father continued. "If it pans out, the engine will have the ability to fire repeatedly; not just once until it burns out. An engine like that would allow ground control to actually steer a satellite into a different orbit." He smiled. "We're all really excited about it."

"Sounds great." Steve smiled back lamely, thinking sadly that he wasn't part of so much that was happening.

"I don't know where GAT would be without Don's innovation . . ."

His father was trying to explain something to him, Steve realized. *I was wrong. Don isn't Pop's "yes man"; it's the other way around . . .*

Outside, there came the sound of tires on the crushed gravel drive. A motor idled. A horn blared.

"Pop, that's my cab. I gotta go. Tell Mom I'm sorry for what happened."

"Maybe you should tell her yourself . . ."

"I can't go in there," Steve said, his hand on the doorknob. He smiled wryly as he stepped out into the night. "I'm not used to losing, Pop."

(Three)

Harrison Household
Brentwood

It was close to four in the morning when Susan Harrision gave up on trying to sleep. Beside her in the double bed Don was snoring soundly. He'd been absolutely contrite during the drive home. Emotionally and physically exhausted, he'd fallen asleep as soon as his head had hit the pillow.

Susan was angry at her husband for what had happened, but she was angry at Steve, as well. Both men had done all they could to humiliate and belittle each other in front of the family, and both men had succeeded.

The wine she'd had at dinner had left her with a parched throat and a headache. Every time she closed her eyes in hopes of dozing off her restless mind replayed that terrible argument, setting her tossing and turning. She gave up and got out of bed, stepping into her slippers and putting on her robe. She was on her way to the kitchen, thinking to make herself a cup of tea, when she noticed light spilling from beneath the staircase door that led up to the attic.

She wrapped her robe around her against the slight chill as she opened the door and went up the stairs. The overhead light was on. In the harsh glare of the bare bulb hanging from the roof rafters she saw her son in his red and white striped pajamas and navy blue corduroy robe sitting cross-legged on an old Oriental carpet. Open beside him was a battered, black and green steamer trunk plastered with travel stickers.

Susan took a deep breath. The attic smelled of dust and cedar and the past. That steamer trunk was where she kept her late husband's things . . .

"I didn't know you knew about that trunk." She tried to keep the resentment she was feeling toward her son out of her voice, but Robbie must have heard it. He looked up at her with his father's penetrating green eyes beneath his touseled black hair.

"Are you mad?" Robbie murmured.

"No . . . yes . . ." She smiled faintly. "Maybe a little . . . It's hard to share," she tried to explain.

Robbie nodded. "I've known about the trunk a long time. I've been going through it for a while now." He paused. "Whenever I'm alone . . ."

She saw that he had pulled out some of the newspaper clippings and photographs, and spread them on the carpet. Beside him was the old shoebox in which she kept her husband's medals, and his letters to her. She knelt down beside her son and pointed to the shoebox. "Have you read those?"

Robbie shrugged. "I started to once, but they were all full of kind of mushy stuff . . . and . . . well . . ." He blushed. "So I didn't . . ."

She put her arms around her son and hugged him. "I appreciate that."

Robbie didn't reply. His fingers brushed over the yellowing, brittle scraps of newsprint that chronicled his father's aviation racing career, and then he picked up a small, faded, black-and-white snapshot of a smiling, tall, dark matinee idol of a man in a tweed suit with too-wide lapels and baggy pants. The man was smoking a cigarette and standing on a beach. In the background, bobbing in the water, was a spindly, single-engine, open-cockpit seaplane.

"This is my favorite one," Robbie said.

"Mine too," Susan confided. "It was taken in 1938. In Venice, Italy. At the—"

"Moden Seaplane Races," Robbie finished for her.

"That's right," she said, surprised.

"That's where you met him . . ."

Susan nodded. "How do you know all that?"

"I asked Grandpa once, and he told me."

"I see . . ."

"Mom, do you ever come up here to look at all this stuff?"

She had the strangest impulse to lie. To say that she never did. "Sometimes . . ."

"When you do, does it make you feel good or bad?" Robbie asked, his green eyes searching.

"It makes me feel, a little *both* ways . . ."

He nodded. "If you could have him back again, would you? Instead of Don, I mean—?"

She closed her eyes. "I can't have him back, Robbie—"

"I know, but if you could . . . ?"

She took hold of her son's hand and squeezed it. "When you get older, those kinds of make-believe games hurt, so you don't play them . . ."

He looked unconvinced. "Mom? When you look at this stuff, don't you feel like you are choosing?"

"I'm not sure I know what you mean." This time she had no problem lying.

"Never mind." He shrugged, and then gestured to the photograph. "If he was here, do you think that he'd be more like Don or Steve?"

It was an intriguing question. "Why do you ask?"

"Because I want to *be* like him," Robbie fiercely replied.

"I see . . . Well, your father was a very good pilot, but he was also a brilliant engineer..." Susan replied. "Did you know that before he went off to the war he was working on a prototype jet engine."

"Grandpa told me . . ."

"Your father would have been a little like both men, I think . . ."

Robbie frowned, puzzled. Susan knew he couldn't accept the notion. Steve and Don had positioned themselves too far apart in his eyes; the boy needed to choose one or the other; of course, he already had.

"I think he'd want me to be a pilot, like Grandpa, and Steve..." Robbie mused. "That's what I think . . ."

"Maybe . . ."

"I don't think he'd like Don at all."

"Have you seen your father's medals in the shoebox?" Susan asked, needing to change the subject.

"Yeah . . ."

"I've always intended that they would someday belong to you. What do you think?" she asked confidently. "Would you like them now? To keep in your room?"

She couldn't believe it when he shook his head.

"I'm going to get my own," Robbie told her.

CHAPTER 13

(One)

Alexandria, Virginia
6 May 1960

Ordinarily Steven Gold got a kick out of the Corvette. It was a 1959, red and white Sports Roadster with a manual transmission. When he toed its throttle the car kicked him back against the tan leather bucket seat like a jet fighter.

It was dark, well after the evening rush hour, when Steve had left his Pentagon office. The roads had been clear, but tonight he hadn't been in the mood to play with the 'Vette's fuel-injected V-8. Tonight, as the Corvette's headlights stabbed the darkness, he was looking forward to a quiet evening in his apartment listening to jazz on the stereo, with no company except for a nice big scotch on the rocks.

He and his staff had been working late every night this week, and it didn't look like there was an end to the work in sight. Sometime last Sunday night an MR-1, a.k.a. Mayfly spy plane, had been shot down over the Soviet Union. The pilot had been taken alive by the Russians. The pilot's name was Chet Boskins, a.k.a. "Lowball" to his friends, not many of whom, including Steve, expected to see their fellow pilot again.

Washington was in an uproar. The Soviets were milking the fiasco for all it was worth, doing their "Imperialist War Mongerers" number at the United Nations and in the international press. The White House, the State Department, and NASA—which was gamely claiming that it had sponsored the overflights for meteorological research purposes—were all putting out conflicting statements. At the Pentagon, Steve, who was the USAF/CIA liaison in charge of technological developments, had been keeping his staff busy working the telephones and typewriters, helping to put out media fires by generating a load of technical horseshit designed to back up NASA's stories. Both the Air Force and the CIA were frantic not to be drawn into it, despite the reports that Lowball had been carrying I.D. and had announced to his Commie captors that he was a civilian pilot employed by the CIA.

Meanwhile, in the Kremlin, Khrushchev was threatening to disrupt this month's Big Four Summit in Paris, and derail the disarmament talks in Geneva. At the United Nations Soviet Foreign Minister Gromyko was demanding an official apology from Ike. Someone with access to the Oval Office had confided to Steve that the President was bullshit that the MR-1 incident would taint his last months in office and throw November's election to the Democrats. At the very least, the incident was expected to give a boost to the Democrats' likely candidate, a senator from New England named Kennedy...

As far as Steve could tell, nobody seemed much concerned about the captured MR-1 pilot, except, perhaps, Jack Horton. The CIA man was telling everyone who would listen that none of this would be happening if Chet Boskins had done "the right thing"...

For his part Steve was sorry he'd ever become involved in the pilot recruitment program. He couldn't help thinking that if he hadn't been so good at his job, Lowball wouldn't now be languishing in a Russian prison cell. Sure he'd taken on the job for self-serving reasons, but he'd also sincerely felt that he was doing his patriotic duty. He'd thought that he was being a good soldier, but Jack Horton and his band of spooks had used him like a fool; a dupe. Not that Steve had any business feeling sorry for himself. The stuff coming in through the diplomatic channels had it that if the United States didn't publicly apologize, the pilot would be tried as a spy. If the Soviets carried through with that threat, Lowball's certain conviction could mean his execution or at best a lengthy prison term.

As Steve drove through Alexandria's quiet tree-lined streets, and then turned onto Prince Street, he wondered what Lowball was thinking right now. Was he blaming Steve for getting him into this mess? It didn't really matter to Steve whether or not Lowball blamed him for his predicament because Steve blamed himself. He was trying his best to make things up to Lowball. He'd been making the rounds up on the Hill, leaking the facts about what had happened to certain influential members of Congress in the hopes that they would push to get the pilot released through diplomacy. Some of the people Steve had talked to had warned that he was pushing too hard; that what he was trying to do on Lowball's behalf could end up hurting his own career.

Steve was certainly worried about that: The Air Force was all he had. Still, he figured he owed Lowball, and he believed in paying his debts.

He was driving slowly along Prince Street as usual, looking for a parking space. As he passed his apartment house his headlights picked up a shabbily dressed character shouldering a knapsack lurking out in front. He found a spot half a block down, and parked the car. Walking back to his apartment he saw that the guy was still there, leaning against a lamppost a few paces away.

A coffeehouse that featured live jazz, and poetry readings

for beatnik types, had recently opened on King Street. Steve figured this guy was one of those. By the light cast by the street lamp Steve saw that the guy was tall and stocky, wearing grimy pants, sneakers, a dark turtleneck sweater, and a torn, brown canvas workman's jacket. He had a dark blue baseball cap pulled down low on his brow obscuring his face, and that knapsack on his shoulder.

In the past, Steve—wearing civies—had dropped by the King Street hipster joint a couple of times for the music, which he kind of liked . . . He'd even picked himself up a set of bongo drums and a how-to book at the local music store . . . But he had use for the poetry, which tended toward leftist political slogans against the so-called military-industrial complex.

As Steve reached his front steps the beatnick detached himself from his lamppost to approach him. *Probably looking for a handout*, Steve thought, cautioning himself to ignore any slurs the guy might cast against his uniform. He was just too tired to get into it tonight; he would think about the scotch on the rocks waiting upstairs—

"Uncle Steve . . ."

Steve paused to stare. "Robbie?"

He and Robbie had been writing to each other, but he hadn't seen his nephew, or any of his family, for a long time. He talked on the telephone with his parents, and now and again his sister called, but since that family dinner when he'd had it out with his brother-in-law, he'd accepted the fact that he was persona non grata back home, and had acted accordingly.

Robbie, grinning, had taken off his baseball cap to give Steve a better look. "Sorry if I scared you . . ."

"You'd scare anybody, buddy." Steve laughed, coming back down the steps. "Look how big you've grown!"

"I'm seventeen now, Uncle Steve," Robbie said quietly.

"What the hell are you doing here?" Steve asked.

"I ran away from home."

"Oh . . ." Steve replied awkwardly, shocked that nobody back in L.A. had seen fit to telephone him with the news.

He supposed that he really *was* out of the family. "Your mother must be frantic."

Robbie looked away. Steve wrinkled his nose. "Whew, when was the last time you showered?"

"Last Sunday morning." Robbie shrugged. "I've been on the road since then."

"You hitchhike?"

Robbie nodded. "Not bad making it across the country in under a week, huh? I got a couple of good rides from truckers."

"Well, come on upstairs," Steve said. "You can get cleaned up, and I'll make us something to eat. You must be hungry?"

"I could eat." Robbie nodded.

"Eggs and bacon are all I have, I'm afraid," Steve said. "I don't do much cooking . . ."

"I ran away because I couldn't take it anymore at home," Robbie was explaining. "The guy was just *at me* all the time." He looked up at Steve for affirmation. "You know how Don can be . . ."

"I know," Steve said wryly.

They were sitting in the living room. Steve was in an armchair, smoking a cigarette. His second and final scotch on the rocks—these days he was limiting himself to two a night—was within easy reach on the end table. Behind Steve in the galley kitchen the sink was filled with the dishes from their supper. Robbie was on the sofa cradling a coffee mug in his hands. He was showered and shaved, his thick, black hair still a damp tangle as he sat wrapped in Steve's blue terry cloth robe. He had asked Steve for a cigarette, and for some brandy in his coffee, and Steve had allowed him both, thinking that his nephew was a man now. You could see it in his stature, and in the reservoir of hurt already apparent in his emerald eyes.

". . . I was having some trouble in school," Robbie continued. "Right away, Don got on my case, getting Mom, and

Grandpa and Grandma all upset by telling them I wasn't going to get into college."

"Are you doing that poorly?" Steve asked.

"In some things." Robbie shrugged. "I'm doing okay in math and science."

"Just okay?"

"Well, I've got a B average in algebra, but I'm just passing in English, and social studies," Robbie confessed. "So I said to myself, the hell with it! Who needs school." He grinned. "I figured I'd be like you—"

"What?" Steve blurted, surprised. "What's that supposed to mean?"

"I want to be a fighter pilot, like you," Robbie began. "You ran away from home when you were about my age. You never finished high school—"

"I got my high school equivalency diploma—" Steve said quickly.

"Okay, then I will, too . . ." Robbie replied. "While I'm taking pilot's training."

"Robbie . . ." Steve hesitated. Lately he'd been thinking about how he might relive his life if he had the chance . . . He'd made some real mistakes in his professional and personal life, shot himself in a foot any number of times, but not getting himself an education topped them all. Now, in a way, he was getting that chance to make things right, through Robbie. There would be a point to his mistakes; they might count for something, if he could keep Robbie from making the same ones . . .

His nephew was staring at him; ready to hang on his every word, but then Robbie had *always* idolized him. Steve had never realized how important to his own self-image his nephew's adulation had been . . . Until now . . .

Steve thought: *Someday I'll learn to appreciate what I have before it's lost.*

"Robbie, it's time you knew the truth about me." He had a hard time looking the kid in the eye as he confessed, "I'm a failure . . ."

"Come on, Uncle Steve . . ." Robbie laughed. "What are you talking about? You're great! You're a double ace in two wars. A Medal of Honor winner. You made lieutenant colonel when you were twenty-eight—"

"And now I'm thirty-six, and I'm still a lieutenant colonel," Steve pointed out.

"What are you talking about?" Robbie demanded, incredulous. "You've got a great job—"

Steve held up his hand to quiet his nephew. "Remember that dinner at your grandpa's and grandma's? When your stepfather and I had it out?"

"Yeah." Robbie grinned. "I'll never forget the way you tore into Don."

"We were arguing over whether I should apply for admission to NASA's Project Mercury astronaut program," Steve reminded him.

"And you really told off Don good!" Robbie chuckled. "I still remember what you said about how those astronauts were going to be white rats in a tin can . . ."

"I'm glad you remember it so well, buddy." Steve frowned. "Do you want to know the *real* reason why I got so hot under the collar that night? It was because I was lying. Don didn't have to tell me about the NASA program. I already knew about it because I'd already *tried* to volunteer—"

"You *wanted* to be an astronaut?"

Steve nodded. "But they turned me down flat, just the way they did at the Air Force Aerospace Research Pilots School at Edwards Air Base."

"I don't believe you—" Robbie said. "Why wouldn't they take you?" He looked near tears.

"Because I don't have the education to make the cut, buddy," Steve said quietly. "The future of aviation belongs to the educated guys, the ones who can hack the math and high-powered engineering that's required to drive today's latest fast movers. I'm talking about guys like your stepfather. You should be looking up to *Don*, not me. Guys like

Don Harrison are going to be tomorrow's aviation heroes: the *hot* pilots."

"All right," Robbie murmured, his eyes downcast.

"And if *you* want to be a hot pilot you've got to go to college, like your folks want—"

"I said all right!" Robbie snapped, his green eyes cool.

And that's what I wanted, Steve thought, leaning back in his chair. *And that's what I got . . .* He stared at his empty glass. *And I guess tonight I've earned myself another scotch . . .*

"I'll call your folks now," Steve said, standing up. "Let them know you're all right . . ."

(Two)

**Steven Gold's Apartment
Alexandria, Virginia
8 May 1960**

Don Harrison flew into Washington National Airport on a rainy Sunday. He took a cab to Alexandria, giving the driver Steve's Prince Street address.

During the ride he pondered the past frantic week. Robbie's disappearance had overshadowed everything, including the superpower confrontation over the downed, GAT-built MR-1 spy plane. As Herman had so tellingly put it to Harrison last week, "When there's trouble in your family, you realize what's really important . . ."

Friday night poor Suzy had collapsed into tears of relief when Steve had called to say that her son was with him, safe and sound. Harrison had gotten on the telephone with Steve to say that he would immediately fly out to get the boy. It had been the first time he'd talked with Steve since that night they'd almost come to blows over two years ago.

On the phone Steve had been cordial, if a bit cool, which

was certainly understandable, and so they'd confined their brief conversation to working out the logistics of Harrison's visit. Not once did Steve reproach him over the fact that nobody had called to inform him that Robbie had run away. Harrison, feeling guilty about that, considering how it had been Steve who had come to the rescue, had been grateful for his brother-in-law's tact.

Then Robbie had gotten on the telephone. The boy had talked briefly with his mother, and then had surprised Harrison by asking to speak to him . . .

The cab was pulling up in front of a brick town house. Harrison asked the driver to wait, and then ducked out of the cab, hurrying through the rain into the front foyer of the building. He rang Steve's bell, and Steve buzzed him in. As Harrison climbed the stairs to the fifth floor apartment he felt himself perspiring under his gray flannel suit and tan trench coat. His blond hair was a rain-damp tangle on his brow. His eyeglasses, their lenses misted by the rain, had begun to fog. He took them off to wipe them clear with his tie as he stood outside Steve Gold's door, and then he knocked.

Steve opened the door. He was barefoot, wearing dungarees and a light blue crewneck sweater over a white T-shirt.

"Hello." Harrison smiled tentatively, offering his hand.

"Hi, come on in," Steve said, turning away, as if he hadn't seen Harrison's outstretched hand.

Harrison quickly let his hand fall to his side. "Nice apartment," he commented, stepping into the living room and looking around. "Beautiful neighborhood . . ."

"Thanks."

Steve didn't offer to take his coat, or ask him to sit down. Harrison stood there in his sweaty suit and damp trench coat, wondering how to begin to talk to this man whom he hadn't seen in over two years. Then Robbie came out of the bedroom, wearing new-looking tan chino slacks and a dark blue windbreaker.

"Robbie's clothes were kind of worn out," Steve explained. "So I picked him up some new things to get him home."

"Thanks." Harrison nodded quickly. He wondered if he should offer to pay . . . Better not . . . "Robbie, there's a cab waiting for us downstairs. Would you go down now? I'd like to talk with your uncle a moment . . ."

"Sure, Don . . ." Robbie hesitated in the doorway, looking at Steve. "Thanks . . ."

"Drop by anytime." Steve smiled.

Robbie nodded, smiling slightly, and then he was off, heading down the stairs.

Harrison looked at Steve. "Uh, on the telephone Friday night, Robbie told me what you'd said to him . . ."

Steve nodded, silent, waiting for him to go on.

"Well, what I wanted to know . . ." Harrison took a deep breath. "Was what you told him true? About trying to get into NASA, and the Air Force's space program, I mean?"

"Maybe it was, and maybe it wasn't," Steve said. "None of this is about me, it's about Robbie doing the right thing for himself . . ."

Harrison quickly ducked his head in agreement. "Well, in any case, what I want to say is that I know that telling Robbie all that had to be a tough thing for you to do."

"I'd do *anything* for that kid," Steve declared. "I don't care what he thinks of me as long as he does the right thing . . ."

"I understand that completely," Harrison said. "Suzy— and I— Well, we don't know how to thank you . . ."

"Don't worry about it," Steve said dryly. "I didn't do it for you, I did it for Robbie." He paused. "He wants a career in the Air Force, you know?"

"That's not a problem as far as I'm concerned."

"Well, I've been thinking," Steve continued. "What Robbie ought to do is try to get into the Air Force Academy at Colorado Springs. He needs to be nominated for consideration by an elected or military official, but between us, we could get him a hatful of recommendations . . ."

"I'd already thought of that," Harrison said. "Trouble is, he hasn't got the academic record to gain admission."

"Yeah, I figured as much," Steve said wistfully. "I don't recommend that he go the military prep school route. It'd mean an extra year of school, and I don't think he's got the stomach for it, and there'd still be no certainty he'd meet the academy's academic standards."

"No, I agree," Harrison said. "So I figured that whatever college he goes to has got to have an Air Force ROTC program . . ."

"Yeah, that's good." Steve nodded. "You should see that he looks into that . . ."

"Well," Harrison began. "I thought we could *both* help him look into that . . ."

"You want me to have a hand in it?" Steve was looking hopeful and doubtful.

"Suzy and I discussed it," Harrison pressed on. "We would very much like your involvement concerning Robbie's future."

"I'd like that," Steve said shyly.

"You've always been like a father to him . . ."

"Well, you've tried to be one to him, as well," Steve mumbled, looking down at the the carpet.

"Yes, I have tried," Harrison said sincerely. "But trying and succeeding aren't the same . . ."

"No, that's true," Steve murmured.

"Maybe between the two of us, we can be the father he deserves . . ."

"Maybe so . . ." Steve nodded.

Harrison was satisfied. "Well, I've got a cab waiting . . ."

"Yeah, you'd better get going . . ." Steve followed him out to the landing, then stood in the doorway. "See you . . ."

Harrison nodded. As usual, he was dumb enough to want to say something more, and maybe muck things up all over again. Fortunately, Steve had the brains not to let him; he shut the apartment door.

(Three)

Harrison Household
Brentwood, California
9 July 1960

Robert Blaize Green was alone in the den, sitting on the floor on the Navaho rug, watching television. His parents were out for the evening. His two-year-old half brother Andy was being put to bed by his nanny. Robert had told the housekeeper that he would make his own dinner, and now he had a FlufferNutter and a Coca-Cola behind him on the coffee table.

He knew that he should have been doing his summer school homework—he was taking English and civics—but he couldn't tear himself away from the television. In awhile they were going to have a special news broadcast about the latest development in the spy plane crisis: Today the Russians had formally charged the MR-1 pilot Chet Boskins with espionage against the Soviet Union. On the news someone had said that the Russians' decision to hold the trial was "a response" to President Eisenhower's economic blockade of Cuba. The politicians they'd talked to on the television had expressed concerns that the "confrontation could escalate." That was another way of saying war, Robert guessed, which nobody wanted. Especially not him.

Not until I'm done with school, Robert Blaize Greene thought, reaching for half of his FlufferNutter. *Let those MIGs stay grounded until I'm ready to bag me some . . .*

BOOK II:
1960–1967

KENNEDY OVER NIXON—
Democrat Takes Presidency by Narrow Margin—
Los Angeles Tribune

U.S. LAUNCHES NAVAHO MISSILE—
Government Extends Contract with GAT Aerospace—
Internal Guidance System Deemed Successful—
Aero-Tech Magazine

BERLIN DIVIDED BY COMMIE WALL—
U.S. and Soviet Union Increase Defense Spending—
Kennedy: "We Stand Prepared to Defend Freedom"—
Miami Daily Telegraph

U.S. CHARGES CUBAN MISSILE INSTALLATIONS—
Soviets Warn Attack on Cuba Could Mean Nuclear War—
Philadelphia Tattler

SOVIET RELEASE IMPRISONED U.S. SPY PLANE
PILOT—
Chet Boskins Exchanged for Russian Spy—
Baltimore Globe

VIETCONG ROUT SOUTH VIETNAMESE TROOPS—
Congress Votes on Gulf of Tonkin Resolution—
President Johnson Given Broad Powers to Strike Back at
Reds—
Providence Herald

MIDDLE EAST BOILS OVER IN SIX-DAY WAR—
Israel Smashes Arabs and Gains Control of Jerusalem—
Egypt Charging American Involvement in Air Attack—
Nasser Severs Diplomatic Relations with U.S.—
Boston Times

CHAPTER 14

(One)

**Near Saratoga Springs, New York
4 November 1964**

The indoor firing range had a cement slab floor and pale green walls. There were two stalls where shooters could stand abreast to fire at targets up to seventy-five feet away. Fluorescent ceiling fixtures lit the range, while a pair of powerful exhaust fans rumbled to suck out the gun smoke.

Steven Gold, wearing heavy flannel trousers, hiking boots, and a green, thick wool turtleneck sweater, stood on the firing line. He wrapped both hands around the black plastic, checkered grips of the stainless steel, long-slide, custom Colt .45, thumbed off the safety, and sighted down on the paper target the full twenty-five yards away: a one-third size human torso silhouette gridded with concentric numbered circles. He steadied his breathing and squeezed off a shot. The .45 rose up, the recoil stinging his hand as orange flame stabbed from its barrel. The auto's report had him wincing, despite the fact that he was wearing hearing protection.

Steve cast a questioning glance over his shoulder at his host.

"Hot load, huh?" Benny Detkin asked knowingly. He was also wearing a foam-stuffed headset to protect his hearing.

"Armor-piercing, you mean." Steve frowned. He transferred the .45 to his left hand and tried to shake the sting out of his right.

"I made those up myself, in case of grizzly bear attacks." Benny smiled broadly. He was wearing boots, tan corduroys, and a blue crewneck sweater over a red chamois shirt. Benny stood about five feet ten inches tall. He was slender but kept himself very fit. He had heavy-lidded, dark brown eyes, a broad, flat nose, and a strong jawline. He wore his thick, black curly hair cut moderately short with no part. Steve, who had not seen his old World War II buddy for some time, had been shocked to see that Benny's hair had become seeded with gray.

"Well, what's the matter, Air Force? Can't handle it?" Benny leaned against the gun locker, obviously relishing Steve's discomfort. "You didn't hear me complaining when it was my turn. And all mine printed tight in the X-ring."

Steve, rolling his eyes, turned back to the target. He held the .45 straight out in front of him with his elbows locked, and emptied it with three double taps. The series of two round bursts set the paper silhouette quivering. The last shot, emptying the gun, left the auto's slide open. Steve removed its magazine, and set both it and the auto down on the firing stall table. As he and Benny removed their headsets Steve activated the overhead electrical pulley that brought his target whooshing back to him.

"That load is brutal," Steve complained.

Benny laughed. "Tell you the truth, I can't stand to shoot them myself. That's why I gave them to you . . ."

"Thanks a lot." Steve took his finger off the pulley switch

as the target reached him. None of his rounds were well grouped. "Ugh, just look at that," Steve said, disgusted.

"Hey, they're all in the black," Benny said. "At twenty-five yards that ain't chopped liver..."

"Yours weren't scattered around like these."

"Don't forget I'm used to the load," Benny said. "And I practice a lot. When was the last time you fired a handgun?"

"Point well taken," Steve muttered.

Benny tapped Steve's target. "If that had been a bad guy, any one of your hits would have done the job."

"What else do you have besides this cannon?" Steve asked.

"Lots of stuff." Benny went over to the gun locker. "A .22 Woodsman target auto, a Browning nine millimeter, a brace of engraved, single-action Colt Peacemakers. Back at the house I've got another .45—"

"I know, in case of grizzly attacks," Steve said wryly.

Benny looked back, smiling. "You can't be too careful..." He turned back to the locker. "Oh, and I've got this pair of Smith and Wesson .38 Special, Combat Masterpieces—"

"Now you're talking," Steve enthused. "Get them out. We'll shoot against each other with those, and I bet I whip your ass..."

"Not a chance." Benny laughed.

Probably right, Steve thought as he studied the shelf of trophies Benny had won in shooting competitions down through the years. "You win most of these with a .38, or a .45?"

"Some of each," Benny replied, handing Steve the guns and a box of cartridges. "But lately I've been concentrating on the .45. Most of the serious shooters are switching over to autos..."

Steve examined the revolvers. They were blued steel, with four-inch barrels, squared walnut target stocks, red ramp front sights, and adjustable, white-outlined rear sights.

"You know, I carried a piece like this during the Korean War..."

"Well, load them, and we'll see how you do," Benny replied, clipping two fresh targets to the pulley system and running them out the length of the range until they were hanging against the backstop.

Steve fed six semi-wadcutters into each gun, and handed one of the revolvers to Benny, who took it into the adjoining stall. Steve replaced his hearing protection, and gripped the Combat Masterpiece with two hands, aiming so that the bright red front blade was level centered in the U-shaped, white-outlined rear sight.

"Whenever you're ready," Benny called.

"Now..."

"Huh?"

Steve replied by squeezing off a round. The .38 barked, spitting fire, but the piece felt as smooth as silk after the .45's mule kick. He emptied the revolver, concentrating on pulling the trigger straight back, not letting the gun jerk right or left as he fired, and resisting the urge to look over his sights at the target to see how he was doing. Benny finished firing an instant after him, and then both men were working their pulleys to reel in their targets.

Steve, grinning, plucked his target from the pulley and confidently strode toward Benny's stall.

Benny met him halfway. "Read it and weep," he said, proudly presenting his own target.

Both men laughed as they compared scores. Each had closely grouped all of his rounds in the center X-ring.

"That's the way we used to do it when we were flying together," Benny said quietly. "Knocking Zeros out of the sky over the Solomons."

"Amen to that." Steve nodded.

"You know, there's no substitute for experience," Benny added. "And we were *there*, old buddy..."

"We surely were," Steve agreed. "And you were one of the best."

During the Second World War Captain Ben Detkin had distinguished himself as a triple ace. He'd flown as Steve's wingman, and had countless times saved Steve's ass in dogfights by waxing the enemy before they could draw their bead on Steve's six o'clock.

"Lately I've been thinking a lot about those days," Benny was musing. "We were just a couple of cocky kids sent to do a job, and we did it, but things were so black and white back then . . ."

"Or maybe they just seemed that way because we were so young," Steve pointed out.

Benny ruefully nodded. "I still can't believe I hit the big four-oh last year."

"And I'm coming up on it this year," Steve said. "But you don't look any different."

"No? What about all this damned gray I'm getting?" Benny demanded.

"Ah, that's nothing," Steve said. "Anyway, a touch of gray suits a big-shot lawyer. It makes you look distinguished."

Benny looked amused. "Well, gray or not, at least I've *got* all of my hair . . ." He squinted at Steve. "You seem to be getting a little thin up top," he said merrily.

"Thank you for pointing that out to me, you sonofabitch—"

Benny laughed. "Come on, let's go back to the house and have something hot to drink. I'll come back later to clean the pieces."

"Good idea." Steve nodded. "It's damned cold in here." When he exhaled he could see his breath. "I thought you said this place was heated?"

"It is, to some extent," Benny said as they gathered up the weapons and put them back into the gun locker, closed it up, and then set the padlock. "This was where they used to keep the cows, and *they* never complained."

"That's right, you said all this was once a dairy farm."

They put on their coats and left the range. Outside a brisk wind was blowing. It was cold, but sunny. It had snowed a few days before, and everything still looked fresh and clean under its white blanket.

"When I saw how long and narrow the dairy barn was, I

thought instantly of having it converted into a range," Benny said, his breath puffing as they trudged toward the house.

"What's the matter?" Steve joked, "You don't like cows?"

"You sound like my wife." Benny chuckled. "When I told Amy what I wanted to do with the barn she said nice Jewish boys shouldn't be playing with guns, but what the hell, punching holes in paper relaxes me . . ."

"Seriously, I think the place is terrific."

"My little hideaway in the country." Benny beamed fondly as they entered the house. It was three stories, with a red shingled roof, a white clapboard exterior, and black shutters on all the windows.

"Do you make it up here much?" Steve asked as they paused in the mud room to stomp the snow off their boots and hang up their coats.

"I'm sorry to say only sporadically during the winter," Benny replied. "But we do get here most every weekend during the summer, when things at the office are slower."

Steve nodded. Benny was a partner in one of the most prestigious law firms in New York City.

Benny led the way into the big kitchen, which had a fireplace, like all the other rooms in the house. The kitchen's walls and cabinets were painted mustard yellow. The floor was covered with red and black checkerboard linoleum that was almost worn through in several spots. Benny's wife Amy had told Steve that the house, furnished with antiques bought locally at auctions, still looked pretty much the way it did when they'd purchased it from the family who had lived here for several generations. "Chic we have in Manhattan," Amy had said. "Here it's anti-chic . . ."

"There's a little airport a couple of miles southwest of here," Benny was saying. "Amy and the girls and I leave early on Friday, and fly up in the Cessna. The local guy I hired to keep an eye on the place meets us, and then here we are. By flying my own plane I bet I can get here faster than some guys I know can make it to their weekend places in the Hamptons, or Fire Island." He paused. "But I know this was a real schlepp for you; I really appreciate you making the trek."

"Hey, thanks for inviting me," Steve said lightly.

Benny winked at him and then turned to open the refrigerator. "How about a beer? Or maybe some hot apple cider?"

"Hot cider," Steve said adamantly, settling down on a kitchen chair. "I've been looking forward to this visit ever since you called," he added as Benny poured the cider into a pan, tossed in some spices and a chunk of butter, and set it on the stove to heat. "I was *ready* for a week in the country. Things have been hectic, to say the least . . ."

"Yeah, that's right." Benny nodded, getting down two big mugs from the pantry. "You were pretty involved with that Chet Boskins, MR-1 spy plane thing for a while, weren't you—?"

Steve nodded. In 1960, the Russians had followed through with their threat to try Lowball, and had found him guilty of espionage, sentencing him to ten years.

Benny had his back to Steve as he stood at the stove, stirring the heating cider. "Some people I know in Washington told me that you ruffled quite a few feathers to get your buddy back home . . ."

"There might have been a little bad blood created." Steve shrugged, remembering how Jack Horton and his CIA buddies newly installed in their Langley, Virginia, headquarters had been looking to put past failures behind them. Horton had spread it around that it would be in the "national interest" to let Boskins molder away forgotten. Steve liked to think that in some small way it was his sincerely made threat to go public concerning all he knew about the MR-1 program that had convinced Horton to be more helpful toward securing Boskins's release. In any event, last year all the hard work had paid off when the Reds sat down at the bargaining table to agree to trade Chet Boskins for one of their own held by the United States.

"The important thing was that we got Lowball home," Steve said.

"That's right." Benny poured the steaming cider into the

mugs and set them on the kitchen table. He then went rummaging in another pantry, bringing out a bottle of rye whiskey. "You help yourself," he said, setting the whiskey on the table between them.

Steve grinned. "Well, I usually don't hit the sauce until after five, but seeing as how I'm on vacation . . ." He poured a healthy dollop of rye into his cider. "When are Amy and the girls due back?"

"Not for hours." Benny chuckled, pulling out a chair and straddling it backward. "When they go antiqueing, they go *antiqueing*."

Steve watched him dribble less than a teaspoon of whiskey into his cider. *To keep me from feeling awkward about drinking alone*, Steve guessed. He knew that Benny rarely drank except for a little wine at dinner.

"I'm glad the wife and kiddies are gone for the day, though," Benny said. "The week's almost over and we still haven't really had the chance to catch up with each other. For starters, how's the Air Force been treating you?"

"Well, after that business concerning Chet Boskins was settled, I began to think again about leaving the Air Force . . ."

"To go to work for your father?"

"Yeah," Steve replied. "I've been getting along pretty well with my brother-in-law . . ." He smiled. "I guess I really earned myself a bunch of Brownie points with the guy when I convinced my nephew to continue his education."

"How's your nephew doing?" Benny asked.

"Okay. He had a rough time of it his freshman year at a four-year school, so he transferred to a junior college." Steve smiled. "I've got to hand it to him. He knew from the outset that he wasn't going to win any academic excellence awards, but he stuck with it, and that sonofagun *graduated*," Steve proudly declared. "He's got himself an associate's degree, and he stuck with Air Force ROTC, as well, successfully completing cadet flight training. He went into the Air Force last year, and now my little nephew is Second Lieutenant Robert Blaize Greene. He was accepted into fighter pilots' training. Now he's learning how to drive the fast movers."

"That's good," Benny said. "But getting back to you, what made you decide to stay in the Air Force?"

"The opportunity to continue flying all the latest fighters, thanks to my pop's old buddy, General Simon," Steve replied. "The general's still involved in Aircraft Development/Procurement out of Wright-Patterson, and had the clout to get me assigned to him. My job is still pretty much the same old P.R. routine of lobbying for appropriations, but the carrot at the end of that stick is my authorization to fly any fighter/interceptor bird I want, when I want, 'for purposes of evaluation . . .'"

"It sounds to *me* like *Simon* is getting the best of the deal," Benny said. "Over the years you've built yourself an invaluable network of contacts in both the government and the aviation industry, and you're still putting all of that at the Air Force's disposal. A guy like you would be invaluable in the business world, either working with your father, or for any company that supplies the military."

"Maybe . . . It's nice of you to say so, in any event." Steve grinned. "I guess I'll find out pretty soon . . ."

"What do you mean?"

"This free ticket I've got courtesy of General Simon won't last forever," Steve explained. "The general's coming up on retirement. When he goes, so will my magic carpet ride. I know the kind of desk duty a light colonel gets saddled with, and I know that's not for me." He noticed that his mug was half-empty, and topped it off with rye.

"What about further promotions?" Benny asked.

Steve shrugged. "They want to send you to war college before they make you a colonel . . ."

"So?"

"So you know that classrooms and I don't mix."

"Not that bullshit again," Benny said impatiently. "I swear to God, I don't see how a fighter jock with your confidence could have such a phobia about education."

"Let's not get into all that now," Steve said.

"No problem." Benny reluctantly dropped the subject.

Steve took his Pall Malls out of his pants pocket, shook a smoke loose, and lit it. Benny got up to find him an ashtray, and ended up giving him a teacup saucer to use; neither he nor Amy smoked.

"Well," Benny began again. "Are you seeing anyone?"

"No one special . . . Anyway, I'm pretty busy. General Simon has me dividing my time between Dayton and Washington. And when I'm not working I'm flying."

"I always thought you and that cute little brunette newspaper reporter—"

"Nah," Steve said lightly, shaking his head. "That's been over for years. Anyway, last I heard she was married, with a couple of kids . . ."

Benny looked perturbed. "You can't stay a bachelor forever—"

Once again Steve was feeling uncomfortable over the turn the conversation was taking. "I'm married to the Air Force," he said and winked. "But enough about me. What have you been doing besides spending your weekends like a country squire on the ill-gotten gains of your shyster legal practice?"

"Nicely put . . ." Benny said sardonically. "Well, Amy and I have always been involved in work on behalf of Israel . . ."

"You've made several trips there with your family, haven't you?" Steve asked.

"Yeah, and those opportunities have been very gratifying to me," Benny replied. "You know, even when I was just a kid growing up in Brooklyn I was always going around shaking the can to collect pennies for Palestine . . . Now that I've become professionally established, I'm able to meaningfully engage in political activity and fund-raising on behalf of Israel. It's really become a major focal point in my life—excepting my family, of course."

"I never thought you were that religious," Steve said.

"I'm not." Benny shrugged. "But it isn't about religion, you see. Remember what I've told you about my childhood? About how during the Depression—before my family moved to Brooklyn—we were stuck in New Jersey?"

"Yeah." Steve nodded. "I seem to remember you saying that it was some kind of mill town . . . and that you were the only Jewish family—?"

"That's right," Benny said. "I spent a large portion of my childhood feeling threatened and lonely; feeling as if we were surrounded by enemies—" The smile had gone from Benny's face. His voice had tensed, and his fists had clenched. "It was a bad time for me. It's no way for a kid to grow up, always ready for a fight every time you walk out of the house, and then always looking over your shoulder, knowing that the chances are that you're going to be out-numbered, so you don't dare make a stand . . ."

Steve, nodding, thought about the shooting range, and the handgun trophies on the shelf. He wondered what Benny thought about when he was putting his tight groups through the X-rings of those target silhouettes; when he was making up his hot loads for "grizzly bear attacks"—

". . . the way it was for me growing up in Jersey, that's the way it is for Israel now," Benny was saying. "Since its independence in 'forty-eight nothing has come easy for Israel." His voice began to rise. "Just look at the map! It's just a little sliver of a country, surrounded by a *sea* of Arab hatred. Nasser and the other Arab leaders are constantly vowing to run the Israelis into the sea."

"Hey, lighten up," Steve coaxed gently.

Benny paused, then nodded, smiling. "Sorry, but when I think of all those Israeli children growing up the way I did, living with their shoulders hunched waiting for the blow to land . . . Well, I get worked up." He snapped his fingers. "Hey, that reminds me! You'll be interested in this! Last spring when we were over there, I visited an air base near Tel Aviv, and got to take up one of their jet fighters—"

"Hold on," Steve interrupted, puzzled. "You're telling me that the Israeli Air Force let a foreigner civilian fly one of their war birds?"

Benny was blushing. "You know I don't mean to brag, but over the years I've made a lot of money—the stock market, real estate investments, and so on—and that's allowed me to *contribute* a lot to Israel . . . What I'm getting at is that over there my family and I get the VIP treatment. Because of my aviation background I mentioned to some people that I would be interested in visiting an air base, which was arranged for me, and when I made it known that I was still an active pilot who enjoyed flying my own plane, I was invited for a ride in one of their dual-seat jet trainers."

"I get it now." Steve smiled. "And now that I think about it, I've got to admit that I've arranged for a few stateside VIPs to go for a ride in the Air Force's two-seaters. Well, how'd you like it?"

"It was incredible!" Benny exclaimed. "The pilot even let me take the stick."

"Now that's something I've never arranged for any of our VIPs!" Steve laughed.

"I tried a few of the aerobatic tricks we used to pull on the Japs." Benny looked proud. "That pilot was surprised to see what I could do!"

"I'll bet he was," Steve said earnestly. "*I'll* tell *you* something, if your Israeli pilot was like any of the youngsters our Air Force is training, he probably thought air combat maneuvers had gone out with the biplane."

"No, it's not like that over there," Benny replied. "You'd like the way they do things, Steve. There's no red tape, no bullshit, you know? They can't afford it. They know that if they ever lose a war they'll have *had* it."

"Sounds like you're ready to re-up," Steve joked.

Benny just smiled. "Anyway, I'm glad we got onto this subject. You see, there's something I need to ask you . . ."

"What is it?" Steve asked. He noticed that Benny was looking troubled. "What's eating you, old buddy?"

"Care for some more cider?" Benny asked. "More whiskey?"

Steve shook his head. "Why do I get the feeling you're buttering me up smoother than you buttered this cider?"

"Because I am," Benny admitted. "I'm about to ask you a big favor . . ."

"Well?"

"I need something from you," Benny began. He took a deep breath. "Actually, I need you to get something from your father. It's no secret that GAT is in partnership with Aérosens to build a jetliner for the European market."

"Yeah, so?"

"Well, Aérosens is the same French aviation company that's been supplying Israel with its jet fighters, the latest being the Tyran II—"

"I'm familiar with that bird's specs." Steve nodded. "She's a beauty. An outstanding, delta-winged fighter. She can carry a variety of ordnance, and a brace of thirty-millimeter guns."

"She is a superb airplane," Benny said. "But she needs one thing to be able to outfight anything in the Arab arsenal, and that's the Vector-A radar ranging weapons firing system. The catch is that the Vector-A is manufactured by GAT, in a co-venture with an independent avionics firm, and there's a United States Government export restriction on the system—"

Steve's stomach sank as he finally realized what his friend was getting at.

"I'd like you to convince your father to defy that restriction," Benny finished.

"You mean convince my father to break the *law* by smuggling Vector-As into Israel?"

"I'd like to think of it as obeying a higher, moral law in order to bring about the survival of one's people," Benny said quietly. "Herman Gold is a Jew, after all . . ."

"And I thought *you* were my friend!" Steve savagely shot back. "Getting around to this was the whole reason why you invited me for this stay, wasn't it?"

"No, of course not—"

"Ah, stop it, Benny. For a successful lawyer, you're a lousy liar . . ."

"Look at me," Benny commanded.

"What?" Steve felt hurt and betrayed.

"If you will speak to your father about this matter a lot of people will be grateful," Benny said. "If you decide you'd rather not, that's that. But I'll *always* be your friend . . ."

"This is real important to you, huh?" Steve sighed.

"The importance goes far beyond me," Benny said. "But if you prefer to think of it that way, then yes; with all you know about me, you should realize that I would never have asked such a thing of you if it wasn't of crucial importance to me . . ."

"Then I'll speak to my father," Steve said. "I can't promise anything, but I'll speak to him . . ."

"Thank you," Benny said happily. "Whatever the outcome, you have the gratitude of an entire nation—"

"What are friends for?" Steve murmured.

(Two)

GAT
Burbank, California
17 December 1964

Herman Gold's secretary buzzed him over the intercom to say that his call to Massachusetts had gone through, and Arthur Zolot was on the line. Herman reached for the telephone, leaning back in his big leather chair and swinging his feet up onto his desk. "Arthur? Yes, it's Herman. How are you, my friend?"

"Who's Arthur Zolot?" Steven Gold asked Don Harrison, who was sitting at the opposite end of the burgundy leather upholstered couch. Steve was wearing a suit and tie and was feeling very businesslike hanging around the executive suite, jawing with his old man and his brother-in-law.

"Arthur Zolot is the founder of Aero-Marine Radio Corporation, one of the foremost East Coast avionics firms," Don said in hushed, reverent tones. "Arthur *invented* the Vector-A."

"No shit," Steve said, thinking that this guy Zolot had to

be really something special to get an egghead like Don Harrison so hot and bothered.

"When you brought all this up last month about smuggling Vector-A radar weapons firing systems into Israel, your father felt that Arthur had to be consulted."

Steve nodded. Thinking of eggheads, he was secretly pleased to see that Don's honey blond hair was thinning faster than his own. Since Steve had last seen him, Don had taken up pipe smoking, and had cultivated a neatly cropped golden red beard that gave him a professorial look that fit in with the tweedy sport jackets he favored. The beard made him look older, more distinguished: Don was a lot easier to take now that he didn't look too young to be so smart . . .

"So, Arthur, you got my letter?" Herman was saying. "Yes, yes, that's why I wrote you. I agree that it's not the sort of thing we'd want to discuss in detail over the telephone."

"And if this guy nixes the idea, that's that?" Steve asked hopefully.

"Yes." Don nodded. "I must say, for someone who suggested it, you don't sound very enthusiastic about this scheme . . ."

"I'm not," Steve replied. He looked around his father's office, at the oil paintings of GAT airplanes in flight and at the glass display cases filled with mementos chronicling the company's history, which was also pretty much the history of aviation since World War I. "I don't like the idea of Pop risking everything he's built by breaking the law. I proposed this matter to him as a favor to a friend. If Pop shoots it down, so be it. I can tell my friend I tried."

"Well, I'm with you," Don said. "I hope that this whole outlandish idea gets shot down."

"Very well, Arthur," Herman was saying. "I understand. No, the risk would be GAT's; I just felt I had a moral obligation to confer with you . . . Yes, right. I understand. Goodbye, Arthur . . ."

"Well?" Steve demanded as his father hung up the telephone.

"He's for the idea," Gold said. "It turns out Arthur Zolot is a member and generous contributor to many of the same pro-Israel organizations as your attorney friend, Benjamin Detkin."

"Oh, great," Don said broodingly.

"Don, have you talked with your counterpart at Aérosens?" Steve heard his father ask.

"Aero-Marine Radio Corporation can deliver an extra forty Vector-A systems within the next twenty-four months," Don replied. "That would pretty much coincide with Aérosens' shipments of Tyran II fighters to Israel."

Herman pondered this. "I guess we could juggle the records to let fall between the cracks an extra forty systems . . ." He glanced at Steve. "We've contracted for hundreds, you see. The Vector-A is just one of the black boxes that's going into our new, twin-seat, Super-BroadSword fighter-bomber."

"I still don't much like it," Steve grumbled, looking at his father. "You still have to figure out a way to get the Vector-As to Israel . . ."

"Jack Horton has a few ideas about that," his father said.

"Horton?" Steve blurted. "What's that CIA rat got to do with any of this?"

"Horton contacted your father to lobby for the idea just a few days after you put it on the table," Don said.

"No shit . . . ?" Steve murmured. "Why would the CIA want us to defy the government's export restrictions on the Vector-A?"

"According to Horton, the United States maintains its position as a friend to all parties in the Mideast," Don said. "Which is why we don't supply things like the Vector-A to anybody in the region."

"But off the record the CIA works very closely with its Israeli counterpart, the Mossad," Herman cut in. "For some time now the Mossad, in cooperation with the Israeli Air Force, has been working on a scheme to get an Arab pilot to defect to Israel with his MIG-21."

Steve whistled. His father nodded.

"The MIG-21 is the Soviet Air Force's top war bird," Steve's father told him. "When GAT proposes a new fighter design, the first question the Air Force's R & D people ask us is can it beat the '21'?"

"Exactly," Don added. "But that's a question that can't be answered. We in the United States have no way of knowing the MIG-21's capabilities, or even more important, its *limitations*, because we can't get our hands on one. According to Horton, the Soviets have recently begun deploying them to their client countries, including those in the Mideast, but with the airplanes go KGB-trained security teams to guard them, and, needless to say, only the most senior, trusted pilots get to fly them."

"So how the hell are the Israelis going to get their mitts on one?" Steve asked.

"That we don't know," Don said. "But according to Horton, and to your boss General Simon, if they should succeed in snaring a MIG-21 the United States Air Force would give its collective right arm to get a chance to put it through its paces."

"Amen to that," Steve agreed.

"Here's the bottom line," his father said. "The Mossad has offered us a deal: If Israel gets its Vector-A systems, the United States will get its look at the MIG when the Mossad snares one."

"*If* the Mossad snares one," Steve corrected.

"Fair enough." His father nodded. "But the CIA thinks it's worth the risk."

"But *whose* risk?" Don demanded. "Certainly not the CIA's . . . Tell me this, Herman: Are you saying that the CIA is going to get us official clearance to ship the Vector-As to Israel?"

"You know they can't do that," Herman quietly replied. "They and the Air Force hope that we'll go through with the deal, but Horton has emphasized the risk. If we're caught, the CIA will disavow all knowledge of the scheme—"

"In other words," Don interrupted, "if we get caught, GAT gets hung out to dry."

"And take it from me," Steve said. "I know from bitter experience that when Horton says he's prepared to walk away fast from any public mess he *means* it. They don't call these guys spooks for nothing."

"All right—" Herman was leaning back in his chair, studying the two men sitting across from him. "I sense that for once the pair of you are on the same side of an issue . . ."

"I guess we are, Pop." Steve chuckled, glancing at Don, who was also smiling and nodding in agreement.

"So talk to me," Herman decreed. "Convince me why I shouldn't go through with this."

"It's a tremendous risk, Herman," Don began.

"Tell me what I don't know," he intoned.

"What's the upside, Pop?" Steve asked. "I mean, say GAT manages to successfully get those black boxes to Israel without getting caught, and say that the Israelis manage to snare their MIG-21 and give the Air Force its peek, what does GAT get out of it?"

"My point exactly." Don nodded. "Any GAT employee involved in this is going to be risking a jail term, and the company as a whole will be risking financial ruin. If we're caught there's no way we'd be able to hold on to our security clearances, which means good-bye to GAT's defense contracts. And for what? Surely not patriotism?"

"And why not patriotism?" Herman queried. "Has this country been so terrible to you that you don't feel you owe it something . . . ?"

"Pop?" Steve asked softly.

"Yeah?"

"Pop, I know that tone of voice," Steve said. "I think you've already decided you're going through with this. So what's up? What's *really* on your mind?"

"All right," his father admitted, smiling. "You're right, I have decided to do it, or at least *try* to do it," he amended thoughtfully. "Exactly why I want to is all mixed up inside of me. Part of it has to do with something Arthur just said on the telephone: 'You can't run away from your roots; who you really are.'" He paused. "Now, I'm almost sixty-six years old, and I realize that all my life I haven't so much been running away as just not looking back."

"You're talking like your life is over," Don chided. "It isn't."

"No, of course not." Herman nodded. "But I am feeling like it's time to take that look back. I've accomplished a lot in my life, and yet I've never come to terms with who I am, and of who I'll be when I die: a Jew, one cut loose and drifted away from a life he's too ignorant to even imagine, but a Jew nonetheless..." He smiled wistfully. "I've come so far, I think I'd like now to take a few steps back, and maybe find a small bit of what's been lost along the way..."

Don was nodding. "And you think helping the Jewish homeland in this way is a first step in that direction? Is that it, Herman?"

"You two are young men," Steve heard his father say shyly. "I don't expect you to understand."

"It doesn't matter," Don said. "You've got to do what you think is right."

Steve felt incredibly touched as his father turned his pale blue eyes toward him. *He wants—needs—my approval*...

The scales abruptly dropped from Steve's eyes, and he saw his father not as he used to be when Steve was a kid, but the way he was *today*. The red was gone from what little hair Herman Gold had left; the red had weathered to wintry silver gray. There were deep lines etched into his father's face; a lifetime's worth of lines...

"I'll tell you what I think, one fighter jock to another." Steve glanced at Don. "No offense meant..."

"None taken," Don acknowledged, smiling.

"I *was* a fighter pilot, once..." Herman murmured.

"*Once* means *always*," Steve firmly insisted. "*Always* means that your entire life you lived according to the fighter jock's credo: *Trust your instincts*. Well, I say you ought to keep on trusting them. You want to do this?"

His father hesitated. Then he nodded, smiling boyishly, and Steve remembered that smile from when he himself had been just a little boy, and his father had been even younger than Steve was now; a robust, powerful man, standing tall beside an open-cockpit airplane . . .

"Sonofabitch, but I don't care about the possible consequences," Herman said. "I *want* to *do* this."

Steve beamed at Don. "What'd I say? Once a fighter jock, *always* a fighter jock." He looked back at his father and winked. "Then you *go* for it, Pop."

"I appreciate the way you backed me up—and Pop—in there," Steve said to Don when they left Herman's office.

"That's okay," Don murmured.

Steve glanced at him, thinking that Don seemed preoccupied. "You're really upset about this Vector-A thing, huh?"

"Not really . . ."

Steve had to laugh. "Well I sure as fuck am. If you're *not* worried then something *really* bad must be on your mind . . . Everything okay at home?"

"Yeah!" Don said too heartily, and then, "Well, maybe not . . . I didn't want to worry your father with it, but Robbie called home yesterday. He was all excited. He's received his Wing assignment."

"And?"

"With all this stuff going on in Southeast Asia since the Gulf of Tonkin thing last August, Suzy and I were keeping our fingers crossed that he'd end up in Europe, in support of our NATO commitment . . ."

Now Steve understood. "But he's not, is he? He's going to Vietnam . . . ?"

Don nodded, frowning, his shoulders hunched in apprehension. "He's going to war."

CHAPTER 15

(One)

Phanrat, Thailand
22 August 1965

First Lieutenant Robert Blaize Greene bolted awake. He sat upright in his cot, clawing at the mosquito netting clinging to his face. He glanced at the luminous dial of his wristwatch: 2:30 A.M.

Robbie looked across the hooch. By the silvery moonlight coming in through the screened windows he saw Captain Stewart Saunders sitting on the edge of his cot. Stew was dressed in a flight suit. As he bent forward to tie his boot laces the moon and shadow turned his shaved head into a bone white skull.

"I was having a nightmare," Robbie murmured. He cast aside the suffocating mosquito netting. He was sweating like a sonofabitch. His sheets were soaked. He resisted the urge to rake his fingernails across the itchy heat rash ringing his neck.

"I was dreaming I was back in high school..." He paused to catch his breath; the humidity made it hard to breathe. "...I didn't know where my classes were, and I couldn't find my locker."

"*Verry interrrresting*—" Stew mimicked a German accent. "*Ver you naked?*"

"What is this, like prison?" Robbie muttered. "They put the new guys in with the perverts?"

"I was just going to wake you anyway," Stew said. "Weather officer predicts clear flying."

"Well, all right," Robbie said gamely.

"It looks like this is going to be your day, kid."

"Yeah, all right..." Robbie trailed off.

Stew smiled. "Don't freak, Lieutenant. Everybody's got to bust his cherry sooner or later."

Robbie nodded. At twenty-two years of age, he was one of the youngest pilots based at Phanrat. He was certainly the most inexperienced.

Five months ago he'd gone from Fighter Weapons School, into a squadron that was part of the Tactical Fighter Wing at McConnell Air Force Base in Kansas. He'd had a gas flattening the wheat fields as he learned the ins and outs of his F-105 Thunderchief, and once the Wing was certified operational in their Thuds, the organization was rotated to Japan. Robbie knew that combat duty was preordained and he was looking forward to it: somewhere in the misty future. Then, just a couple of weeks ago, the Air Force's all-powerful computers had whirred, spitting out Robbie's card, and he'd found himself in Thailand ahead of the rest of his buddies, filling a slot in the 609th TFS, one of the three tactical fighter squadrons that called Phanrat home.

My first combat mission, Robbie thought as he switched on the lamp on the little folding camp table beside his cot. At once the winged things that ruled the Southeast Asian night began thumping insistently at the window screens.

"You know, Stew, when I arrived I was really feeling gung

ho," Robbie began nervously. "But now I'm feeling kind of rusted up . . ."

"Yeah, well, it was a tough break you got," Stew said. He was at the mirror, carefully twirling wax into the handlebar curves of his luxurious mustache. "I guess it would be best to get here and just jump right in, but rules are rules."

Robbie nodded. Since he'd arrived at Phanrat he'd been parked on the shelf, with nothing to do but swat bugs and bite his nails worrying about how he would react when he finally did see action. He'd been grounded because of a string of bad weather and the relative difficulty of the targets that Saigon Command had seen fit to send the 609th's way. His squadron's commander, Lieutenant Colonel Owen Farris, believed in an easy break-in for buck pilots. Farris wanted Robbie to bust his cherry on a target in a less fortified area, during daylight, and in good weather, so that Robbie could maintain visual flight rules. Robbie had begun to think that his opportunity would never come, but now here it was . . .

All the years of daydreaming, and the hard work to get through school, and then fighter pilot training . . . Robbie climbed out of his cot and padded barefoot in his boxer shorts and T-shirt to his footlocker in order to grab his kit. *It's taken so long to get to this day; the first mission.* He stepped into his unlaced boots and headed for the door. *Just let me do okay . . .*

He noticed Stew watching him. "I'll just hit the showers, and then I'll meet you—"

"No," Stew said.

Robbie, his kit in hand, paused in the doorway. "No, what?"

"No shaving, no brushing your teeth, no shower, and no deodorant."

"Why the hell not?" Robbie demanded. Outside the hooch he could hear the voices of the other pilots drawn for the morning's mission as they walked by on their way to the mess. He glanced out the window. Here at the hooches it was too dark to see much beyond a few glowing cigarettes bobbing like fireflies, but off near the hangar complex harsh lights were staining the night sky. Robbie could hear the clanging of ordnance being fitted and the whine of the electric carts as the maintenance crews hustled to prepare the fighters for takeoff.

"Why can't I shower, for chrissake?" Robbie repeated. "I'm sweaty as hell. I've got plenty of time to make briefing..."

"Gomer doesn't brush his teeth," Stew replied. "And he doesn't take showers, or use deodorant, except for maybe splashing a little fish sauce in his armpits to attract the little gomer girls. Should you have to punch out over unfriendly territory all that minty clean Ipana smell coming off you will let gomer sniff you out in that jungle of his like a bird dog on a quail..."

"Come on..." Robbie shivered, and then laughed weakly. "You're kidding, right?"

"Just get dressed and come grab yourself some breakfast," Stew said evenly. "Be plenty of time to shower later."

Jesus Christ, it's really happening, Robbie thought numbly. *Oh, please let me just get through this day...*

The civil engineers who were busy messing around with Phanrat would be working on the base long after Robbie's tour of duty was over. They'd already done a good job on the fighter maintenance/ordnance areas adjoining the spaghetti tangle of concrete taxi ramps and runways, but the rest of "The Rat" was still nothing but a wide expanse of tramped-down dirt hacked out of the emerald jungle. The base had elevated wooden sidewalks that floated in the mud, some rusting trailers where the senior officers berthed, and prefab, hangar-type buildings that housed the mess and the officers' club, both of which functioned twenty-four hours a day. Near the ready line were the pilots' personal equipment shack, and the Operations center, which was where Robbie was now, along with the other pilots selected from "The Rat's" several squadrons to take part in this morning's strike. The main briefing room was a large, fluorescent-lit auditorium with sky blue walls, and an acoustic tile ceiling. The room had a raised platform equipped with lecterns, blackboards, and maps, and a lot of those uncomfortable combination folding chair/writing desks . . . Just like a high school or college lecture hall, Robbie thought, remembering his dream.

". . . The primary target will be the Song Sen Bridge . . ." the operations commander was announcing.

Robbie was chain-smoking. The eggs, toast, and coffee he'd forced down were churning in his gut. He was sure that everybody could tell how nervous and afraid he was, but when he looked around nobody seemed to be paying attention to him.

". . . Song Sen is the name of the village where this bridge spans the Song Ca River southwest of . . ."

Get your shit together, Robbie told himself. *Listen to the briefing.* Up on the raised platform the operations commander and his support staff—weather, intelligence, and weapons officers—were talking specifics concerning their areas of expertise about the primary and alternate targets if for any reason the Song Sen Bridge could not be struck.

Robbie tried to concentrate, dutifully shuffling through his maps and navigational cards and the mimeographed reports and their update inserts, but he couldn't focus. All he could think about was winning medals, or disgracing himself by acting cowardly.

The Wing briefing broke up. The pilots left the auditorium for their individual squadron briefings held in smaller rooms around the corner from the main hall. As Robbie entered his squadron briefing he saw Lieutenant Colonel Farris talking with his senior officers.

Farris was in his early forties. He had red hair, freckles, a pug nose, and blue eyes. Behind his back the guys called him Howdy Doody, but Robbie thought the commander looked like Robbie's grandfather Herman Gold must have looked in his younger days. Robbie took that as a good omen.

Farris must have felt Robbie's eyes upon him. He glanced up, then winked at Robbie before returning his attention to his staff. *Another good omen*, Robbie thought, settling into a chair/desk.

"All right, this should be an easy one, gentlemen," Farris began once the rest of the pilots had arrived and were seated. "The weatherman tells us that visibility should be excellent. Intelligence suggests that the enemy has most of its defenses concentrated over a hundred klicks to the north, at the Dragon's Jaw . . ."

Robbie began flipping through his maps. He couldn't find anything called Dragon's Jaw, but then map reading had never been his strong point . . .

"But before I go any further, I want to make a personnel change," Farris said. "Lieutenant Greene—"

Robbie, his heart pounding, wondered if he was going to be scratched from the mission. He looked up from the crumpled maps littering his desktop and his lap. "Sir?"

"Since this is your first mission, I want you where I can keep an eye on you," Farris said. "For today you'll be part of my flight. Our radio call sign is Warrior . . ."

"Yes, sir."

Farris moved on. "Major Gleason's flight call sign is Rambler. Major Goldblum is Dasher . . . Major Lawrence is . . ."

It was almost 4 A.M. when Robbie and the other pilots got to the personal equipment shack. The others were talking and joking as they drew their gear. Robbie stayed out of it. He really didn't feel like he had any right to be among these men who had all passed the ultimate test: The least among them had twelve combat missions under his belt . . .

Robbie emptied the pockets of his cotton flight suit and stowed his personal belongings in a locker. He began donning his equipment. First he laced on the chapslike, waist-high, G suit. Next came his vest, its many pockets bulging with survival gear, including canteens and his beeper radio. He strapped on his chute, and a .38 revolver, then drew the weapon from its holster to make sure it was loaded.

He stared at the gun, thinking about the survival training

he'd received, and his target practice at the range. He'd gotten to be a pretty good pistol shot, just as he'd gotten to be highly accurate at delivering dummy ordnance and cannon fire during flight gunnery practice . . . But shooting at paper targets or bombing circles painted on the ground wasn't anything at all like attacking a flesh and blood enemy who was going to be shooting back at you—

Eahhhhhhhhhh—

A high-pitched wailing, the electronic equivalent of fingernails on a blackboard, startled Robbie. It was one of the pilots fiddling with his rescue radio. If you punched out over gomer land it was that mournful cry that Search and Rescue would lock onto in order to find you and pull you out—if they could . . .

The pilot switched off the radio. He saw Robbie staring at him, and winked as he said, "It's a good idea to check out the battery. . ."

Robbie was anxious to please, but the thought of hearing that despairing keening coming from his own radio was unbearable. "I'm not going to need it," he said loudly.

He grabbed his helmet and satchel full of paperwork, and strode out of the room. On his way to the van that stood waiting to take the pilots to the aircraft he patted his vest to make sure that his radio was there—

It was just dawn as the pilots were ferried to their parked aircraft. The line of F-105 Thunderchiefs, their fuselage racks bristling with ordnance, their wing pylons heavy with extra fuel tanks, were parked with their canopies raised up, as if in salute to the arriving pilots.

Robbie's bird was near the front of the line. Like the others, she had a tricolor camo paint job: green and tan up top, with a ghost gray belly. The Thud had a conical needle nose. She was huge for a single-seat fighter, sixty-four feet long, which was almost the length of a DC-3, with a thirty-four-foot wingspan. A man could comfortably stand beneath one of those wings without having to duck his head, and just climbing the ladder and settling into the cockpit put you about twelve feet off the ground.

"Good morning, Lieutenant," the crew chief said, saluting Robbie as he approached.

"Sergeant." Robbie nodded. The chief was wearing green fatigue pants and an oil-smeared, white T-shirt, and was looking tired and pale beneath the outdoor lights. Robbie sure hoped the guy had been awake—not hung over or anything—when he'd been doing his job checking out the bird. "How's everything?"

"She's ready to go, sir . . ."

Robbie nodded in what he hoped was a knowing manner, set down his satchel of paperwork, and began to walk around the aircraft, pretending to be sagely giving it the once-over. It was a joke, of course. He knew there wasn't a snowball's chance in hell of his spotting anything the maintenance people might have missed. He didn't know why the other pilots persisted in peering and poking at their bird, kicking the goddamned tires like they were on a used car lot or something, but they did it, so Robbie was damned sure he was going to do it as well.

One thing Robbie did notice: There were only six 750-pound bombs nestled beneath the Thud's belly. The bombs were painted drab green, with banana yellow noses. Safety clips dangling long red ribbons were attached to the fuses.

The crew chief came up behind him as he was staring at the paltry war load. "Sarge," Robbie began. "This airplane can carry up to six tons of ordnance—"

"There's a bomb shortage, Lieutenant," the chief said in a whisper. "Between us, I'm surprised the old man even let you have those six."

"Huh?"

"If I could speak frankly . . . ?" the sergeant looked uncomfortable.

"Go ahead."

"The old man doesn't like to send out his buck pilots loaded up until he's sure that pilot's got the balls to go the distance."

"I understand now," Robbie replied quietly. The facts were the facts. It was his first mission, so nobody, including himself, could know for certain how he would react in combat. Perhaps he would lose his nerve, and toggle off short of the target, shredding jungle . . . Like the crew chief had said, there was a bomb shortage . . .

"Time to strap in, Lieutenant . . ."

"Right . . ." *Let's get the fucking thing over with*, Robbie thought as he climbed the ladder.

He settled into the cockpit, strapped himself in, and then put on his helmet and sunglasses. He was reviewing the preignition checklist on the pad clipped to his knee when the chief came scrambling up the ladder with his satchel.

The chief didn't say anything; he didn't have to. Robbie, feeling like a fool, snatched the bag. He stuffed the more important things, like his navigational cards to help him find the alternate targets, into the nooks and crannies around the instrument panel. The knee pads of his flight suit were already filled to capacity with more paperwork.

He heard a clicking sound in his helmet as the chief plugged his mike into the Thud's belly in order to go through the lengthy starting procedure. Fifteen minutes later the Thud's engine was droning.

The chief radioed. "You're all set, Lieutenant. Now you go get them, and then you bring my bird home safe and sound to me . . ." He disconnected his radio, took several steps back, and threw Robbie a salute.

Robbie felt a shiver travel his spine as he saluted back, thinking, *Chief knows he may not be seeing me again* . . .

Robbie eased his throttle forward. As the Thud got rolling the chief used hand signals to guide Robbie through the gray dawn light, out of the parking area and safely past the orange painted weapons and maintenance carts, onto the taxi ramp. There, Robbie paused to allow other ground crewmen to make one last check that nothing had gone wrong or come loose, and for the armorer to pluck the red-ribboned fuse safeties off his bombs and his cannon.

Holy shit, Robbie thought happily as the armorer held up

the red-ribboned bundle for his inspection. *This is for real. When I drop these bombs they're gonna explode. For the first time I'm being sent out to put some wholesale hurt on the enemy.*

"Warrior Four, hold position," the tower radioed.

No! Now! Let's go now!

"Warrior Four, cleared for takeoff," sounded in Robbie's ears.

Robbie joyfully began trucking down the runway. He built to full power, and then jerked his throttle sideways, activating his afterburner. The kick in the pants flattened him against his seat as his Thud leapt forward, trailing a cone of orange fire. The big bird hurtled along, eating up the concrete, and at 190 knots he lifted off, retracting his gear. Then he was traveling at 250 knots, 290, 300; charging into the sky, eager to join the rest of the strike force on its way to war.

A half hour later the strike force was at 25,000 feet, approximately seventy minutes from the primary target. Warrior flight was in the vanguard of the five chevrons of Thuds that curved across the mottled Asian sky. Flying ahead of Warrior flight were F-100 SuperSabres from Danang, assigned weather recon and advance flak-suppression. More SuperSabres from South Vietnam flew MIG-CAP escort, weaving protective swallow-tail patterns above the strike as they searched for enemy fighters. A recon flight brought up the strike's rear to photograph the damage done to the target once the bombs had been dropped.

"Warrior lead, to Warrior flight," Lieutenant Colonel Farris radioed, cutting through the random exchanges from the various flights that cluttered the frequency. "Weather recon says we've got clouds coming together up ahead. It looks too big to fly around or over. Looks like we're going to have to tough it out going right through." He paused. "In honor of our new young buck, let's practice a channel switch to another frequency. Go manual— *Now.*"

Robbie hurriedly double-checked the list of call signs and

frequencies, and then tuned his radio to the channel that had been exclusively assigned to Warrior flight.

"—ior flight check," Farris was saying. "Warrior flight check."

Robbie listened as the other members of the flight sounded off, and when it was his turn clicked his mike and said, "Four!"

"Attaboy, Warrior Four," lead said. "Are you close to element leader?"

"Rog, boss," Robbie said succinctly, anxious to impress Farris with his radio discipline. He was flying as wingman to Captain Strauss. Over the target area Robbie would become his own man for the seconds it took to execute his attack dive and toggle his bombs, but going and coming it was his job to stick to Warrior Three like glue.

So far I've been able to manage that, Robbie thought worriedly as he watched the rugged green and brown landscape that was the border between Thailand and Laos passing beneath his wings. He had easy tallyho with Strauss; for that matter, he had visual contact with the entire flight. But even with visual contact he was using every ounce of concentration and skill to stay in formation. Back at Fighter Weapons School the instructors had concentrated on teaching straight-on, low-level, nuclear weapons strike delivery techniques. This morning Robbie had not flown a straight course for more than a few minutes.

Robbie understood that the flight commanders had to have their people zigzagging all over the sky if the strike was to avoid known enemy concentrations of defenses, but that didn't help him to stay in formation. He invariably strayed during the abruptly announced course changes, and then had to stoke his burner in order to catch up. It was no big deal because he could *see* where his element lead was, but if visibility should decrease to the extent that the strike had to resort to instrument flight rules he was going to be one harried buck pilot . . .

"Warrior flight," Farris called. "We're coming on enemy territory. Start your music."

Robbie scanned his flight checklist just to refresh his memory, and then set to work flicking the numerous switches necessary to activate his weapons systems. He watched his weapons indicators go green, signifying that his ordnance was "hot."

"Warrior Four, how's your fuel situation?" Farris asked.

"Boss, you read my mind," Robbie said, startled. All that maneuvering and extra afterburn had cost him fuel. For a while now he'd been anxiously eyeing his steadily dropping fuel gauges.

Farris laughed. "The new guy always uses the most fuel. You've probably been leaning on your afterburner to maintain flight integrity."

"Rog."

"Let me just get the coordinates on our tanker and we'll get us all gassed up . . ." There was a pause. When Farris came back on the air his voice was fraught with concern. "Ah, Warrior flight, especially you, number four. We've got a little problem . . ."

"Don't tell me, let me guess," Robbie muttered. "That cloud front is moving faster than anticipated."

"Affirmative, Warrior Four. I'm going to turn you around, Lieutenant. You can make an emergency landing at—"

"Boss, don't send me back—" Robbie pleaded.

"Got to, son. It looks like we're going to have to go to Instrument Flight Rules."

"I can handle it—" Robbie began.

"Negative," Farris said. "You're not ready for IFR, and *nobody* is ever really ready for aerial refueling in the soup, but especially not bucks on their first time out."

He's right about that, Robbie thought. Standard procedure for a new pilot was to become an old hand at cycling on a tanker before trying it in the murk. The sensible thing to do would be accept his boss's decision and go home—

"Boss, I can handle it," Robbie insisted.

"Warrior Four, you're having enough trouble learning the kicks in the chorus line in the sunshine. How are you going to—?"

"Moot point, boss," Captain Strauss cut in. "The slop's found us."

Maybe it won't be too bad, Robbie hoped as the first fingers of cloud began caressing his canopy.

"You're right, Three," Farris said. "Kid'll never be able to find his way home in this . . . Warrior flight, make sure your lights are on," he said worriedly.

The sky ahead was fading to white. When Robbie looked down, the ground appeared as if it were being viewed through quickly increasing folds of white lace. Robbie looked for Warrior Three, and could scarcely see him through the cloud wrapping around his Thud like a blanket of cotton wool.

Then all he could see was the light on the end of Warrior Three's wingtip . . .

Then even that faded from view.

"Uh, boss," Robbie transmitted, peering blindly through the gray mess. "Uh, boss, this is Four—"

He was having trouble getting through the radio clutter. Every pilot in the strike was suffering through the same situation and anxious to make contact with his flight mates.

"Warrior flight, go to channel seven—" Farris managed to transmit during an abrupt second of silence.

Robbie tuned to that relatively quiet frequency. "Warrior check," Farris commanded to make sure that all his birds had followed him to seven, and then gave flight coordinates.

"Ah, boss, this is Four," Robbie began tentatively, feeling bashful about hassling his boss after he'd pleaded to be allowed to stay. "I've got bingo fuel, boss."

"I'm looking for those tankers, son."

Robbie was sweating now. He felt claustrophobic flying through the cloud mass pressing in from all sides against his canopy. He kept watching his fuel gauges; the needles were settling toward empty. He studied his instruments, trying his best to hold to the course Farris had set for the flight. He had a feeling in the pit of his stomach that he was diving, even though his instruments were telling him otherwise. The feeling was so *strong*. He *had* to be diving. His instruments were wrong!

"Warrior lead, this is Four. I've got negative instrument—"

"No, you don't," Strauss cut him off.

"But you don't even know what I was going to say—" Robbie protested.

"You were going to claim that your instruments are fouled up; that you're climbing or falling or doing barrel rolls, am I right?"

"Affirmative—" Robbie said, stunned.

"I just had momentary tallyho on you, and you're flying right. Your mind is playing tricks on you, kid. It's vertigo. Like a hallucination. Happens all the time when you're flying blind. Just try to ignore what your senses tell you and maintain IFR—"

"Warrior Three, get off the channel," Farris said impatiently. "Here's the coordinates to our tanker..."

Robbie set the new course. "My gauges are bouncing on empty, lead," he heard himself chattering needlessly as if Farris could do something about it. *Oh, well, so much for radio discipline*, he thought.

"Warrior flight, this is Blue tanker, we've got you on our scope—"

Talk about your last chance gas station, Robbie thought, relieved.

"We've found a little break in this soup," Blue radioed. "A clear spot right in the middle. We're circling within it. Here's the coordinates..."

As Robbie steered the way he was told, Farris said, "Four, you take on some gas first..."

"Boss, we're all hurting," another pilot, whom Robbie thought was Warrior Two, cut in.

"Rog, Warrior Two," Farris said. "Warrior Four, I'm sorry about this, son, but what you're going to have to do is take on just enough to keep your engine going, then cycle off to let somebody else have a chance. When everybody's set you'll cycle back on for a complete fill, got it?"

"Rog, copy," Robbie transmitted, sighing in relief as his Thud broke out of the cloud mass. "I see the tanker!" he crowed.

"Go get him, son," Farris ordered.

"And make it quick, Lieutenant," Warrior Three, Captain Strauss, interjected. "I'm coming up on empty."

It was as if the clouds were a doughnut, and the clear space in which the big jet tanker was circling was the hole in that doughnut's center. The clearing was low, less than a thousand feet, and only a couple of miles around; a flattened oval of visibility hanging suspended in a milky white sky.

Robbie nudged forward the throttle to catch up with the tanker, holding his breath all the while. He knew that he was already flying on fumes, and that he could expect to flame out at any second. As he closed on the tanker's tail he thought the big jet airlinerlike craft looked familiar, but he didn't know why, and then he put the matter out of his mind. He couldn't afford any distractions as he settled into position behind and a little below the tanker's tail. Banking off his starboard wing in staggered formation were the three other thirsty birds of Warrior flight, anxiously waiting their turn at the watering hole.

Robbie could see the tanker's fuel boom operator lying on his belly, peering out at him like a gunner through the big window in the turret beneath the tanker's tail. The operator began working his controls and the boom began extending down toward the fuel receptacle in the Thud's nose. The twin rudders on the boom twisted around like rabbits' ears as the operator adjusted his aim. Robbie activated the control that opened up the filler tube on his Thud's nose and concentrated on making the connection.

The boom touched the receptacle and then slid off. It swung wide, retracted, and then extended maddeningly slowly again.

And again Robbie missed.

"Come on, Warrior Four," Farris coaxed urgently. "We haven't got the time, son. We're *all* on empty now, and visibility is decreasing."

Robbie didn't bother to reply. He'd already noticed that the little oasis of visibility had begun to contract; that was his problem. He'd refueled in flight before, but never when he and the tanker he was chasing were racking around in an ever-shrinking racetrack oval. The boom was reacting to the increasing centrifugal force, veering sideways as Robbie tried to make the connection. The boom operator would have to work his rudders to compensate—

And this is my last try, Robbie thought. He could hear the change in his engine's pitch. He was going to flame out. If he blew it this time he'd have to bail out . . . become a prisoner of war, if gomer didn't skin him alive . . .

He held his breath as he angled up his Thud's nose toward that life-saving boom, and then the operator, God bless him, shoved it home.

"Yeah!" Robbie cried out in triumph, and then his engine flamed out. He felt the airplane begin to fall, then stabilize. The boom's hydraulic locks had clicked into place. The tanker was towing his Thud as it took on fuel. Robbie watched his gauges rise to a fraction above empty, and then restarted his windmilling engine.

"Come on off, son," Farris said urgently. "We've got to—"

Robbie froze. The boom operator had disconnected. The boom was hovering, waiting for the next customer, but Robbie could not bring himself to relinquish his position. *It took me forever to make the connection,* he thought. *I've only taken on a few minutes of fuel—*

"I'm going to flame out!" Strauss cried.

Visibililty is almost gone. I won't be able to connect again, Robbie thought distractedly. He was panicking, he knew, but he couldn't help it. *Got to take on more gas now—*

"Get off that tanker!" Warrior Two was shouting.

"Everybody shut up!" Farris ordered. "Lieutenant Greene, you listen now," he said calmly. "I realize that you're Herman Gold's grandson and that this is a GAT AT-909 Aero-Tanker—"

Robbie smiled. He *knew* there'd been something familiar about the tanker.

"But just because your grandpa built this gas station," Farris continued, "doesn't mean you own it . . ."

Robbie laughed, and in the process of laughing found the handle he needed to gain control over his fear. He dropped away from the tanker. Strauss instantly replaced him, and within seconds the veteran combat pilot was hooked to the boom and taking on fuel.

"Boss, everyone. I'm sorry," Robbie muttered thickly.

"We'll talk later," Farris said. "Now get your mind right, kid. We still have a target to hit."

"We still going for the primary?" Strauss asked. He had taken on enough fuel to keep him flying and was in the process of disconnecting from the tanker, to be replaced by another Thud.

"Let's find out," Farris replied, giving the order for the flight to tune back to the main communication channel. Together, Warrior flight monitored the advance recon reports.

Sounds clear over the target right now, Robbie thought, watching as Farris cycled onto the tanker and filled his tanks. Then it was Robbie's turn to go back on, this time to take on all the lovely fuel he could carry.

He was pleasantly surprised to find that hooking up this time was no big deal. He guessed that a lot of this business was kind of like working an automobile's clutch: It was easier to do if you didn't think about it, but just did it . . .

"We'll do a fly-by," Farris told his pilots as the flight veered away from the tanker to rejoin the strike force. "The way this freak weather system has been acting, there's just no way to tell what we'll find when we get there . . . In about ten minutes, I'd say . . ."

The weather had cleared. Visibility was excellent. The word had gone out across the strike force that the primary target was a go, and the swarm of Thuds had banked west, to follow the Song Ma River to the trestle bridge at Song Sen.

"Warrior flight, drop down to fifteen thousand."

Robbie felt his spine tingle. They were on attack approach. Their flight would be the first in.

Robbie clicked his mike. "Boss, shouldn't we punch our tanks?"

"Negative, son," Farris replied kindly. "You only want to do that when MIGs are around. This far south they're pretty rare."

No MIGs? Robbie thought, disappointed. This combat initiation was not turning out at all the way he'd hoped . . .

"Let's have some radio discipline now," Farris said.

Robbie understood the need for quiet. A few months ago the enemy had introduced a new weapon: SAM, for Surface to Air Missile. The Thuds had electronic gear to warn of a SAM launch, but once those thirty-foot-long telephone poles were airborne the only way to keep them out of your tail pipe was to eyeball them early, take evasive action, and spread the word so that the other Thud drivers could duck and feint. The radio had to be clear of chatter if any pilot was going to be able to sound that alarm.

"Warrior lead, this is Lodestone lead," the radio crackled. Robbie listened. Lodestone was the call sign of the flak-suppression F-100 SuperSabre flight.

"This is Warrior lead," Farris said. "We're three minutes from Initial Point—"

"Warrior, we've got a problem," Lodestone overrode. "There's enemy barges parked underneath the bridge. We think they're heavily armed. We tried to hit them, but our cannons and rockets can't penetrate the bridge—"

"I copy, Lodestone," Farris replied. "What about the ground defenses?"

"Same old story," Lodestone replied, sounding frustrated. "Gomer's got his guns placed in his *so-called* village on both sides of the river. Just like you guys, we're not allowed to hit *villages*, even if they do have more gun barrels than chimneys sticking up."

The enemy was so fucking sly, Robbie thought in disgust. *And our politicians are so fucking dumb—*

The politicians back home cringed whenever gomer went whining to the press about how the big, bad, war-mongering Imperialist American pilots were stomping on their peace-loving, rice-farming peasants. Accordingly, the politicians had tied one arm behind the Air Force's back by formulating strict rules of engagement. MIGs could not be shot at unless they were in the air, and SAM sites could not be attacked unless they had already launched their missiles. The worst of it, however, was that nothing even remotely resembling a civilian-populated area could be attacked, even *if* those peace-loving, rice-farming peasant types happened to be firing at the war-mongering pilots . . .

"All the jinking we've been doing to avoid the flak has us low on fuel," Lodestone lead said. "Afraid we're out of here, Warrior."

"Well, thanks for trying, Lodestone," Farris radioed.

"Rog, Warriors. Happy hunting. Lodestone out."

"I've seen this before," Farris announced. "Gomer likes to move those barges around, depending on where he thinks we're going to strike. Expect pedestal-mounted heavy machine guns, and lots of automatic small-arms fire. Gomer will try to hit us with flak all the way coming in and all the way going out, but those barges will come into play when we're at our most vulnerable: just coming out of our attack dive at about three thousand feet, when our noses are up and our bellies are exposed." He paused. "I wish Intelligence had apprised us of those barges," he muttered.

"Yeah," Strauss cut in. "We could have arranged for flak suppression to have escorted us *during* our attack instead of prior to it. A little cover fire would give those fuckers on the barge something to think about . . ."

I can do that, Robbie thought. He clicked his mike. "Boss, this is Four. I can do that—"

"What are you talking about, son?" Farris demanded. "There's no way a Thud carrying a full load of ordnance can—"

"But I'm not carrying a full load," Robbie said. "All I've got are a half dozen bombs."

"That's right, boss." Strauss chuckled. "You wanted the kid to fly light his first time out, remember?"

"That's one thing I *do* remember," Farris argued. "It *is* his first time out—"

"I can go in with you and your wingman during your attack," Robbie said. "Then, once you've toggled off, you can do the same for Strauss and me."

"Think about what you're saying, Lieutenant. You'll be exposing yourself *twice* to the enemy."

"I'm willing to do it," Robbie said firmly, all the while trying to control the trembling in his voice. He wasn't totally sure he had the balls to expose himself *once* to the enemy.

"It's totally against standard procedure," Farris said worriedly.

"One minute to IP," Strauss said quietly.

"Sonofabitch," Farris cursed. "Okay, kid! We'll try it your way! We'll come in as planned. You come in from the southeast." He laughed. "From out of the sun, you fucking cowboy."

"Affirmative, boss." Robbie began working the switches to go from air-to-ground bombing mode to gun mode.

"And Lieutenant?"

"Yeah, boss?"

"If this works . . . I'll buy you a beer when we get home . . ."

Farris tersely informed the other flights about Warrior's change in tactics. This was necessary because the strike force's attack specifics were all set during the briefing. The slightest unanticipated change in that complex choreography would cause major foul-ups down the line.

They were almost over the target now. The top of the two-lane steel trestle bridge was coming into view from out of the jungle. Robbie could see the first white, puffy balls of flak expanding in the sky from the 37-millimeter guns nestled in the village; the guns the SuperSabres had been restricted from attacking. Blue puffs of smoke—from larger 57-millimeter guns—added to the fireworks display. Then small-arms gunfire began pouring from the twin jumbles of thatched-roof shacks and huts clustered around the roads leading onto the bridge. Already the muddy riverbanks were obscured with a drifting haze of gun smoke.

Robbie peeled away from his element lead, Captain Strauss, then racked his Thud across the river, groaning in pain from G-stress as he whipped the mammoth jet into its tight turn. He did a sideslip barrel roll, letting his nose drop down, and began his strafing run. As he did so, just for the hell of it he glanced at his watch: 9:11. *Punch your time clock, Lieutenant. Welcome to the war . . .*

A half dozen barges bristling with weapons had moved out from beneath the bridge. Their many guns were now tracking Farris and his wingman, who were executing their attack dive following the course of the river, perpendicular to the bridge. The sensible approach would have been an angled dive traveling the *length* of the bridge, but that approach had been forbidden by the big shots safe behind their desks in Washington, who'd warned that there would be hell to pay if any bombs overshot the bridge and landed in the villages on either side.

As the bomb-laden Thuds screamed down, the heavy machine guns on the boats opened fire. The red tracers crisscrossed upward, joining with the flak coming from both riverbanks. Then the automatic rifles on the barges began to wink. Gomer had added the last fine strands to the net of death he'd woven to pluck the Thuds from the sky.

Robbie, meanwhile, was hurtling down upon the unsuspecting barges from the opposite direction. He waited until his red pipper gunsight was centered on the middle barge, and then he squeezed the trigger. The M-61 Vulcan gun mounted beneath the Thud's nose sounded like the world's biggest electric shaver as its six barrels began revolving, spitting 20-millimeter slugs at the rate of one hundred rounds per second. The rounds were falling short. A curtain of splashing water was rising up behind the barge. Robbie nudged back the stick, the Thud's nose rose a little, and the slightly elevated gun buzz-sawed the barge until there was nothing left but wreckage and a gradually expanding oil slick. He kicked rudder, the Thud's nose yawed to left and to right, and the swinging cannon hosed down the two barges on either side of the first. One of them exploded in a geyser of flame, igniting the oil slick. Now the river itself was on fire.

Nose-up, Robbie thought. *Get the fuck out of here.* He released his trigger, hauled back on the stick and lit the afterburner. He was thinking about how he'd been firing for only five seconds but had already expended half the ammunition in the one-thousand-round drum nestled behind the gun—

—when Farris and his wingman toggled off their bombs.

The noise was incredible as the river erupted in a mushroom cloud. Steam and smoke hung in the air; there was zero visibility; as Robbie clawed his way upward at a sixty-degree angle he could only hope that he would not blindly run into flak or small-arms fire, or debris—

—or Farris and his wingman, who were now somewhere close by, struggling to regain the relative safety of the same upper reaches of the sky.

Robbie burst out of the smoke to see the rest of the strike force; an orbiting cartwheel of glinting specks against the blue. High on adrenaline and feeling sassy, he stood his Thud on its tail and went into a vertical roll in order to scan the sky for the rest of his flight.

"Very fancy maneuver, Lieutenant!" Farris called.

"Thanks, boss." Robbie laughed. "Where are you?"

"Try eight o'clock, a little low."

Robbie looked, saw the rest of Warrior flight, and fell over into a dive. His element lead, Captain Strauss, saw him coming, and began setting up for their dive bomb attack.

"We're heading east to take out the rest of those barges," Farris called. "Hope we do as well as you did, son . . ."

Robbie didn't exactly know how to reply to that, so he just busied himself double-checking his switches to make sure he'd depressed his sight and was ready to drop his bombs. Then he caught up to Strauss and positioned himself on the captain's wing.

"Let's go, Four," Strauss murmured.

"Rog." Robbie gritted his teeth as they began their run.

As they plummeted toward the bridge Robbie was disappointed to see that although Farris and his wingman had scored several direct hits the structure looked to be only slightly damaged. Meanwhile, it seemed like every gun in North Vietnam was aiming at him as he followed Strauss down. Glowing worms of tracers slithered past his canopy. Red fireballs of flak floated up at him. He could see the flak rounds exploding; see the angry orange eyes of destruction reaching out for him with tentacles of black smoke as the shock waves shook his Thud. He borderline-registered that Farris and his wingman were spewing 20-millimeter cannon fire at the remaining barges. It didn't seem to be making much of a difference in the volume of fire coming his way, but then he guessed that having even one guy shooting at you was one guy too many...

Toggle the bombs, he thought. *Toggle them early. Who gives a flying fuck where they land. Cut them loose and get the hell away from these people doing their best to kill you—*

But then he thought about how in a situation like this you either bought it, or you didn't; it was totally out of your control. There was only one thing you *did* control, and that was the bomb load hanging from the Multiple Ejection Rack beneath your bird's belly.

Maybe he couldn't push the fear entirely out of his mind, but he *could* cage it—within the crimson, concentric circles of his bombsight.

Not yet, he thought as his Thud screamed toward the harsh embrace of the enemy's guns. *Not yet*, as the flak explosions buffeted—

The Thud's red pipper lazily floated, then superimposed itself upon the bridge.

Oh yes. Now—

He bottomed out at three thousand feet, toggled off, and lit the afterburner, jinking like crazy, kicking rudder and moving the control stick every which way, doing everything he could to zigzag and throw off gomer's aim, short of throwing himself out of the sky.

He climbed out of the righteous firestorm that was a combination of the enemy's guns and his own exploding ordnance, and then looked around for Captain Strauss. He saw that his element leader was safe and sound on his ten o'clock. He glanced at the bridge. It was still standing, but he could have sworn that there were a couple of more craters in it where his red pipper had been only a few seconds before.

The next rotation of Thuds was already beginning their bombing run as Farris called, "Warrior Four, tighten it up, son. It's a crowded sky, and there ain't no traffic lights."

"Rog, copy," Robbie transmitted. As he came around a stray pair of Thuds startled him by streaking across his nose. *A crowded sky, all right.*

"Boss, you finish off those barges?" Strauss asked.

"Affirmative." Farris chuckled. "Let's start home."

"I'm light on fuel, boss," Robbie said as he regained his position on Strauss's wing.

"We're heading for the tankers now, son . . ."

Robbie glanced at his watch: 9:17; exactly six minutes in combat. *Well, they say that time flies when you're having a good time . . .*

He'd never imagined that six minutes could last an eternity.

(Two)

Officers' Club
Phanrat

Robbie, showered and shaved and wearing a fresh flight suit, was sitting alone at a corner table in the officers' club. He was smoking a cigarette, nursing a beer, feeling glad that the first mission was over, and apprehensive about the next ninety-nine. The radio behind the bar was on: Dionne Warwick singing "Walk on By."

It was only one o'clock in the afternoon, but it might as well have been one in the morning from the atmosphere inside the club. The place was always dimly lit; the round tables always filled with pilots unwinding after coming off a mission. The club even had waitresses: a couple of Thai girls in their late teens. They were both less than five feet tall; perfect little doll women, with long black hair straight as horses' manes, high cheekbones, and small, impenetrable, onyx eyes. The girls spoke no English; they simply giggled as they flitted from table to table with their beer-laden trays. They answered, interchangeably, to "Hey-you" and "Come-mere," and wore Air Force castoffs: worn-out fatigue pants cut off at the knees and old white T-shirts shrunk so small that the girls' round breasts and cherry nipples poked through the thin cotton.

Every pilot liked to talk about pronging these two, but Robbie knew that nobody ever actually would. The girls were fresh and innocent; perpetual kid sisters. Nobody wanted that silvery giggling to stop.

"I owe you one of these..."

Robbie looked up. It was his boss, Lieutenant Colonel Farris, holding a pair of long-necked beers. Robbie started to get to his feet in order to come to attention and salute.

"Forget about it," Farris said. He set the beers on the table and grabbed a chair. "You can stop me if I'm wrong, Lieutenant, but I'd wager you're feeling a little depressed about now... Am I right?"

"Yes, sir." Robbie nodded. "I guess I am..."

"That's normal," Farris assured him. "It's kind of like postcoital depression. Do you read me...?"

"Uh, yes, sir..." Robbie said awkwardly. "I guess..."

Farris studied him. "You got something else on your mind, now's the time to spit it out."

"Well," Robbie hesitated. "I feel really bad about today,

and with all due respect, I don't think it's post— Well, what you said . . ."

"Go on," Farris coaxed, taking a sip of his beer.

"A couple of times during the mission I almost lost it, sir . . ."

"You saying you were scared?"

Robbie thought about how he'd frozen up after that first midair refueling, and the way he'd felt while executing his bombing run. "I guess I'm saying that I was so scared that I thought I was going to die of fright."

"That's good," Farris said. "Any man who isn't scared doing what we do is too damned ignorant to be here. The important thing is you didn't let your fear win."

"But—"

"Listen to me, Lieutenant. Today, thanks to the luck of the draw, you were up against flight conditions that would have taxed my most veteran pilot—"

"None of my training prepared me for what I had to do this morning—"

"That's right." Farris nodded. "But you handled it. Sure you had a few moments there when things were maybe a little touch and go, but you hung in. You more than did your job."

"Did I?" Robbie asked. "I've been thinking about the recon film we saw after debriefing. That bridge was still standing after the strike."

Farris shrugged. "That's how it is. A bridge is just about the hardest target there is to knock down. It's built to take punishment, and if a bomb doesn't land directly on it, all that happens is the bridge gets wet. Anyway, we'll be going back to Song Sen in a couple of days," he added indifferently.

"Back *there*? So *soon*?" Robbie asked, surprised.

"Photo recon shows stacks of construction materials in the village. Gomer will have his bridge back in shape in no time flat."

Robbie shook his head. "I just don't get it, sir. Here I am

being asked to fly missions requiring skills in which I've received no training, and restricted from defending myself from the enemy, in order to bomb targets that the enemy can rebuild more easily than I can knock them down—"

Farris toasted him with his beer bottle. "Welcome to Vietnam."

CHAPTER 16

(One)

Wright-Patterson A.F.B.
Near Dayton, Ohio
5 March 1966

Major General Howard Simon's office was large but seemed too small to contain all the proud memories and tradition spanning his forty years of service. Normally, Lieutenant Colonel Steven Gold felt like a kid turned loose in a candy store whenever he visited this office, but not today.

Steve was standing at attention in front of the general's desk, waiting for his boss to finish reading the report he'd just delivered. As Steve waited, he tried to imagine the office as he'd known and loved it.

Up on the walls had been photos of the general when he was a seemingly impossibly young, fledgling lieutenant, and later photos of him as a confident-looking colonel in a leather flight jacket standing proudly with the bomber crews under his command in Europe during the war. There had been photographs of the general taken with the war birds that he had nurtured during his tenure at Wright-Patterson's research and design center; photos of him wearing his first star; photos taken with Truman, and with Ike; photos of him as a two-star general, conferring with JFK, and with Lyndon Johnson.

And the photographs of Howard Simon with famous men and famous airplanes in fabulous places were only a small fraction of what there had been to see. There had been the complete collection of Army Air Corps and USAF insignia, and the scale models of airplanes. There had been vintage leather flying helmets, first-edition flight manuals, dummy ordnance—

But now the office was in disarray. Dust motes hung and twirled like dogfighting biplanes in the sunlight streaming through the picture windows that looked out on the airfield. There were open, half-filled packing cases and pads of wrapping tissue littering the carpet. Ghostly rectangles stained the walls where the photographs had only recently hung. The office was in this sorry state because it was being disassembled.

Steve's boss was retiring.

"Excellent report," Simon said, setting the folder aside.

"Thank you, sir." Steve had been relocated to Wright-Patterson for the past few months, living out of temporary officers' quarters on base as he worked closely with the general. Simon was putting his professional affairs in order, closing out the books on his long career of service to his country.

"Pull up a chair, Steve," Simon invited. He was a tall, gaunt man in his sixties, with a shock of snow white hair and bright blue eyes. "That is, if you can manage to find one in all this mess . . ."

"Yes, sir." Steve removed the framed set of RAF-embroidered insignia from a straight-backed chair and leaned the collection against some World War I vintage aircraft identification charts that were already stacked.

"I spoke with your father this morning," Simon began as Steve sat down. "Do you know the old boy offered me a job selling GAT airplanes to the government?"

Steve chose to assume the general's question was rhetorical, but actually he had known about the offer. His father had discussed it with him before making it to Simon. "It's not such a bad idea, sir," Steve offered.

"Could you ever imagine me a salesman?" Simon laughed. "I can just hear my sales pitch now: 'You'll buy these airplanes, and that's an order!'"

"Yes, sir. Maybe it wasn't such a good idea after all, sir..."

Simon laughed again. "Your father mentioned that the Vector-A matter was proceeding on schedule, but he was understandably loath to go into the specifics over the telephone about how he was managing to get the weapons firing systems into Israel. He said you could fill me in..."

"Yes, sir, well, it's kind of complicated—"

"And risky," Simon interjected. "I must say, I have to admire Herman's courage in going through with it."

"Well, my father's never shirked from doing his duty for his country," Steve said proudly. "Anyway, like I said, it's complicated, and I'm not all that clear myself on the specifics, but basically what's happening is that the partially disassembled Vector-A systems are being sent to Israel by way of France. The stuff leaves America hidden in GAT shipments to Sky Train Industrie—"

"That's the name of the commercial jetliner consortium that GAT belongs to, isn't it?" Simon asked.

"Yes, sir, along with the British firm of Stoat-Black and the French company Aérosens," Steve replied. "It seems the Aérosens directors are sympathetic toward Israel—"

"Well, they ought to be," Simon snorted. "They're making a fortune selling the Israelis Tyran II jet fighters..."

Steve nodded. "Anyway, Israel is paying a premium price for its Tyran IIs. In exchange Aérosens' directors have agreed to look the other way so that Mossad operatives working within the company can hide the Vector-A components among the Tyran II spare parts shipments destined for Israel."

"And that way the Aérosens directors can have their cake and eat it too." Simon scowled. "They get the money, and if the French Government should catch on, all the directors have to do is point the finger at Israel, claiming that the Mossad had infiltrated their company without their knowledge. The only ones who'd end up screwed would be the Israelis . . ."

"And my father," Steve amended politely.

"Yes, that's right." Simon nodded. "That's why I meant it when I said your father is a brave man. He's risking a lot for his country, and for no personal gain. That makes him the finest kind of patriot."

"He is a patriot, of course, sir, but he's also having himself a great time." Steve grinned. "He's done all this research on Israel, you see; especially the history of its struggle for independence. That's where he got the idea for the entire roundabout smuggling scheme. It seems that back in the forties, during the period leading up to Israel's independence, American Jews managed to smuggle munitions to Israel despite the United States Government's restrictions by hiding the stuff in hollowed-out farm equipment, and so on." Steve paused. "I just hope the Israelis come through with their part of the deal."

"You mean delivering on their promise to snare a MIG-21?"

"And letting us have our look at it, sir."

"I have confidence they will," the general said. "Don't forget they need to know what they're up against concerning the 21 for their own survival, not to do us any favors."

"Yes, sir," Steve said respectfully, although privately he had his doubts about the whole thing. If the Israelis ever did manage to coax a MIG driver to defect, and then manage to expedite his successful flight from heavily guarded Arab airspace, it would be a miracle on a par with Moses parting the Red Sea.

"I was hoping to be able to hang around here long enough to get a look at that MIG-21," the general said longingly. "It would have been edifying to know what my Soviet counterparts have been up to, but it wasn't meant to be . . ."

"I was hoping you'd be sticking around longer, as well, sir," Steve said.

"Well," Simon said briskly. "The bottom line is that I'm not, which leads to another matter: your future in the Air Force . . . Steve, I'm sure you realize that I have the clout to arrange for you to be sent to war college—"

"Excuse me, sir," Steve interrupted.

"What?" Simon sharply demanded.

"Begging the general's pardon, sir, but that's not for me," Steve said.

"What isn't for you, son? Career advancement?" the general asked disdainfully.

Steve frowned. The Air Force's war college was located at Maxwell A.F.B. in Alabama. It was there that the officers who the Air Force was grooming for great things studied aviation warfare set against an overall general background of national policy and strategy.

". . . you know that your career has hit ceiling unless you're willing to attend . . ." the general was saying.

"I'm only a high school graduate—"

"Doesn't matter. I can finesse that part of it for you, as well," Simon assured him. "Don't forget that what we do here at Wright-Patterson falls under the umbrella of Air University Command—"

Steve held up his hand. "Permission to speak frankly, sir?"

"Go ahead," Simon muttered.

"Howard, it's *school*," Steve burst out, exasperated and embarrassed. "I don't want any part of it!"

"May I ask why?"

Steve hesitated. "I don't want to go because I know I can't hack the program . . ."

"That's a lot of bullshit—"

"It isn't . . ." Steve paused, thinking: *Why do I have to go into this*? "You—you really don't know me . . ."

"Don't *know* you?" Simon echoed in disbelief. "Get serious, son. You've been on my staff for almost five years."

"You don't know how tough school was for me when I was a kid—"

"You don't think you're smart enough, is that it?" Simon demanded. "You don't think you've got what it takes to be a full colonel, or higher?"

"Maybe not."

"Then try this on for size," the general replied evenly. "During the past months I've had you here at Dayton you've been doing a bird colonel's level of work—if not higher— and doing it better than anyone I've ever had working for me, and that includes a brigadier general whose name I won't mention."

"Really . . . ?" Steve was flabbergasted. "I don't know what to say . . ."

"Say yes to this opportunity I'm holding out to you," Simon urged.

Steve shook his head.

"You're still not convinced?"

"Don't get me wrong, sir. The fact that you're pleased with my work means a lot, but . . ." Steve trailed off, shrugging.

"All right, then. You had your opportunity to speak frankly. Now it's my turn," the general said fiercely. "You're forty-one years old. You've got almost twenty-two years in. If you're not going to give yourself the opportunity to advance, then get the hell out."

"I've been thinking about doing just that."

"You have?" Simon looked surprised.

"You see, when *you* go, my clearance to fly fighter/interceptors will go as well," Steve replied. "And the opportunity to fly is about the only thing that's kept me in this long."

"I see . . ."

"As a matter of fact," Steve began, "I was hoping you

could pull some strings to get me assigned back to Operational Command..."

"A TAC squadron leader, huh?" the general asked thoughtfully.

"Well, yes..." Steve said. "Preferably with an outfit that's seeing some action..."

"Hmmm, you're talking about Vietnam?"

"Yes," Steve replied hopefully.

"I don't know about that... You've been out of Operational for a long time... Since Korea..." the general added meaningfully.

"Sir, I've kept my hand in flying."

"The real problem is that you've cut yourself out of the loop. They're handing out operational assignments to those officers on upward career paths."

"There is one way..."

"Well, go on," Simon demanded. "Spit it out, son..."

"General, there's a memo from Pacific Air Force headquarters in your in-box..."

"Now what the *hell* are you doing rummaging around in *my* in-box?" Simon challenged.

GAT, here I come, Steve thought, guessing that he would soon be perfecting his civilian sales pitch unless he could sell the general right now.

"Sir, I was in your office the other day to find some files I needed, and the memo in question was lying right on top of the pile of stuff in your box. It had 'Vietnam Air Combat Volunteer Request' across the top in bold letters, so it caught my attention, you see..."

"Go on, I'm listening," Simon grumbled.

"The memo says PACAF is looking for someone to act as a troubleshooter on a tour of our bases in Thailand."

"It sounds like things are going wrong over there if a troubleshooter is needed," the general said, looking concerned.

"Things *are* going wrong." Steve nodded. "I, um, took the liberty of making a few telephone calls using your name..."

Simon rolled his eyes. "Go on . . ."

So far, so good, Steve thought, relieved. "Well, sir, it turns out that there's a serious morale problem permeating our fighter wings. There's concern about it at the highest levels. We've been losing so many people going up against very heavily defended targets that our squadrons have begun to back off, to stroke it. They've been dropping their bombs too high, killing palm trees, or whatever it is they have over there, instead of the enemy."

"It's not like the Air Force to back off just because the job is a little tough," the general said.

"Well, I don't totally put the blame on our fighter jocks," Steve continued. "I've been looking into the situation, sir."

"You have?"

Now why the hell is the old bird smiling like that? Steve wondered. "Anyway, sir, in my opinion, the fault lies not with our pilots, but with the politicians back home. What's needed is for our Air Force tigers to be unleashed. They need to know that they've got total backing to steamroll the enemy. You ask a guy to go up against a stone wall with a rubber mallet when what's needed to do the job properly is a sixteen-pound sledge; he's just bound to get tired and discouraged after a while." Steve paused. "But I also realize that thanks to the way Washington has been losing the propaganda war to the enemy, nothing like that is about to happen."

"That sounds like a perceptive analysis of the situation, Steve." The general nodded. "So, then, what does PACAF want this so-called troubleshooter to do, exactly?"

"Visit for a while with each fighter wing, give a pep talk, and then fly a few missions in order to lead by example."

"The fighter wings are flying Thunderchiefs, aren't they?" Simon asked.

"The guys who are being given the tough armed reconnaissance missions are, yes, sir." Steve nodded.

"And, of course, since you spend every spare moment in the air, you've been checked out on the Thud, haven't you?" the general asked dryly.

"I have, sir." Steve couldn't quite muffle his smile.

"I suppose you think that's all that's needed to make you the right man for this job?" Simon challenged.

"No, sir—" Steve said earnestly. "I'm the right man for the job because I know what I'm talking about, sir. I've *been* there. I did the job in the Second World War, and in Korea. I'm a fighter pilot by vocation, and I've been at my trade longer than some of these pilots we've got in Vietnam have been *born*."

"Speaking of young pilots," Simon began. "I believe your nephew is currently in a Thud Wing over there . . . ?"

"Yes, sir, he is," Steve said and then smiled. "I have to admit, General, the possibility of getting to fly in combat with my nephew only adds to the assignment's allure."

"Hmmm . . ."

"Speaking man to man, General, it's what I want. Do you think you could swing it for me?"

Simon looked thoughtful. "Maybe there *is* a way . . ."

"Sir?" Steve perked up.

"Seeing as how you're adamant about not taking my suggestion concerning war college . . ."

"With all due respect, sir, I *am* adamant about that."

"Well, then . . ." The general nodded. "I'm owed a few favors. Might as well call one of them in while I'm still wearing the uniform . . ."

"Thank you," Steve said.

"You realize the assignment is only temporary," Simon warned.

"Yes, I know." Steve nodded. "I'm prepared for that, but I figure the opportunity to fly a fighter in a third war is just too good to pass up. If it comes down to it, I'm prepared to accept this assignment as a fitting coda to my Air Force career." He paused, suddenly puzzled. "But how would *you* know that, General?"

"Know what?"

"That it's a temporary assignment," Steve replied. "I mean, if you haven't read the memo, or heard about any of this before now, sir?"

Simon shrugged. "I just assumed as much. By it's very nature a troubleshooting assignment is temporary."

"I see," Steve said slowly. "I suppose so, sir . . ."

"Now, get out of here," the general gruffly commanded. "Let me start making those telephone calls on your behalf . . ."

"Yes, sir!" Steve got to his feet and came to attention. "Thanks again." He saluted smartly and then left the office, thinking about how great it was going to be to see combat one more time.

(Two)

You can lead a horse . . . Major General Howard Simon thought.

He waited until Steve left the office, then pulled open the bottom left-hand drawer of his desk and took out a fifth of Jack Daniels and a glass. He poured himself a generous shot of sour mash, then knocked it back.

The whiskey burned pleasurably going down. Simon knew that later on there'd be hell to pay for indulging when his ulcers began kicking up, but he figured his bad heart was going to get him long before his gut had the opportunity to do him in.

He reached back into the drawer, this time for a cigar. He had a box of Macanudos stashed there. They weren't as good as the Cubans he used to smoke, but everybody had to make sacrifices in the war against communism, and anyway, the good old days were long gone.

The doctors had firmly told him to stay away from the booze and cigars, and he had just as firmly told them to go to hell. He didn't want to live forever. His wife had passed away several years ago. His only child, his daughter, was married to an investment banker Simon didn't get along with, and living in New York City, a place Simon despised. He had grandchildren, but they hardly knew him. The few times he'd been around them they'd called him "sir," and tended to hide behind their mother's skirts.

The hell with it, he thought, nipping the tip off the stogie and firing it up. He'd been terrible with his own daughter when she was a child, so what the hell kind of chance was he going to have with children a generation removed? He was too old to change, and anyway his airplanes were his children—

But the powers that be had decreed that he was too old for his profession. Just what in hell was he supposed to do with himself?

The doctors couldn't answer *that* question, of course. They didn't even understand why he would ask it. They didn't understand how frightfully hollow his life in Texas was to be; about the loss of his wife, and how that terrible emptiness was only underscored by this forced retirement from the Air Force. The goddamned doctors were maintenance people, preoccupied with keeping the machine running, without the slightest clue to what purpose. Simon had seen their kind before: well-meaning but narrow-minded men too involved in their areas of authority and expertise to see the big picture—

But Steve wasn't like that, Simon ruminated, puffing steely blue smoke rings into the air. Steve could see the big picture, all right. Take his insightful analysis concerning the morale problem among fighter wings operating in Vietnam. Steve was able to gather the input necessary to come to the correct conclusion: that the pilots were dispirited because they believed they did not have the full backing of the politicians. Even more important, Steve was then able to use his experience to deduce that because there was nothing to be done about the underlying cause of the problem, what was needed was another way to get the pilots motivated: to appeal to their esprit de corps . . .

Oh yes, Simon thought. *Steve was going to make an outstanding colonel, and eventually, God willing, a splendid general officer . . .*

He had already arranged for Steve to receive the trouble-shooting assignment.

He had been aware that Steve was coming into his office at odd times to use his files. For that reason Simon had left the memo prominently displayed in his in-box, going so far as to repeatedly move the memo to the top of the pile of the daily incoming blizzard of paperwork. He'd waited patiently for Steve to see it, and then to make the appropriate tele-phone calls to find out what the job entailed...

You can lead a horse to water...

Simon knew that he'd almost given away his scheme to Steve when he'd let slip that bit about the assignment being temporary. Steve had picked right up on that; Simon had been forced to scramble to get himself out of that hole. It was important that Steve think this was all his own idea; that *he'd* convinced *Simon*, and not the other way around. Steve could never know that Simon had orchestrated all this—

The telephone rang, startling Simon. The call was from the Air Force Museum in Dayton. Simon had offered them his entire collection of memorabilia. They wanted to know when to send a truck around...

He worked out a date with the museum representative and hung up, feeling sad as he looked around the office at his things. It would be disquieting not to have these mementos of his career close at hand. It would make the momentous transition he was about to experience irrefutably real.

Well, to hell with it— Only thing worse than a crotchety old fart was a sentimental, crotchety old fart, he thought, disgusted. Goddamned junk would only gather dust at the ranch. Who was he going to show it to down there...?

He cheered himself with another drink, and with thinking about how surprised Steve was going to be when he found out that his new assignment called for him to receive a tem-porary, spot promotion to full colonel. This was necessary because a troubleshooter by definition ruffled feathers; he *criticized*. If Steve went throwing his weight around those bases as a light colonel he wouldn't need to worry about the North Vietnamese on his six o'clock; his own fellow officers would wax him. The troubleshooter would have to outrank the lieutenant colonels who commanded at the squadron level if they, and the pilots to whom he'd be delivering his pep talks, were to take him seriously.

You can lead a horse to water, but you can't make him drink...

Simon leaned back in his chair, feeling smug as a riverboat gambler holding a royal flush. Steve's promotion to bird colonel would be as temporary as his assignment, but maybe the opportunity to wear a full colonel's eagles would bring Steve to his senses. Simon was banking that once Steve had a taste of them, he'd want those eagles permanently. That meant war college, and once Steve got past that hurtle, Simon was confident that there'd be a general officer's stars in his future.

Major General Howard Simon was retiring, but he intended to leave two things in his stead: his aviation collection to the Air Force Museum, and the man he'd chosen to be his protégé—Steven Gold—to the Air Force, itself.

Simon laughed out loud as he enjoyed his cigar. It was true that Steve was something of a hard case, but like he'd explained to his protégé, the Air Force never backed off just because the job was tough...

CHAPTER 17

(One)

**Muang Chi, Thailand
18 July 1966**

Steven Gold arrived at Muang Chi Air Base at 2200 hours on a balmy, rain-swept, summer night. He'd been in Thailand for a little over a month. This was the third stop on his troubleshooting tour.

The drone of the GAT cargo airplane's turboprops was still in Steve's head as he lugged his bags down the transport's ramp. He was exhausted, and tomorrow was a big day. In the morning he would give his pep talk, and in the afternoon he'd fly his first mission here. A few days from now he'd move on to the next stop on his itinerary...

There was a fine mist falling as Steve turned up the collar of his trench coat, shouldered his bags, and began to cross the rain-slickened concrete. He heard the roar of auto engines and a horn honking. He turned, shielding his tired eyes from the glaring headlights as a pair of Jeeps came toward him. As the Jeeps pulled up, he saw three pilots in each. By the fog-shrouded glare of overhead arc lamps Steve saw that the driver of the Jeep closest to him was a young black man, wearing pilot's wings and gold second lieutenant's bars.

"Colonel Gold?" the driver asked, saluting.

Steve grinned. After all those years as a light colonel he still wasn't used to the fact that he'd come up in the world. No point in getting too used to being a full colonel, however. The promotion was as temporary as this tour of duty.

"What can I do for you?" Steve said.

"I'm Lieutenant Lincoln Ritchie, sir. We thought you might like to unwind after your flight. Maybe have a drink, talk about a few things . . . ?"

Steve nodded, trying hard to forget how tired he was. What he really wanted to do was hit the sack, but he felt it was part of his assignment to listen to pilots' complaints, and a lot of guys were more comfortable talking off the record, as opposed to the more formal exchanges that went on in the briefing room.

"Are the beers cold in your O club, Lieutenant Ritchie?" Steve asked.

"So cold they serve 'em on a stick, sir." Ritchie grinned.

What the hell, Steve thought resignedly. These guys were going to have to be up just as early as he. If they felt what they had to get off their chests was all that important, he'd hear them out.

"Tell you what, then, Lieutenant. Give me a lift over to Operations so that I can let them know I'm here, then let's swing by my trailer so I can drop off my bags. Then we'll investigate this cold beer situation, firsthand . . ."

(TWO)

The Muang Chi officers' club was dimly lit, just like every other O club Steve had been in during this stint. Come to think of it, just like every club he'd been in, period.

He was sitting at a table with the six pilots who'd intercepted him. He was smoking a Pall Mall. A beer, a bowl of pretzels, and a jar of Cheese Whiz—his dinner—was in front of him.

Behind Steve were a couple of guys sitting hunched over their drinks at the bar, but otherwise the club was empty. Because the weather had been lousy all day there had been no missions flown out of Muang Chi. That explained the lack of pilots straddling bar stools and hitting the sauce to come off their postflight, adrenaline highs.

It hadn't taken long for the six pilots who'd shanghaied Steve to get to what was eating them: their profound dissatisfaction with the tactical limits and support they'd been receiving from up the chain of command.

"The way I see it, things here are like what we experienced in Korea," Steve said. "In those days, we were going up against Stone Age logistical and communication systems with state-of-the-art airplanes and ordnance."

"You'd think we'd be on top of the situation on account of that," said one of the pilots, a lieutenant named Dave Toback.

"We figured it would all go our way in Korea, as well," Steve replied. "But we were wrong, just like you guys. It was like we were trying to take out a hornet's nest with a tommy gun."

"*Tommy gun*—?"

Whispered snickers from a couple of the pilots at the opposite end of the table:

"Who is this guy: Audie Murphy?"

"What war does he think he's in—?"

Steve chose to ignore it.

"Sure you can blast open the nest," he continued. "But you don't kill many hornets doing it, and tomorrow that spit and paper nest will be rebuilt, so what have you accomplished, besides blowing off a couple of clips of rounds?"

"And taken a hell of a lot of stings in return," Lieutenant

Ritchie added, nodding. "Okay, but maybe in Korea you guys didn't know any better," he added. "But now we *do* know better, or at least we're supposed to, but somebody forgot to tell the brass."

"You tell 'em, Linc—" one of the others declared.

"I hear you," Steve sighed. "I know the Air Force seems to have a short memory. Every time we go into action we seem fated to make the same mistakes, and then play catch-up. It happened that way in World War Two, and in Korea. Now it's happening in Vietnam. I don't know why that's the case, but it is." He shrugged philosophically. "You don't like it and I don't like it, but this Air Force happens to be the only one we've got. You want to fly Uncle Sam's jets, you have to take the lumps with the sweet stuff."

"We all know that, sir," began one of the other pilots. "We've trained to be fighter jocks. We've walked the walk and talked the talk, and now we consider ourselves the fortunate few who've been given the chance to put it to the test—"

"He's right," Dave Toback said. "We're *happy* to be here, Colonel."

"We just don't understand what we're supposed to be doing," Lincoln Ritchie picked up. "From the start, we were ready to take the fight into the enemy's backyard, hitting him where it hurt—at the source of his supplies into the theater—but we weren't allowed."

"Come on now," Steve chided. "It's gotten better... You guys have been socking it to the enemy's POL facilities..."

Back in the spring the Joint Chiefs had lobbied Washington to allow the Air Force to bomb North Vietnam's petroleum, oil, and lubricant industrial facilities. Secretary of Defense McNamara and President Johnson had been hesitant to give the go-ahead because most of the targeted POL sites were in the Hanoi and Haipong areas. The DOD and the White House were concerned that the increased bombing might cause excessive civilian casualties, and might harden the enemy's resolve. It was Johnson's strategy that the bombing be taken as a warning: a relatively mild slap that hinted of the knock-out punch being held in reserve. That strategy would crumble if the escalated bombing effort prematurely caused the enemy to have nothing left to lose in his northern home ground. Eventually, however, the bombing was approved. The first POL strikes had taken place at the end of June.

"We hear that Washington is claiming the POL campaign is a success." One of the other pilots was scowling.

"You guys saying it isn't?" Steve asked, looking around the table.

"It's too little, too late, man—" Ritchie fervently began, and then paused, looking worried. "Sorry, no disrespect meant, Colonel, sir."

"Hold on, son," Steve said. "I'm wearing these eagles because they buy me the right to stick my nose where I please, and say what's on my mind. I don't want them to make you tongue-tied. We're all on a first-name basis here. We're all Thud drivers trying to do the job we've been handed."

"All right, then . . ." Ritchie nodded, smiling slightly. "Like I was saying the trouble with the POL campaign—and this is something we all know, and LBJ is gonna find out—is that it's too little, too late."

"Wait a minute," Steve interrupted, puzzled. "Intelligence is claiming that almost three quarters of the enemy's facilities have been destroyed, and project total destruction within a few weeks . . ."

"The Defense Intelligence Agency and the CIA don't understand the enemy any better than LBJ."

"You saying that hitting those facilities hasn't crippled the enemy?"

"It's irritated him all right," Ritchie said. "But no way has it crippled him. Oh, sure, maybe if we had hit those facilities in the beginning we might be somewhere now," he acknowledged. "But we didn't, and in the interim we've given the enemy time to decentralize his stores—"

Steve listened closely, aware from his exchanges with the brass in Saigon that this firsthand information hadn't yet made it up the chain of command. *Hadn't made it*, he thought, *or had been stifled . . .*

"Now there's buried POL stockpiles and little oil refineries all over the fucking country," one of the other pilots said. "They've stashed the stuff in towns and villages, where they know we can't touch it, and so we're reduced to hanging our asses out over the combat zone. We throttle back, extend flaps, turn overselves into fucking targets for any rice farmer packing a weapon more sophisticated than a bow and arrow, and all that's just to drop ordnance on any oxcarts and bicycles loaded with a couple of gallons of kerosene that we happen to spot."

"Meanwhile, the enemy is still importing plenty of POL, thanks to the Russian and other supposedly 'neutral' tankers off-loading in Haiphong Harbor," Lieutenant Toback grumbled. "We can't touch any of those tankers crowding the harbor, not even if they shoot at us—which they do—unless they're flying the North Vietnamese flag—"

"Which they don't." Another pilot scowled.

"There's another aspect to all this," Ritchie said. "The fact that we're allowed to hit so few enemy targets means that gomer can concentrate his defenses where he knows we're going to be," Ritchie said. "We're taking state-of-the-art stuff: radar-directed AAA, and SAMs . . ."

"I haven't yet encountered a SAM," Steve admitted, frowning, thinking that remote-controlled Surface-to-Air Missiles hadn't been around in Korea.

Knowing chuckles swept the table. "You'll encounter them tomorrow, Colonel," Toback said. "Route Pack Six is SAM country."

Steve nodded. Back around the end of '65, North Vietnam had been divided into six areas called "route packages." So far Steve had flown missions over the relatively lightly defended Route Pack One: the area near the DMZ separating North and South Vietnam; and Route Pack Five, which was well to the west of Hanoi. Tomorrow would be his first venture into the hottest route pack of them all, number six.

"Tomorrow you'll be striking at the heart of the beast,

man." Lincoln Ritchie winked. "Tomorrow we go downtown, to the Yen Lam POL rail depot, in beautiful *Hannnnoi*."

"Right on, brother," Dave said. "SAM is thick at Yen Lam."

"What about Iron Hand?" Steve asked.

Iron Hand was the code name given to the anti-SAM search and destroy program run by the "Wild Weasels": F-105 Thunderchiefs with modified fuselages stretched an extra five feet to accommodate a second man in the cockpit. The Weasels flew advance strike escort. Their motto was "First in and last to leave," and it was true. The twin-seat Thuds were equipped with electronic countermeasure equipment pods designed to lock onto SAM site radar. They'd fly over the strike target just in advance of the strike, acting as decoys to get the SAM site to switch on its radar. If the SAM site did, the Weasels would fire off a radar-homing Shrike air-to-ground missile to keep the SAM crew occupied, while backup F-105s came in with follow-up ordnance, including CBU cluster bomb units.

"The Weasels do a great job," Dave said. "The best job they can. But the Weasel crews are learning the game as they go along. Meanwhile, gomer is getting all the Soviet-built SAMs he needs, so when we show up he just fires off a volley of the fucking things. If the Weasels manage to take out a few SAM sites in the process, gomer figures that's just the cost of doing business."

"I understand that the way to beat the Sams is to fly in low, beneath their effective envelope," Steve volunteered.

There was more knowing laughter. "Colonel, you come in *that* low, gomer's guns are going to shred you," Ritchie replied. "As a matter of fact, we've come to the conclusion that SAM's main purpose all along has been to force us down low enough to let those guns reach us—"

"Or else get us to jettison our bombs early," one of the others said.

"In order to have the speed to outrun SAM," Lieutenant Toback explained.

"I hear the flak around Hanoi is much worse than anything the Germans managed to put up around Berlin," Steve said.

Toback nodded. "The first Thud drivers were told that there was no way an enemy gun could track a fast mover, and that's true, as far as it goes, but the Russians and Chinese have given the enemy so *many* AAA batteries that all he has to do is put up a curtain of fire and let us fly into it."

Steve grimaced, thinking back on what the flak had been like in Korea. This was going to be much worse. "What about MIGs? I haven't seen any yet."

"You'll see them tomorrow," one of the other pilots said. "Gomer keeps his fighters up north. It's MIG-16s and 17s mostly, but now and then a 21."

"No shit." Steve smiled, thinking that things weren't all bad if there was the chance to mix it up with enemy fighters . . .

"Gomer has a solid radar net up over Hanoi," Toback was saying. "He sees us coming and sends up MIGs to meet us. The MIGs like it up high. They can't compete with a Thud down low on deck. Our F-4 Phantom top cover escort does a fine job, but some MIGs always manage to get through."

"Bet you're glad of that." Steve chuckled.

"Come again, sir?" Toback asked, looking blank.

"Well . . . I mean, aren't you glad that you get the chance to do a little dogfighting?"

"Sir, the MIGs' objective is only to harass us into dropping our ordnance early," Toback began, using that excruciatingly polite tone usually reserved for the elderly or the infirm. "They'll make a swooping pass or two, but you'll be too busy setting up your attack dive to do anything about it."

"We'll see about that," Steve said, thinking: *Wouldn't it be something to be a triple scorer? To shoot down the enemy in three wars . . . ?*

"Colonel, the MIGs don't stick around to dogfight," one of the others was saying. "You almost never see them too near the target. They don't like mixing it up with their own SAMs."

"SAM's like my pecker." Someone laughed. "Get him fired up and he'll drill any hot pipe he can catch—"

"And gomer is more than willing to hose off SAMs even if there are MIGs in the vicinity," Lieutenant Ritchie added. "But then, he's got plenty of airplanes, since we're not allowed to hit his airfields."

"Fuck it, man," Dave said scornfully. "Even if they let us, they probably wouldn't let us use the right ordnance . . . "

"The protests back home are on the politicians' minds," Steve said, thinking about how the headline-grabbing demonstrations at Dow Chemical and the other munitions manufacturers had led the government to ban the use of napalm and certain other weapons in the north.

"Speaking of protest demonstrations," Steve continued, choosing his words carefully. "Maybe they've got you thinking that there's no sense in playing the game all out, if we're not playing to win . . . "

"You talking about those reports concerning how some of the guys have been stroking it?" Toback asked, looking sour.

"Yep." Steve nodded. He was sitting with his back to the bar, but he'd heard the squeak of a bar stool swiveling. At least one of the guys at the bar was tuning in on the conversation. Steve decided to pretend not to notice. If the guy wanted to pull up a chair and join in, he would.

"Look, Colonel. We don't want you to take what we've been saying the wrong way," Ritchie began. "Most of us do our job the way it's supposed to be done, but sometimes because of the difficult circumstances under which we're being asked to operate, some of us get a little sidetracked. Maybe we divert a little attention away from the target, and toward looking out for each other." He smiled. "I mean since the odds are stacked way against us, if we don't cover each other, who's gonna?"

"It doesn't work that way." Steve shook his head. "If we start concerning ourselves with covering our asses we might as well exchange our ordnance for leaflets telling gomer he's won this thing, and then turn in our wings."

"Colonel—" Ritchie tried to interrupt.

"Hold on, son," Steve growled. "I'm not finished yet." He looked around the table, drilling each pilot with his eyes. "You guys fly fighters. That means that you make your living by stretching your neck across the chopping block. Of course it's dangerous," he spat disdainfully. "Of course the odds are stacked against you. Hell, if it were easy, everybody would be doing it!"

The table stayed silent as Steve paused to light a cigarette. "You know, my father flew a fighter during the First World War," he resumed, exhaling smoke. "In those days a pilot's life expectancy was measured in weeks. Things weren't much better for the men of RAF Fighter Command, back when they were trying to save London from the Luftwaffe—"

"Begging the colonel's pardon," Lincoln said evenly, "but you can save the history lesson."

"Is that right, son?" Steve scowled.

"Yeah, man, that's right." Ritchie nodded vigorously. "You're handing us this stiff upper lip stuff, man, but you don't know *shit* about what you're talking about—" he spat, disgusted.

"Easy, Linc," Dave warned, casting a worried glance at Steve.

"No, let him talk," Steve said. "I said I wanted you guys to level with me, and I meant it."

"Thank you, Colonel, I appreciate that—" Lincoln began, sounding like he was calming down.

"But before you proceed let me also say that I *have* seen some action in my time," Steve added wryly. "I was shot down and wounded over the Pacific, and shot down twice in Korea..."

"We all know your record, Colonel," Lincoln replied. "And I don't mean to take away from it, but that was *then*. This is *now*. By your own admission, all you've flown over here so far have been chicken shit strikes. You ain't danced with SAM—"

"*Tell him, Linc—!*"

"You ain't ever seen the flak as thick as summertime flies on spilled honey—"

"*Right on, Lincoln, my man*—"

"Or heard the call, 'MIG on your six!'" Ritchie continued. "And you so loaded down with ordnance you know your Thud's a sitting dead duck."

He paused, his dark gaze locked onto Steve. When he resumed speaking the strident street patter was gone, replaced by the quiet voice of an intelligent, educated young man who had seen more of hell in his twenty-odd years than most people experienced in a lifetime.

"I don't care what wars you've fought, sir," Ritchie declared, "because you haven't fought *this* war, which means that you've never experienced what you're going to experience tomorrow."

"I hear you." Steve nodded. "And while I've been a lot of places, I understand that I haven't yet been *there*. That's why tomorrow I'm gonna strap a Thud to my ass and go leave my calling card with Uncle Ho."

Steve glanced at his watch: It was midnight.

"Oh, shit," Dave Toback said hurriedly. "We didn't mean to keep you up all night, sir..."

"No problem." Steve smiled. "I enjoyed the conversation."

"So did we, sir," Ritchie replied, straining to sound polite.

Tonight I'm an adversary, Steve thought as the table quickly broke up. *But tomorrow I'll be one of them.*

He was following the other pilots out when a familiar-sounding voice coming from behind said sarcastically, "... calling card with Uncle Ho?—"

Steve turned. His eyes widened. "Robbie?" he stammered, staring at his nephew.

"Hi ya, Uncle Steve." Robbie grinned, sticking out his hand. "Welcome to Vietnam, the wholesale hurt capital of the world."

"Colonel?" Lincoln Ritchie called from where he was waiting near the door. "You going to need a ride?"

"You guys go on," Steve said, and then turned back to his nephew. "What the hell are you doing here at Muang Chi? I didn't expect to see you until next month, when I got to Phanrat . . ."

"The 503rd needed an element leader," Robbie explained. "So I'm here on loan until they can get one of their own guys up to speed."

"They needed an old hand, eh?" Steve grinned. "How many missions have you flown, nephew?"

"Depends on who you ask." Robbie grinned. "Officially, seventy-six."

"No shit . . ." Steve nodded, impressed. "Over three quarters through your tour."

"Yep, but that's the official tally. Actually I've flown over eighty. I arranged for some of my flights not to be recorded." Robbie blushed. "I guess I kind of like it here . . ."

"I hear you," Steve said, laughing. "That's just great!" he enthused. "My little nephew, an element lead!" He paused. "But do you mean to say you've been sitting at the bar this whole time?"

When Robbie nodded, Steve demanded, "Why didn't you come over?"

"I wanted to hear what you had to say to those guys." Robbie smiled. "Watch how you handled yourself."

"Uh-huh . . ." Steve studied Robbie's face, pretending concern. "But what's *that*?"

"What?"

"Is that a caterpillar crawling across your upper lip?" Steve reached out as if to swat it away.

Robbie, blushing, intercepted Steve's hand, and then protectively stroked his black mustache. "A lot of guys grow 'em. I'm working on a handlebar. You like?"

"I think it looks fine." Steve forced himself to smile, but now that he'd had the chance to study his nephew he was shocked to see how much the kid had aged. It wasn't just the mustache. Robbie's face looked drawn and weathered. There were lines etched around his mouth and at the corners of his green eyes. Thinking about it, Steve reminded himself that the fighter pilot's job had always tended to age men before their time.

Robbie pulled out a pack of Marlboros and a cigarette lighter. As he lit his cigarette the captain's bars pinned to his shirt collar reflected golden in the lighter flame.

"Holy shit!" Steve exclaimed. "You made captain—?"

"Uh-huh." Robbie chuckled. "The promotion came through a few weeks ago."

"And you didn't tell anyone, you little shit?" Steve feigned rage.

"I knew you were coming." Robbie shrugged shyly. "I wanted to surprise you."

"Goddamn, a captain..." Steve shook his head. "This fucking Air Force must be really hard up..."

"I knew you'd have something appropriate to say." Robbie laughed. "Anyway, you've been promoted as well."

"Mine's temporary." Steve shrugged. "Yours is for real."

"*Yours* could be real, as well," Robbie said meaningfully.

"Yeah, yeah..." Steve cut him off, and then gestured toward the bar. "Come on, I'll buy you a beer to celebrate."

"I guess one more won't kill me." Robbie smiled as they grabbed a couple of bar stools.

"First thing tomorrow you write home and tell your folks," Steve instructed as he signaled the bartender for a pair of beers. "*And your grandfather*—got it?"

"Yes, sir." Robbie laughed. "But not the first thing tomorrow, I'm afraid. In the morning I've got to listen to your bullshit, and then I happen to be scheduled to fly tomorrow afternoon's strike."

"You flying with me?" Steve asked.

Robbie, smiling, shook his head. "Nope. *You're* flying with *me*. When you check with Operations you'll see that you've been assigned as my wingman."

"Aha!" Steve laughed, tickled by the notion of being his nephew's number two. "And I suppose this assignment was a coincidence?"

Robbie winked. "Let's just say that I had a favor to call in. I figured Mom would never forgive me if I didn't look out for you. Downtown Hanoi's a tough neighborhood, you know."

"You little twerp," Steve said fondly. "We're gonna have ourselves a great time... Say, you *said* you were listening in on the exchange between me and those other guys, so what did you think?"

"About what?" Robbie asked, sipping at his beer.

"Come on," Steve chided. "Those guys were coming on like they don't *enjoy* themselves flying strikes." He nudged Robbie in the ribs. "We both know flying combat is better than sex, right?"

"I like sex better," Robbie murmured. "You don't need a chute in case you have to punch out."

Steve laughed. "It's gonna be you and me tomorrow, kid," he enthused. "Maybe we'll just sidle off and bag us a pair of MIGs."

"Uncle Steve —"

"How many have you bagged so far?" Steve demanded.

"None, dammit!" Robbie exploded.

"Hey, kid, take it easy," Steve said, startled by his nephew's angry reaction.

"Those guys were right!" Robbie said, swiveling his bar stool in order to confront Steve. "You *are* living in the past. You can forget about what Grandpa experienced flying with the Red Baron, or what it must have been like for my father dueling with Me-109s, or what it was like for you mixing it up with Zeros over the Pacific, and even what you experienced sporting around in your BroadSword over MIG Alley—"

"War is war, kid," Steve argued. "I know how to handle myself."

"Dammit, you keep that attitude, you're *asking* for an extended stay at the Hanoi Hilton."

"They'll never take me alive," Steve said lightly.

"Right, just keep it up . . ." Robbie sulked.

"Why are you getting so steamed?" Steve asked, bewildered.

"Because you don't seem to care whether you live or die."

"Come on," Steve demanded. "Don't tell me you're like the rest of these guys: all dressed up like fighter jocks, but with accountants' souls. You all sound like you're afraid of your own shadows—"

"And what are you afraid of, Uncle Steve?" Robbie asked softly.

"I'm not afraid to die, and that's for sure," Steve growled.

"I know that," Robbie countered quickly. "How do you feel about living?"

"What's that supposed to mean?" Steve warily demanded.

"Grandpa writes me all the time, lets me know what's going on. He told me that General Simon has retired, and what the general has to say about you: that you ought to get on the stick, and get your ass into war college. Grandpa told me that you're afraid, and *why*..."

Steve could feel his temper boiling over. Why did everyone—especially Robbie—have to know all his dirty laundry?

"Fuck it—" He forced a grin as he put his arm around his nephew's shoulder. "I'm not *afraid* ... It's just that all that classroom stuff is for sissies, right? Maybe after this tour is over I'll get out, go to work at GAT."

"You've been threatening that for as long as I can remember," Robbie said.

"Yeah, but maybe this time I'll really make good on my threat—"

Robbie shook his head. "Grandpa's told me that as much as he would love to have you in the business, he'd much rather you did what made you most happy. That's why he's hoping that you'll come to your senses and let the Air Force send you to school. He'd love to see you wearing a general's stars."

"Oh, so Pop's got me promoted to general already, has he?" Steve asked sourly. "Somebody better tell him he's dreaming..."

"It's *your* dream, not his," Robbie insisted. "But it doesn't have to be just a dream..."

Steve struggled not to lose his composure. "I don't want

to talk about this war college crap anymore—" he muttered. "I'm full up to here with it, get it?"

"All you have to do is get over this last hurdle," Robbie persisted. "There's no telling how high you could rise."

"Right!" Steve snapped, losing his temper. "Nothing to it, huh?" he sneered. "I've got to say it's kind of funny hearing *you* promote the value of higher education. You didn't exactly end up at the head of the class in *junior* college—"

Steve regretted the remark as he saw the hurt flare in his nephew's eyes. "Hey, I didn't mean anything," he tried to joke. "You were just pushing too hard. You hit a nerve, you know...?"

"No problem." Robbie shrugged, looking away.

"Come *onnn!*" Steve joshed, again putting his arm around Robbie's shoulder. "You and me flying together like you'd said you've always wanted. Remember how you used to talk about it happening someday during our hunting and fishing trips? Well, tomorrow's the day. We're gonna tear up the sky. We'll make a *great* team. After all, we're two peas in a pod—"

"You know, I always thought we were alike," Robbie said slowly. "But now I'm not so sure."

"What does *that* mean?" Steve challenged.

"Maybe we'd better change the subject again," Robbie warned.

"I asked you a question!" Steve demanded, growing angry all over again.

"Okay . . . If you really want to know . . . It means that unlike you, I'm not willing to admit that something's beaten me without first trying my best," Robbie said.

"Like school, you mean?" Steve eyed him.

"Yeah, like school," Robbie declared. "Sure I didn't do so great in school, but at least I tried, and I got past it, and I'll tell you something else," he continued fiercely. "If *I* ever get the chance to go all the way to the top, I'm not going to throw it away like *you*." He stood up, tossing some money on the bar.

"What's that? . . . I said I was buying you a drink—"

"I think I'd rather buy my own," Robbie said quietly.

"Come on." Steve grabbed hold of his nephew's sleeve. "Don't leave things this way."

"I don't know what you mean," Robbie insisted. "Things are cool. It's just late, and we've got some flying to do tomorrow."

"Yeah, sure. You have it your way, kid." Steve nodded, not looking at him.

"Good night, Uncle Steve."

"Good night, then."

Steve sat there for a long time after Robbie had left the officers' club, thinking about what the kid had said to him. Who the fuck did his nephew think he was? Steve wondered resentfully.

And when had Robbie gotten so smart . . . ?

CHAPTER 18

(ONE)

**Over Thud Ridge, near Hanoi
North Vietnam
19 July 1966**

"Float like a butterfly and sting like a bee," said Cassius Clay, or as he was calling himself these days, Muhammad Ali . . . The tactic had worked for the boxer up against Sonny Liston, thought Captain Robert Greene from the cockpit of his Thunderchief. Maybe it would also work for this Thud strike up against the Yen Lam oil depot and railroad yard . . .

There were four flights of Thunderchiefs in the strike force that was just now cruising at seven thousand feet, hugging the steep brown spine of rock the pilots called Thud Ridge. The strike had left its Thailand base at thirteen hundred hours, approximately ninety minutes ago. Once all sixteen heavily bomb-laden Thuds had thundered aloft into the clear blue sky, the strike had navigated a course over Laos, where they'd refueled off the fleet of waiting, orbiting tankers. Continuing on, the Thuds were careful to give wide berth to the thirty-mile buffer zone paralleling North Vietnam's border with Communist China. As they flew they ran constant flight checks, and double- and triple-checked their weapons systems as they banked over the craggy, dun-colored mountains and lush green jungle. They crossed the glittering silver thread that was the Red River, and then approached Thud Ridge, the mountain range landmark that pointed the way like a skeletal finger, southeast, to Hanoi.

"Rio go to prestrike frequency," radioed the flight leader, Major Wilson. "Rio check."

"Two," sang out Wilson's wingman.

"Three," Robbie said. He was Rio flight's element lead.

"Four—" Robbie heard his Uncle Steve crisply announce.

Robbie glanced out the canopy to assure himself that his uncle was maintaining proper wingman position. Yep, Steve's Thud was tucked in nice and tight. His uncle saw him looking and waved. Robbie quickly waved back, anxious to communicate as much friendliness as possible.

Robbie felt terrible about last night's argument at the O Club. Last night he'd been positive that he'd been right, but in the cold light of day he wasn't so sure, and during the briefing he'd concluded that regardless of who was right, the fact remained that he'd been sticking his nose in where it didn't belong. Sure it was frustrating to think that Steve was cutting the legs out from under his own career by stubbornly refusing to go to war college, but just imagine how frustrated Steve must be! Seeing it from his uncle's point of view, Robbie had an inkling of how tough it was for Steve to admit his fear, even to himself. Anyway, Robbie knew from past experience that the surest way to get his uncle to dig in his heels was to try and pressure him. Robbie wished that there was some less confrontational way of convincing Steve to do the right thing for himself, and he hoped that Steve had forgiven him for stepping out of bounds. His uncle had seemed to have forgotten all about last night's blowout.

He'd been as warm and friendly toward Robbie as ever during the briefings.

A tense radio exchange snapped Robbie out of his brooding.

"Champion two, we got another SAM, ten o'clock."

"Champion four, watch out. SAM on your six!"

Robbie, monitoring the urgent transmissions, could only cross his gloved fingers, wishing the members of Champion flight the best. Champion was a Wild Weasel flight in advance of the strike, just now approaching the target, and, he hoped, soaking up all the SAM action.

"Drover lead to Drover three—"

Robbie listened. Above the Thuds were the hulking, twin-seat, F-4 Phantoms of Drover flight, on MIG Combat Air Patrol. The MIG-CAP Phantoms had no guns but were armed with close-in (two-mile effective range), heat-seeking Sidewinder air-to-air missiles, and longer range (up to ten miles), radar-guided, Sparrow A/As.

"Drover, this is Three—"

"Three, We've got two—No!—Make that four MIGs at eleven o'clock."

"Drover, this is Rio lead," Robbie heard Major Wilson cut in. "Are they MIG-21s?"

"Affirmative," Drover lead replied. "They're giving us a wide berth so far."

"They're likely trying to draw you off," Wilson warned. "Don't you guys fall for it. They likely have buddies— probably 17s—waiting in the wings . . . Rio three, come in."

Robbie clicked his mike. "Rog, Rio lead. This is three."

"Three, you monitored Drover?"

"Rog." Robbie knew that the MIGs' favorite tactic was to lure off the Phantom escort by dangling in front of the F-4 crews the possibility of bagging a coveted MIG-21, in the process leaving the main strike force vulnerable to the enemy's workhorse airplane, the MIG-17. The 17 usually carried only cannons, but it was a very agile craft. A Thud driver's best defense against the 17 was his bird's superior speed at low altitudes, but to use that speed the Thud driver had to prematurely jettison his bomb load. If a MIG driver could force you to toggle off before you reached your target he'd won the battle, regardless of who ultimately bagged whom.

"Rio three, green up your Sidewinders," Wilson ordered.

"Rog, lead." Robbie set to work throwing the series of switches that set up and armed the pair of Sidewinders slung from beneath his wings. Because of the preponderance of MIGs in the Hanoi area the flight leader and element leader Thuds in each flight were armed with the heat-seeking missiles, and, of course, all the Thuds had their cannons.

The strike, flying "downtown" from a southeasterly direction, was approaching the northern outskirts of Hanoi. The ground below was a tan and green checkerboard pockmarked with bomb craters; a desolate moonscape of rubble and death. The enemy, as if to thumb their noses at American air power, used the bomb craters as revetments in which to shelter their smaller AA guns.

"Rio, this is four," Steve said. "Light guns at two o'clock."

Robbie saw pinpoints of red flame sparkling amid the debris-littered bomb craters. *Machine guns*, he thought, and shuddered. Pretty soon gomer would start in with the heavy stuff . . .

The Yen Lam depot was located to the north of the city. It would have been a relatively easy task for the strike force just now closing fast on that part of the city to use the advantage of surprise to hit the facility before the enemy could put up a solid cone of defensive fire. Unfortunately, Command Directives stated that all attack runs had to be executed coming from the *south*. The directive was meant to protect Hanoi's civilian population—any bombs that might overshoot the target would fall away from the city's residential districts—but it put the pilots at increased risk. The Thuds would have to execute a banking turn over the city in order to achieve the required northerly attack heading, and that would give the enemy plenty of time to set up his guns and SAMs.

"Rio, this is four," Steve repeated. "What are those below? They look like groves of trees—"

"Negative, four," Robbie said. "Those are AAA batteries —likely eighty-five-millimeter guns. Gomer likes to tie palm fronds around the barrels for camo purposes."

"Don't remember that in Korea." Steve chuckled. "Of course, there weren't any palm trees . . ."

As if on cue, the AAA batteries opened up. The "trees" sprouted geysers of fire. An instant later the first ragged boulders of black smoke blossomed and hung in the air. A second barrage of flak, this volley impacting closer to the Thuds, generated shock waves of explosive force that buffeted the war bird.

"No SAM activity yet, huh?" Robbie heard Steve ask.

"It's early yet," Robbie said.

"Maybe the Weasels got them all . . .?"

"Maybe so," Robbie replied evenly, privately very much doubting the possibility.

"Rio, go to strike frequency," Wilson cut in, and then ran a flight check to assure that all of Rio's ducklings were in a line.

Robbie thought that Steve had sounded cool and collected when he'd asked about SAMs. Anybody else monitoring the exchange would have been fooled, but Robbie knew his uncle well enough to hear the undercurrent of tension in his voice. For Steve, SAMs were the only unknown. Everything else—enemy guns and enemy planes—he'd dealt with in Korea.

"Rio, this is Pogo, we're over the target—"

"Rog, Pogo," Wilson replied. "What you got, son?"

Every pilot down the line waited to hear what Pogo lead had to say. His was the strike's lead flight; the first to try and set alight Yen Lam's giant fuel tanks. Whatever defenses the enemy had kept quietly hidden from the Wild Weasels would now be going into action.

"Heavy guns. Negative SAMs—" Pogo lead muttered. "Executing attack dive now!"

"Rio, check," Wilson called.

"Two."

"Three," Robbie said.

"Three, green up your air-to-ground mode," Wilson said.

"Rog." Actually, Robbie had already switched over from air-to-air Sidewinder capability to bombsight-in/release mode. From previous experience he knew that there was very little likelihood of MIG interference over Hanoi.

"Four," Steve said, checking in.

Robbie saw a giant plume of oily black smoke rising up thousands of feet into the blue sky. Pogo flight's bombs had found their target.

"Pogo withdrawing," the flight leader announced, sounding understandably relieved.

"Rio, roll in for attack setup," Wilson ordered. "Let's get this over with."

Rio's four Thuds would attack simultaneously. Yen Lam was a sprawling complex of huge fuel tanks, warehouses, and freight car yards. During the main briefing the depot had been divided into four separate sectors, one to each flight. Each sector had then been subdivided into targets for each individual Thud at the squadron level briefings.

"Four, you stay tight with me," Robbie cajoled.

"Rog, li'l nephew," Steve replied lazily.

Robbie pushed the stick sideways and kicked rudder, going to afterburn and pulling hard Gs as he skidded his Thud across the sky fifteen thousand feet over Hanoi. His screaming bird carrying its four-and-a-half ton load of explosives stood on a cone of orange flame as it nosed up in a 180-degree popover.

"Stay with me, stay with me," Robbie groaned to Steve as his Thud slithered through the maze of bursting flak. His safety harness cut into his shoulders as he jinked and turned. His eyes felt like they were going to pop out of his head. His gut felt like he'd just swallowed a rancid bowling ball.

"Think of me as your shadow from here on in, my boy..." Steve said lightly.

Jesus Christ! Robbie thought. Steve sounded like they

were taking a leisurely Sunday afternoon drive through the country. *Is the guy immune to Gs?*

The city of Hanoi cartwheeled beneath Robbie. From this altitude the narrow, twisty streets and gabled rooftops looked weirdly like the aerial views of Paris that he'd seen in picture books. Looking down, he saw sparkles of light like flashbulbs popping off: He guessed every small arm in Hanoi was just now firing straight up at the Thuds hanging overhead. *Let's get this over with was right.*

"Kind of nice to think that all that sizzling hot stuff they're firing up at us is going to fall right back down on their little sloped heads." Steve chuckled.

Robbie couldn't get over how relaxed Steve was sounding. It really did sound as if the Gs he *had* to be suffering weren't bothering him in the slightest. Robbie glanced out his canopy, thinking that maybe Steve was swinging wide, in that way sparing himself the worst of the G punishment ... He should have known better: There Steve was, glued tight on Robbie's wing; any closer and they'd be sharing the same airspace.

Robbie would have smiled if he weren't so busy wincing in pain: The fucking birds weren't as at home in the sky as Steven Gold ...

"Commence attack!" Wilson ordered.

The four Thuds of Rio flight dived toward their target sector through the white and black clouds of flak and the streams of tracer fire like crisscrossing strands of sparkling rubies. As always was the case during these few seconds spent attacking, the war-torn, fiery, noisy world receded, and Robbie felt an odd, inner calm.

From the reading he'd done he'd come to the conclusion that the inner peace he felt was a meditative, Zen warrior kind of thing. Usually there were so many anxieties, concerns, and ambitions buzzing around inside his mind. During these intense moments of life or death it was a relief to be able to quiet his soul by focusing on the only thing that mattered: working stick and throttle and rudder to get that red pipper smack where he wanted it on his target.

The pipper was moving into position now, crimson against the half dozen circular fuel tanks arranged in two rows of three. The tanks glinted like silver coins in the shrouded sunlight and wafting smoke. Steve hoped he would be dropping his bombs on the airplane hangarlike complex of buildings that housed the fuel-pumping machinery, just to the right of the tanks. Rio lead and Rio two would be zeroing in on the freight cars and the railroad track-switching apparatus several hundred yards to port.

Robbie waited until the last possible second, and then unleashed his twelve 750-pound bombs. As he pulled out of his dive at 2,500 feet he saw Steve toggling off his own four-and-a-half tons of ordnance, and then both Thuds were twisting and turning, trying to throw off the infuriated hornet swarm of flak and tracer fire as they clawed for altitude.

Back up at fifteen thousand, Robbie banked his Thud around, and had the satisfaction of seeing the fuel tanks and pumping stations billowing flame and smoke: Rio element's targets had been destroyed. Then he and Steve were out of the immediate vicinity.

"Rio, flight check!" Wilson demanded anxiously.

After all four Thuds had sounded off safe and sound, the major happily announced to the two remaining flights, "Rio withdrawing," and then, "Rio, go to poststrike frequency."

After another flight check to make sure that everyone was tuned to the right radio channel, Wilson took the flight up to twenty thousand feet, saying, "Next stop is a gas station. I'll see if I can get us one with a rest room," he added cheerfully.

"Never mind a rest room," Two cut in. "I could use a dry cleaner. At some point back there I think I wet my pants."

Robbie found himself laughing hysterically. Probably everyone else was, as well. The dumbest jokes provoked a giddy response in the emotionally charged rush that came when a flight managed to successfully complete a mission unscathed.

"Our Tankers are waiting for us at the prearranged poststrike refueling area." Wilson paused. "Four, how'd you like your first taste of downtown Hanoi?" he asked amiably.

"I've got to say it wasn't as bad as you all led me to believe," Steve replied.

"To tell you the truth, I was surprised at the lack of SAM activity," Wilson confessed. "It's very unusual for the Weasels to get them all."

"In a way, I'm kind of sorry the Weasels did such a good job," Steve said. "I was hoping to get my SAM initiation over and done with."

"Bite your tongue, Colonel," Rio two cut in, laughing.

Amen to that, Robbie thought, as he anxiously studied the outlying city districts below for signs of SAM. The sites were usually made up of four to six launchers arranged in a circle, with a radar/communications van a few yards away.

They left Hanoi behind, coming upon what looked like a large agricultural area. There was a small village, partly smoke-shrouded by its myriad cook fires, and hemmed in on all sides by a green patchwork quilt of rectangular garden plots, bordered by dense, green jungle.

"Let's give that village a wide berth," Wilson said. "SAM could be down there."

"They put them in villages?" Steve asked skeptically.

"Affirmative, Four," Wilson said.

There was no sign of SAM, but Robbie knew that being able to spot the missiles before they were launched was highly unlikely, and that Wilson was right: There could easily be SAMs hidden among the thatched-roof huts in that village. In the beginning, the Russian-built, concrete installations had been easy to spot, but with the advent of Iron Hand, the enemy had taken to camouflaging his SAM sites. The village was a perfect place because the Rules of Engagement under which the Thud drivers operated decreed that SAMs couldn't be hit near so-called civilian areas.

As a matter of fact, the more Robbie studied that village, the more something—call it a sixth sense born of his seventy-six missions—warned him that SAM was close by, lying in wait to rise up and snatch the Thuds out of the sky. The sooner that village was put behind them, the better. Just now Rio Flight was at 22,000 feet, which was within SAM's envelope, but high enough to allow for evasive action should SAMs appear—

Provided the launch was spotted soon enough—

"Sure would like to get a crack at those MIGs that were pestering us before," Steve mused out loud. "Here I am in a real blue balls-type situation—"

"Meaning?" Robbie demanded.

"Well, there, nephew, meaning I've got an ammo drum jam-packed with rounds hanging low beneath my cannon, and I'm feeling frisky and light now that those bombs are away."

"You're feeling light because you're low on fuel," Wilson said pointedly. "Anyway, don't expect to see any MIGs, Colonel . . ."

"Oh, no, Major?" Steve asked innocently.

Robbie began swiveling his head, searching the sky all around him. Once again something in Steve's tone had tipped him off. Growing up, Robbie had heard his uncle use that same tone of voice during their hunting trips. It was the teasing tone Steve had used when Robbie had been ready to swear that there was no sign of game anywhere in the woods, and Steve was about to prove him wrong . . .

Clearly, Steve knew—or *saw*—something as yet unknown to the rest of them.

"The thing is, Colonel," Wilson said patronizingly, "the MIGs know better than to try and tangle with us once we've dropped our ordnance."

"You know that and I know it, Major." Steve laughed. "But someone forgot to tell those two, swept-wing beauties at one o'clock low—"

"Huh?" Wilson stammered.

"What? Where?" Rio two was demanding.

Robbie stared in the direction that his uncle had indicated. Just as had always been the case in the woods, he'd been looking that way a moment ago and had seen nothing, but now that Steve had pointed out what there was to be seen he wondered how he could have missed it. The pair of MIGs was maybe two miles off. They were arranged in a loose echelon, making a wide turn heading away from the flight, back toward that village. They looked to be down around fifteen thousand feet, which was unusual for them. They didn't like it down low, where the Thuds had the speed advantage, as long as the latter didn't try to match gomer's turning ability . . .

Robbie, studying the MIGs, caught movement out of the corner of his eye. It was Steve's Thud, peeling away from the flight.

"Be right back," Steve said cheerily.

"Steve, no!" Robbie blurted.

"Negative, Rio four!" Wilson demanded. "Four, you get back here—"

Don't waste your breath, boss, Robbie thought angrily as he watched Steve's tail pipe light up. Steve had gone to afterburn to close the gap between him and the MIGs.

"Where does that fucker think he's going?" Wilson demanded angrily.

"He isn't *thinking*," Robbie muttered as he watched Steve follow the MIGs back toward the village. "He's like a fucking hound onto the scent of quail. He's just doing what he was born to do . . ."

"Boss, I'm getting low on fuel . . ." Rio two called.

"Rog," Wilson began. "Hey! Three! Where are you going—?"

"I'm gonna watch my uncle's back," Robbie said, slinging his Thud around in a tight turn to set a course toward the MIGs.

"Negative—" Wilson began.

"Boss, you know as well as I do he could be heading into a trap. There could be more MIGs waiting to drop down onto his six o'clock."

"Three, come back here! Now, goddammit!"

Robbie, ignoring his flight leader, went to afterburn to try and catch up to Steve, never minding the fact that his own fuel gauges were beginning to warn that he'd better take it easy on the juice or he'd find himself hitchhiking home. As he hurtled forward he set up his Sidewinders, just in case cannons alone weren't up to the task of getting them out of this.

Robbie was close enough now to the unsuspecting MIGs to see that they were 17s. Both were a dirty gray aluminum color, highlighted with red on their snouts and tails.

Thank heavens for small favors, Robbie thought, his gloved fingers nervously twitching at his missile and cannon triggers. The Thuds didn't have the gas to start shaking it up with state-of-the-art MIG-21s.

"Trust that's you behind me, Three?" Steve said calmly.

"Roger." *Fucking guy's got eyes in the back of his head*, Robbie thought.

"Closing on the rear MIG, now," Steve said. "You hang back, make sure I'm not being boxed in."

"Three, we've got to leave the vicinity," Wilson called. He and his wingman were orbiting where Robbie had left them. "Two and I are both getting real low on fuel—"

"Roger," Robbie replied. "You guys go on, and ask that tanker to alter its course to meet us as close to hostile territory as it dares to come. I'm gonna be flying on farts by the time I manage to rope in my crazy uncle."

"I heard that," Steve murmured. "Don't worry. This won't take long."

"The colonel's closed on the rear MIG!" Rio two blurted.

Robbie saw that Steve had positioned himself above and to the rear of the MIGs. He was closing at an angle. Robbie guessed his uncle intended to rake a single continuous burst of cannon fire across the upper wings and cockpits of the tightly grouped MIGs.

"He's opened fire!" Two yelled.

Robbie saw smoke and fire spewing from the cannon chin pod of Steve's Thud. The 20-millimeter rounds hosed the rear MIG, shearing off its port wing. The dirty silver plane dropped away, spewing black smoke. Steve shifted to the lead MIG, which was now rolling and jinking in the general direction of that village in order to throw off his aim.

"Steve, get out of range and I'll fire off a Sidewinder," Robbie called.

Steve ignored him. *Greedy bastard wants them both*, Robbie thought.

Donnononononononog—

"Jesus Christ! SAM launch—" Robbie bellowed.

Donnononononononog—

The droning electronic tone reverberating in Robbie's headphones was coming from the anti-SAM, Electronic Countermeasure gear mounted in his Thud. The ECM gear was sensitive to the SAM's radar tracking signal, which the SAM crews switched on a few seconds before firing.

Robbie looked for the telltale dust cloud that would indicate a launch but couldn't find one. He realized why he hadn't seen the launch as a trio of SAMs trailing fiery exhausts spiraled crazily from out of the smoky haze over the village—*that fucking village*—running like a pack of hungry wolves up toward the belly of Steve's Thud.

"Steve, three-ring circus at four o'clock!" Robbie urgently called as he watched Steve continue spraying the fleeing MIG with cannon fire.

"Just another second . . ." Steve muttered. "I almost got this sucker . . ."

"There's no time, dammit!" Robbie cried. "Break now!"

"Got 'em!" Steve cried triumphantly as the MIG's tail section blew off. The enemy fighter slashed a bold back line of smoke across the blue sky as it fireballed toward the earth.

And SAM has you, Robbie thought sadly, knowing from experience that Steve had waited too long to begin evasive tactics.

The SAMs, each thirty feet long and carrying 350 pounds of explosives, had separated from their boosters. The missiles began to accelerate on their stubby little wings as they tracked Steve, their heat-seeking guidance systems zeroing in on his tail pipe. Steve broke hard left, going to afterburn to try to gain some altitude, but it was too late; the SAMs were already above him and were now arcing down for the kill. Steve racked another hard left, and then a right, jinking like crazy. The SAMs coming down at him from out of the sky followed relentlessly.

Oh, he's good, Robbie thought in admiration. He's turning on two planes at once in order to confuse the SAMs' tracking systems. He's doing everything he's supposed to, but there's three of them boxing him in. If he manages to throw off one, another can easily take over.

Only seconds had passed since the electronic SAM alarm had sounded in Robbie's ears, and it would only be a few more seconds before this duel between man and machines was decided.

Robbie fired off a Sidewinder, thinking that there was a slim hope that the Sidewinder's trail of fiery exhaust cutting across the dwindling bit of sky between Steve and the trio of Sams might jam or confuse the latter's infrared gear. *Yeah, it was a long shot, but what the hell*, Robbie thought. Again, the odds were long that the Sidewinder's own heat-seeking guidance system would lock onto Steve's tail pipe. Anyway, at the moment, Steve didn't have much to lose.

The Sidewinder hurtled forward on its thrashing tail of fire. Robbie watched it dwindle in size, seeming to dip, and then arc up on a general course toward the SAMs. Soon the Sidewinder's exhaust was only a glowing speck, and then even that faded from view in the sunny sky.

Steve's frantic maneuverings had dropped him to ten thousand feet and the SAMs were coming down at him. One was angling in toward his nose, one in the general direction of his midsection, and one was converging on his tail pipe. The enemy missiles looked like three fiery fingers spread to scratch Steve out of the sky.

There was a brilliant burst of light as the SAMs on Steve's six o'clock exploded prematurely. *My fucking Sidewinder must have locked onto it*, Robbie thought, grinning despite the seriousness of the situation as he watched tendrils of black smoke radiating out from the blast's center. *I may be the first pilot in history to have shot down a SAM—*

Meanwhile, Steve seemed to be outracing the remaining two SAMs dropping down on him. The one on his nose abruptly flamed out and hurtled past well ahead of him, on an irrevocable course to the ground. The SAM his tail was struggling to make the course corrections necessary to stay locked on his exhaust.

He's gonna make it, Robbie thought. *The lucky sonofabitch has more life than a fucking cat. Gomer's going to miss his bull's-eye—*

The SAM site's radar must have revealed that their target was on the verge of escaping because the enemy controllers chose that instant when Steve was sandwiched between the two SAMs to detonate the missiles.

Robbie watched horror-struck as the twin blasts—one just a few hundred feet beneath Steve's airplane, and one just a hundred yards behind—engulfed Steve's Thud in a smoky, blood red fireball, totally blotting his airplane from view.

It's all over, Robbie thought in shock, but then, incredibly, he saw Steve's Thud arrowing up out of that spreading hell of smoke and fire.

"You fucking made it, you wild man!" Robbie crowed, but he shut up fast. He could see from the way Steve's Thud was handling that something was wrong.

"Steve, come in!" Robbie frantically transmitted. "Steve—"

There was no reply. *Had something happened to Steve's radio?*

Robbie looked around for the rest of the flight, but they'd gone. *We're all alone, over enemy territory*, he realized. He checked his fuel situation: not good . . .

He glanced back toward Steve in time to see his Thud still climbing, but then it faltered as its engine flamed out. The Thud dropped into a stall, and then the sleek war bird was transformed into almost twenty-five tons of flying brick as it began to fall out of the sky.

"Steve, you're out of control. Get out!" Robbie cried, hammering his mike button.

Maybe Steve was only semiconscious, he thought. *Maybe his radio could receive, if not transmit. If he were only a little stunned, Robbie's voice in his ears might snap him awake.*

"Get out, Steve!" Robbie screamed hoarsely. "Get out! GET OUT!"

Robbie saw the Thud's canopy blow, and then Steve, punching out. As his chute blossomed its beeper began emitting its doleful, electronic cry of despair. The high-pitched wailing seemed transformed in Robbie's earphones into a keening: *don't-leave-me/don't-leave-me/don't—*

I won't, Robbie vowed silently. He was already on the horn, broadcasting a Mayday.

(Two)

Call it bravery, or call it defiance, but Steve Gold knew as soon as he'd spotted those MIGs that he was going after them. Shooting down enemy airplanes was what he did best. Not dropping bombs, or giving pep talks to hotshot young jet jockeys who thought he was a prehistoric relic, or trying to make sense out of his future as past choices inexorably closed in—

Steve knew what was right for him, and what was wrong. He knew he really *didn't* have the kind of smarts it took to make it at war college, and that once this tour was over he really would have to make good on his threat to leave the Air Force. But that was all in the future. What was here and now were these two fat, juicy MIGs that the good Lord had seen fit to put within reach of his gun.

Wax those two birds, Steve thought, *and you will have counted coup on the enemy in three wars . . .*

"Be right back," he told the flight, arming his cannon as he banked his Thud toward his prey.

"Steve, no!" he heard his nephew cry out.

"Negative, Rio four!" Major Wilson ordered him. "Four, you get back here—"

Steve ignored them. Ahead stretched a long future during which the world could tug and prod him to its heart's content, but this was *his* moment. Here in the cockpit of his war bird, with his finger resting lightly on his cannon's trigger, he was supreme.

There were various electronic shrieks, beeps, and drones coming from his ECM and navigational gear, competing for his attention with the multiple, garbled exchanges from the other pilots on the airwaves, and the controllers back in Thailand. Steve flicked the switches to silence the electronic bedlam, until only his radio was left on. *What a relief! How'd they expect a pilot to hear himself think through all that black-box racket?*

It was time to get back to basics, Steve thought. To remember that first and foremost a fighter plane was a platform for its weapons systems. All the black boxes in the world couldn't take the place of a man who knew how to shoot . . .

The MIGs were now about a mile away. *Hold on,* Steve thought. *Don't get overeager; a thousand feet is optimum range.*

So far, so good: The MIGs still seemed unaware of his presence. His cherry red, notched circle gunsight was closing in on them like some luminous UFO intent on joining their formation.

The MIGs were 17s. With their short, swept wings, blunt, piglike air-intake snouts, and bubble canopies they looked a lot like the Commie birds Steve had tangled with almost fifteen years ago in Korea. He knew that the 17s usually carried a pair of cannons in a chin pod. They were a lot slower than his Thud, but much more maneuverable. Going up against them without a wingman was risky. If they got behind him his only alternative would be to go to afterburn and get out of here.

He glanced at his fuel gauges. At least he could run as far as he could on what little gas was left in his tanks.

And if these MIGs do bag me, so be it, Steve told himself, brooding on how poor old Howie Simon had been forced to retire to Texas to spend the rest of his life with nothing to keep him company but his aching ulcers and bum heart. Hell, if that was what a man's future held once the Air Force was done with him, Steve could think of worse ways to die than with his finger on the trigger of the baddest-assed popgun in the history of breech-loaders, riding 49,000 pounds of war bird into the afterlife . . .

I may be afraid of a classroom, Steve thought, still smarting from the memory of the look in Robbie's eyes during last night's argument, *but I am not afraid to fight, and if necessary, die for my country—*

Something began tickling the hairs on the back of Steve's neck. Someone—he hoped without fish sauce and rice on his breath—was on his six o'clock.

He punched his mike button. "Trust that's you behind me, Three?"

"Rog—"

Robbie was sounding a mite pissed off, Steve noticed, but the important thing was that he was there.

That's my boy, he thought fondly. He'd always believed that Robbie would be there to back him up. "Closing on the rear MIG now," Steve said. "You hang back, make sure I'm not being boxed in."

It had crossed his mind that this might be a trap. That the MIGs he was chasing were the lambs staked out to lure the tiger into an ambush.

"Three, we've got to leave the vicinity," Wilson called, sounding harried.

Steve chuckled, thinking that the major was probably too pissed at him to address him, as well.

"Two and I are both getting low on fuel—" Wilson was saying.

"Rog," Robbie replied. "You guys go on, and ask that

tanker to alter its course to meet us as close to hostile territory as it dares to come."

Good idea, Steve thought, nervously eyeing his fuel indicators. With all the afterburn he'd been doing, that tanker was going to have to meet him more than halfway...

"... I'm gonna be flying on farts by the time I manage to rope in my crazy uncle," Robbie added.

"I heard that," Steve said absently, grinning as the red dot pipper floating in the center of his gunsight's red circle moved into position on the rear MIG, just behind the canopy, smack between the wings. "Don't worry," he added. "This won't take long."

"The colonel's closed on the rear MIG!" Steve dimly heard somebody shouting as he squeezed the trigger, feeling the recoil reverberating up through the cockpit floor as the Vulcan's six revolving barrels began spitting 20-millimeter rounds. The individual tracers looked like glowing orange beads as the cannon spewed a fiery rope that ran between the nose of Steve's Thud to the backbone of the thrashing MIG.

"Mississippi one, Mississippi two," Steve counted out loud to himself as he held down his trigger. He was aware that his cannon could empty its thousand-round ammo drum in ten seconds. He still had another MIG to wax.

The 20-millimeter rounds were pelting the MIG. The multiple hits raised sparks and left ugly black pockmarks on the enemy plane's drab silver aluminum exterior.

"Mississippi three, Mississippi four—"

The MIG banked hard to starboard, trying to escape the lethal circle of Steve's gunsight. Steve let the red pipper in the center of the circle slide onto the MIG's port wing, and watched his cannon shear it clean off at the root. He released the trigger as his first kill dropped away, knitting its own mourning shawl of thick black smoke. Steve shifted to the lead MIG, which was now rolling and jinking in the general direction of that little village they'd passed some time ago.

"Steve, get out of range and I'll fire off a Sidewinder," Robbie called.

Steve ignored him. *No way am I surrendering a kill to a*

fucking machine, not while I'm in control of this airplane, with ammo in my gun. Watch and learn, li'l nephew—

His bright red gunsight was chasing the MIG. *Just a little too low,* Steve mused. He eased back a hair on the stick. The Thud's nose lifted. The retreating MIG was framed like a cameo in the gunsight's circle. The red pipper became lost in the glowing exhaust emanating from the MIG's tail pipe.

"Got'cha!" Steve laughed. He mashed the trigger. The Vulcan gun chattered maniacally. The MIG went to afterburn, writhing as flaming 20-millimeter gunfire tore relentlessly at its red-painted tail.

"Jesus Christ! SAM launch—" Robbie abruptly bellowed.

Huh—? Where—? Steve guiltily pondered the ECM gear that he'd muted. *Spilt milk,* he thought. He did not take his eyes off the MIG in his gunsight.

"Steve, three-ring circus at four o'clock!" Robbie was shouting, sounding terrified.

"Just another second..." Steve muttered, counting to himself *Mississippi six, Mississippi seven...*

The pipper was staying glued to the MIG's tail. "I've almost got this sucker..." he told Robbie. *And shooting down airplanes is what I do—*

Mississippi eight— He was totally relaxed now. His mind was clear. He was not consciously trying to anticipate what the MIG would do, and yet he was able to stay locked on his quarry, as if the 20-millimeter strand of gunfire connecting the hunter to the hunted was a towrope. Steadily the MIG's red tail was being whittled away, decreasing its pilot's control. There was nowhere the MIG driver could go where Steve wouldn't be there at precisely the same moment.

Mississippi nine— The MIG went into an inverted reverse turn. Steve followed him around, pleased at the way his fuel-light Thud was responding.

"There's no time, dammit!" Robbie yelled. "Break now!"

Mississippi ten— "Got 'em!" Steve cried elatedly. The last of his tracers had blown off the MIG's crimson-painted tail. The ruined MIG cartwheeled across the sky in flames, trailing a freight train's length of black smoke.

Steve scarcely registered the MIG's earthward plummet. He was too busy searching for the SAMs coming to get him. He saw them at twelve, three, and six o'clock high, riding herd on the sky as they streaked down to intercept his Thud. He went to afterburn, jinking like crazy; maybe even panicking a little. It was weird and scary to know that those things adjusting their aim to track him were not being piloted by men, but by electronics.

I'm up against mindless machines, he thought. *I can't outsmart them. I've to outfly them.* He was enduring maxium G as he slalomed his Thud in two directions at once. Still the SAMs closed on him.

It was a SAM that shot down Chet Boskins in his Mayfly spy plane over the Soviet Union, Steve remembered, even as he realized just how well the SAMs had boxed him in. No matter where he put his airplane, that particular piece of sky was well within the lethal vectors of at least one of the three SAMs looking to put the bite on him.

He dived and twisted, putting his Thud through paces like a hooked trout leaping from a stream. It was like being in a brawl and trying to fend off three assailants at once; it was like being chased by hornets. The SAMs seemed alive, and yet it was not life as man could understand it. Like enraged insects, these thirty-foot-long, buzzing, winged things racing so swiftly and cunningly to destroy him seemed possessed of an implacably malign, alien intelligence . . .

Steve heard and felt the explosion as the SAM on his tail detonated. "Lucky, lucky, lucky—" he repeatedly chanted to himself in a whisper. The sweat was running in rivulets down his back, dripping down his forehead from beneath his helmet. Trying to escape the two remaining robot birds was taking everything he had.

He saw the SAM angling down toward him from his twelve o'clock flameout. Afraid he was going to run into it, he popped his speed brakes. The SAM slashed past his nose, its stubby, triangular wings making it look like an arrowhead.

He retracted his speed brakes and cobbed the throttle,

pushing it sideways to go to afterburn. His fuel gauges were on empty. He had to be flying on fumes. He didn't care. The one remaining SAM closing on his six o'clock had to be getting low as well. All that mattered was outrunning it.

I'm going to make it, Steve began to think. *I'm going to beat these machines—*

And then the two SAMs exploded—

The double blast of thunder and light engulfed Steve, deafening and blinding him. He blacked out as his stomach corkscrewed around his spine, and his skull rattled like a pea in its pod inside his helmet. His Thud was batted straight up by the first explosion, and then smacked tail over nose by the second ferocious detonation.

He was only semiconscious as his trained body went on auto pilot. He struggled reflexively with rudder/stick/throttle to regain control of his airplane. As full awareness slowly returned he realized that his cockpit was filled with angry insectile buzzings he didn't immediately comprehend. His vision returned, to show a sky gone from blue to a shade of red as raw as an open wound.

Tumbling through the Sams' twin fireballs, Steve's mind thickly registered. *Thud's glistening with droplets of fire . . . Lucky my fuel's just about gone; that I've got no ordnance left, and no ammo, else I'd have exploded.*

As it was, bits of the flame cloud pressing in against his canopy had somehow wormed their way into the cockpit—

"No, those are warning lights," Steve mumbled, struggling to clear his head as the red fire outside dulled to a black, smoky fog. "Those are amber malfunction lights and red fire lights on the panel," he said out loud, just to hear himself; to know he was okay. The buzzing he'd been hearing was his warning signals going crazy.

He battled the Thud's controls as he burst free of the spreading smoke cloud, regaining blue sky. He was climbing, but he knew from the feel of his controls that his Thud was in trouble. He scanned his gauges, saw he was losing hydraulic pressure. *Control lines must have been severed by the blasts. This bird is never going to make it home—*

He looked around for Robbie, saw him about two miles off, and punched his mike button at the exact same moment as his fuel-starved engine flamed out. "Robbie, come in! Robbie—!"

Nothing. His radio had evidently been deafened and muted by the blasts. The Thud, its engine dead and its control surfaces locked due to lack of hydraulics, slowed in its climb. The war bird seemed to poise motionless in midair for a split second, and then began a twirling belly flop. The ground some twelve thousand feet below began spiraling up.

Got to step out, Steve thought. *Thank God Robbie's there to see me and send a Mayday.*

He hunched down, pulling up the hand grips on both sides of his seat to release the canopy. As the canopy lifted away the shrill wind whipping through the cockpit created a paper blizzard of the charts, reports, and navigational cards he'd received during that morning's briefing. He brought his knees up toward his chest, leaned his helmet back against the headrest, tucked in his elbows, and squeezed the seat-ejection triggers. His pressure suit was automatically inflated as the explosive charge blew his entire chair straight up out of the cockpit at close to one hundred miles an hour. He had a momentary, bird's-eye view of his massive Thud augering in for its embrace with the earth, and then his seat harness automatically released, and another, smaller, explosive charge ignited, kicking him free of the chair. He tumbled helplessly through the sky, his legs pumping furiously, his arms swinging, his fingers spread to claw futilely for purchase in the thin air. As he fell his own involuntary howl trilled within the confines of the rubber oxygen mask. Then his chute deployed. He heard the cruel whip-snap of nylon catching wind, and clenched against the bone-cracking, sudden halt of his downward plunge. He tore away the sour, spit-wet rubber oxygen mask as he hung, gently swinging like a pendulum from beneath that blessedly billowing parasol.

It was then that he saw his mighty Thud go to ground. From his vantage point his airplane disappeared to a clap of thunder. The Thud seemed like a majestic, olive and tan mottled sea bird, cleanly piercing the emerald ocean that was the jungle canopy.

The plane's gone, Steve realized. *Time to think about my own survival.*

He was going to be coming down very near that village, and that was bad news. The villagers were likely watching his descent, and preparing search parties to trap and capture him.

No way, he thought, shuddering. He'd die before he'd let himself be taken a P.O.W.; to spend the rest of the war eating fish heads and bug-infested rice in the Hanoi Hilton, or worse . . .

He'd descended to about three thousand feet. He looked down between his legs. He was pretty much over where the jungle met the North Vietnamese-tilled fields. If he spread his legs, his left boot was over the patchwork quilt planted area; his right boot was over green jungle. He glanced toward the village. People looking like ants were threading out into the fields. *Yeah, it was going to be quite a welcoming committee*, Steve thought grimly.

Two thousand feet— Steve looked up, and saw just beyond the edge of his chute a tiny glinting speck in the sky: Robbie, watching to see where he went down.

Fifteen hundred feet— He was tugging on the chute's risers, trying to steer himself a little bit away from the jungle and a little more toward the planted field. What he hoped to do was make a relatively safe landing on cleared, level ground, and then run into the nearby jungle to avoid being captured until he could be rescued. He had no doubt that Search and Rescue would make the effort to get him out. They would come. He knew they would—

But it was up to him to survive until they arrived . . .

Five hundred feet— It was no good. The wind carrying him toward the jungle was too strong. He was going down into the trees—

One hundred feet— He drew himself up into a ball and squeezed shut his eyes, lacing his fingers protectively across his face as he crashed through the first, thin, leafy branches of the giant trees that ruled the jungle. The noise sounded like pistol fire as the ever-thickening branches snapped beneath his cannonballing weight. As he fell the barbed vegetation slashed at his thin cotton flying suit. It scraped with bony fingers against his helmet. He yelled out in fear and defiance, thinking that at any moment he would be impaled by some upward jutting branch—

And then his chute's harness bit into his armpits as he was jerked to a stop. He opened his eyes to see a sunlight-dappled, silent, green world. On a branch at eye level, less than a yard from his face, a blue and yellow parrot was staring at him with head cocked, as if to ask what he was doing here.

"Good question, pal," Steve muttered. He looked down to where his boots were dancing in midair ten feet above the jungle floor. He looked up to where his chute had become tangled in branches, checking his fall.

"Lucky, lucky, lucky," he murmured. His heart was pounding. He took deep breaths to try and steady his nerves. *Lucky, all right—so far.*

He drew his survival knife from out of its sheath and began to saw through the risers, one by one. As each rope unraveled and then parted beneath his blade, he dangled a little more lopsidedly. When only one riser remained, he stared at vegetation-carpeted ground ten feet below, uttered a short but heartfelt prayer against broken ankles, and cut the last rope.

He hit the ground with his knees bent, and fell sideways, rolling away the impact in the soft ground cover. He got to his feet and discarded his helmet. He drew his emergency radio—a small black walkie-talkie with a stubby, rubber-coated antenna—from his mesh survival vest. He thumbed the beeper signal, hoping that Robbie was still up there somewhere, and could home in.

(Three)

Robbie had hardly finished broadcasting his Mayday before his radio began exploding in reply. First on line was Major Wilson, Rio flight's lead.

"Do you see a chute, Three?" Wilson demanded.

"Rog, boss. I see his chute. I repeat. I see his chute. He's going down into the jungle," Robbie said excitedly. "Look, I'm low on gas! The only reason I've got anything left is because I've been flying at reduced throttle in order to keep watch—"

"That's just great," Wilson muttered, sounding pissed. "You're flying just above stall speed, presenting yourself as a target. That's one hot area." Wilson paused. "As you and the colonel now well know. . ."

"Look, I need someone to take over to fly ResCap—" Robbie demanded. "We need Search and Rescue—"

"Settle down, Three," Wilson ordered. "I'm refueling now, and will immediately return. I've got another tanker heading toward you at this moment, and number two is on Rescue frequency. A Spad is on the way, and a chopper's waiting on the border."

"Rog," Robbie said weakly, vastly relieved that somebody had set the Search and Rescue ball rolling. "Thanks, boss . . . What's the Spad's E.T.A.?"

"About a half hour," Wilson said.

"Rog."

"Spad" was the nickname for the prop-driven, A-1 Douglas Skyraider. The A-1 was based on a design so old it reminded the jet jockeys of the famous S.P.A.D. biplane fighter of the First World War. The Skyraider had originally been intended as a torpedo diver bomber, created to see action in World War II. It had missed that war but had served admirably in Korea. In Vietnam, the Spads were used for close air support and rescue missions. During the latter, the Spad drivers flew dangerously low, and at suicidally slow speeds over hot areas in order to visually spot downed fliers, so that the rescue helicopter could get in, grab the guy, and get out in the shortest possible time. The Spads could carry up to four tons of ordnance in addition to its four 20-millimeter cannons. During rescue missions the weapons were used to protect the chopper, and, if possible, to keep the enemy from capturing the pilot waiting to be rescued.

"Three—Rio lead here," Wilson said. "I've finished refueling. Rio two and I are on the way to take over. E.T.A. seven minutes."

"Rog," Robbie said. He did some quick calculations. Chances were he could hightail it to his tanker, gas up, and be back in time to rendezvous with the Spad. Robbie figured it was pretty important that he be on hand when the Spad arrived in order to convince its pilot—if need be—that a rescue attempt was feasible; that the odds of getting Steve out were good enough to risk exposing a chopper and its crew. It was up to the Spad drivers to make that call, and though most of them were great guys, willing to give a downed pilot the benefit of the doubt, this particular situation that Steve had gotten himself into was pretty sticky. The area was very hot, and Steve had gone down very close to an enemy village. The village had sheltered SAMs, and where there were SAM sites there were usually soldiers . . .

Yeah, Robbie thought. *Considering the situation, it wouldn't be a bad idea at all to be present when the Spad showed up in order to be able to do a little fast-talking hard sell on Uncle Steve's behalf . . .*

Meanwhile, Robbie's Thud was no Spad, but he had his bird throttled down, and puttering along pretty damned low and slow as he crisscrossed the patch of jungle where he'd seen Steve's chute go in. The chute's beeper had cut off—probably torn loose and broken—as soon as Steve had hit the trees.

Robbie canted his port wing in order to study the wall of jungle where it met the clearing, but he saw nothing. He canted starboard wing and looked toward the village about a half mile distant. People were running toward the jungle, but they were too far away for Robbie to be able to make out if they were soldiers or civilians.

He considered buzzing over and using his cannon to slow them down. He didn't much like the idea of shooting civilians, if that's who they turned out to be, but Robbie was prepared to do whatever it took to give Steve a chance of being rescued—

The shrill beeper echoing in his headphones filled Robbie with hope. He almost dropped his airplane into a stall as he came around as tight as the stripes on a barber pole, frantic to get a good directional lock on the signal in case it abruptly faded.

"Rio four, Rio four," he radioed, once he had the signal pinpointed. "This is Rio three. If you read me, turn your beeper off—"

The beeper shut down, and Robbie heard Steve saying softly, as if he were afraid of his voice carrying too far: "This is Rio four. I read you loud and clear. I'm okay . . . I repeat, I'm okay . . . Think you could call me a taxi?"

"Rog, Four," Robbie replied, grinning. "You're a taxi."

His uncle's soft laughter coming through his headset sounded so clear and close it reminded him of the laughs they used to have together huddled around the campfire during those hunting trips— Oh, they seemed so long ago . . .

"Three, I sure hope you can get me out of here . . ." Steve murmured.

"Four, we've got fighters, and a Spad on the way," Robbie said encouragingly.

"They'd better hurry. I spotted a welcoming committee on its way out from the village on the way down."

"Rog, Four. You stick in the jungle to hide, but don't go too deep. You want to be able to get to the cleared area on the double when that chopper gets here."

"Rog." A pause. "It's tree city where I am. Where is the cleared area?"

"You got your compass?" Robbie asked.

"Rog."

Robbie was just finishing giving Steve the coordinates he needed to get a fix on his own position in the jungle when Major Wilson broke through his transmission.

"Rio three—Rio lead. We're above you flying top cover. Negative MIGs."

"Rog, boss, I'm on my way to meet that tanker," Robbie

said, giving Steve's coordinates to the two newly arrived Thuds. Rio two further relayed the directional fix on the rescue frequency to the Spad on its way in. As Robbie was pulling up to head off toward where his tanker was waiting he remembered the hunting party coming from the village. "Boss, there's enemy personnel going into the jungle to try and capture Four. Use your cannon—"

"Negative," Wilson said. "It's too late. We see them fading into the jungle right now . . ."

"Oh, shit," Robbie muttered fearfully. "Four, you monitoring the situation?"

There was no verbal reply, but just a sharp, crisp *click-click*. Robbie recognized the sound: Steve had pressed twice on his radio's transmit button.

Yeah, Steve knew the score, all right, Robbie thought. What's more, the enemy had to have been awfully close by for Steve not to have wanted to risk being overheard by replying verbally.

Hang in there, Uncle, Robbie thought. *Just hang loose. We'll get you out . . .*

(Four)

"—Four, you monitoring the situation?"

Steve, hunched down in the elephant grass, immediately squelched the volume on his emergency radio as he heard the soft chitterings of the enemy calling to each other. He studied the tangle of green all around him, wondering if it was his imagination, or had he really seen movement in the jungle undergrowth?

He punched his radio's transmit button twice to indicate to Robbie that he'd read his nephew's last transmission, and then began to retreat deeper into the jungle. As he ran he crouched low, ducking under hanging vines, using his compass. He did not want to wander too far from the jungle's edge . . .

He came upon a decent-looking hiding place: a shallow depression behind several fallen palm trees. He settled in, using some of the yellowed palm fronds to cover himself. He drew his gun, a .38 caliber Smith and Wesson Military & Police Model 10, with a four-inch barrel. He cocked its hammer. He pressed the squelched volume radio up against his ear, listening to the whispery exchanges going on between the Thud drivers flying RESCAP. He waited to hear that the Spad had arrived.

With his free ear he tried to listen for the enemy. It was going to be tricky, all right. He could remain silent for now, but when the Spad arrived he was going to have to signal, so that it could get a fresh directional fix, and then make verbal contact to prove that he was still okay: When the enemy captured a downed pilot they sometimes used his emergency radio's beeper to lure the vulnerable Search and Rescue chopper into a trap. That was why the Spad had final say concerning whether the chopper should come in. Usually the Spad driver required visual contact with the downed pilot. Steve could only hope that the driver he got would be a bit more flexible concerning this particular situation.

The forest around him was as thick as if he'd gone down in the Amazon, but Steve figured that he was no more than one hundred yards from the clearing. When the time came, after he'd convinced the Spad driver that he was savable, and the chopper was close by, he was going to have to make it back to the clearing in order to be picked up.

The problem was that the enemy knew that, as well. Most likely that had fanned out in a long—and, he hoped, thin—line between Steve and the jungle's edge. Most likely their intent would be to intercept him when he made his run for it. If he could succeed in breaking through their line the jungle would keep them from having a clear shot at him—

Until he reached the clearing. After that, he would just have to trust to his luck, and the guns of the airplanes flying low cover...

And the chopper *would* come, he told himself firmly, even

as he sweated and the palm fronds tickled his face, making him want to sneeze. Not *if* the chopper came, but *when*.

He could hear boots crunching grass. Snapping twigs. Gomer was sure conducting a noisy search . . .

Hell, why not? Steve thought. *This is their turf. They don't have to be quiet. I do.*

How long for the Spad to get here? Steve wondered. *Maybe another fifteen, twenty minutes. How long until Robbie got back from refueling? Maybe another ten . . . Sure wish he'd hurry up and get back.* For some dumb reason the thought of his nephew being close by comforted him . . .

He felt a tiny pinprick of fire on the inside of his wrist. He glanced at the spot. A bug—a reddish ant of some kind—had hooked into him with curved mandibles. Steve, grimacing, plucked it away.

Another dart of fire, this time on the back of his neck. His fingers danced madly to find the bug before it bit again. He glanced down and saw more ants crawling across his knees, exploring the tears in his flight suit. *Jesus Christ! The logs he was hiding behind must be their nest!*

He suffered more stinging bites. The pain was maddening. He wanted to run from this place, but he couldn't risk it: He could end up running right into the enemy.

Grin and bear it, he told himself as he tried without causing too much movement of the fronds camouflaging him to brush the bugs from his body. It was no use. He was crouched up against the logs and the bugs within the rotting wood were swarming over him. He could feel them in his hair, prowling the collar of his flight suit. He started to panic, thinking about what it would be like when they found their way inside his clothes to his cock, his rectum—

Stop it! Stop thinking about it! He clamped down on his imagination. *Deal with it. A few bug bites are nothing. You'll live. The choice is yours. You can take this, and in a little while you'll be having yourself a nice hot shower and then a scotch on the rocks. Dinner will be steak cooked medium rare, and fries with ketchup. Or you can move, and that decision will be the last one you'll make as a free man for who knows how long . . .*

"Rio four, this is Three . . ." the radio murmured in his ear. Robbie was back! "Four, this is Three, do you read?"

Steve took the radio away from his ear and listened hard. The enemy seemed to have moved off. Either that, or they were playing the same game he was: sitting quiet and listening for him to give himself away.

Fuck it, Steve thought. *Got to take the chance.*

He pushed the transmit button and hissed, "Three—Four. I'm okay. Can't talk. Enemy close."

"Rog," Robbie replied. "Spad will be here anytime now. Hang on."

Steak medium rare, and fries with ketchup, Steve kept repeating to himself silently as he huddled in his hole, the ants crawling and feasting on his flesh. *Steak and fries; a shower and a nice soft bed, not fish heads and rice and a filthy bamboo cage—*

He heard the North Vietnamese resuming their active search.

Please let that Spad get here soon!

(Five)

". . . Hang on," Robbie transmitted, flying a low orbit.

"Spad is here," Wilson radioed. He and his wingman were flying top cover to protect the Search and Rescue airplane from any MIGs that might decide to drop by.

"Rog," Robbie replied happily as he pulled back on his stick to join in flying top cover. "Four, you copy? Spad is here."

"Rog," Steve whispered. He sounded near the breaking point. Robbie wondered how close the enemy was.

"Hi, Rio four," the Spad driver called out brightly. "Mountie here. You know why they call me Mountie? 'Cause I always get my man . . ."

"Mountie—Four." Steve laughed thinly. "Don't let me ruin your record, pal . . ."

"No way, Four," Mountie reassured. "Okay. Turn your beeper on."

Robbie watched from his vantage point high in the sky as the Spad driver racked his little prop-driven relic around in a corkscrew in order to get his directional steer on Steve. Robbie began to feel optimistic. Everything about the Spad driver, his friendly patter and the way he handled his bird, led Robbie to think that this guy knew his business.

"Four—Mountie. Okay, pal, I got a real good fix. Shut off your beeper."

"Mountie, this is Rio three," Robbie interrupted. "You bringing in a chopper?"

"Chopper was waiting just outside the area. Already called it in on my second radio. You copying, Four?"

Click-Click.

"Mountie—Three," Robbie addressed the Spad driver. "You know the situation? There's enemy in the woods looking for him."

"Rog, Three," Mountie replied. "Four? You copy?"

Click-Click.

"I'm sorry, pal, but I need a verbal reply," Mountie said. "I need to know you're still okay so that I can keep that chopper coming . . ."

"*I'm here. I'm okay*—" Steve hissed. "They're right on top of me . . ."

"Rog. Chopper E.T.A. is five minutes," Mountie tried again to reassure Steve.

Robbie glanced toward the village. "A couple of trucks coming from the village," he muttered.

"Fuck!" Mountie swore savagely. "This sucks totally. By all rights I should cancel this—"

"Don't sweat those trucks!" Robbie implored, arming his cannon and banking his Thud around toward the village. "I'll take care of them."

"All right! Listen up, Four. I've got the chopper on my

other radio. E.T.A. three minutes. Move out to the clearing! Move out!"

(Six)

"Move out!"

Steve, huddled beneath the palm fronds with his radio pressed against his ear, didn't dare move so much as his finger on the transmit button. There was an enemy soldier standing on the opposite side of the logs. The soldier was facing in Steve's direction. Steve was hiding literally under the guy's nose.

The soldier was maybe five feet eight inches tall. He looked like he weighed all of one hundred thirty pounds, soaking wet. He was wearing black pajamas, and a pith helmet. He wore a thin mustache, its ragged ends curling over his protruding upper lip. Across his chest in "present arms" position was an automatic rifle with a shoulder sling, a wooden stock, and a curved, banana-style, ammo clip. *Soviet-manufactured, AK assault rifle*, Steve thought.

"Four, do you read?" Mountie was demanding harshly in Steve's ear. "Move out!"

Got to do it, Steve thought. *Can't wait for this guy to move on. Got to make my break for it now. I've got to reply to Mountie's transmission, else he'll think I'm done for and call off the chopper—*

His cocked .38 was clutched tightly in his hand. *Got to take this guy out with one shot, and then make tracks.*

He wondered how close the other soldiers were. It didn't matter. It was now or never.

Steve sprang up, scattering the palm fronds. The startled enemy soldier involuntarily stepped back. The rest of it happened in seeming slow motion. The soldier was bringing around his rifle as Steve lunged forward, blocking the rifle's barrel with his left arm, almost dropping his radio in the process. He jammed the .38's barrel deep into the fleshy area underneath the soldier's jaw, and pulled the trigger. The .38 boomed, and blood, brains, hair, and bits of skull exited the top of the enemy soldier's pith helmet. As the soldier twisted, the front blade sight on the revolver's barrel caught in the man's helmet chin strap. The gun was torn from Steve's sweaty fingers as the dead soldier crumpled. The revolver tumbled, disappearing into some weeds.

Got to have a gun, Steve thought. He scooped up the fallen AK rifle, slinging it over his shoulder as he ran.

"Mountie—Four!" he screamed into his radio, digging into his pocket for his compass. "On my way! On my way!"

"Rog, Four!" Mountie shouted back. "Chopper ETA ninety seconds!"

Steve could hear shouts and gunfire coming from behind him. He didn't look back, but just ran headlong through the jungle, his eyes on his compass, stumbling and staggering to keep his balance as he tripped over vines, ignoring the branches raising welts and cuts as they whipped across his face.

He broke through the jungle and into the clearing. The air was filled with the sound of gunfire as enemy bullets coming from the jungle whizzed past. He zigzagged across the field, toward the green and tan mottled HH-3 chopper coming in low toward him.

They've got to hit me anytime, Steve thought as he ran, but then the small-arms fire being directed at him was overwhelmed by the deep thunder of the Spad's quartet of 20 millimeters. Steve glanced up over his shoulder to see Mountie in his blue and silver, prop-driven dive bomber racking his bird along the jungle's edge, hosing down the trees to suppress the enemy.

The camo-painted chopper was setting down about thirty yards away. The chopper looked bottom-heavy thanks to its auxiliary fuel tanks. Its rotor wash flattened the weeds and plants all around it.

High in the sky Steve saw two Thuds orbiting on MIG-CAP cover. Flying much lower was Robbie's Thud sweeping down over the two canvas-sided trucks barreling toward the chopper. The Thud's Vulcan cannon began firing, and 20-millimeter tracer rounds began sending up geysers of dirt all around the trucks. The trucks' windshields imploded under the cannon barrage. They swerved wildly, spilling men. One of the trucks turned over on its side. The other exploded as Robbie's gun ignited its fuel tank.

Steve was at the chopper now.

"Let's go, buddy!" yelled one of the chopper's crew. He was wearing a drab green flight suit and matching helmet, and was waving frantically from the open bay door. Another crewman dressed similarly was firing a pedestal-mounted M-60 machine gun at the North Vietnamese soldiers advancing out of the jungle.

"Hey, I know the meter's running." Steve laughed as he threw himself into the chopper.

"Go!" the crewman yelled into the mike built into his helmet. The chopper began to lift off. The M-60 gunner kept up his lethal field of fire as the chopper swung free of the ground and began to veer away.

Steve studied the AK rifle for a moment, then braced it against his shoulder, aiming at the line of enemy soldiers, and experimentally squeezed the trigger. The assault rifle bucked, its barrel climbing rapidly as he fired off several bursts of full automatic fire that quickly emptied the thirty-round banana clip. He tossed the AK out the chopper as the M-60 gunner retracted his weapon and slid the door closed. Several of the AK's ejected shell casings were rattling around the chopper's floor. He picked one up and put it in his pocket. *Souvenir.*

The chopper gained altitude. As it left the vicinity the Spad pulled in close in order to fly escort.

"We're all right now," the crewman shouted to Steve over the noise of the chopper's eggbeaters. "You want any first aid for those cuts and scratches you got?"

Steve shook his head. "I can wait until we land." Exhausted, he curled up in a corner of the bay. "Could use a smoke, though. You got a smoke?"

The crewman nodded, settling down beside Steve and handing him a package of Salems. "Hey, I hear you bagged a pair of MIGs before you went down."

"Yep."

"Far out." The crewman grinned in admiration.

Steve nodded. The menthol cigarette tasted great. Steve looked at the bug bites on the backs of his hands. *No big deal*, he thought, smiling. *I made it. I'm out!*

"Bet you're looking forward to a nice hot shower and a drink when you get back to base, Colonel," the chopper crewman said, winking.

"You read my mind," Steve replied. *And a steak, medium rare . . .*

(Seven)

Muang Chi Air Force Base
Thailand

The steak came out of the kitchen somewhat well-done, but Steve Gold was in no mood to complain.

He'd arrived back at Muang Chi about 7 P.M. Steve had showered and changed and gone to the infirmary, where the medics treated his bumps and bruises and then sent him on his way to debriefing. There, he was told that his two MIG kills had been confirmed, and that credit for them would be added to his record.

Steve was glad to hear that, even as he waited apprehensively for the downside. It didn't matter who held the higher rank on the ground. In the air, the flight leader was the boss. Rio flight's lead, Major Wilson, had given Steve a direct order not to chase those MIGs, an order that Steve had disobeyed. When would the base commander get around to telling Steve what disciplinary action he faced?

It turned out that nothing was said about his dereliction, for which Steve was thankful but mystified as he left Operations and headed on over to the mess. He had his steak and fries, and then went over to the perpetually twilight-lit officers' club.

"Monday, Monday" by the Mamas and the Papas was on the jukebox as Steve entered the crowded, smoky club. He looked around and spotted Robbie and Major Wilson having themselves a couple of beers at a table beneath a neon Coca-Cola sign.

"Well, I'm glad to see your ugly face." Robbie laughed, standing up to embrace Steve as he came over.

"Roger that," Major Wilson said as he stood up to shake Steve's hand. Wilson was in his late thirties. He was clean-shaven, with thinning, curly auburn hair and light blue eyes. "Glad you made it back, Colonel."

"Thank you, Major. I owe it to my nephew here, and you, and Search and Rescue, of course," Steve replied. "I wish I could personally thank Mountie . . ."

"Spad drivers are like the Lone Ranger." Wilson laughed. "They never hang around for thanks."

Steve nodded. "Uh, Major . . ." he began uneasily. "During debriefing I kept waiting for someone to say something about how I bugged out on you guys in order to go MIG hunting, but it was like the brass never heard that part of the story—"

"Yes, well . . ." Wilson smiled thinly. "Let's say that I forgot to mention that little item during my own debriefing. According to my report, you had my permission to chase those MIGs."

"Thanks, Major," Steve said gratefully.

Before the major could reply, Lieutenants Ritchie and Toback, two of the pilots from last night's rap session, called out to Steve from the bar.

"Congratulations, Colonel!" Toback shouted.

"You sure showed 'em, my man, Colonel, sir!" Ritchie was grinning. "Right *on, brother!*"

"You see?" Wilson said quietly. "That's why I left your insubordination out of my report. Your exploits today have already taken on legendary status. You bagged two MIGs and almost outran three SAMs. On account of you the Thud drivers around here are walking with their heads held high for the first time in months. And our pilots will make what you accomplished today even more wondrous as they retell it to the new guys as they rotate in." Wilson shrugged. "You did us a big favor, Colonel. You did your job. You fired us up by setting an aggressive example. You've got the spirit, and you've instilled a bit of it into our guys. I didn't want to cloud the issue by hauling you up on insubordination charges. We've already had more than enough of that sort of schizoid, Simon says bureaucratic, red-tape bullshit coming out of Saigon and Washington . . ."

"Yeah, well, thanks again," Steve said softly.

"And your nephew here has made a pretty good reputation for himself in his own right," Wilson added. "The way he hung in for you, and knocking out that SAM with a Sidewinder, and the way he took out those trucks . . . Well, he's impressed a lot of important people by illustrating the proper, aggressive way to back up a fellow pilot. He's being put in for the Silver Star, and I'd wager that he's going to get it."

"Like I said," Steve responded, smiling at Robbie, "I owe him my life."

"I'd say that you do." Wilson nodded firmly, shaking Steve's hand a final time before taking his leave. "I'd say that you do . . ."

"There's nothing I wouldn't do for this kid . . ." Steve called out after Wilson as the major walked away.

"Is that a fact, Uncle Steve?" Robbie asked innocently.

Steve put his arm around his nephew. "That's a fact. Anything you ever want from me, you just name it," Steve fervently swore.

"Far out," Robbie enthused. "Hey, listen up, everybody!" he shouted. "My uncle's going to war college!"

"You little sonofabitch!" Steve gasped, looking around balefully at the other pilots, who were now all grinning at him, and *applauding*, for chrissakes. "Come *on*!" Steve hissed. "When I said anything, I didn't mean—"

"No way, Steve." Robbie grinned devilishly. "I'm not letting you off the hook . . ."

"Sonofabitch," Steve grumbled. "You're gonna be the death of me . . ."

"Hey, you said yourself that I saved your life, right? You owe me, Uncle. Going to war college and doing your best is the way I expect to be repaid."

Steve stared darkly at his nephew.

"You gonna back down, or you gonna keep your word, Uncle Steve?" Robbie demanded.

Sonofabitch— "You want it," Steve mumbled, pausing to take a deep breath. "You got it . . ."

"What?" Robbie teased. "I couldn't hear you?"

"I said you want it, you got it!" Steve roared, feeling like a guy who just got roped into making a high dive into a very shallow pool . . . "*Sonofabitch!* I need a drink, and I mean a *real* drink, not one of those piss-assed beers—"

"Colonel Gold?"

Steve turned to see a young Air Force sergeant standing at attention. "What can I do for you?" he asked.

"Orders for you just came into Operations," the sergeant replied. "I was told to get them to you on the double, sir."

He handed Steve the sheaf of papers, which Steve quickly scanned.

"Holy shit . . ." he murmured.

"What's up?" Robbie demanded.

"I said I'd pay you back for saving me by going to war college, and I will," Steve said. "But it's going to have to wait a bit."

"How come?"

"The rest of my tour here has been canceled," Steve said. "I'm to get back to the States ASAP." Perplexed, he stared at his nephew as he held up his orders. "Robbie, it says here I'm going to Israel . . ."

CHAPTER 19

(One)

**Gold Aviation and Transport
Burbank, California
11 September 1966**

"This way, Steve," Herman Gold said, leading his son out of the bright California sunshine into the cool, dark quiet of the deserted, unlit hangar.

It was a Saturday afternoon. Gold was informally dressed in brown corduroy trousers, a moss green and white vertically striped shirt-jac (vertical stripes were supposedly good camouflage for a stout belly), tan loafers, and a loden green leather car coat. He'd grown a beard, which had come in crimson, and which he kept closely trimmed, like the short ruffle of red curls that now wreathed his ears. Erica had taken to calling him her "strawberry Falstaff."

Gold began flicking switches on the light panel near the

door. One by one the fluorescent banks hanging from the steel ceiling rafters flickered to life above a large, sleek, jet airplane. The airplane was seventy-four feet long and seventeen feet high. She was painted ghost gray, with scarlet and turquoise detailing on her nose and tail. On her wings and rear fuselage were the Stars and Bars, and the X-prefix number that set her apart as a prototype.

"There you are, Steve," Gold said. "The GAT X-11 Super-BroadSword."

Steve whistled softly. "She's a beauty, all right, Pop."

"Isn't she, though . . ." Gold smiled. "You know, as far as I'm concerned there's still nothing like the thrill of bringing a new airplane into the world."

He walked around to the stern, to point up toward the double tail pipes. "Those are twin turbofans, each rated at twelve thousand pounds of thrust. She's got a seventeen hundred mile-per-hour top speed, and a service ceiling exceeding sixty thousand feet. Range exceeds thirty-five hundred miles on internal fuel, and that's carrying up to fifteen tons of ordnance."

"Whoo-wee!" Steve exclaimed. "And I thought the Thud was a workhorse . . ."

"The Thunderchief was, in her day," Gold remarked. "But it's a new day dawning. The day of the Super-BroadSword. The first airplanes off our production lines are being delivered to the Air Force this week. They're calling her the F-110. We've got high hopes she'll make a big difference to the war effort."

Gold watched his son slowly circle the aircraft. Steve was wearing wheat-colored jeans, black sneakers, a gray sweatshirt, an L.A. Dodgers baseball cap, and a battered leather A-2 flight jacket circa World War II, still emblazoned with Steve's Pacific Theater squadron markings.

"She's got the same Vector-A system that you sent to Israel, isn't that right?" Steve asked.

"The Vector A is only one of the many aces up this airplane's sleeve," Gold said. "She's loaded with innovations. First and foremost, she's got variable sweep, swing wings.

The pilot can electrically pivot the wings into swept forward position for takeoffs and low-speed ground support strafing runs, or he can sweep the wings back right up against the tail's horizontal stabilizers, to form what in effect is a solid delta wing that is ideal for supersonic flight."

"So now the pilot's got one more thing to think about," Steve said. "I pity tomorrow's fighter jocks; they're gonna need three hands to deal with all the gizmos these birds carry."

"That's why she's a twin-seater," Gold said. "She had to be. There's just too much instrumentation. You need an electronics/weapons officer on board."

"A bear," Steve mused.

"Huh?"

"That's what the pilots call their backseaters in Vietnam, bears, as in trained bears."

"I see..." Gold nodded, trying hard not to react negatively to Steve's attitude. "Well, the Super-BroadSword's backseater will be sitting *side by side* with the pilot. We've gotten very good reaction on another innovation. In the event that the crew has to bail out the entire cockpit becomes an escape capsule. It lifts off by means of explosive charge, and even carries a chaff dispenser to help ward off enemy radar tracking. On the ground the cockpit can be used as an emergency shelter..."

"That sounds cool, Pop," Steve said softly.

"And as I was saying before," Gold pressed on. "She's got a full complement of black-box technology. Enough, we hope, to take her well into the next decade of electronic warfare..."

"Black boxes," Steve scoffed. "What about guns? You were always a main advocate of guns on airplanes. The more guns the better, you always used to say."

"Oh, the Super-BroadSword will have a gun, don't you worry. We're not going to make the same mistake that Brower-Dunn made with the Sun Wolf jet fighter," Gold added firmly, thinking back on how during its initial design phase Brower-Dunn had made provisions for its Sun Wolf to carry a gun, but then scraped the provision in favor of a fuller complement of short- and long-range air-to-air missiles. In Vietnam, however, Sun Wolf pilots learned just how handy a cannon could be during close-in dogfights, so now the Air Force was scrambling to retrofit their Sun Wolfs with external gun pods.

"You know what, Pop?" Steve sighed. "Someday you guys are going to invent a black box to fly the airplane, and then what will happen to us pilots . . . ?"

"That will never happen," Gold scoffed. "No machine will ever replace a good pilot."

"I don't know . . ." Steve mused, more to himself than to Gold. "Those SAMs on my ass handled themselves pretty good . . ."

The Vietnam thing again, Gold thought, frowning with concern. Steve was here on interim leave, staying with Gold and his wife at their Bel-Air home, so Gold was aware that his son was seriously troubled. Steve used to eat like a horse, but these days he picked at his food. He was drinking fairly heavily, as well, Gold knew, but what most concerned Gold was that Steve was having trouble sleeping because of nightmares.

Gold had been putting off bringing up the subject of what was bothering Steve because he didn't want his son to think he was prying. On the other hand, he knew Steve . . . His son wasn't going to open up unless he received a little coaxing.

"I guess you went through a pretty rough experience over in Vietnam," Gold began. "Being shot down and all . . ."

"Hell, I didn't have it hard at all," Steve replied, sounding almost pugnacious. "The pilots who go down and *don't* get rescued are the ones who have it hard."

"Yes, I know that . . ." Gold said quietly, trying to defuse his son's seeming hostility.

Steve turned away from his examination of the Super-BroadSword to walk back toward Gold. "I'm sorry for my tone of voice, Pop." He hesitated. "I guess I've been acting a little down in the dumps, huh?"

"Your mother and I are concerned about you," Gold agreed. "I don't mean to pry, but I wish you'd talk to me, son."

"No, that's okay. I want to talk about it...I guess..." Steve pulled a pack of cigarettes out of his jacket's flapped patch pocket, then paused, looking back at the aircraft. "Can I smoke in here?"

Gold nodded. "But go on, you were saying—?"

"Right," Steve said, lighting his smoke. "But let's keep what I'm going to say to yourself, okay, Pop? I don't think Mom could understand..."

"Okay..."

"Well..." Steve looked uncomfortable. "It might sound crazy to you, but what's gotten to me is that soldier..."

"That...soldier?" Gold echoed puzzled.

"The one I shot."

"Ah...Yes..."

"Now, before you say anything, Pop, let me tell you that I *do* know that I had to do it. I mean, it was him or me, I understand that, and I'm really glad that it was him..." He paused, shaking his head, his brow furrowed and his lips compressed into a flat line. "This is really hard to explain, but I'll do my best. You see, Pop, I felt great for a while just after the rescue, but pretty soon I began to feel different. Kind of depressed...I began remembering little bits and pieces of the experience. You know the way a fighter pilot will flash on aspects of a dogfight after the fact?"

Gold smiled reassuringly. "Let me tell you, I'm sixty-eight years old, and to this day I have such flashes about the dogfights I experienced during the First World War...It's perfectly normal for something that intense to stay with you—"

"Mostly what I flash on is the look on that guy's face just before I pulled the trigger," Steve cut him off. "Now I can't help thinking that maybe he wasn't a regular soldier at all. Maybe he was just some little gomer farmer who was peacefully minding his own business, you know? And then I got shot down, and somebody in the village militia or something shoves a rifle into this guy's hands and tells him he's got to forget about weeding his garden for now, and go help search for the big, bad, war-mongering American." Steve dragged deeply on his cigarette. "You know what I'm saying, Pop? Maybe that poor jerk was standing around out there in the jungle right on top of my hiding place because he was scared shitless, thought he was safe where he was, and didn't know what else to do with himself. From his point of view I was probably some cross between Attila the Hun and Dracula." Steve paused. "And from his point of view, he turned out to be right..."

"They say on the news that over there it's almost impossible to tell who's a civilian and who's military," Gold quietly pointed out.

"Yeah, that's true, but so what?" Steve demanded impatiently. "I mean, it doesn't make me feel any better..."

"I think that if that soldier had been given the chance, he would have captured or shot you," Gold firmly continued. "You were in a war, son, but maybe because you dipped in and then out of it so fast you didn't get the chance to emotionally prepare yourself—get the proper mindset. The facts are that you've been in three wars now. You've shot down so *many* planes. How many of those pilots you bagged in the Pacific or over Korea lived to tell the tale?"

"I hear you," Steve acknowledged. "I know I've killed before, but never like this. Christ, Pop! It was so *close*, you know? I guess it was being on the ground that made all the difference. That little guy was standing no farther away from me than you are now. I looked into his *eyes*, Pop. I saw him die." He shivered. "I tell you, I thank God I'm a fighter pilot. I don't think I could have hacked it as a ground soldier. I take my hat off to all those guys in all those wars, on *both* sides."

"I've always felt exactly the same way," Gold confided. "Sure, we fighter pilots put up with our own special risks, but at least we know that when we tangle with an opponent up in the sky our adversary is trained to be there. It's a fair fight..." He paused. "But you know, it was a fair fight as far as you were concerned in that jungle. No! I take that back. It wasn't *fair*: The odds were stacked way against you!"

Steve smiled tentatively. "Thanks, Pop. Thanks for listening."

"You've got to get an emotional handle on this . . ."

"I know," Steve admitted. "What's gonna help is to become involved with something. That's why I'm looking forward to going to Israel, and climbing into the cockpit of that MIG-21 . . . Best thing for me, I think; to be out and doing something active, to be able to *fly* . . ." He smiled. "I've got to confess, all the time when you were smuggling those Vector-A systems to the Israelis I never thought there would be a payback; that the Israelis would manage to get their hands on a MIG-21, the Russians' most advanced fighter plane."

"*I* knew they would," Gold smugly stated. "They're an amazing people, and the country is an amazing place. I look forward to your reaction to Tel Aviv . . ."

"I'm sure I'll have a great time. Why not? You evidently had a ball there . . ."

"They treated your mother and me like royalty."

"And rightfully so." Steve laughed. "They should have erected a statue to you considering what you did for them . . ."

"I did what I thought was the right thing." Gold shrugged. "You know, your mother didn't want to go, but I talked her into it, using the excuse that I needed to see how those Vector-A systems were fitting into the Israelis' Tyran fighters. Once we were over there Erica had a ball sightseeing . . . By the way, did you know I've started taking Hebrew lessons?" he added proudly.

"Mom told me." To Steve's credit, he kept a straight face, but Gold could see the amused sparkle in his eye.

"Well, knowing another language never hurt," Gold said defensively.

"Right on, Pop . . ." Steve chuckled.

"Hmmm . . . You know what they call it when you come home to Israel for good?" Gold asked. "An *aliyah*."

"Pop, L.A.'s my home," Steve chided affectionately. "I'm only going for a little while, and anyway, I'm not even Jewish."

"You're half Jewish," Gold responded adamantly. "You're my son, and blood is blood."

Steve was studying him. "Gee, you're really getting into this, aren't you?"

"It's like I told you once," Gold mumbled. "A man's heritage—his roots—becomes more important to him when he gets old."

"*Older*," Steve corrected him firmly. "You're not old yet."

"Right," Gold replied wryly. He heard someone entering the hangar, and turned to see Don Harrison and his son Andy in the doorway. "Listen," Gold whispered quickly to Steve as the others approached. "You let me know if you want to talk more about that other thing."

"Will do, Pop," Steve said, putting his hand on Gold's shoulder. "Thanks—"

Gold pretended not to hear. "Hello," he called out in cheerful greeting to his son-in-law and grandson. "What are you two doing here on such a lovely Saturday afternoon?"

"We called the house," Don Harrison replied, smiling. "Erica said you were here."

For the past year or so, Don had been gradually letting his blond hair grow down past his shirt collar and over his ears. He'd also cultivated a broad, curving mustache, and had replaced his tortoiseshell eyeglasses for a pair of gold wire rims. Gold's daughter Suzy had been nagging her husband to start dressing "mod," but Don was sticking stubbornly to his Ivy League wardrobe. Today he was wearing tan chinos, a sky blue button-down collar cotton oxford shirt, a plum-colored crewneck sweater, and mahogany penny loafers with no socks.

"Your grandson wanted a visit with you," Don said. "So here we are . . ." He looked down at his son. "Right, boss?"

"Right!" Andy exclaimed. The boy ran toward Gold, who bent to embrace him.

"What do you think?" Gold winked at Steve. "Your nephew is big for eight years old, right?"

"He's tall, all right, Pop." Steve pretended to frown. "I think he's gonna be too tall to be a fighter pilot when he grows up."

"No way!" Andy said hotly. He had blond hair like both his parents, and his mother's big brown eyes. He was dressed in elastic-waisted corduroy jeans rolled up at the cuffs, a polo shirt, and an L.A. Dodgers warm-up jacket that was way too large. "Grampa, can we go flying today?"

"Well, I don't know..." Gold said, sounding troubled.

"What's the matter?" Steve asked.

"I've been laying off flying for a little while," Gold murmured to his son. "I've been on this damned high blood pressure medication, you know... There's some side effects..." He shook his head. "I don't trust myself soloing anymore. Especially not with the boy in the airplane..."

"You want me to take him up?" Steve suggested.

"Would you mind?" Gold said gratefully. "The Cessna's here on the company airstrip, all ready to go." He looked down at Andy. "How about it, Andy? You want to fly with your uncle? He's a colonel in the Air Force, you know..."

"Sure!" Andy said. He looked back at his father. "Daddy, can I?"

"Sure, if your uncle wants to take you..."

"My pleasure," Steve said. "This trip home has been the first opportunity I've had to spend time with Andy. He's a great kid..."

"Well, Suzy and I think so." Don smiled.

"You coming flying, Daddy?" Andy asked.

Don shook his head, laughing. "I build 'em, I don't fly 'em... You guys go on."

"Come on then, Andy," Steve said. "Let's go—"

As he and the boy walked away, Gold saw Steve take his Dodgers cap off and put it on Andy's head. "Here, you'd better have this," Steve told the boy. "It goes with your jacket..."

(Two)

Harrison watched his brother-in-law walk away with his son. As always, he felt the stab of anxiety for the boy's well-being he suffered whenever Andy was out of his presence.

"You really don't mind, do you?" Herman asked as Steve and Andy left the hangar.

"I said I didn't, and I meant it," Harrison replied, maybe just a little too stridently as he tried to force the anxiety out of his mind.

"Thanks," Herman was saying. "Being with kids seems to relax Steve. It always has."

"I know," Harrison said, smiling. "He was the same way with Robbie when he was growing up, remember?"

Herman nodded, sighing. "Too bad Steve never found the right girl," he mused. "He could have benefited from kids of his own... It would have grounded him..."

"Is that an intentional pun, or wishful thinking?" Harrison asked, laughing.

"Huh? Oh! Grounded... I see..." Herman chuckled. "No, I guess I meant having kids of his own would have *rooted* him, given him something to fall back on when the time came. A man can't be a fighter pilot forever, you know..."

"I know," Harrison said quietly. "Having a son of his own to raise might have made that difficult transition a little easier." He brightened. "But it's not too late for him. He's only forty-two, and he looks ten years younger—"

"That he gets from his mother." Herman laughed.

"Except, of course, for his receding hairline," Harrison teased.

"*That*, he got from me," Herman sighed. "But seriously,

you really think it's not too late for him to meet the right woman? You and Suzy don't happen to know a likely candidate, do you?" he added hopefully.

Harrison pondered it. "Not really, Herman." He laughed uneasily. "I mean, no offense, but it would take one tough lady to put up with the likes of Steve on a permanent basis, wouldn't it . . . ?"

"Tell me something I don't know," Herman sighed. "Anyway, it really *is* very kind of you to let him spend time with Andy."

"If Steve does half the job with Andy that he did with Robbie, my boy will be a better man for it," Harrison said earnestly.

"Yes, Robbie has turned out to be quite something, hasn't he?" Herman said proudly. "He got the Silver Star. And he's a captain . . . I just wish he and Andy were closer," he abruptly blurted.

Harrison's smile faded. Robbie had always been cold and aloof toward his half brother, barely acknowledging Andy's existence. Harrison and his wife had brooded about it many times. Psychological explanations sprang easily to mind, but all the Freudian mumbo jumbo in the world didn't alter the fact that the schism existed.

"Don't get me wrong," Herman said hurriedly. "I'm very glad that you were able to make your own peace with your stepson. You've been a good father to him—No! Not just a good *stepfather*," he said. "A good *father*, period."

Harrison blushed. The way he saw it, he didn't deserve any credit for finally coming around and doing just what he'd been obligated to do all along once he'd married Suzy. "Robbie sure grew up to be a damn fine pilot, didn't he?" he said, anxious to change the subject. "And I don't say that just because he saved Steve's ass in Vietnam . . ."

"And he saved it for a good cause, too." Herman chuckled. "I loved the way Robbie roped Steve into agreeing to go to war college."

"Right?" Harrison laughed. "When Robbie wrote us to tell us about it he said that it felt good to return the gesture. You know, he's never forgotten how Steve convinced him to go to college years ago . . ."

"First things first, though," Herman remarked. "Israel is at the top of Steve's agenda."

"What I still don't get is why the Israelis asked for Steve specifically," Harrison mused. "I'd think it'd be far more useful to send an aviation engineer to look over that MIG . . ."

"Like yourself, you mean?" Herman gleefully challenged.

Once again Harrison felt himself blushing. "Well, *yes* . . . I don't mind admitting that it would be intensely interesting to find out what makes our adversary's fighter planes tick . . ."

"The government is interested in finding out the MIG-21's *capabilities*, not what makes her tick," Herman pointed out. "And that calls for a *pilot*; one who can take the MIG to the true boundaries of her performance envelope and then bring her back in one piece. There's no one better suited for that job than Steve."

"Assuming what you just said is true, that still doesn't explain why Steve was chosen. There are so many full-time test pilots out there, why select a fighter pilot to do the job?"

"The MIG's a fighter, not an experimental plane, so why *not* choose a fighter pilot to put her through its paces?" Herman argued. "And don't forget, this is a very sensitive international situation we've got on our hands. The Russians are already hopping mad at Israel for stealing the plane from Iraq in the first place. If they ever found out that the Israelis were sharing their secret with us, all hell would break loose."

"I get your point," Harrison said. "The CIA and Air Force are not increasing the security risk by using Steve because he's already privy to the Vector-A deal we struck with the Israelis, and he's got CIA experience . . ." He paused. "Still, for the Air Force to pull Steve out of Vietnam the way it did . . ." He snapped his fingers. "Oh, I get it, *now*—Herman, did you put in the fix for Steve? Is *that* how he got this assignment?"

"Me? Mix in?" Herman protested.

Harrison fixed him with a skeptical look.

"Well, anyway, not *this* time..." Herman said weakly. "Honestly, Don. All I know is what Jack Horton at the CIA told me, which was confirmed by my contacts in the Air Force. The Israelis specifically insisted that Steven Gold be sent to examine the MIG, and the United States was so happy to be getting this opportunity that the government would have sent the Mickey Mouse Club if the Israelis had asked."

CHAPTER 20

(One)

Lod Airport
Tel Aviv, Israel
12 December 1966

As the jetliner descended, Steven Gold caught a glimpse of the glinting, deep blue sea, and then the urban sprawl that was the city of Tel Aviv. He leaned his forehead against the oval plastic window to watch the jet's shadow racing across the yellow sand dunes, and heard the electric drone of the jetliner's landing gear being lowered. A few moments later the airliner touched down on the runway.

"Ladies and gentlemen," the intercom crackled. "Trans European Airlines welcomes you to Israel. The temperature is sixty-four degrees. The sky is clear. Thank you again for giving us this opportunity to serve you, and we hope that . . ."

Steve tuned out the rest. He ignored the flashing seat belt sign, standing and stretching to get out the kinks as the lumbering GAT 909I jetliner taxied to a stop. He ran his fingers across his scratchy beard. He could do with a shower and a shave. The past forty hours he'd flown from L.A. to New York, endured a two-hour stopover before his flight to London, and then boarded this flight to Tel Aviv. It had been an eye-opener and a nuisance dealing with airlines' booking agents for a guy used to traveling the Air Force way, but both the CIA and the Mossad had insisted that Steve arrive here incognito, like any tourist. Evidently everybody had the heebie-jeebies about the *Russians* finding out the *Israelis* were letting the *Americans* take a peek at their MIG-21 . . .

Steve shrugged into his jacket, grabbed his carry-on bag, and left the airplane. Outside the breeze was warm and dry. He put on his sunglasses against the bright glare of the Mediterranean sun, and then joined the rest of the airliner's bleary-eyed passengers trudging across the tarmac toward the customs building.

At least Steve *thought* it was the customs building. Who could tell? All the signs were in hieroglyphiclike Hebrew. *Too bad Pop isn't here with me*, he thought, chuckling, *assuming the old man has gotten far enough in his Hebrew primer—*

A man wearing wire-rimmed aviator sunglasses, and dressed in brown corduroys, a white turtleneck, and a khaki bush jacket fell in beside Steve. "Mister Gold?" the man murmured so softly that only Steve could have heard him.

"Yeah?"

"Shalom, Mister Gold. I'm here to meet you . . ." The guy took Steve's arm and gently steered him away from the rest of the passengers. Only then did he flash a picture I.D. "I'm Dov Sachar. Lieutenant Sachar, of the IAF."

"Israeli Air Force?" Steve murmured, looking the guy over. He was in his thirties, thin, and hawk-nosed, with longish, auburn hair.

"I apologize for not addressing you by rank just now, Colonel, but as you're aware, we'd much prefer that your visit here pass unnoticed."

"Sure, I understand. How'd you recognize me?"

"I had a picture, not that I needed it." He smiled. "We don't get many tourists wearing one of those."

Steve looked down at himself. He was wearing white sneakers, tan chinos, a navy blue cotton polo shirt, and his A-2. "You must be referring to my flight jacket . . . Sorry about that. I know I'm not supposed to be in uniform, but I figured an old World War Two jacket wouldn't give me away."

"No problem," the Israeli said.

"Thanks." Steve smiled. *Because I'm not giving this jacket up*, he added to himself. He'd worn the A-2 during his stint in the Pacific and in Korea, and in both war zones things had gone just fine. The only time he hadn't had this jacket was in Vietnam . . . "I've gotten kind of superstitious about having it with me, you see . . ."

"Like I said, no problem," the Israeli repeated. "Leather jackets are very popular here, although I must say that I've never seen one like yours," he added, studying the squadron and USAAF patches that adorned the jacket's front and shoulders, and looking at the faded, painted design that took up almost the entire back: a turquoise shield emblazoned with two large, scarlet vees in its upper left and lower right corners. Connecting the vees, running diagonally from upper left to lower right was a scarlet lightning bolt.

"What's this stand for, Colonel?" the Israeli asked, pointing to the shield.

"The Vigilant Virgins," Steve replied.

"The *what?*"

Steve shook his head, smiling. "It's a long story, pal. It starts in the Solomon Islands, around 1943. Maybe we can get into it another time . . ." He paused. "I'm sorry, but what'd you say your name was?"

"Dov."

"Got it." Steve nodded. "Like the bird."

"Good one!" Dov grinned obligingly. "If you'll follow

me, we can skip customs and passport check-in. Your bags are being collected. They'll be waiting for us at the car."

"You speak English fairly well," Steve remarked as Dov led him out through a guarded gate toward the parking area.

"I ought to, Colonel. I was born in Albuquerque."

"I see . . . and your folks named you Dov. . .?"

"My parents named me Leon, Colonel," the Lieutenant replied patiently. "I changed my name when I came here to live." He paused in front of an old-looking, dark blue Mercedes-Benz four-door sedan. "Well, here we are."

"This is the car?" Steve murmured.

"Yeah." Dov opened the trunk, and then stood aside so that Steve could check to see that all of his luggage had been loaded. "You look perturbed, Colonel. Are we missing any bags?"

"No, nothing's wrong . . . But I do have a question . . ."

"So ask."

"Well, this is a *Mercedes*," Steve began. "A *German* car," he added carefully. "Pardon me for saying this, but considering what happened to the Jews in Germany, and all . . . Well, I'm kind of surprised the IAF would—"

"Yeah, I get the idea," Dov cut him off. "Look, in this country we must be practical, Colonel. We cannot afford otherwise." He smiled. "Why bite off our own nose to spite our face? Mercedes builds good cars."

Steve gestured to the front passenger side of the Mercedes. "Can I ride shotgun?"

"Climb in, Colonel."

"Call me Steve," he said as he settled back against the Mercedes' red leather upholstery. His father had told him about how informal the Israelis were concerning titles.

Dov started up the engine and pulled away. "What's next is up to you, Steve. We can go directly to the flat in Tel Aviv where you can get some rest, or we can go out to the base where we've got the MIG—"

"Let's go to the base," Steve said, taking out his cigarettes. "I want a look at that MIG." He winked at Dov. "That way I'll have something to dream about when I do go to sleep."

"The base it is," Dov said.

"Smoke?" Steve asked, offering the pack to Dov.

"Is the Pope Catholic?" Dov replied, reaching for a cigarette.

They followed a blacktop road out of the airport, through a densely settled rural area. The traffic was heavy, the drivers aggressive in their worn-out midget, foreign automobiles and trucks. Seemingly oblivious to the strident mechanized traffic were the Arabs in their ancient-looking horse-drawn carts plodding along the road's shoulder. Mixed in with the stink of engine exhaust and horse manure was the salty tang of the sea, the scent of eucalyptus, and the aroma of oranges.

"I didn't know the Arabs still wore all that Sheik of Araby stuff," Steve remarked. "The flowing robes, and that headdress thing, and all . . ."

"Here, the more things change, the more they remain the same," Dov said as he slowed, and then turned off onto a dirt road pretty much vacant of traffic. "Downtown Tel Aviv is just a couple more kilometers the way we were going," he said as the Mercedes bounced and rattled its way over the mounds and ruts. "Forgive the condition of the road," he added, glancing at Steve. "The rainy season has ended only a few weeks ago. The damage done has yet to be repaired."

Steve studied the terrain. They'd left the ocean breezes and towns and villages behind. Here the hilly landscape was covered with thorny, dark green scrub above which oak trees with thick, gnarled trunks spread their branches wide.

"What's that sweet smell?" Steve asked.

"Carob," Dov replied. "Usually it grows northward of here, but we've planted some to see what'll happen."

"This all reminds me somewhat of the American Southwest."

"Somewhat," Dov agreed. "Like certain parts of Arizona, maybe . . ."

"Right." Steve chuckled. "I keep forgetting you were born in America."

"Don't worry about it." Dov smiled. "Lots of times I forget, too."

The Mercedes slowed to turn left onto an even narrower road, and rounded a bend to come upon a checkpoint gate barring the way. A pair of bearded soldiers armed with matt black machine pistols, and wearing berets and desert camo uniforms, appeared from out of a tent along the side of the road. The soldiers gave the Mercedes a hard look as it rolled to a stop. Steve heard Dov and the sentries grunt and cough their way through an exchange in Hebrew, and then the guards waved them on.

"All of our air bases are secret, of course," Dov explained wryly as they drove away. "But this one is *really* secret . . ."

Over the Mercedes' mellow rumble Steve heard the buzz saw sound of higher-pitched engines revving. He looked back to see another pair of armed soldiers astride motorcycles quickly overtaking them. The cyclists managed to find the room on the narrow road to whizz past, and then took up escort positions in front of the Mercedes.

"This way no other sentries will challenge us," Dov said.

They drove a few more kilometers, rounded another bend in the road, and the air base came into view. The setup reminded Steve of the rugged, World War II frontline bases the Seabees had racheted together for the Marine VMF and the USAAF fighter squadrons in the Pacific. The Israeli base's facilities were spread out, to decrease the likelihood of losing everything in an air attack. Hidden among the groves of trees was a squat, prefab, flight control/operations complex surrounded by skeletal radar and radio towers, and a half dozen low-slung airplane hangars. Camouflage netting strung high from poles and tree branches formed a protective canopy over the vehicle and airplane parking areas. As they drove past, Steve heard the high-pitched whistle of a jet engine, and saw a dun-colored, delta-winged, Tyran II fighter emblazoned with the blue and white, six-pointed Star of

David taxiing out from beneath the netting, toward the concrete runways.

"She's a beauty, isn't she?" Dov asked, gesturing toward the plane.

"You bet." Steve glanced at him. "I never asked you, Dov. Are you a pilot?"

"No," the Israeli said sadly. "I wish I were. Like most of us in the Air Force I tried to take the training—we need fighter pilots desperately—but I washed out. So I serve in administration."

"You live here full time?"

"No, only the pilots and maintenance crews live here," Dov said. "Over there on the other side of the control tower are a number of flower gardens. Interspersed among them are the living quarters."

"Who did all the landscaping?" Steve asked.

"The pilots and the air crews, of course," Dov said, sounding as if he'd been surprised by the question. "They do it in their spare time."

"I can't imagine American Air Force personnel spending their off-duty hours gardening," Steve said, amused.

"Here, we're glad to do it," Dov replied seriously as he pulled up in front of a tan-painted hangar. He shut off the motor and then turned slightly in his seat to face Steve. "You see, we *never* tire of tending to our country. For so very long we didn't have one, so now we don't take anything for granted."

"I understand," Steve said softly, feeling a bit ashamed about all the things that Americans took for granted.

"Well, you go on into the hangar and take your first look at the MIG," Dov said. "I'll run over to Operations and let them know you're here."

Steve got out of the car and went into the open hangar. His heart was pounding with excitement. She was there, all right, caged beneath the ceiling lights—

A MIG-21—The delta-winged beauty was the latest brilliant product of the awesome collaboration between Artem Mioyan and Mikhail Gurevich, Russia's premier aircraft designers. It was the MIG-21 that was the burr under the blankets of the Thud drivers and Phantom crews in Vietnam's mist-shrouded skies, and until now, U.S. Intelligence had been forced to make do with grainy, blurred, recon photos of the Soviets' most advanced war bird on the ground or in flight—

Until now—

Steve slowly walked around the MIG, luxuriating in the opportunity to meticulously look her over. It was hard to concentrate; he couldn't believe his luck. To a fighter jock there could be nothing more desirable than being given the opportunity to check out the competition . . .

Steve heard a car pulling up outside the hangar. *Probably Dov, come back to hijack me to some boring briefing,* he thought, and hurried to finish his preliminary inspection.

The MIG's exterior was drab gray. She had until very recently belonged to the Iraqi Air Force, but now that country's insignia had been expunged from the MIG's wings and fuselage, replaced by the Star of David. She was just a bit over fifty feet long, with a stubby, twenty-four-foot wingspan. Like earlier series MIGs, the 21 had a wide snout that served to duct air to her engine, but unlike any other jet fighter that Steve had seen, the 21 had a conical radar pod protruding out of the nose duct's center, the way the ink tip protrudes from out of the barrel of a retractable ballpoint pen. Her canopy was unique as well. It was neither bubble-shaped like earlier MIGs, nor the teardrop design favored by most U.S. fighter designers. Instead, the 21's canopy extended flush and level from the jet's dorsal spine.

A questionable design choice, Steve thought. *Sure, drag would be somewhat reduced, but rearward visibility would be poor to nil, and in a fighter, visibility was life—*

"Well? What do you think?" A male voice demanded from the hangar's doorway. "Is she everything you thought she'd be, and more?"

Steve whirled around in disbelief. "Benny?" he called out. "Benny Detkin—?"

Benny came over to embrace Steve. He was wearing gray wool trousers, a tan shirt, and a pine green pullover sweater. Steve thought his old friend's short-cut, thick black hair was only slightly more seeded with gray than the last time they'd met.

"Welcome to Israel—" Benny said. "Or should I say shalom, old buddy?"

"You can say anything you want," Steve shot back fondly. "As long as you also say what the hell you're *doing* here—"

"And just look at that jacket you're wearing!" Benny was laughing. "Man, that old A-2 brings back memories! I don't have mine anymore," he complained. "Amy threw it out on me when I wasn't looking."

"That's what you get for being married, but you still haven't told me why you're here. Are you on vacation, or here for some kind of charity work?"

Steve knew that Benny was a big wheel in stateside Jewish philanthropies, and pro-Israel political lobbies, but he realized none of that would explain what his friend was doing wandering around this supposedly top-secret air base . . .

"This is going to be hard for me to explain, Steve . . ." Benny awkwardly began. Just then Dov Sachar stepped into the hangar.

"Excuse me . . ." Dov called out. "Colonel?"

"*Yes?*" Both Steve and Benny said in unison.

"Sorry." Dov smiled. "I meant Colonel Detkin . . ."

"You meant *who?*" Steve blurted weakly, staring at Benny.

"Major Yakkov has a little more paperwork to get out of the way but promised to meet you in the mess," Sachar continued.

"Thanks, Dov," Benny replied.

"What the fuck are you a colonel *of?*" Steve demanded as Dov left the hangar.

"Of the Israeli Air Force . . ." Benny said.

"You can't be! You're an American citizen—"

"It gets worse, old buddy," Benny reluctantly confessed. "I'm also in the Mossad."

"I became a Reserve Status IAF colonel, and a Mossad agent, five years ago," Benny was telling Steve.

It was late afternoon. The two men were seated at a table in the largely deserted air base mess. There were mugs of strong tea, and slices of honey cake on the table in front of them, but Steve, despite the fact that he was tired and hungry, hadn't touched the food. He was too pissed off to eat.

"You see, I already had the perfect cover," Benny continued. "Over the years I'd established a legitimate history of traveling frequently to Israel on behalf of various causes—"

"All of which are totally legal, aboveboard activities," Steve sharply interrupted. "Endeavors protected by the U.S. Constitution, which by the way, specifically condemns what you've done . . ."

"Why are you sounding so angry?" Benny asked mildly.

"I find out my best friend is a fucking foreign spy, why shouldn't I be angry?"

"I'm *not* a spy," Benny said patiently.

"I thought you were an *American*!"

"I am—"

"Oh yeah? Answer me this," Steve demanded. "If there was a war between Israel and America, on whose side would you be on?"

"That's a stupid question . . ." Benny grumbled.

"You mean it's one you can't answer."

"Look, Steve, I'm telling you that I'm not a spy. I'm a—" Benny paused. "I guess you'd call me *a fixer* . . . I smooth things out, put people in touch with one another. Get things done—"

"*Illegal* things!" Steve scowled, lighting a cigarette.

"Things like getting your father to cooperate in smuggling the Vector-A systems to Israel," Benny quietly amended.

"Yeah, and that was against the law—and you a lawyer!"

"Technically, yes, like most of what I do for Israel, the Vector-A project was against United States law," Benny admitted. "But if we asked your father, I think he'd agree that we were conducting ourselves according to a higher moral imperative. This is not a game where Israel can play by the rules. Survival is what's at stake."

"Oh, man—" Steve winced, disgusted. "Don't you *see*? The Arabs could say that, as well . . ."

"Listen a minute," Benny insisted. "You read the papers, you watch the news on television. You know the score. For a year now the border skirmishes between the Arab states and Israel have been increasing. Now, once again, our old Egyptian friend Nasser is rattling his saber, making speeches to his Arab neighbors about how it's time to make another stab at driving the Israelis into the sea."

"That's why the U.N. is here," Steve said.

"The U.N. can't be depended on," Benny countered. "Last month this country defended itself by striking at a Jordanian village from which Arab guerillas were conducting border raids. For that, Israel received an official censure from the U.N., but nobody is censuring the Arabs. Believe me, when Nasser says jump, the only question the U.N. will ask is how high. When the Arabs are ready for war, the peace-keeping force will pull out, and Israel will once again be on its own."

"You keep referring to the Israelis as 'they' and 'them,'" Steve observed. "Don't you consider yourself an Israeli?"

"Of course I don't," Benny said. "Why would I? I'm an American. Sure, I love what Israel stands for, but I also love my native country. I've tried to serve America all my life. I served her in war, as you well know—"

"Sure, I know that, Benny," Steve sighed.

"—and I truly believe I'm serving America now, by aiding Israel. Israel is America's only steadfast ally in this part of the world."

"I can't argue with that, either."

"So?" Benny smiled tentatively. "You still mad?"

"No . . . I was never *mad*, I was just . . ." Steve trailed off, not knowing how to explain it, and not sure he wanted to. As a warrior he'd always seen things in black and white: America was right and everyone else was wrong, *period*. That mindset had held up through World War II, and against the Commies in Korea, but it had started to become unglued after his experience in Vietnam. Now, hearing about what Benny had been up to all these years, he no longer knew what to think. Benny had broken the law, and yet he knew his old friend to be a stand-up guy . . . Maybe there *wasn't* always a right and a wrong side to things. Maybe the end sometimes *did* justify the means . . .

"Anyway, you should be glad I'm in the Mossad," Benny was saying. "It was my contacts in the organization that allowed me to persuade the Israeli Air Force that you should be the one sent to check out the MIG."

"So *you're* the one who set that up?" Steve said.

Benny nodded. "When I first brought up with you the idea of smuggling Vector-A systems into Israel, I did promise you that you'd be paid back if you relayed Israel's interest in the matter to your father . . ."

"So you got me this assignment."

"You are my best friend." Benny smiled. "I figured this opportunity would make you happy . . ."

"It does," Steve acknowledged.

"It's making the United States happy, as well," Benny added. "I told you that I consider what I do to be of benefit to both America and Israel. I would never betray the United States—"

"You don't have to prove anything to me, Benny," Steve stopped him. "Forget I said anything, okay? I mean, what the hell do I know? I'm no one to judge you. You live your life the way you think is right." He shook his head. "I guess I'm just getting old . . . The only time I can make sense out of anything these days is when I'm in a cockpit."

"What do you mean *these* days?" Benny joked, and they both laughed.

"But speaking of flying, that reminds me," Steve said. "What's this about you being in the Israeli Air Force?"

"Like I said, only as a Reserve officer," Benny explained. "And even that is on a quasi-official status, but having access to Air Force headquarters in Tel Aviv has made my work easier. Most everything I've done for Israel has concerned aviation. And there's one other aspect to it. You know that here fighter pilots are in very short supply—"

"Yeah, I heard this country's hurting for jet jockeys."

"I felt that I should lend my expertise in that area," Benny continued. "I've helped to formulate a training program, and now and then I keep my hand in by leading a training flight."

"You checked out on the Tyran II?" Steve asked.

"Oh, sure," Benny said proudly, and then smiled. "Maybe you and I can do a little mock dogfighting? If you're not too scared, that is . . ."

"Scared? Of you? I'll wax your ass," Steve growled.

"Oh yeah? You wouldn't want to bet your flight jacket on that, would you?"

"I would, but what do you have valuable enough to put up against it?" Steve demanded.

Benny was looking past Steve. "We'll have to continue this another time. Here's Captain Yakkov—"

Steve, glancing over his shoulder, did a double take. The captain so purposely striding toward their table was a stunningly beautiful dark-haired woman in her late twenties or early thirties. She was tall, with legs that seemed to go on forever, and looked lean and muscular except for her ripe breasts. She was wearing a khaki uniform: snug-fitting trousers and an open-necked shirt with a cloth flight jacket over her shoulders. Her captain's bars were pinned to the jacket's epaulets.

"Colonel Steven Gold, may I present Captain Rivka Yakkov," Benny said as both he and Steve stood up.

"Shalom, Colonel Gold," Rivka said in thickly accented English. She offered Steve her hand. Her fingers only brushed his palm before fluttering off like a bird thinking twice about landing. "I am pleased that we will be working together."

"The pleasure's mine, Captain."

"Please, call me Rivka. I feel like I know you already, Colonel." She nodded, setting her shoulder-length hair billowing in chestnut waves that framed her heart-shaped face. "As Benny's administrative assistant I have done much research concerning your impressive career . . ."

"Research on me?" Steve smiled. "I'm flattered. Maybe you and I ought to go somewhere private for a one-on-one interview—?"

"Not necessary, Colonel," she said evenly. "We will have ample time to talk while working together."

"You're going to be working with me?" Steve asked her, and then glanced at Benny.

"I'll be in and out of Israel during your stay," Benny explained. "I've got a life and a family to deal with back in America, after all, so I've arranged for Rivka to be assigned as your assistant. Turn to her for anything you might need."

"Hear that, Rivka?" Steve winked. "Your boss says anything I need . . ."

"I will certainly do my best, Colonel—" she replied, her wide-spaced, almond-shaped brown eyes revealing no sign that she was aware he'd been flirting.

"Well, you can start by calling me Steve. Next on the agenda would be a set of wheels."

"Pardon?" She looked questioningly at Benny, who machine-gunned some Hebrew her way.

"Oh yes! Of course! A car! I'm aware that your time will be spent here at the base, and at Air Force headquarters in Tel Aviv. For that reason I found you housing—a flat—close to headquarters, and I have already arranged for a car."

"Very efficient," Steve complimented her. "But I hope the car you got me is something a little more sporty than Dov's Mercedes . . . Tell me, Rivka, do *you* like sports cars?"

She merely smiled politely, and then her eyes fell on Steve's flight jacket draped over the back of his chair. She studied the shield design. "Please? What is the significance of the vees—?"

"It stands for Vigilant Virgins," Benny told her. "It was the nickname they gave our fighter squadron during World War Two."

"But why in the world would they call you virgins?" she asked. Her eyes were large with amused curiosity, and this time a genuine smile was playing at the corners of her pink rosebud mouth.

"It's a long story," Steve said. "I think I should tell it to you over dinner..."

Her smile broadened. "I think that I would do well with a jacket such as this," she murmured, fixing Steve with her penetrating stare, the pupils of her eyes grown so large that her gaze seemed almost black. "It would save a *lot* of men a lot of pointless effort."

"Rat-tat-tat..." Benny chuckled softly.

"Now, if you'll excuse me," Rivka said. "I have work waiting."

Steve watched her walk away, her rump working sleekly beneath the snug khaki. He waited until she was out of earshot, and then asked, "Do you think she really is?"

"Is what?"

"A virgin."

"I really couldn't tell you," Benny said, startled.

"I figured you Mossad guys knew everything."

"There are some places even the Mossad doesn't stick its nose."

"Good idea, leave that to me."

"You are a hound." Benny laughed, shaking his head.

"Me?" Steve protested. "What about *you*? Don't try to tell me you made her your assistant because she's a great typist—"

"She's no secretary. It so happens that Rivka received her degree in aeronautical engineering from the Israel Institute of Technology. She's my assistant because my main area of concern these days is Israel's project to develop a home-grown jet fighter largely based on the French Tyran II, but incorporating whatever international aviation technology is worthwhile."

"Then that's why she's here?" Steve asked. "To see if there's anything worthwhile copying from the MIG-21?"

"Yes, but as I said, she's also here to assist you. She will be your liaison—and when necessary your interpreter— with the rest of the Israeli air defense establishment. The two of you together should make an excellent MIG-21 evaluation team."

"So there's nothing between the two of you?"

"Have you been listening to a word I've been saying?" Benny frowned sternly.

"Sure, so she isn't your mistress, or anything like that?" Steve persisted.

"In the first place, Amy knows Rivka," Benny declared. "Not that I would cheat on my wife in the second place—"

"Okay!" Steve said, beaming. "Your loss is my gain."

"I think the laugh is going to be on you." Benny smiled.

"Wanna bet?"

Benny gestured toward Steve's jacket still draped on the chair. "Rivka meant it when she said she ought to have a jacket like this to ward off would-be Romeos. That young lady has shot down more guys than your old man's wartime buddy the Red Baron."

(Two)

In the sky over Israel
5 February 1967

Steve flipped the MIG-21 over into a high G barrel roll, feeling the joyful push of the turbojet as he went to afterburn. The altimeter read fifty thousand feet. Below him, Tel Aviv looked like a jumble of children's building blocks scattered along the sand-banded, blue curve of sea, while the land to the east was a tapestry of crimson and gold, flecked with green.

Well away from Steve, orbiting warily, were a pair of armed IAF Tyran IIs. The Mossad had warned that the loss of the MIG had so infuriated the Russians and humiliated the Arabs that a surprise Arab air strike to destroy the airplane could not be ruled out. The dun-colored Tyran IIs were assigned to baby-sit Steve. They would hold the fort in case the Arabs somehow managed to come in undetected by the Israelis' extensive early warning system, and before the main force of Tyran IIs waiting on deck could scramble.

Steve came out of the barrel roll at 55,000 feet, which was close to the MIG's ceiling, and put the nimble little Russian bird into a low-speed yo-yo, a steep dive that took the MIG to the limit by trading altitude for speed. As he watched his altimeter unwind he felt the MIG rocketing earthward as solidly steady as a locomotive on a downhill stretch of track.

This was Steve's forty-second flight in the MIG. During the weeks since he'd first made the proud Russian war bird's acquaintance he'd taken his time in wooing her. Patiently, carefully, he'd become only a little more forward on each flight, so that now he felt that he knew all of her eccentricities; what liberties he could take and remain unscathed; what insults would earn him a slap in the face . . . Or worse.

Now Steve felt he knew the MIG's pure, simple pleasures. Due to her uncomplicated instrument panel, her lack of a HUD Head-Up-Display beyond a weapons sight, or any sophisticated avionics at all, she was in many ways a throwback to an earlier, simpler time in jet-propelled warfare.

That was not to say that this Russian aristocrat was perfect. He'd never quite gotten used to the MIG's poor visibility in air-to-ground mode due to her strange snout, and the almost total lack of rearward sight lines thanks to that flush-mounted canopy. . .

He pulled out of his dive, moving the stick back between his legs and cobbing the throttle. The MIG climbed like a squirrel up a tree. At 45,000 feet he leveled off, feeling a mix of exhilaration and sadness. This passionate affair between an American fighter jock and a Russian war bird was fast coming to a close—

Very simply, the MIG had nothing left to tell him. All of her secrets had been revealed, as he and the Israelis now knew.

Last week Benny Detkin had returned to Israel from the United States. Just now Benny was waiting for Steve back at the base. Benny had mentioned something about dinner in Tel Aviv this evening with some Israeli Air Force bigshots. Steve guessed that this was going to be the Israelis' way of letting him know that he'd overstayed his welcome; that it was time for him to go home. Steve was sorry to see his visit here coming to an end. He loved to fly, and on this assignment he'd spent almost the entire time in the air.

He had Rivka Yakkov to thank for that. As Benny had predicted, Rivka had been an outstanding assistant. Her engineering and design savvy had nicely dovetailed with Steve's hands-on experience. Together they'd created a thick folder of valuable MIG specification/evaluation reports that had been regularly sent back to the Air Force.

Benny had been right about what a great team Steve and Rivka would make, and, sadly, Benny had been right about one other thing, as well: No matter how hard Steve had tried, he hadn't been able to get to first base with the beautiful Israeli...

Steve pushed his lewd fantasies about the girl out of his mind and tried to get his thoughts together about the MIG. Chances were that at tonight's farewell dinner the IAF brass would expect him to say a few words about what he'd learned.

The bottom line was that the MIG was an agile sports car of a fighter, but her lack of avionics put her at a distinct disadvantage to the Tyran II. Like the MIG, the Israelis' French-built Tyran II was delta-winged, small, and maneuverable, and the Tyran IIs had also been just as limited by their lack of electronics—until GAT had come through with the Vector-A radar ranging system. The Vector-A was the ace in the hole the vastly outnumbered IAF needed to have a shot at taking control of the sky during a war.

Could the U.S. fighters currently rolling off the production line compete with the MIG-21? This was the question that the USAAF would soon be asking him, and it wasn't nearly as easy to answer, Steve thought as he brought the Russian airplane around in a gentle banking turn toward the air base.

The American aviation establishment's majority thesis was that one elaborately equipped state-of-the-art fighter could wax any number of smaller, cheaper, less sophisticated enemy war birds. Steve wasn't so sure about that. There was no question that in a hypothetical, one-on-one duel with equally capable pilots in both cockpits, the MIG couldn't touch anything currently in the U.S. Air Force's stable. The problem was that air wars weren't decided by a single, gladiator-type duel. Wars were won by getting lots of airplanes into the fray, and that required machine reliability.

Steve knew that you couldn't judge a production line's entire output by only one sample. For what it was worth, however, this particular MIG had proven supremely reliable *despite* the punishment that Steve had unwittingly inflicted upon her by putting her through her paces without the benefit of flight manuals or instructors. He couldn't help comparing the MIG's rock-solid reliability to that of the Thuds he'd flown in Vietnam. The Thuds were always suffering downtime, or going negative on this or that piece of black box black magic just when it was most needed, despite preventive maintenance . . .

Yeah, what it all came down to in a war was the ability to get your airplanes flying, and the caliber of the men in the cockpits . . .

Steve glanced out at the pair of Tyran IIs flying escort. *Speaking of the caliber of men in the cockpits, since this is likely going to be my last time out with the MIG, why not have a little fun?* he thought.

The Israelis had forbidden any mock dogfights between the MIG and Tyran IIs. They felt that their MIG was irreplaceable, which was true, but Steve thought they were wrong about not wanting to take the rather unlikely risk of the MIG being damaged or destroyed participating in the rough-and-tumble of a mock furball. The bottom line was the MIG was only as valuable as the amount of knowledge concerning Soviet aircraft capabilities that could be wrung out of her. Steve could execute solo high-speed maneuvers from now until doomsday, but it wouldn't tell him as much as would a single dogfight up against some capable opponents.

Thinking about capable opponents, Steve reminded himself that the Tyran II drivers baby-sitting him were supposed to be as good as the IAF's. Steve guessed it was time to find out just *how good*. Chances were that they were going to have to prove themselves for *real*, sooner or later.

In the past few weeks there had been a gradual but steady increase in the number of border incidents between Israel and its Arab neighbors. Even more ominous, IAF fighters defending the integrity of Israel's airspace had on several occasions played a tense game of chicken with Syrian and Egyptian jets. So far no shots had been fired in the sky, but Steve knew that it was just a matter of time before one side or the other made a mistake, and the shooting did start. From his conversations with Israelis Steve knew that most in this country were resigned to the fact that war was inevitable.

Steve had made some friends here. He wanted to know for his own peace of mind that the IAF jet rockets had what it took, but there was another, more practical reason for his defying the Israeli Air Force authorities by using the MIG to engage in a mock attack upon his Tyran II escorts. When Steve got back to the States he knew that the CIA and the Air Force would debrief him on what he'd learned about the Israelis' air combat capabilities. When that time came, Steve wanted to have the answers.

He brought the MIG up and around to gain some altitude, and get behind the unsuspecting Tyrans. He couldn't warn the Israeli pilots about what he was about to do. The MIG had been equipped with IAF communications gear, but Steve wasn't allowed to use it except in a dire emergency because he couldn't speak Hebrew. The Israelis knew that the Arabs had Soviet personnel operating high-tech/long-range surveillance equipment. If the Russians were to monitor Steve's obviously American transmissions coming from the MIG, international diplomatic hell would break loose.

Steve hadn't missed the lack of communications. It had been very enjoyable to have made all of these flights in heavenly silence. *And it's certainly to my benefit that we can't communicate today*, Steve thought. *They can't tell me to stop—*

It was not going to be a fair fight for the Israelis, he reminded himself as he began his intercept course on the pair of Tyran IIs. Each Tyran was loaded down with twin 30-millimeter cannons and a pair of extended-range fuel drop tanks. The MIG had no drop tanks, and though she had been equipped with 23-millimeter cannon, the weaponry had been removed for analysis by Israeli weapons specialists. The decreased weight gave a speed and maneuverability advantage to the MIG. On the other hand, score a two-against-one advantage for the Israelis.

The pair of Tyran IIs was typically arranged with the leader flying lower and somewhat ahead of his wingman. As Steve closed the gap he knew that the Israeli pilots were watching him. He settled onto the wingman's six o'clock and waited.

The pair begin to jink, most likely trying through an aerial pantomime to get Steve to disengage. He patiently stayed on their tails, aware that because he couldn't radio the Israeli drivers a challenge, it was going to take them awhile to figure out what was happening.

Through his helmet headset he could hear the two pilots conversing in their national tongue with each other, and with ground control. Then Steve heard Benny Detkin's unmistakable voice joining the Hebrew conversation. Steve didn't know what anyone was saying, but from the tone of the various exchanges he could tell that nobody was terribly angry. As a matter of fact, one of the pilots was chuckling—

The pair of Tyran IIs abruptly broke apart into a defensive split. The high man—Steve immediately dubbed him Alpha —went to afterburn, zooming up toward the sun. The low man—Beta—banked sharply, and barrel-roll dived away from the fray.

Steve, grinning, kicked in his own afterburner, and went after the high man, knowing that he would be the most immediately dangerous. It would take Alpha far less time to drop down on Steve than it would low-breaking Beta to circle around and then climb to set up an ambush.

The Alpha Tyran was already whipping around in a vertical reverse: topping out in his climb, fluttering in the sky as all speed was lost, and then ruddering his bird sideways and around into a steep dive. Steve had to give the IAF pilot credit as he watched the guy successfully complete his move. Delta-winged aircraft were not at their best at the sudden low speeds characteristic of the vertical reverse. In less capable hands the Tyran might have gone into a stall.

Alpha was now diving toward Steve, who was simultaneously zooming up toward the Tyran in a head-on game of chicken. Steve craned his neck, cursing the MIG's poor visibility as he searched the sky for the Beta Tyran. Finally he spotted the jet, and saw that he still had time to deal with Alpha before Beta became a concern.

The Alpha Tyran was still coming head-on. Steve decided on an offset head-on pass; a maneuver for which the agile MIG was born and bred.

He waited until the Tyran II loomed huge in his foreward windscreen and then Steve veered to the left, angling slightly below the attacking jet. In quick response, the Tyran broke right. Now both jets were banked sharply in opposite directions, but Steve, by stressing the MIG to the utmost, was able to corkscrew around in the tighter turn. The Alpha Tyran was still skating around when Steve was able to straighten out and settle on its six o'clock.

Alpha began jinking, trying to lose Steve. Steve, keeping

an eye peeled for the Beta Tyran, managed to stay locked onto Alpha for five seconds. He then had to break as the Beta Tyran began to close on his tail.

As Steve banked away from the Alpha he knew that he'd won the first part of the mock dogfight. Five seconds would have been plenty of time to blast the Tyran out of the sky with a cannon. He had no camera on the MIG to record his mock victory, but he knew that downstairs they would have been watching the whole thing. He wondered what Benny and the Air Force operations people at the base were thinking . . .

Steve also wondered what the Alpha pilot was thinking. Would he continue the fight, or withdraw, as honor dictated he should do because he had hypothetically been waxed? Steve was pleased to see the Alpha pilot do the right thing, banking away from the fight, although he did stay in the vicinity. Steve understood the reason for that: The Tyran II pair's original purpose for being here was to protect the MIG against a possible Arab attack.

It was time to deal with Beta—

Steve put the MIG into a vector roll: He pulled up hard, banked into a turn, and then barrel-rolled his airplane so that it was suddenly twirling in the opposite direction from that turn. The Tyran pilot, realizing that he had been set up to overshoot, disengaged by breaking into his own turn in order to regain the speed and altitude he would need to once again come down on Steve's six o'clock.

Steve quickly stood the MIG on her ear, whipping her around so that she resembled a dog—a borzoi—chasing her own tail. The sharp maneuver put the MIG behind and above the still-banking Tyran. By dropping the MIG's nose Steve could set up for what would have been a fairly decent deflection shot.

The Tyran pilot immediately realized Steve's advantage, and broke sharply in the direction of Steve's attack approach. Steve, all the while gaining velocity in his dive, cursed himself for falling for the IAF pilot's trick as the MIG duly overshot the Tyran. Now Steve found himself once again below and behind the Israeli jet, which had quickly reversed, in order to attack the MIG. Steve executed his own reverse turn in order to deny the Tyran a firing opportunity. The Tyran immediately copied Steve's reverse turn, so that now *he* was back on *Steve*'s six o'clock. Steve reversed, and now the horizon was spinning like an airplane's prop as he and the IAF pilot repeatedly exchanged positions, playing out their scissoring ballet across the sky.

Finally, Steve's lighter, more maneuverable MIG gained the advantage, forcing the cannon and drop tank burdened Tyran II out in front. Steve stayed locked onto the Tyran's six o'clock until its driver waggled his wings, indicating that he knew he'd been shot down.

Good fight, son, Steve thought. He pulled abreast of the Tyran II. Once he had the IAF pilot's attention, Steve waved to him and then waggled the MIG's wings in order to salute the guy for leading him on such a merry chase.

As Steve headed back to base he thought that the furball he'd just engaged in was likely nothing to what he would soon be experiencing on the ground.

Steve brought the MIG down, turned her over to the ground crew who would check her out before towing her into her hangar, and then went to the pilot's personal equipment shack to change out of his gear. He was stowing his equipment in the locker when a tight-lipped Benny Detkin came into the shack.

"Benny, I know what you're going to say," Steve began quickly, hoping to head off his friend's tirade.

"Do you now?" Benny asked coolly, his expression deadpan.

"I know I disobeyed orders by challenging those Tyrans," Steve hurriedly continued. "But I did it for a good reason—"

Benny nodded. "What you mean is that you did it because you wanted to—"

"No!" Steve protested. "Well, I mean, sure I *wanted* to." He couldn't help grinning.

"Hmmm . . ." Benny scowled knowingly.

"But I also learned a lot of valuable stuff about the MIG—" Steve quickly added as the pilots who had been flying the Tyran II's that he'd just waxed came into the shack to change out of their gear. "Hi, guys." Steve grinned. "No hard feelings, right?"

"No, of course not." One of the pilots smiled.

The other pilot was also smiling, nodding his head in agreement. They were both skinny, dark-haired guys. The one who'd been nodding had a bad case of acne. They both looked like they should be in high school, not in the cockpits of fighter jets.

"If that fight had been for real, you would have been carrying auxiliary tanks and weapons," the pilot with the acne good-naturedly accused in thickly accented English. "Loaded down as I was, your MIG would not have had the advantage."

"Sure I would have," Steve said softly. "If that fight had been for real, I would have punched my drop tanks," Steve explained. "Cleaned up, my MIG would have gotten the better of you just the way it did just now, and then I would have taken you out with my cannon."

"You would have wasted auxiliary tanks?" the Israeli pilot asked, appalled. "They cost so much money—"

"Look," Steve interrupted. "I know this country has to scrounge dearly to find the funds to buy weapons . . ."

He paused, wondering if he had the right to continue with what he wanted to say. He glanced at Benny, who nodded.

"Okay, listen guys—" Steve began again, returning his attention to the two young pilots. "When you're in a dog-fight, you can't be thinking dollars and cents. Take the situation we were just in, what's the better choice? To waste a couple of drop tanks, or lose a pilot and his aircraft?"

"He's right," Benny interjected. "If you're going to do the job you must have your priorities straight." He paused. "We'll talk more about this later. For now, would you men excuse us for a few moments? I'd like to speak with the colonel in private."

Steve waited until the two pilots had exited the shack and

then said, "Look, Benny, let me save you some trouble. I know what this dinner you've got planned for tonight is all about."

"You do, huh?" Benny asked skeptically.

"Sure, it's intended to be my kiss-off, but that's okay. I'll finish up here, head back to Tel Aviv to pack up, and—"

"Just shut up a minute," Benny said. "It so happens that's not at all the purpose of tonight's dinner. The purpose of the dinner is to convince you to stay—"

"Huh?" Steve stared blankly. "What are you talking about?"

Benny hesitated. "Ah, what the hell. If you can break a few rules, so can I . . . I'm going to tell you what's been planned for tonight so that you'll have a little more time to think about it, but I'd appreciate it if tonight you'd act surprised when the subject is brought up. The IAF is going to ask you to stay on for a few more months, in order to head up a training program for our fighter squadrons in combat techniques."

"You're shitting me?" Steve blurted happily. "I can't believe it!"

"Why not?" Benny shrugged. "It's not that unusual. There are American military advisers training armed forces in Indochina and South America, so why not one working with an ally like Israel? The Air Force brass here have been watching you put that MIG through its paces for some time now. What you accomplished dogfighting today—despite the fact that you were specifically told not to—will only strengthen the IAF's resolve to keep you on. If you're agreeable, the IAF will make an official request to the USAF that you be allowed to remain."

"I'm agreeable, I'm agreeable," Steve said quickly. "The more flying I get to do the better, and the opportunity to spend my time concentrating on nothing but fighter strategy and tactics makes me happier than a pig in shit."

Benny winced. "Just try and think up a little bit nicer reply for when the offer is put to you at dinner tonight," he icily suggested, turning to go.

"Roger, old buddy!" Steve said. "Oh, and naturally I'll need Rivka to continue acting as my assistant when I set up this training program—?"

"Naturally." Benny nodded, straight-faced. "It's a given that fighter jocks are more aggressive when they've got lots of pent-up, frustrated sexual energy."

"She can't deny me forever." Steve laughed.

"Famous last words," Benny said gloatingly. "Oh, and by the way, I'll be participating in the training whenever I'm in Israel . . ."

"You want to see if something of the old master can rub off on you, huh?" Steve asked innocently.

Benny winked. "I just want to keep you properly humble; although it appears that Rivka is accomplishing that quite well on her own."

CHAPTER 21

(One)

Gold Aviation and Transport
Burbank, California
3 June 1967

Herman Gold's desk was piled high with work. It was a Saturday afternoon, but lately Gold had taken to coming into the office on weekends in order to catch up.

The GAT production lines ran seven days a week around the clock, and Gold suspected that if he went down to the design department he'd find a couple of engineers busy at their drafting tables, but on weekends the executive and sales offices were closed tight. The lack of ringing telephones and people at Gold's office door allowed him the uninterrupted time he needed to clear the decks for the coming week.

Because the office was officially closed, Gold was

dressed casually. He was hunched over in his chair, working an adding machine as he slugged his way through some ponderous cost analysis sheets. The Air Force had been complaining about design defects in the Super-BroadSword. The cost analysis sheets itemized the contemplated running changes that must be made in the GAT production lines to try to rectify the problems.

"Grandpa?"

"What is it, Andy?" Gold asked, glancing up over his bifocals.

His nine-year-old grandson, dressed in white tennis shorts, a T-shirt, and blue sneakers, was sprawled out on a sofa, idly flipping through a comic book. "How much longer do we have to stay, Grandpa?"

Andy's parents had gone away for the weekend, so Gold and his wife had volunteered to take the boy, in lieu of leaving him in the care of the Harrisons' housekeeper. Gold had known better than to bring the kid to the office with him, but Andy had begged and pleaded, and it tickled Gold that his grandson seemed interested in the business.

"I *told* you when you insisted on coming that I'd be here a long time!" Gold snapped.

He saw the boy flinch, and immediately regretted his gruffness. "I'm sorry, Andy. I'm not mad at you," he softly reassured. "I'm mad at myself, I guess . . ."

"How come?" Andy asked.

"We're having some problems with the Super-Broad-Sword," Gold muttered. "That's our latest military airplane?"

Andy nodded. "It's broken?"

Gold smiled thinly. "You could say that . . ."

"When my stuff gets broken you fix it," Andy said. "You gonna fix your plane?"

"I'm going to try." Gold forced patience into his voice. "But I need you to be quiet, okay . . . ?"

The more Gold thought about the trouble the full-production Super-BroadSword had been causing for the last several months, the more he could feel his gut clenching.

Just about everything that *could* go wrong with the damned airplane—from its aerodynamic drag to its engines—*had* gone wrong. It was becoming impossible for his design and production departments to stay on top of the mess. Just last week a new batch of complaints had flooded in concerning a potentially life-threatening in-flight malfunction of the variable-sweep swing wing. Gold couldn't account for the gremlins. He'd had Don Harrison and his best people heading up the design process. The components had all been checked and double-checked. The parts had all been perfect. Hell, they *still* were, and yet when those parts were assembled into a Super-BroadSword they just didn't seem to want to hang together . . .

"Grandpa, I'm bored—" Andy was complaining. He'd tossed aside his comic book, and was restlessly swinging his heels against the sofa.

"I wish there was something around here for you to do," Gold murmured. His elegant office with its oil paintings, dark wainscoting, and leather furniture was not exactly set up to be a playroom . . .

His eyes fell on the newly installed glass display case in the office's far corner. The case was filled with scale models of all the airplanes that GAT had designed and manufactured in its forty-two-year history. The models had resided in Teddy Quinn's office back when Teddy was chief engineer. When Don Harrison had stepped into the job he'd moved the model case onto the main floor of the engineering department. Gold, feeling sentimental, had recently had the case moved up here.

"I've got an idea." Gold pointed toward the model case. "Would you like to play with the airplanes?"

"Sure!" Andy hopped off the sofa. "Can I?"

"You bet," Gold replied, standing up and walking to the case. He slid open the glass doors and stepped aside, grinning as he watched his grandson carefully lift from its stand the twelve-inch-long, cast metal replica of a prop-driven, open-cockpit G-1 Dragonfly.

"That was the first airplane we ever built," Gold said as

the boy held the silvery model up to the light. "We called it the Dragonfly. We sold a bunch of them to the Post Office, and to private freight transport companies. For a while it was used all over the country to deliver the mail."

"It must have been fun to fly one of these, huh, Grandpa?"

Gold nodded. *More fun to fly them, and more fun to build them in those days,* he sadly added to himself. He would have liked to play with the models along with his grandson, reminiscing about old, and better times. *You've got work to do,* he reminded himself. He trudged back to his desk, intent on dealing with today's problems instead of losing himself in yesterday's fond memories.

He spent another quarter hour staring at the goddamned columns of numbers, then tossed aside his pencil and shut off the adding machine. He couldn't concentrate, and it wasn't just because Andy was sitting on the carpet by the display case, making airplane noises as he played with the models.

Gold leaned back in his chair. He was feeling exhausted. This Super-BroadSword fiasco was keeping him up nights with worry. He was also feeling a bit sorry for himself—

Despite all the problems, things could have been smoothed out if old Howie Simon was still in charge of procurement, Gold brooded.

He'd shared twenty years of aviation history with Howie. The two men had understood each other. Howie would have known without question that Gold would work day and night to set things right . . .

But Howie was gone, put out to pasture in Texas. The general had been replaced by a team of snot-nosed young officers who didn't have the aviation savvy in their entire bodies that Howie had possessed in his little finger. And the way those young bastards had talked down to Gold! Just thinking about it was enough to set his pulse pounding all over again . . .

Yeah, he could have worked things out with Howie. The problems could have been rectified without tarnishing the reputation of the Super-BroadSword and the reputation of his company. But the new people in charge of Air Force procurement hadn't been interested in the way things had always been done—

On Gold's desk was the telegram notifying him that the Air Force had temporarily suspended acceptance of Super-BroadSword deliveries pending an evaluation of the design changes, and a reassessment of the unit costs.

The trade publications would soon get wind of it—if they hadn't already, Gold thought sourly. He supposed that once the headlines broke, the politicians in Washington would want to stick their noses into it, as well. He also knew that once the Air Force had pinned the lemon label on the airplane, it wouldn't matter how hard GAT worked to rectify the problems. The company could still kiss good-bye its future foreign orders . . .

God, it was all so needless! The Super-BroadSword was a good airplane. Frustrated, he balled his hands into fists. *It was all so aggravating!*

Calm down, he told himself. It wasn't like the Super-BroadSword was the only thing he had to worry about. Dealing with the Europeans concerning the Skytrain Industrie jetliner consortium of which GAT was a part was always an exhausting burden. And then there was the ever-sharpening competition from Boeing and McDonnell-Douglas in the domestic jetliner market. Sure, Don Harrison was eager to take some of the burden off Gold's shoulders, and the other executives in the company did their jobs, but Gold had always had trouble delegating responsibility. He was the top man after all . . . The buck stopped at *his* desk, goddammit. Nobody else's; *his*—

And it all used to be fun, Gold thought, *but not anymore*. Pondering it, Gold realized that it hadn't been fun for a long time. It seemed that increasingly his pleasures were diminishing, while the unpleasant aspects of life continued to increase—

For instance he couldn't fly anymore. When he'd turned sixty-nine last month his wife, his daughter, and his son-in-law had all ganged up on him. They'd sat him down and explained the facts of life: that the various medications Gold was taking for this or that damned ailment had made flying simply too risky.

It had hurt like hell to listen to that. It had hurt even more to realize that what they were saying was true. *Dammit!* He'd been flying since he was eighteen years old. He was a combat *ace* before he was twenty...

With flying denied to him, Gold had concentrated on his religious studies for relaxation. At home he had dozens of books on Judaism, and he'd really enjoyed his Hebrew language lessons. It was too bad that he'd had to cut them out when this Super-BroadSword mess developed. There simply wasn't enough time to do everything—

"Grandpa?"

"Yes, Andy..." he sighed.

"Would you play with me?" Andy was still sitting on the carpet by the display case. He'd removed most of the airplane models from their stands and had them scattered on the level green runway that was the carpet.

"Play?" Gold muttered. "I don't know... Play *what?*"

"We could play... Dogfight!" Andy held up one of the airplane models he'd removed from the case. "You could pick one and I could pick one and we could have a dogfight—"

"I've got so much work to do here..." But Gold trailed off, thinking, *Screw the work.*

He got up from his desk and walked over to the case. "Dogfight, huh? I ought to remember how to play that..." He winced from the jolt he felt in the small of his back as he laboriously lowered his girth to the carpet.

"Grandpa, what plane did you fly in the war?"

"I flew a lot of different planes, but my favorite was the Fokker triplane."

"Is that like a Mess-o-shit?"

Gold burst out laughing. "No, the Messerschmitt was in the Second World War. I fought in the First World War..." He gently brushed Andy's unruly blond hair out of the boy's brown eyes. "I think that was a little before your time, right?"

Andy nodded solemnly. "How many planes did you shoot down?"

"Twenty." Gold smiled. The boy asked him that at least once a week.

"Wow," Andy gravely replied, as he always did.

"Okay," Gold said, looking at the models spread out on the carpet. "Pick the plane you want to use for our dogfight."

"Which one is the one you flew in the war?"

"What? The Fokker? It's not here . . ."

"How come?"

"Because I flew it in the war, but I didn't design and build it."

"So what?"

"Sew buttons," Gold said. "Now pick."

"Okay. I'll take this one."

"You're going to dogfight with *that*?"

"Sure, why not?" Andy demanded. "It's big, right?"

Andy had chosen the twin-engine, prop-driven, BuzzSaw Combat Support attack bomber. The CS-1 had been a successful design that GAT had put into production back in '39.

Gold pointed at the newest addition to the model collection. "You sure you don't want Super-BroadSword?"

"I'm sure," Andy said.

"You and the Air Force," Gold mumbled. "Okay, then! For our dogfight I'm choosing this one!" He picked up the GC-909I intercontinental jetliner.

"But it doesn't have any guns," Andy pointed out.

"Yes, it does. This one has hidden guns," Gold said seriously.

"Hidden where?"

"In the wings," Gold said. "Fifty of them. Fifty fifty-caliber machine guns. Twenty-five to a wing—" He hauled himself up. "So you'd better watch out, mister, because here I come!"

"Uh-uh!" Andy laughed, springing to his feet and making

varoom-varoom noises as he began running around the office.

"Bogie at five o'clock high!" Gold yelled, feeling silly, and enjoying it. He held the model jetliner out in front of him, keeping its nose pointed at Andy as he ran after his grandson.

"Bang-bang-bang-bang!" Andy chanted, aiming his model at Gold as the boy swung around a pair of armchairs, almost knocking a lamp off an end table in the process. Gold, grinning, faked one way, and then quickly tried to catch his grandson by coming around the other side of the chairs.

"Don't let me get on your tail, mister!" he gasped, laughing so hard he could barely catch his breath.

"Bang-bang-bang!" Andy yelled nonstop, running toward the desk with his bomber pointed over his shoulder back toward Gold.

"Here comes an Immelman turn!" Gold yelled, maneuvering the jetliner in the air as he chased Andy around his desk.

The boy stopped to thrust his airplane out like a pistol across the desk. "Bang-bang-bang! Take that, you mess-oh-shit!"

Gold, laughing so hard he thought he was going to bust, lunged across the desk, scattering papers as he tried to grab hold of Andy. The boy, giggling, lightly twisted away, dashing to the far side of the room. Gold straightened up and came lumbering after him, the sweat running down his heaving flanks beneath his flapping shirttails. "I'm gonna get you now, mister!" he roared. "Here comes fifty machine guns—"

The chest pain hit him so abruptly that he was still laughing even as the sledgehammer blow brought him short. *What is it?* He stood stock-still, afraid to move; afraid even to breathe—

The pain eased. *It's nothing. A cramp. It'll go away—*

The pain hit again and he doubled over. The jetliner slipped out of his grasp and crashed to the carpet, snapping off a wing. *This is not happening,* he thought as the pain wrapped its fingers into a fist around his chest and *squeeeeezzed*—

"Grandpa?" Andy was calling, sounding very far away.

The pain struck a third time. It began as an implosion in Gold's chest and then radiated through him. He was staggering blindly toward the nearest chair when the pain brought him to his knees.

"Grandpa?"

As Gold knelt in supplication to the pain he could dimly see Andy standing quietly beside the display case. The boy's face was pale. His eyes were the size of saucers.

Call someone— Gold waited, staring at the boy, who was still just standing there. *Didn't say it*, Gold realized. He was still on his knees. His arms were laced around himself to try and contain the pain. *Got to try to talk*—

"Andy—" he managed to whisper. "Dial 654 . . ." He toppled over, his face pressed against the carpet. Moaning, he rolled onto his back.

"Grandpa! Grandpa!" Andy was standing over him and crying.

"Andy, phone on the desk." His grandson's hot tears were splashing Gold's face. "Dial 654—"

The boy disappeared from his line of sight. Gold stared up at a spiraling white circle in a growing field of purple. The pain was grinding its heels into him as he heard squealing casters—*Andy, shoving the desk chair out of the way*—and then his grandson fumbling with the telephone.

"*654*—" Gold wheezed, closing his eyes. He was drifting now, floating on his back on a warm sea. Now and again the dark waves would wash over him . . . then . . . slowly . . . recede . . .

"*Security*—"

Andy must not have been holding the telephone up against his ear because Gold clearly heard the male voice on the other end of the line repeat, "This is Security. Is there anyone there?"

"My grandfather!" Andy sobbed. "My grandfather's sick—!"

"I love you, Andy," Gold murmured. Another wave turned him facedown into the dark warmth and carried him away.

(Two)

Tel Aviv, Israel
4 June 1967

On this clear, warm Sunday evening, Dizengoff Street, which was Tel Aviv's main drag, offered more entertainment than a three-ring circus. Schiff's Sidewalk Cafe, one of the many eateries on Dizengoff's north end, was the perfect place to watch the summer night's boulevard show roll by.

Steve Gold and Rivka Yakkov had a candle-lit table on Schiff's flagstone-paved front patio. The table was back under the striped awning. It was separated from the sidewalk by a wide flower box, but it had an unobstructed view of the street. There was soft jazz playing over an outdoor loud-speaker mounted in the patio's corner. The music worked as an accompanying background for the crowds strolling by, and for the city lights coming to life. The lights glowed like cool jewels in the gathering purple dusk.

Steve and Rivka had been there for the last hour. They were having an early dinner: roast lamb, rice mixed with pine nuts, and salad. Steve noticed that the bread basket was empty. Rivka saw, and was about to signal the waiter, but Steve stopped her.

"Watch this." He winked. Steve got the waiter's attention, and when the man had come over to their table he managed, in very halting Hebrew, to ask for more pita bread.

"Not bad," Rivka said in English, her dark eyes glinting with amused approval. "Not *good*—but not bad . . ."

"Hey, I'm trying to impress you. Am I succeeding?"

Her soft laughter was reward enough for his efforts. She was wearing a turquoise sundress with an elasticized bodice that clung to her luscious curves and left her tanned shoulders bare. Her thick, dark hair was loosely bound, revealing her dangling, crimson earrings. A matching strand of beads encircled her long, graceful neck.

She looked incredibly beautiful, Steve thought, gazing at her. But then she always did, no matter what she was wearing: an alluring dress or IAF khakis. Slowly over the last few months her manner toward him had thawed, to the extent that they'd had several such dinner dates together. Unfortunately for Steve, dinner—and a chaste handshake at evening's end—was as far as the relationship had gone.

"Have you actually been *studying* Hebrew?" Rivka asked skeptically.

"Me study?" Steve made a face. "But I was always pretty good at picking up phrases by ear. Forget about trying to learn it out of a book, though." He grinned, shaking his head. "Anyway, if I'm going to look like an Israeli, I might as well try to sound like one . . ."

He was wearing brown basket weave sandals, tan linen trousers, and a white short-sleeved shirt with an open, flat collar. In his spare time he'd gradually purchased a small wardrobe to round out what he'd brought with him to get through his extended stay. It amused him that when he was wearing his locally bought clothes, he could walk down the streets of Tel Aviv and nobody gave him a second look—until he opened his mouth, of course. But hell, a couple of times Israeli out-of-towners had actually stopped him to ask directions . . .

"I think you look handsome," Rivka told him. Her eyes over the rim of her wineglass had suddenly grown as huge as the moon over the dark Mediterranean. "But should I tell you that? Will it go to your head?"

"I think it might," Steve softly admitted. "Far more than this wine ever could."

They were working on their second bottle. Like so many in this city by the sea they were celebrating life by blowing off a little steam. For the past week the commercial radio broadcasts had been full of ominous bulletins about the Arab armor and artillery being massed along the borders of the Sinai and Gaza. Here in Tel Aviv, the Israeli Army's tanks and personnel carriers were clogging the narrow roads as they headed south to the Negev.

Enjoy the day, the Israelis seemed to be telling each other, evidencing the fatalistic humor characteristic of these eternally hard-pressed people. This is the calm before the storm, so enjoy yourself now. We are two and a half million against forty times that many. Enjoy now. The war is coming...

To Steve, it did look as if war was imminent. It had been a tense few months since he'd begun training several carefully selected squadrons of the most promising IAF fighter pilots. As far as he was concerned, the shit had hit the fan in April, when some of his personally trained boys had mixed it up with some Syrian MIGs, waxing a half dozen of the Commie/Arab bastards. Back at the base that night, the backslapping celebration had been joyous, but short-lived. On May 18, Nasser had demanded that the U.N. forces withdraw from the Egyptian-Israeli border. As the U.N. pulled out, Israel mobilized, calling up its reserve forces. A week later Nasser announced a naval blockade, closing the Gulf of Aquaba to Israeli shipping. Meanwhile the Mediterranean was filling up with American and Russian warships. The super powers were all urging Israel to show restraint, but from his vantage point inside the country Steve knew that the Israelis had to do something very soon. Each day of mobilization was costing Israel twenty million dollars that she didn't have.

"I think you may have become part Israeli," Rivka suddenly said.

"Hmm?" Steve asked, pushing the dark thought out of his mind. "How so?"

"You've got that same look in your eyes that we all get when we think about the situation we're in. Well? Am I right? Is that what you were thinking about?"

"It doesn't take much to guess that." Steve shrugged. He pushed away his plate, his appetite gone. "How can anybody think of anything else? Look! There goes some more of them—"

They watched as out on the street a World War II vintage truck slowed to a crawl, vainly beeping its horn as it tried to clear a path for itself through the crowds. The truck's side-railed bed was filled with heartbreakingly young-looking soldiers. They had rifles, and were wearing over-size khaki uniforms and high-crowned, duck-billed cloth caps.

"Reservists from the kibbutzim," Rivka observed as the truck finally rolled past. "You can tell by the hats, and the awkward way in which they hold their guns . . ."

"Farm boys," Steve sighed. He took out his cigarettes, lit one, and placed the pack and his matches on the table within Rivka's reach. "It's hard to see how they're going to stand a chance up against the Arabs."

"But a chance is exactly what they do have," Rivka said. "Provided, of course, that the Air Force can help them. That is why what *you've* been doing here is so important, Steven . . ."

"Maybe," Steve said, unconvinced. "You've seen the Mossad's latest estimates?"

"Of course I have," Rivka said.

Steve watched her help herself to a cigarette but did not try to light it for her. He'd once offered her a light and for his trouble had almost received his head handed to him, along with a stinging lecture about equality. The waiter came to take away their plates. Neither one of them wanted dessert, but they ordered coffee.

"The Mossad thinks your fighter jocks are going to be up against odds of five to one in the air," Steve continued. "Do you think your guys have what it takes to win against odds like that?"

"You're the one who trained them," she countered as the waiter returned with their double espressos.

"Sure I did, and they took well to the training, but when it comes to odds like that, it isn't about what's up here." He tapped his forehead. "It's about what's down here." He patted his heart.

"The Air Force will do its part," Rivka said, sipping at her espresso. "It always has, just as it has always faced overwhelming odds. You've seen the old airplanes enshrined on bases throughout the country, yes? The Piper Cubs, and the Czechoslovakian war surplus Messerschmitts our boys flew in 'forty-eight, during our war of independence? You've seen the photographs from those days at IAF headquarters here in the city? The pictures of our boys loading gasoline bombs to throw out the Piper Cubs' windows? And remember the pictures showing our pilots in their overalls standing in front of their ME-109s?"

When Steve nodded, she continued.

"Well, what the photos don't tell you is that those overalls were Nazi war surplus, just like the Messerschmitts. What the photos don't show is that on some of those overalls those brave boys wore into battle, you could see right here"—she touched her left breast—"right on the pocket, the terrible outline where the embroidered swastika had been razored off!"

"How would you know something like that?" Steve chided. "You were no more than a toddler back then."

"I know because I asked," she said simply. "It's every Israeli's obligation to ask, and to know, and to remember the heroes."

"And who is *your* special hero?" Steve asked. The strong espresso had counteracted the wine, reviving him. He felt alert and immensely intrigued by his beautiful and provocative dinner companion. He couldn't remember the last time he'd had a conversation with a woman this desirable, and had concentrated on what she was saying, instead of what he might next try in order to get her into bed.

Yeah, he thought. *Rivka is different from all the others . . . Or maybe it was he who was changing . . .*

Rivka's gaze had turned inward as she smoked her cigarette. "For me, Steven, I suppose that my special hero is a woman," she began. "Oh, I know those who take up arms and risk their lives in battle are very brave—" she added quickly. "They are certainly worthy to be called heroes, but in this hard world it is *expected* that a *man* should fight for what is right, while women are expected to be docile. That's why when a woman does great things, it is all the more heroic, do you see?"

"Sure." Steve nodded. "Women do have to start from behind, although during my short time in Israel I have seen women in all facets of life, including the military. They all seem heroic to me. Who out of all of them is special to you, Rivka?"

She smiled, her eyelids fluttering. For the first time since they'd met she looked shy, almost unsure of herself. "When I tell you, don't laugh—It is Golda Meir."

"Oh, sure." Steve nodded. "I've heard of her . . ."

"*Heard* of her, have you?" she scolded playfully. "*Only heard?*"

"I mean I know who she is," Steve said, laughing.

"For many young women *here* she is like, say, an Abe Lincoln would be to you," Rivka explained. "She is a great soldier for our cause. She fought in her own way during the war of independence by going to America and winning public opinion over to our side," she continued, growing in enthusiasm as she spoke. "After liberation she was elected to Israel's first Knesset—which is like your congress in America—and then moved to a cabinet-level post in the Government. For almost ten years, up until 'sixty-five, she was our Foreign Minister. I think for many people all over the world she symbolizes the State of Israel . . ."

"I think that's true . . ."

"Sometimes," Rivka said softly, "I imagine that I could follow in her footsteps . . ." She stopped abruptly, staring at Steve, as if daring him to mock her.

"I think you will," he said earnestly. "You've got the intelligence, the opportunity, and most important—" He again tapped his heart. "You've got it here . . ."

"Ah!" she said dismissively, suddenly businesslike again. "All girls here want to be the next Golda. We'll see who the next one will be . . ." She smiled. "But what about you? Who is your hero?"

"I've had many, at different stages of my life," Steve admitted. "John F. Kennedy, of course, and in the Air Force there have always been fighter pilots—men of action—to look up to . . ." He paused. "But now, well, nowadays, I think my hero is my father."

Rivka was smiling at him.

"I've pretty much had things my own way all my life," Steve continued. "But my father didn't. He started without a dime in his pocket. Hell, he didn't even have a birthright to call his own—"

"He is now a hero of Israel for what he has done for us," Rivka said.

"And what he's done for Israel is *beans* compared to what he's done for America," Steve said. "And meanwhile, he's overcome some pretty heavy odds on his own part. He's been knocked down a number of times, but he's always picked himself up, dusted himself off, and gone right back to doing what he believes in. And despite all the important things he's done, he's always been there for my sister and me." Steve nodded. "Yeah, these days my hero is my father . . ."

"Have you ever told him?" Rivka asked.

"Nah." Steve blushed, shrugging.

"You should, you know."

"I will . . . Someday . . . It's hard for me to say something like that to him . . . I guess because my pop and I have locked horns more than a few times . . ."

"Steven—Tell him!" she admonished sternly.

"Okay, okay." He grinned. "I promise I will . . . Can we change the subject?"

"Yes, of course."

"Maybe you can answer this for me. No one's ever told me the story of how Israel managed to get the MIG-21 out of Iraq in the first place . . ."

"The Arab pilot was brought here through a honey trap."

"Pardon?"

She laughed. "It is an espionage term. It means when a beautiful woman—or, I suppose, a handsome man—

charms the victim into whatever course of action is desired. I am not Mossad, so I know only a little, but in this case, it seems the Iraqi pilot was approached by a beautiful Mossad agent. She is a woman with an American passport, it so happens..."

"Goddamn, another one like Benny," Steve said sadly. He'd come to know and like the Israelis, but he still had mixed emotions about his friend's dual loyalties.

Rivka shrugged noncommittally. "In any event, this woman mixed easily within diplomatic and military circles, so she had little trouble making the acquaintance of the pilot. You know, of course, that only the highest-ranking, most trusted Arab pilots are allowed to fly the MIG-21?"

"That's what makes it all so mind-boggling," Steve said.

"Well, this agent learned that the pilot was critical of his government's actions toward the Kurds—"

"Whoah, slow down," Steve demanded.

"The Kurds are a minority people who live primitively in the mountains of Iraq. They tried to maintain their independence from Baghdad, so the Iraqi Government set out to exterminate them. This pilot had flown some bombing missions against the Kurds, and was deeply troubled concerning this policy of genocide he was being asked to carry out."

"So the guy had a motive for defecting..." Steve mused.

"And as the months passed, the Mossad agent helped strengthen that motive by becoming romantically involved with the pilot," Rivka continued. "He was married, with children, but in Iraq, I suppose, the aristocracy is allowed certain liberties," she added, her tone primly disapproving. "Anyway, the pilot and the Mossad agent traveled together. In Europe the honey trap was sprung. If he was willing to fly to Israel with his MIG-21, he would be paid handsomely, and he and his family would be given a new identity and settled somewhere in this country..."

"And if he wasn't willing?" Steve asked.

Again Rivka shrugged. "As I told you, I am not Mossad, so I don't know how these things go."

"So he went for it, obviously." Steve nodded. "But how did they get his wife and kids out?"

"Prior to his defection it was arranged for one of his children to travel to England to receive medical attention for some nonexistent ailment. With the child of course the mother would go, and with the mother, why not the other child, as well?"

"They just let the guy's family out like that?"

"It's very common practice. Medical care is not all it could be in Iraq." Rivka chuckled. "And don't forget, this man was highly placed in the Iraqi Air Force. The right to medical treatment abroad is just one of the privileges such Arabs enjoy over the unfortunate masses."

"So his family boarded an airplane to England—" Steve began.

"But they never got there," Rivka finished. "They got *here*, instead. Soon after, the Iraqi got into his airplane for a routine patrol, and flew to Israel. It happened so fast that by the time the Arabs realized what was happening the pilot had already linked up with his IAF protective escort. And that was how we got our MIG," she finished.

"Poor guy," Steve said.

"Hardly," Rivka scoffed. "He and his family are well taken care of, I am quite sure. Israel's reputation depends on her holding up her part of the bargain in such matters." Her smile turned devilish. "But I do understand why a man such as you might empathize with that pilot."

"Meaning what?" Steve demanded.

"Meaning that you can easily see yourself being hoodwinked in just the same way," she teased, licking her pink lips as she regarded him.

"Are you saying that I could be wrapped around some female's little finger, Captain Yakkov?"

"Oh, absolutely I am saying just that, Colonel Gold." She nodded adamantly. "It would be even *easier* to take advantage of *you*."

"How so?"

She leaned toward him across the table. He could feel their knees suddenly touching.

"Because, Steven, *you* think it is the natural course of affairs that every woman to whom you have ever paid attention should tumble into bed with you."

"Hmmm." Steve nodded. "Until *now*, of course . . ."

"Until now, of course," she echoed, deadpan mimicking him.

"Honey trap, huh?"

"Honey trap." Rivka impishly nodded.

"Well, you know what they say." Steve smiled brightly. "You can catch more *fliers* with honey than you can with vinegar—" His laugh died in his throat as he saw her staring blankly.

"*Who* says that . . ." Rivka asked, puzzled.

"In America! It's an old saying! 'Flier' instead of 'fly,' as in 'housefly' . . ." Steve rolled his eyes. "Ah, the hell with it . . ."

Rivka glanced at her watch. "We should go. Do you have your car?" she asked. She had met him at the cafe.

"It's parked around the corner," Steve told her.

"Then would you take me to my flat—?"

"Now you're talking!" Steve beamed.

"—and drop me off there," she added, wagging her finger at him like a schoolteacher. "I have IAF paperwork to catch up with tonight, Colonel, sir."

"Rivka," Steve groaned. "This has got to stop. The way you're keeping me at arm's length is making me *miserable*. And I *thought* it was your job to make me *happy*—"

"That *is* my job, Steven . . ." She reached across the table to skate a figure eight with her fingernail on the back of his hand. "But *when* I do it is up to *me*."

The car they'd given him was a Citroën 2CV. It was a bug-eyed, little tin can of a thing, painted a cream of pea soup shade of pale green. The Citroën had serious wrinkles in all four of its rusting bicycle fenders, a balky, push-pull gear shift lever mounted on the dash, and a black canvas sunroof that Steve kept open all the time because it couldn't block the rain worth a damn, anyhow. Inside the car there was more of that black canvas, this time cut into strips and crisscrossed around hollow, curved metal tubing: lawn furniture where in a real car the padded upholstered seats would be. Beneath the hood was a minuscule 300 cc engine: Steve had seen bigger power plants on lawn mowers. The car could do maybe forty-five miles an hour, provided, of course, the road was level, the wind was at your back, and you stuck out one foot and helped scoot her along.

Despite all that, careening around Tel Aviv in what he had affectionately taken to calling his "little green crab louse" was kind of fun. On the other hand, Steve was grateful that his "other car" was a Tyran II jet fighter—

He dropped Rivka at her apartment building, a rickety-looking tenement located on a side alley off the southern end of Hakovshim Street, near the old port of Jaffa. Rivka had told him that her flat was on the top floor, and that her bedroom had a beautiful view of the sea.

If there's a God, I'll someday get to find that out for myself, Steve thought as he drove back to his own apartment. It was furnished studio equipped with a small kitchenette, located on the second floor of a building on a side street off Petah Tikvah Road, near the railway station. The place was a little grim, but all in all it wasn't bad. The apartment was clean, and it faced the rear, overlooking a little courtyard, so it was quiet.

He parked the Citroën in front of his building and used his key to open the locked front door. His head was full of lustful thoughts of Rivka as he climbed the two flights of stairs.

He stopped short on the second-floor landing.

There was light coming from beneath his door. Steve thought about it: He'd left early this morning, and had spent the day on his own, sight-seeing. He *knew* he hadn't left any lights on.

He moved quickly and quietly to his door and tried the knob. It was unlocked. He pushed it open and stepped inside. Benny Detkin, a very somber expression on his face, was sitting in the rocking chair by the window.

"I'm disappointed," Steve said, shutting the door behind him. "I was looking forward to meeting a Jewish burglar."

"Jewish burglars are like all the rest," Benny told him. "More successful, maybe..."

"When'd you get back?" Steve asked, standing in the center of the room.

"Just a couple of hours ago."

"You ready to do some flying tomorrow?" Steve challenged him. The past few months, whenever Benny had been in Israel, he'd managed to find the time to come down to the base and fly training missions along with Steve and the rest of the pilots. Steve had been gratified to find that his old friend still had the right stuff. Benny today was every bit as sharp in the cockpit as he had been over twenty years ago when he'd helped chase the Zeros back to Tokyo.

"Steve..." Benny began, looking worried. "When I checked in at IAF headquarters, there was a cable for you."

"A cable? What about?"

"Steve—"

"What?" The look on Benny's face froze him. "What's happened?"

"It's your father," Benny said, his voice thick with sadness. "He had a heart attack—"

"Oh, God—" Steve staggered back. His vision dimmed. He could feel his legs sagging. His head was filling with a steadily building roar, like that of a jet plane approaching—

"My father's my hero—" he'd told her.

"Then you should tell him—" Rivka had said.

"Plenty of time..."

His earlier chuckles echoed perversely, melding with his hoarse moan of grief—Plenty of time...

"Steve!"

He opened his eyes to find himself lying flat on his back

on the carpet. Benny, looking petrified, was kneeling beside him cradling Steve's head in his hands.

"You fainted," Benny said. "You all right now?"

"Yeah . . ." Steve said thickly. "Jesus, is my father *dead*?"

"No—"

"Huh? What?" Steve shook himself, trying to clear his head.

"I said no! He's not dead! Listen to me! Will you?"

Steve nodded slowly. "I'm okay now." He sat up gingerly and rubbed his hands across his face. "When did it happen?"

"I don't know, exactly, but it was yesterday. Sometime during late afternoon." Benny paused, studying Steve, as if he still wasn't sure how much of what he was saying was getting through. "I'm talking about Saturday *California time*," Benny added.

"Yeah, of course . . ." Steve muttered. "Late afternoon on the West Coast would make it three or four in the morning here . . ." He frowned. "That's still hours ago! Why wasn't I contacted?"

"No one knew where you were all day."

"When did the cable come in?"

"According to the log, mid-morning our time."

"And that's hours after you said it happened!"

"Calm down!" Benny commanded. "Think it through. I'm sure it was some time before they knew anything, and *then* they had to first reach somebody in Washington—and this is on a Saturday night—who knew how to get a message to you. When you add in the time difference, I'm surprised they got to you as soon as they did. Someone must have stayed up all night trying to pull all the pieces together."

"I guess you're right," Steve said, getting to his feet. "Damn! I wish I knew what was happening!"

"Come on," Benny said, heading for the door.

"Where are we going?"

"IAF headquarters. The cable had a number for you to call. I left a man standing by in Communications to patch you through . . ."

(Three)

IAF Headquarters, Tel Aviv

The Communications Room was a small annex off the amphitheaterlike, map-lined, computer-laden War Room. Both were in the basement of the nondescript, gray stone building like so many others in the heart of the city. Steve and Benny waited anxiously in the windowless, fluorescent-lit, belowground cave lined with electronics as the radio man seated at his console fiddled with his dials. On the sound-proof wall behind them the rows of clocks showing the time all over the world ticked relentlessly.

"I've got the connection," the radio man suddenly said in English, whipping off his earphones and handing them to Steve. "Use this mike here—" He indicated a microphone angled out on a pivoting arm above his control panel. "Talk fast," he added in warning as Steve adjusted the earphones on his head. "We could lose the connection anytime."

"Hello? Hello?" Steve called loudly, grimacing as static pouring from the headphones filled his ears.

"I'll pipe it through the overhead speaker," the radio man was telling Benny.

"—Steve? It's Sus—" The rest was lost in a burst of angry static.

"Susan? Can you hear me? Damn—!" Due to some glitch in the thousands of miles of wire linking him to his sister half a world away, Steve's own voice was echoing in his ears a split second after he spoke.

"—Yes. I can hear you—" Susan said. "—been waiting forever for you to call! No one knew how to reach you—"

"Susan, tell me about Pop," he demanded.

"—heart attack," she said. As she continued she was peri-odically drowned out by the noise over the line. "—awake, resting comfortably—intensive care—blocked artery—

no operation—too old—but the doctors say he should recover—"

"How's his spirits?" Steve shouted into the mike.

Suddenly, miraculously, all interference on the line ceased. Susan's voice came through the headphones as clearly as if she were in the room with him.

"He's taking it very well, considering," she said. "Mom and Don have talked to him. He knows he has to retire. When they told him, his reaction was funny. He seemed almost *relieved* to be turning over the business." She began to laugh and cry at the same time. "Oh, Steve, wait until you hear! You'll never guess what he intends to do once he's well: He wants to be Bar Mitzvahed—"

The roar of static cut in. "Susan? Hello? Are you still there!" Steve shouted, glancing questioningly at the radio operator.

"That's it, we lost it." The guy frowned. "We were patched in through London, believe it or not. From there over the cable to New York, and across to California. I'm surprised the linkup lasted as long as it did. I could try to get it back . . ."

"Not necessary," Steve said, plucking off the headset. "Thank you for what you did manage."

The operator nodded, breaking into a grin. "Thank God your father is going to be all right. And better than all right! He's going to be a Bar Mitzvah!"

"Bar Mitzvah literally translates into 'man of duty,'" Benny said as they left the IAF building. It was now close to eleven o'clock, and the city was quieting down. The street they were standing on was deserted.

"Traditionally, a boy is thirteen when he is a Bar Mitzvah . . ." Benny continued, pedantically lapsing into what Steve imagined was his friend's courtroom style. ". . . But, of course, there is no set limit to how old a man might *be* when God sees fit to summon him to finally take on the religious duties of a good Jew—"

"I know all that," Steve cut him off.

"You do?" Benny asked skeptically.

"More or less." Steve shrugged. "Look, I've got to get home."

"Are you sure?" Benny asked.

"What do you mean, am I sure?" Steve echoed, pausing to stare at his friend. "Of course I am. My father needs me—"

"You can't do anything for your father by his bedside," Benny said. "But you can do a lot for him here."

"What are you talking about?" Steve impatiently demanded.

"Listen," Benny urgently began. "It's been decided. Tomorrow morning Israel is making the first move. The IAF will execute a preemptory strike against all the Arab air bases."

"Jesus, that's a lot of targets spread out over a wide area. It'll take all your airplanes to pull it off."

"They know."

"It will leave Israel's airspace virtually defenseless."

"They know that, too." Benny nodded. "But they feel it is worth the gamble, and I agree with them. The odds against the IAF will be overwhelming if it allows the Arabs to get their planes off the ground. They feel the only way to take control of the sky is to destroy those MIGs and bombers while they're still parked."

"Okay, but what does that have to do with me?" Steve asked. "My part's done. I've trained your guys to the best of my ability."

"The IAF would like you to stay, in case this gamble doesn't work. They feel that your experience would be of great value in deciding how to utilize whatever remaining airplanes they'll have left if the Arabs do manage to take to the sky."

"Please try to understand, Benny." Steve frowned. "It's hard for me to concentrate on this with my father lying in a hospital bed."

"Your sister said the doctors thought he was going to be all right," Benny argued.

"Sure, that's what the doctors *think*, but what if they're

wrong?" Steve countered. "Benny, he's my father. There are things I want to tell him; this might be my last chance."

"Forgive me for speaking bluntly, but there's little time," Benny began. "If you stay another few days, and your father lives as is expected, you'll have the chance to tell him what's in your heart. But if you stay, and God forbid he should die before you get home, think about what he would tell you to do, if he only could. You just heard from your sister that your father wishes to devote his future to his religion. You already know that Herman Gold has worked very hard for Israel's survival. Taking all that into account, don't you think you would be telling him quite a lot about how much you love him by remaining here, furthering his work on Israel's behalf in its time of need—?"

Steve nodded uncertainly. He'd been in touch with Washington through a continuing exchange of coded cables. Back in May, when the news about the U.N. pulling out was breaking, Steve had asked for permission to continue training the IAF pilots. Washington had been quick to agree. The most recent cable he'd received just a couple of days ago relayed orders for him to cooperate with the Israelis in every way possible short of actually entering into combat. Of course, he knew that those orders would be rescinded if he were to plead personal hardship concerning his father...

"Think a moment on what I've said, and you'll realize that I'm right," Benny was telling him. "Your father risked his reputation and freedom to work for Israel. I'm sure that right now he is very proud to know that his son is doing the same."

If that's true, and I think it is, Steve mused, *I know what might make him even happier—*

"Okay, I'll stay," Steve said. "On one condition . . . We give my Pop a *real* Bar Mitzvah present."

"What are you talking about?" Benny asked, perplexed.

"Come on." Steve smiled. "I'll tell you on the way. If this raid is happening in just a few hours from now we'd better get over to the base—"

CHAPTER 22

(One)

IAF Base, outside Tel Aviv
5 June 1967

Dawn was brightening the Mediterranean sky as the coded word went out from IAF headquarters to the secret air base where Steve and Benny were waiting, and to similar bases all around the outskirts of Tel Aviv. The preemptive strike would begin at 0745 hours.

Inside the brightly lit Operations Complex's main briefing room, Steve and Benny stood staring at a large map of the area, along with the twelve Tyran II pilots in khaki flight suits who were scheduled to fly. IAF Captain Rivka Yakkov was there as well. She was looking pale and somber, her uniform uncharacteristically rumpled, and her eyes still puffy from sleep. Like most of the administrative and operations people assigned to this base, she had been awakened just a few hours ago by an IAF courier banging on her door with the news that war was about to begin.

Steve took a moment to look over the pilots as the briefing began. He'd trained every one of them, and dozens more assigned to other bases. He'd done the best he could to give them the advantage of his hard-won, aerial combat experience.

"Here are your targets," Rivka was saying, using a pointer to indicate the Egyptian air bases at Abu Fayid, on the Sinai Peninsula's Mediterranean coast; and at Suez, on the far side of the Gulf. The briefing was being conducted in English for Steve's benefit, so that he could participate if he wished by giving some last-minute observations or suggestions to the men. The pilots were all proficient in English; that had been a prerequisite, practical necessity for participating in Steve's training program.

". . . The eight aircraft of Flight Orange and Flight Blue will attack Abu Fayid," Rivka was continuing. "Flight Yellow's four planes will join with other flights from other bases to attack Suez. You'll find the specifics of your missions in your briefing kits . . ."

"We'll need auxiliary fuel tanks to reach the Suez," observed the leader of Flight Yellow.

"Call them *drop* tanks," Steve interrupted. "And remember to *drop* them if you have to, dammit. To hell with the cost—"

"I've learned that lesson." Flight Yellow's lead pilot nodded, smiling. He was the pimply-faced kid who Steve had outfoxed in the mock dogfight back in February.

"The other two flights won't need drop tanks," another pilot murmured. "Abu Fayid is no more than fifteen minutes' flight time from Tel Aviv—"

"And it's no more than fifteen minutes from Abu Fayid *to* Tel Aviv, should you leave any MIGs or bombers there intact," Rivka added meaningfully. "Each Tyran will be carrying two, five-hundred-pound bombs which are to be used to destroy the Arab runways. After you have released your ordnance you will use your cannons to strafe. Are there any questions?"

The pilots were shaking their heads.

"Don't forget what I've taught you guys," Steve said. "Don't make me look bad." He winked. "I used this as my home base, so I expect a little more from all of you. Don't let me down—"

"Good luck, and God go with you," Rivka said, glancing at the bank of clocks on the briefing room's wall. "The nation's hopes rest in your hands."

The pilots were busy gathering up their charts and briefing papers. Steve waited until Rivka's back was turned, and then touched Benny's arm. "Let's go," he whispered. Together they slipped out of the briefing room and left the Operations Complex.

Outside the base was stirring with commotion. The quiet dawn was being shattered by the banshee wail of taxiing fighters, and the air stank from jet fuel vapors and diesel fumes. Ground crew chiefs were running around screaming in Hebrew at their people. Ordnance carts were hauling bombs toward the ready line, and pilots were double-timing it to the personal equipment shack. Steve and Benny headed that way, as well.

"I don't know how I let you talk me into this," Benny was complaining.

"I talked you into it because you *wanted* me to talk you into it." Steve chuckled. "You should have seen the gleam in your eye when I first suggested it . . ."

"I just can't believe we're really going to do this," Benny grumbled. "Me, a lawyer from New York, and you, a United States Air Force colonel, flying a combat mission on behalf of Israel—"

"Keep your voice down," Steve hissed. "We aren't flying yet, and we won't be if you announce it to the world!" Steve slapped Benny on the back. See that? There they are, waiting for us just like I said they would be . . ."

A pair of young pilots assigned to Flight Blue were nervously loitering outside the personal equipment shack.

Steve, after checking the flight roster to learn who was scheduled to fly, had cornered these two earlier this morning to ask if they would allow Benny and him to take their places on the air strike. Of course, they were initially horrified at the idea, but after Steve had leaned on them awhile they'd relented.

He'd known they would because Steve had once been in their shoes. As a young apprentice fighter jock he remembered how he'd idolized the older, more experienced guys who had a seemingly impossible to match number of kills under their belts. Steve remembered how those top dogs, top guns had enjoyed a mesmerizing hold over him . . .

But that was all yesterday. Since then the years had flown by with the speed of an F-105 Thunderchief hugging the deck on a strafing run. To the Israeli pilots who Steve had so recently shepherded through the sky, *he* was now top dog. To them, he was the quintessential fighter jock: an ace in two wars, a veteran of three. Steve had arrived here a legend to the fledgling IAF fighter pilots, had proved himself by mastering the intricacies of the MIG-21, and had stayed to become their mentor. He had taken them under his wing and taught them everything. In return, his protégés would do anything for him . . . As these two pilots so anxiously fidgeting outside the personal equipment shack were now about to prove—

"Shalom, Colonel Gold, Colonel Detkin," one of them said softly.

"Yeah, shalom, boys." Steve nodded. "You're both clear on what you're supposed to do, right?"

"Just as you told us, Colonel, sir." The pilot nodded as he and the other IAF flier handed Steve and Benny their briefing kits. "We will go directly to our quarters and stay there. You two will come to us directly upon returning and prep us for the mission debriefing."

"You got it, boys." Steve nodded. "Don't worry. It'll go smooth as silk. Now beat it."

The two pilots quickly walked away. Steve watched as they took the long way around to get to their quarters without going near the Operations/Administration complex.

Once they'd disappeared into the trees, he said, "Well, that's that—"

"I sure hope they'll be all right," Benny said worriedly.

"They will be. First of all, we're not going to get caught. And second of all, even if we do get caught, we'll take the heat, not them."

"And what will happen to us?" Benny demanded.

"Nothing." Steve shrugged. "I hope . . ."

"I just hope you know what *we're* doing—"

"Benny, I may not always know what I'm doing, but I always do what I want." Steve laughed. "Like I told you before, my father is going to appreciate the fact that I'll be able to give him a firsthand account of how the Vector-A system works in a real combat situation, and he'll flip when he hears that I flew this mission to honor him. You said yourself that he's solidly in Israel's corner—"

"I have a big mouth," Benny said morosely.

"Just think how pleased my father's gonna be when he finds out that his flesh and blood actually struck a blow on Israel's behalf."

"Have you picked up enough Hebrew to get yourself through the preflight check?" Benny asked.

"I ought to have; I've heard these guys go through it enough times."

"Just remember that once we're in the air, if you can't say it in Hebrew, then don't say it at all. If the Arabs or Soviets monitoring our transmissions should get wind that Americans are involved in this . . ."

"I know, I know." Steve nodded. "We'll be in deep shit with both the Israeli and United States Governments."

The two men stood to one side as the pilots filed out of the shack. The IAF fliers were loaded down with flight gear, and were wearing helmets, dangling oxygen masks, and sunglasses.

When the last man was out, Steve and Benny ducked inside. They quickly donned the khaki flight suits and gear they'd been issued for the training program. A few moments later, two more pilots, their faces masked by helmets and sunglasses, came out of the shack. Silently, these last two members of Flight Blue joined their comrades who were just now climbing into the droning Tyran IIs trembling in readiness on the flight line.

(Two)

At 0745 hours the twelve Tyran IIs thundered aloft. The four jets of Yellow Flight banked away to begin their journey to Suez. The remaining eight arranged themselves into groups of four, with Orange Flight in the lead, and then banked west, curving far out over the sparkling blue Mediterranean.

This is gonna work out fine, I can feel it, Steve thought. He was flying as Blue Flight's number three man, the element lead. Benny Detkin was flying as his wingman. The weather was perfect. The morning sun had burned away the dawn haze to reign supreme; a blazing fireball hanging in a flawless, turquoise sky.

The idea to wait until a quarter to eight in the morning to launch the attack was a brilliant one. Surprise raids paradoxically traditionally took place at dawn, so by now the Egyptians would most likely have called in their own, early morning combat air patrols. With any luck, the Egyptian radar operators sitting at their consoles would assume that these eight Israeli planes flying out to sea were on just another routine training run. Steve himself had many times taken his students out over the sea to practice combat maneuvers.

Meanwhile, Steve's own surprise scheme seemed to be turning out well. The preflight check had gone without a hitch, and now his Tyran II felt rock solid in the air; as comfortably familiar as his old leather flight jacket. He was positive that nobody suspected that he and Benny had tagged along. Mission protocol was contributing to his strategy: Strict radio silence was in effect.

Steve studied his instruments. Everything was green, including the Vector-A radar ranging system. It was represented in the cockpit by a shoebox-size rectangular console that was studded with switches and knobs arranged around a five-inch diameter porthole-shaped CRT screen. The gizmo was mounted on the instrument panel, just below the forward windscreen, below the Tyran's gun sight. During furball, close-in dogfighting, the Vector-A system remained off, and the fighter's original equipment gun sight was used to aim its brace of 30-millimeter cannons. The Vector-A came into its own during air-to-ground attacks. Once the pilot had locked the Vector-A on target, he could concentrate on jinking to avoid ground defenses. The Vector-A, by means of radar equipment mounted in the jet's nose, calculated the proper instant to automatically release the ordnance. The Vector-A could also control Air-to-Air missile weapons systems, if the Israelis happened to have any, which they didn't. The Tyran IIs were equipped to carry such missiles, but because AAs cost tens of thousands of dollars each, the Israelis couldn't afford them. The Israelis had to pay for everything they got from their sole arms supplier, France. The Arabs got all the weapons they could use from Russia through "foreign aid."

Steve checked his altimeter. The strike force was now at twenty thousand feet, and taking its time cruising along at three hundred knots, both to conserve fuel and to give the Egyptians a nice long look. The hope was that the Egyptians, not especially known for their attention span, would get bored and decide to play a little backgammon or something to pass the time.

Steve checked his maps. Just another few moments . . .

He watched as far ahead the Tyrans of Orange Flight abruptly dropped into a steep dive. Blue Flight's lead element next followed suit. The two, dun-colored, delta-winged craft wearing the Star of David hurtled like arrowheads toward the sun-dappled azure sea.

Here we go, Steve thought as he shoved the stick forward to follow Blue Lead's plunge. He glanced out the canopy to check on Benny. His old buddy was tight on his wing, following him down.

At fifty feet the two flights leveled off. Element by element, the Tyran IIs whip-snapped around onto an easterly course, back toward the coastline. The Israeli jets were now committed to their attack approach. For the next five minutes they would fly a beeline, skimming the waves toward their target. Steve hoped they were now flying below the enemy's radar. Steve, busy greening up his weapons systems, also hoped that his Tyran II had been waterproofed. She was just now flying so low that she was feeling more like a speedboat than an airplane. He was having a hard time seeing out of his canopy due to the salt spray being kicked up by the after-wash of the jets ahead of him.

The Egyptian coastline was looming ever larger as the eight Tyran IIs hurtled onward. *Feet dry*, Steve thought as the strike force quickly left ocean and then beachhead behind. Now the strike force was hugging the Sinai's yellow sand dunes, kicking up dust and gravel as the jets shrieked across the scrubby green and gold desert.

This was it. Abu Fayad Air Base was only a few klicks away. Steve glanced at Benny, who was still flying on his wing. Benny saw him looking, and gave him a jaunty wave.

Stick tight, old buddy, Steve silently told him. *We kicked ass over the Pacific, and those Zero drivers were a pretty tough bunch ... We shouldn't have any trouble with these camel drivers—*

Ahead Orange Flight went to afterburn, rocketing skyward to begin their bombing run. Steve watched for Blue Lead's tail pipe to spit fire, and then cobbed his own throttle, feeling the kick in the pants as his Tyran leapt to one thousand feet, which was the ceiling for this bombing run. The Egyptians had Soviet-supplied SAM missiles, but they were useless below two thousand feet.

As the dunes dropped away Steve saw the target. At the far end of the base he could make out Abu Fayid's bunker-like control tower complex. It was bristling with radar and radio antennae. Surrounding the tower were the airplane hangars, and branching off from them was a cloverleaf complex of concrete runways. What looked like barracks-type housing lined the base perimeter, and about one hundred yards away from the control tower and hangars were probably the fuel and ordnance depots. Tanker trucks and ordnance vehicles were parked nearby the second runway cloverleaf fronting the depots.

It seemed as if the Egyptians were being taken by surprise. The concrete revetments lining the runways were filled with parked aircraft. There were at least thirty silvery MIGs, and a dozen of the Soviet-built, TU-16 Badger bombers. The TUs dwarfed the MIGs, and looked a little like the F-105 Thuds that Steve had flown in Vietnam.

Orange Flight was already executing its dive bomb attack. There was no longer any need for radio silence, so the IAF pilots were now all excitedly chattering away to each other in Hebrew as they went about their work. Below, Egyptian personnel looked like ants pouring out of a broken nest as they ran from the buildings, dashing madly to their planes, and to the sandbagged anti-aircraft gun emplacements scattered about the base. As the Tyran IIs screamed down sporadic tracer fire rose up to meet them. The tracer fire increased as more of the gun emplacements came on-line. Steve watched Orange Flight continue its attack run, skillfully jinking its way through the wildly criss-crossing ground fire.

And that's thanks to you, Pop, Steve thought. *It's the Vector-A systems that are getting us through.*

Orange Flight released its bombs over the runway cloverleaf near the fuel depot. Steve watched as the eight, five-hundred-pound bombs hit and detonated, the massive explosions linking together into a smoky black anvil that abruptly blossomed forth its own tower of orange flame as the nearby stores of fuel and ordnance caught.

Our turn, Steve thought as Blue Flight spread out four abreast and nosed down toward the base. Their target was the complex of runways near the control tower.

Steve fine-tuned his Vector-A, tracking the glowing green

Aim Point target image through the drift-stabilized sight on the portholelike CRT screen. He aligned the Vector-A's cross hairs on the Aim Point and "froze" it in place, pressed the target insert button, and locked down his bomb-release. He then turned his attention to avoiding the fiery beads of tracer fire so hungrily reaching out to him. No matter how much he weaved and bobbed, the Vector-A kept the Aim Point aligned in its cross hairs. As Steve flew over the target his ordnance was automatically released. He nosed up, coming around hard at five hundred feet, scarcely escaping the shock waves as his own bombs detonated, tearing up the runway.

Steve switched off the Vector-A. He checked to see that Benny was still with him, and then rejoined Blue Lead and his wingman. Orange Flight was already busy strafing what remained of the parked planes. Steve could see their dual cannons hosing down the revetments with twin streams of 30-millimeter firepower. The helpless MIGs and TU-16 bombers were hammered into scrap metal. Fires sprouted and quickly spread as the ambushed planes' fuel tanks ignited.

Steve, orbiting the base, noticed a sandbag gun emplacement still operating. He skated the Tyran around onto an attack approach, and centered his gun sight's luminous red pipper on the barking machine gun. He pressed his trigger, and felt his Tyran II shake as its belly-mounted twin cannons lashed out like twin, striking rattlesnakes. The gun emplacement was quickly blown away.

Steve eased back on the stick to climb a bit, careful, however, to stay below two thousand feet, just in case there were any SAMs around. As was his habit, he routinely scanned the sky; that was when he saw the sun glint on four silvery specks coming in fast from the east, at about five thousand feet.

Jesus Christ, those are MIGs, he thought. *We're gonna be bounced.*

His punched the mike, ready to call out a warning. The words died in his throat. *He didn't know the Hebrew. If he called it out in English whoever was monitoring would know that American personnel were involved in the attack—*

Steve looked around wildly at the other Tyran IIs so busily buzzing the base like angry hornets tormenting an enemy. The boys flying those planes were all good pilots, but right now, in the excitement, they'd forgotten what he'd taught them about watching each other's backs. They were all too drunk on their first taste of combat to do anything but concentrate on their targets. Steve was willing to forgive them for their youthful enthusiasm, but he was totally pissed at Benny, who was a seasoned veteran, and should have known better than to forget about watching the sky—

Especially since Benny was supposed to be flying as Steve's wingman, and could have alerted the strike force in Hebrew!

Fuck it, Steve thought, punching on his mike. *You play, you pay.* If he was going to be found out, so be it. He wasn't about to put his Air Force career above the lives of these pilots—

"Listen up," he growled into his mike. "Bandits, five o'clock high."

There was no immediate reply. Steve could imagine the shock the other pilots were experiencing as they heard their trainer's familiar voice coming over their helmet headsets.

"Goddammit! Steve!" Benny blurted. "You weren't supposed to talk!"

"Fuck you, pal!" Steve shot back. "You weren't supposed to be bounced like a goddamned rookie!" Steve pulled back on the stick and swung his Tyran around to meet the incoming MIG-21s head-on. "Open your eyes, everyone! Bandits! Coming in fast."

"Rog, Steve," one of the other pilots replied in English. "Coming to join you now..." The pilot paused. "And everyone! Remember to speak English like we...uh...planned!"

"Yes, to confuse our Egyptian enemies—!" another pilot quickly added.

"Yes...uh...Bob—!" still another pilot chimed in. "This is...Tony! Like Steve, we must all remember to speak the English, and use our English code names to confuse the enemy—"

Nice improvisation. Steve grinned. *Thanks, fellows . . .*

He got his mind back on business, lassoing one of the oncoming MIGs in his gun sights' luminous red circle. The MIG began firing at him with its own cannon. Steve did his best to ignore the enemy tracers, which from his point of view looked like flaming baseballs being lobbed past his wings. He had to make his shots count. The Tyran II carried only 125 rounds per gun. The other guys had all been doing the lion's share of the strafing, so they had to be pretty low on ammo. It might be up to him to defend them from all four of these bandits . . .

Got'cha—The red pipper landed smack on the attacking MIG-21's weird snout, just above the flashing barrel of its cannon. Steve pressed his trigger and watched his rounds pelt the nose and canopy of the MIG. The enemy pilot veered away, exposing his underside to Steve's guns. Steve stitched an ugly line of holes along the bandit's belly, gutting the MIG. It came apart in a crimson explosion.

Steve saw Benny drop down on a MIG's six o'clock, and then cut loose with his guns. The MIG jinked for all it was worth, but there wasn't a pilot on earth—Steve excepted, of course—who could get away from Benny Detkin. A few seconds later, and Benny's MIG had disintegrated under his Tyran's guns like a clay pigeon shattered by buckshot.

"Does that make up for my screwing up back there?" Benny radioed in apology."

"I forgive you." Steve laughed.

The rest of the Tyrans had ganged up on the remaining two MIGs. Steve watched his boys go to work just like he'd taught them. It wasn't long before that last pair of 21s had been turned into smoky fireballs, streaking mournfully toward the shifting desert sands.

"Time to go home, everybody," Orange Lead radioed.

"Rog, let's go home," another pilot replied.

They're all still speaking English, God bless 'em, Steve

thought. *Still keeping up their valiant effort to save my skin—*

Yeah, they were a good bunch of boys, all right. Steve was proud to have trained them. *And come what may, I'm glad I was with 'em when they drew first blood—*

Steve took up his place in his flight's formation as the victorious IAF pilots banked away from the ruined Egyptian base. Benny settled into position on Steve's wing, and together the two war buddies set their course for home.

(Three)

Tel Aviv
11 June 1967

It was twelve noon on a Sunday. Steve was in his Tel Aviv flat, busy packing his belongings. He was going home. He was scheduled aboard an El Al flight departing Lod Airport for London at five o'clock. In London, he would be met by American embassy personnel. The Air Force brass in Washington had arranged for Steve to be hustled directly to a waiting USAF transport plane that would then whisk him across the Atlantic. His reports on the MIG-21 had long ago been sent via diplomatic pouch to Washington. He himself was scheduled to be in Washington to begin his debriefing on Tuesday.

Steve had already said his good-byes at IAF headquarters. Thinking about that, he had to smile. Everyone had seemed genuinely sorry to see him go, but also more than a little relieved to be rid of him. He had become one hot potato since embarking on his impromptu combat mission four days ago . . .

As Benny had feared, the enemy had been monitoring radio transmissions that day. Within twenty-four hours, Nasser had gone public with his charge that the reason the Egyptian Air Force has suffered its ass-whipping was because United States air power had intervened on the Israelis' behalf.

The United States, of course, had denied the charge, rightfully insisting that they had no idea what Nasser was talking about. Nasser, unconvinced, had retaliated by breaking diplomatic ties with the U.S., and closing the Suez Canal. Syria and Iraq quickly followed suit, and Kuwait suspended its oil shipments to the West . . .

To Steve, the idea that he'd personally caused all this was mind-boggling to say the least. It seemed a little funny . . . but mostly appalling—

Actually, the incredible ramifications of what he'd done were scaring the hell out of him. Sure he'd ruffled a few feathers, maybe made a few waves, and maybe pissed off a few people in his life . . . But this was the first time he'd ever caused entire goddamned *nations* to sever ties with one another . . .

Well, Benny told me so, Steve reminded himself. Now the dirty deed was done. If his government found out what he'd done, he was prepared to accept the consequences. Meanwhile, Steve would look forward to Pop's reaction when he heard all about it . . .

The strikes flown against the other Arab air bases that Monday had all gone as successfully as the one against Abu Fayid in which Steve had participated. Within hours the air forces of Israel's various Arab enemies had ceased to exist. The Star of David ruled the sky.

Ironically, a lot of very important people in the IAF thought that a good deal of the credit for their success over the Arabs belonged to Steve, due to the job he'd done training the IAF fighter pilots. Steve wasn't totally convinced. As he'd told Rivka, he'd taught those pilots what he could, but they'd brought their own drive and determination—their own heart—to the job their country had asked them to do.

Nevertheless, some of the IAF bigshots were insisting on comparing Steve to David Marcus, the American Army colonel who had done so much for Israel's ground forces during its '48 war of independence. Privately, Steve thought that his being compared to a legend like David Marcus was a bit much. On the other hand, he just now wasn't inclined to argue with his IAF fans because in their enthusiasm they had prevailed on their government to protect him. The official line coming out of IAF headquarters in response to Washington's inquiries concerning Nasser's charges was that no Americans had taken part in combat.

Now Steve didn't think that Washington was totally buying the line they were being handed, but the Israelis' goodwill efforts on his behalf had at least created some doubt in the minds of his superiors. Steve had been in the military long enough to know that where there was doubt, there was usually room to worm out of a predicament—

Maybe I'll get out of this without being branded the man who pissed off 110 million Arabs after all, Steve thought as he continued packing. *If not, well, screw the camel drivers if they can't take a joke . . .*

The truly important thing as far as Steve was concerned was that the war had continued to go so well for the Israelis. On that first day of fighting, Israeli armor had been able to advance thirty miles into the Sinai. On Tuesday, the Israelis had captured important Jordanian cities, and taken the high ground north of Jerusalem. On Wednesday, the U.N. proposed a cease-fire that Israel tentatively accepted and the Arabs rejected. The Israelis then proceeded to take Gaza, advance across the Sinai, and capture the West Bank of the Jordan River, uniting Jerusalem under the Star of David. That ended things on the Jordanian front.

The only real blot for the Iraelis came on Thursday, Steve mused as he finished packing the last of his bags and set them with his others by the door. It was on June 8 that IAF jets mistakenly attacked an American Navy communications ship, the *Liberty*, killing thirty-four Americans, and wounding many others. It truly had been a terrible mistake, and one for which Israel had quickly apologized, offering financial compensation for the loss of lives and damage to property.

Later that same day, Egypt and Syria accepted the U.N. proposed cease-fire.

Isolated skirmishes continued throughout Friday, and part of Saturday, but for all intents what the international press was dubbing the "Six Day War" was over as of yesterday. Last night, people here were rejoicing; dancing in the streets. Meanwhile, news reports had it that the Arab world was in turmoil. Their defeat had been astonishing, humiliating, a total wipeout on every front.

There was a knock on Steve's door. It was the IAF man Steve was expecting. The airman was here to collect Steve's luggage and ferry it to the airport. Steve himself would be leaving for the airport around three. Rivka was going to come by in the Citroën, to give him a ride.

Once the IAF man had left with his bags Steve decided to go out for a final walk around the city. He'd be back in plenty of time to meet Rivka. He grabbed his leather A-2 jacket and left the apartment. He was surprised to bump into Rivka in the building's front vestibule.

"What are you doing here so early?" Steve asked. "I wasn't expecting you for a few hours yet."

"I know, but I thought that before you left Israel you might like to do a last bit of sight-seeing . . ."

She was giggling, which was odd . . . Rivka was not the giggly type. For a moment Steve thought that she was drunk, but then he decided that she was just in a giddy mood like the rest of the city because of Israel's miraculous victory.

"Speaking of sight-seeing," Steve began. "That's quite an outfit you're wearing . . ."

Rivka's obviously unfettered breasts were straining the buttons of her white blouse. Steve could clearly see her dark nipples pressing through the thin cotton fabric. Her navy skirt fit tightly around her fine hips and sassy rump. The skirt's hem banded her smooth, tawny thighs at least five inches above her knees.

Very nice, Steve thought. He had seen other Israeli girls wearing miniskirts, but never Captain Rivka Yakkov . . .

"You don't like this outfit?" she asked nervously.

"Oh, I like it fine." Steve chuckled.

She blushed furiously, and made a furtive attempt to tug down the hem of her skirt to cover a bit more of herself but quickly give *that* up as a lost cause.

"But what *other* lovely sights did you want to show me?" Steve asked.

"Well . . ." She seemed unable to look him in the eye. "For instance, my flat," she said softly.

"Your flat . . ."

She nodded, still looking down. "It has a beautiful view of the sea, you know . . ."

"Yeah, I've heard that." Steve smiled. He could feel his heart begin to pound and his groin stir. "But I think that view was from the *bedroom* . . . ?"

Rivka looked up at him, her eyes shining. "Yes."

The sun-splashed living room of her flat had white stucco walls hung with colorful Arab prints. Fresh flowers in vases were everywhere. The worn, wide floorboards were covered with scatter rugs, and she made do with big pillows on the floor for furniture. There was a beaded curtain hanging in the doorway to her small kitchen, where atop the refrigerator her languid cat the color of champagne watched with golden eyes as Steve put his arms around Rivka and kissed her.

"Come, Steven," she whispered, her breath moist against his ear. "To the bedroom, come . . ."

Steve shrugged off his leather jacket and let it fall to the floor. The cat leapt gracefully off the refrigerator and padded over to the jacket to curl up on it. Rivka took Steve's hand to lead him out of the living room. He walked beside her in a daze of passion, hypnotized by the sensual flow of her body beneath her scant clothing. He couldn't believe that this beautiful angel was about to be his . . .

Her white stucco bedroom was carpeted with a blue and gold threadbare Persian rug. There was little furniture: only a chest of drawers, a nightstand, a mirror on the wall, and her bed, which was narrow, and covered with a pink and black print cotton spread. It had only a single, thin pillow.

It reminded Steve of a young girl's bedroom; a child's place to sleep. The room seemed a stranger to lust. It seemed as pure and innocent as its owner.

The bed was positioned beneath the wide casement windows that overlooked the great expanse of sea. On this warm June day the windows were swung open, letting in the tangy ocean breeze along with the shrill clatter of the gulls swooping over the waves, and the crash of the surf clamoring against Jaffa's ancient stone piers.

Rivka turned to him, her eyes locked with his as she slowly unbuttoned her blouse, then let it fall from her shoulders. Her breasts were large and round, her nipples startlingly dark against her breasts' alabaster skin. She shyly stepped close, hesitating an instant before she put her arms around his neck, pressing herself against him. Steve held her gently, his hands caressing the strong, supple curve of her back. He buried his face in her thick hair, inhaling her spicy scent. His knees grew weak. The aching swell in his groin was both delicious and unbearable.

"Oh, I've wanted you for so long," he whispered, his voice thick with passion, the blood pounding in his veins. "Oh, you are so beautiful and I've wanted this for *so long*—"

She tilted up her head, smiling at him, taking her time doling out kisses. Her tongue tasted cool and sweet. Her pearly teeth nibbled at his lips.

"Steven, you are my first," she murmured. "My first. My hero—"

What? Steve thought. *Hero—? Is that what this is about?*

She'd unbuttoned his shirt. Her fingers were fluttering across his chest and stomach. Her touch dropped to his belt buckle.

"Rivka, tell me," he pleaded. "What do you mean I'm your hero?"

"You know..." She laughed softly. "You know what they are saying about you, about what you've done for my country. You are a great hero. They compare you to David Marcus! *David Marcus*—" She took his hands and began to pull him insistently toward the bed.

And Steven looked at the bed again—the child's bed—and he thought about how lovely Rivka was, and how his own life was passing, and how there wouldn't be many more girls like this leading him to love . . . He thought about how much he wanted her, and what difference did it make why she wanted him—

Why she wanted him . . .

I'm not a man to her at all, Steve realized. *I'm a legend. I'm not desirable for who I am, but for what I symbolize; like David Marcus—Goddamn it, like Golda Meir!*

It made him want to laugh when he thought about it. It made him want to weep when he looked in the mirror and saw a man holding a girl young enough to be his daughter; a girl who would always remember him, although how and what she remembered depended on what he did next. Depended on what he was willing to deny himself. What he was willing to *give*—

"Steven? What is it?" Rivka asked as he gently, sadly, extricated himself from her heavenly embrace.

"I'm—I'm going to leave." The confounded look in her eyes made him smile. "Yeah." He nodded. "I'm not sure I understand why either, but I am sure that I've got to go."

"But I thought you wanted me." She shook her head, her dark eyes growing wet. "I thought *you* thought I was beautiful—"

"I do—" He was fumbling at buttoning his shirt with fingers grown too clumsy for the job. His groin was aching. Her taste was in his mouth, her scent in his nostrils, her touch seeping into his pores. *Got to get out of here,* he thought. *Got to go before I surrender to my greed, before I take what isn't mine—*

"I thought you wanted to love me—" she whispered pleadingly.

"Maybe if I could stay, Rivka, darling . . ." He paused, chuckling ruefully. "No, it's too late for that, as well. But maybe if I were fifteen years younger..." He shrugged. "I don't expect you to understand—hell, *I* didn't, until just now—so you just listen. I've been a go-as-I-please, selfish sonofabitch my entire life, but it's time for me to make a change. You are one wonderful thing I'm going to leave for someone else. You find someone you really love, Rivka. If not forever, at least for that instant, but the important thing is that you should love him for who he *is*, not what you think he *stands for*. That's what you deserve, and so does some lucky guy somewhere in the world." He sighed. "When you *do* find yourself that guy, chances are that he'll have a few less miles on him than *me* . . ."

"You really are a hero . . ." she said, awestruck.

"You put on your blouse now," Steve told her. He felt heartbroken because the look in Rivka's eyes told him that he was doing the right thing. Told him too much about the roads of his youth so recklessly well traveled; the roads he wouldn't be going down again.

Dressed, she followed him out to the living room. "Don't you want me to take you to the airport?"

"No." He smiled, shaking his head. "I'd rather say good-bye to you here. Anyway, I've got plenty of time. I think I'll go walking for a bit, and then I'll grab a taxi."

She nodded. The cat scooted away as Steve bent to pick up his flight jacket. He slung it over his shoulder. He was at the door when he stopped, looked at the jacket for a moment, and then at Rivka.

"Here," he said, tossing the jacket to her. "Catch!"

"You are giving it to me?" she asked as she caught it.

"It's got that Vigilant Virgins logo on the back, right?" Steve shrugged. "Remember what you said when we first met?"

She nodded, her eyes growing wet all over again as she murmured, "I said I could use a jacket like this to discourage . . ." Her voice changed, melting down the scale into something that was half laughter and half a sob. She only shook her head, rubbing her teary eyes.

"You let that jacket keep you safe and warm," Steve said. "Until you find the right guy to take over the job—"

"And even then," Rivka said adamantly, hugging the jacket. "Even then—"

Steve nodded. "Well, I guess I *would* take it kindly if from time to time, you could see your way clear to favor me with your thoughts . . ."

He felt something warm and furry against his ankles, and looked down to see the champagne cat with the wise eyes weaving between his feet. "And if this cat doesn't like the guy you're thinking of, you boot him right out of here." Steve winked. "Because it's plain this animal knows how to judge a man who's got the right stuff."

He turned away then, and let himself out of her flat and out of her life, closing the door gently but firmly behind him.

(Four)

Lod Airport

Steve was about to board his flight when Benny Detkin intercepted him at the gate.

"What are you doing here?" Steve asked. He'd already said good-bye to his friend at IAF headquarters. They were planning to get together back in the States.

"I have something for you," Benny said. "Something that's pretty much guaranteed to get you off the hook with the big boys in Washington . . ."

"Well, I don't know if I *am* going to be on the hook," Steve said. "The IAF has pretty much covered my ass concerning our little escapade."

"Well, this is going to close the books on it once and for all," Benny confidently replied. He took an envelope out of the inside breast pocket of his linen sport jacket and handed it to Steve. "Go on," he urged excitedly. "Open it."

Inside the envelope was a color snapshot of several circular, concrete enclosures out in the desert. Inside each enclosure was a missile on a launch ramp.

"SAM sites?" Steve asked.

"Sure." Benny nodded. "But not just any old run-of-the-mill SAMs. Those are SAM-12s, the most advanced version. When the Egyptians turned tail in the Sinai they left those launch sites virtually intact. The Israelis got it all, right down to the instruction manuals for the radar guidance equipment."

"That's great," Steve said. "But what does it have to do with me?"

"Only this." Benny grinned. "The Israeli Government has communicated to Washington its decision to share this particular bit of plunder with the United States, as a gesture of appreciation on behalf of Colonel Steven Gold's services."

"You're shitting me . . ." Steve looked down at the photograph in his hand. "The brass would kill their own mothers to get the scoop on what the Russians have in terms of surface-to-air missile technology."

"They don't have to kill their mothers now, though, do they?" Benny winked. "They're going to have it all laid out for them on a plate by the Israelis, who have made it clear that the brass has Steven Gold to thank for their good fortune."

"Benny, this is going to make my career," Steve quietly said. He shook his head, overcome with emotion. "I don't know what to say, how to thank you . . ."

"You don't have to thank me." Benny laughed. "You don't have to thank anybody. This is just the Israeli Government's way of thanking *you*. The actual technical material will travel through the normal channels," he added. "Consider this photograph a memento of our little adventure together."

"Yeah, I will . . . thanks . . ." Steve listened as the final boarding notice for his flight was called over the airport's public address system. "I guess I better get going—"

"Yeah." Benny nodded. "Say, speaking of mementos, where's your flight jacket?"

"Oh ..." Steve shrugged. "I gave it to Rivka. Kind of a present ..."

"Uh-huh." Benny had a funny look in his eyes. "Tell me more ..."

"Well, there's nothing to tell," Steve said quickly. "Except that you were right when you said I'd never get anywhere with her. I tried every trick I knew, but she shot me down ..."

"Oh, *she* shot *you* down, eh?" Benny shook his head. "Before you say anymore, I should tell you that I happened to run into her at IAF headquarters just before coming here."

"Oh, fuck." Steve winced. "What did she do? Tell you everything?"

Benny shrugged. "What can I say, I have that kindly sort of visage that makes girls see me in a fatherly light." He grinned. "You better be careful, Steve, a couple more episodes like the one you had this afternoon and girls will be turning to *you* for fatherly advice."

"Jesus, Benny, just don't tell anyone else, okay?" Steve pretended to gruffly plead, although he couldn't keep the smile out of his eyes. "I got my reputation as a hound to uphold."

Benny laughed. "You better get on your plane ... You *hero*, you—"

As Steve walked through the gate he couldn't help thinking that this hero stuff wasn't all that it was cracked up to be.

CHAPTER 23

**Gold Household
Bel-Air, California
7 August 1967**

Herman Gold was in his second-floor study. He was seated in his leather armchair with a yellow legal pad on his lap and a pen in his hand. He was surrounded by stacks of books: Hebrew primers, Judaic histories, English translations of the Old Testament and the Torah. Occupying a place of honor in Gold's bookcase was his latest acquisition: a custom leather-bound, encyclopedic, thirty-five-volume set of the Talmud. It was the recently published English language edition, translated by Soncino.

Gold enjoyed being in this book-lined den, even if the room did have something of a split personality. Look into the space, with its fireplace, dark paneling, brass lamps with green glass shades, and heavy mahogany and leather furniture, and you might think you were in the library of an old English country house. Turn toward the french doors opening out onto the balcony, however, and you had a typically Southern California view of the swimming pool and landscaped patio.

The only thing Gold didn't like about the second-floor study was the goddamned chair lift they'd installed onto the staircase railing to carry him up here. Stair-climbing as well as most other physical exertion was off-limits for him since his heart attack. He understood the reasoning behind the prohibitions, of course, and he'd pretty much come to terms with them. Hey, he was grateful to be alive. Nevertheless, he found the chair lift especially galling. Settling into that thing and switching on the electric motor was a hell of a comedown for a man used to airplane cockpits.

Grateful to be alive—Gold wrote across the top of the legal pad. He stared at it a moment and then savagely crossed it out. It was just too trite to use as a Bar Mitzvah discourse . . .

Gold had been toying with the idea of being a Bar Mitzvah ever since his involvement in the scheme to smuggle Vector-A systems into Israel had kindled his interest in his religious heritage. Initially he'd dismissed the idea, afraid of the ridicule he was certain to face from his friends and business associates—and, yes, even from his family—if he attempted to carry it out. After all, thirteen-year-old Jewish boys take part in the Bar Mitzvah ritual, not seventy-year-old men . . .

It was, of course, his heart attack that had changed his point of view. Ridicule seemed a very small thing after you'd been locked in a chest-crushing wrestling match with death. As he'd recuperated in his hospital bed he'd realized how little it mattered what other people thought. You were only on this earth for a short while . . .

Once he'd decided to commit himself to the course of study that would lead to his becoming a Bar Mitzvah, he knew that he had to go all out. He'd found the finest scholars to teach him, because he was fervently committed not just to *do*, but to *understand* . . .

Gold had been to Bar Mitzvah celebrations in Los Angeles. As often as not they were Hollywood-inspired extravaganzas. To Gold they had seemed like yards of cotton candy—the catering, the liquor, the gifts, the band—wrapped around a puny little popsicle stick core—an apple-cheeked boy in a brand-new suit spending a quarter hour in a synagogue mumbling beneath his breath a phonetically learned portion of the Torah, and then squeaking, ". . . Today I am a man . . ." just because his parents had said he had to.

Gold, however, was no apple-cheeked boy. He was a man of substance; *material* substance at least—He had never in his life done anything halfway, and he was not about to start now. It would be at least another year before he was a Bar Mitzvah, because he fully intended to *understand* and *feel* the *truth* of what he was doing. More than that, his teachers had mentioned that at one time in Europe it was customary for the Bar Mitzvah to deliver a meaningful discourse to the congregation assembled to witness his right of passage.

Gold intended to follow in that tradition. Hence the pad on his lap, the newly purchased edition of the Talmud on his shelf, and the puzzled look on his face as he contemplated the still-blank page. It was not a moment too soon to begin honing his discourse, and he'd been trying to begin for days, *but what to talk about?*

The teachers had suggested something pertinent . . . Gold put his pen to paper and scribbled: *changing of the guard—*

Since Gold's heart attack, Don Harrison had lifted the burden of running GAT from his shoulders. Gold was pleased with the job that Don was doing, and the respectful way in which he was doing it. Don Harrison was not coming on like gangbusters, further unduly upsetting an already jittery executive staff concerning the transition of power. Don always thought twice before he spoke, and always seemed to take into account other people's feelings and points of view—

What was most important, Don had made it his habit to consult with Gold before making any important decision. Gold was grateful that he was not destined to be a King Lear scorned by his children; the ungrateful inheritors of his domain.

*Changing of the guard—*Gold pondered it awhile and

then thought: *No, it won't do. What he had to say on that topic concerned his children more than himself . . .*

"Children," Gold murmured softly. "The welfare of one's children is a concern . . ."

Especially when your children carried arms for their country—

Gold's eyes moved across the room to the newspaper still lying unopened on his desk. These days he could hardly stand to read the international headlines. He had a son and a grandson in the Air Force, after all, and both men were fighter pilots; frontline warriors in the most crucial battle-ground of the modern era—the sky. How could Gold bring himself to read about the dozens of places around the world where his son and grandson might fight and die? There was Vietnam. The Mideast. The uprising in the Congo. The revolt in Greece. The revolutions in South America—

And wherever duty called, Gold knew his boys would be, taking command of the sky on behalf of their country . . .

Gold's reveries were interrupted by a knock on the door. "Come in," he called.

The door opened and in walked his grandson Andy carrying what looked to be a cake box. "Grandpa?" Andy began. "Grandma said that you were studying, and that I shouldn't disturb you . . ."

"Uh-huh." Gold laughed.

Andy took a step closer to Gold. "*Am* I disturbing you?"

Gold shook his head. He took off his glasses and put them aside, along with his writing materials. "You could never disturb me, sonny-boy," he said lovingly.

Andy grinned. "I have something for you." He held out the cake box. "I made it all by myself," he added proudly.

Gold peered at the box in Andy's outstretched hands. "You made me a cake?" he asked dubiously.

"*Noooo!*" Andy giggled. "Mom just gave me the box to *use* to bring your *present*." He ran to Gold and plopped the box down on his lap, then took a step back. "Open it!" Andy demanded, breathless with excitement.

Gold opened the box and looked inside. "Oh, Andy . . ."

He gently lifted out of the cake box a model of a World War I vintage Fokker Dr.I triplane.

"It's like the one you flew in the war. Right, Grandpa?" Andy eagerly asked.

"It is, Andy," Gold murmured, holding the airplane up to the light in order to better see it. "Oh, it is . . ."

The model itself had been put together from one of those airplane model plastic kits that came with instructions. The kind that you could buy for a few dollars at any hobby shop. Examining it, however, Gold could tell that Andy had assembled the model with incredibly painstaking care for a nine-year-old. What was even more amazing about the model was its enameled paint job. The triplane had been painted scarlet everywhere but on the sides of its fuselage and its wings, where it was painted sky blue. On both rear side quarters of the model were teaspoon-size, bright yellow ovals, each showing a tiny, but perfectly rendered, centaur —a mythological creature, half man and half horse—rearing up on its hind legs to do battle. Just forward of the centaurs, and on her wings and tail, the model wore black Iron Crosses, edged in white.

"Andy, these were my colors *exactly*," Gold said in wonderment. "The Fokker I flew looked exactly like this . . ." Gold stared at his grandson. "How could you have known—?"

Andy was beaming with pleasure. "I asked Uncle Steve . . ."

"Ah." Gold nodded. His son Steven was here in Los Angeles, staying in one of the Malibu beachfront houses the family owned as an investment. The Air Force had given Steve a well-deserved extended leave after the fabulous job he'd done in service to his country, and his country's ally, Israel. When Steve had told Gold how well the Vector-A system had worked, and how he himself had fought to protect the Jewish homeland—Well, Gold would not be ashamed to admit to anyone that tears had come to his eyes as he'd contemplated his beautiful son.

For the past month since Steve had been home he'd come

to visit Gold every morning. They would sit in the sunny garden off the solarium, near the splashing marble fountain, and talk quietly about life and what the future held.

Steve was going to the Air Force war college at Maxwell Air Force Base in Alabama in September. Gold had been gratified to hear his son confidently predict that he would be graduating at the head of his class come the end of the year-long course—

"...I never thought I could do it, Pop, but now I know I can. I did a lot of even tougher work when I was on General Howie Simon's staff. And I did a lot of managerial administration and writing in Israel, in order to set up that pilot training program..."

"Yes, son...I always thought you were capable..."

"I know you did, Pop. You always believed in me. But sometimes it just takes awhile for stuff to sink into a guy, you know...? Once I thought there was a limit to what I could be, but now I know that's not true...Things change, Pop ...Things change..."

"So my boy really will be a general officer someday...?"

"And you'll be there to see it, Pop. I promise. You'll be the one to pin the stars on my uniform..."

And sometimes the two men didn't talk at all but were content to merely sit together in each other's company... Things change, Steve had said. Things change...

"You really like my present, Grandpa?" Andy was asking.

"Like it?" Gold exclaimed. "Andy, I love it!"

"At the office that day you got sick, you said that you didn't have one like this..." The boy was looking proud. "And I *remembered* you said it, so I *made* you one—"

Gold stood to cross to the fireplace. "It's going right here on the mantel, where it will be safe, and where I can see it whenever I want..."

Gold positioned the model, and then went back to embrace his grandson. "Andy," he murmured into the boy's silky blond hair. "Do you know what? I think your gift must be the best airplane ever built by a Gold—"

"Grandpa?" Andy had tilted back his head to look up at Gold. "Someday I'm gonna be a fighter pilot like *you*—"

"Is that right?" Gold laughed with pleasure.

"Yeah, and like Uncle Steve—"

"And like your brother, Robbie?" Gold coaxed.

Andy frowned. "Maybe . . ." he said reluctantly.

Gold sighed. He'd been afraid of this. Andy was now old enough to be aware of his half brother's coolness toward him, and had begun to reciprocate in kind. Maybe it would help if Robbie and Andrew could spend more time together, but that wasn't in the cards.

USAF Captain Robert Blaize Greene, winner of the Silver Star, had completed his tour of duty in Vietnam, and had been rotated stateside. Robbie was currently stationed at Seymour Johnson AFB in North Carolina, where he was a flight leader in a TAC wing of F-4 Phantoms.

As much as Gold was disturbed by the rift between Robbie and Andy, he knew that there was nothing he could do about it. The two would someday have to work out the conflict between them. Meanwhile, Gold would be somewhat comforted by the memories of the rifts between him and his own son, now healed. Robbie and Andy would make their peace someday, Gold was sure of it. The underlying foundation of this family was strong. Famiy ties would ultimately bring the half brothers together.

"Tell you what, Andy," Gold began brightly. "Seeing as how you want to be a pilot, *I've* got a present for *you*." He went over to his desk and began rummaging through its center drawer. "If I can only find it," he muttered. "Ah! Here it is—" He motioned the boy over, and then handed him the tarnished, silver dollar-size circle of metal. "That was my flier's breast badge from the Imperial Air Service. I wore it on my uniform during the war."

Gold watched his grandson study the medal. It showed in relief a Taube monoplane flying over a landscape contained in a laurel and oak leaf wreath, with the Prussian royal crown at the top.

"You keep it, Andy," Gold said. "I wore it through all

twenty of my victorious dogfights. After the war I kept it, bringing it with me to America. It was in my pocket when I met your grandmother. When I began the business. When my children and grandchildren were born, all of you healthy and strong. It has always brought me good luck. Perhaps it's blessed my life. I hope it does as much for you . . ."

"Thank you, Grandpa," Andy whispered. "I love you."

"I love you, too . . ." Gold nodded, the depth of his feelings so strong it was painful.

Gold watched his grandson leave the study, the flier's badge clutched tightly in his palm, and then he turned back to the fireplace mantel to contemplate the Fokker triplane model—his *new* lucky charm . . .

Looking at the model, Gold couldn't help pondering how his life had begun, and now seemed to be moving full circle. He'd started as a wide-eyed boy in love with the sky, and now it appeared as if that love had been transferred intact to a third generation of Golds.

Yes, life had been so good to him; so full . . . As vast as the sky, which itself had always been a friend to the Gold clan . . .

He turned away from the mantel, his brow furrowed with thought. Themes were evolving, slowly taking shape in his mind as he wandered back to his armchair. He put on his glasses, picked up his pad and pen, and began to write, tentatively at first, but faster and faster as the ideas flooded into his being.

Thanks to a little boy full of love, and a model airplane, he had found the topic for his Bar Mitzvah discourse.

Gold, muttering thoughts to himself, hurried over to the bookcase where he scanned the Talmud's bindings in order to pluck the first volumes he would need from the shelf. He took the books and his writing materials to his desk so that he could begin work in earnest.

The spiritual seed germinating so long within his soul had sprouted. For Herman Gold, another great adventure was beginning.